a reluctant roommate

ANGELA CASELLA

Babes of Brewing

Best Served Cold

Worst Nanny Ever

Unlucky in Love

The Love Fixers

The Love Bandits

The Love Losers

The Love Destroyers

The Thief Who Saved Christmas

Finding You

You're so Extra

You're so Bad

You're so Basic

You're so Vain

Fairy Godmother Agency

A Borrowed Boyfriend

A Stolen Suit

A Brooding Bodyguard

A Reluctant Roommate

Bringing Down the House (Nicole and Damien's story)

Highland Hills

(co-written with Denise Grover Swank)

Matchmaking a Billionaire

Matchmaking a Single Dad

Matchmaking a Grump

Matchmaking a Roommate

Bad Luck Club

(co-written with Denise Grover Swank)

Love at First Hate

Jingle Bell Hell

Fraudulently Ever After

Matchmaking Mischief

Asheville Brewing

(co-written with Denise Grover Swank)

Any Luck at All

Better Luck Next Time

Getting Lucky

Bad Luck Club

Luck of the Draw (novella)

All the Luck You Need (prequel novella) by Angela Casella

DREW

SOMETHING inside of me dies as Andy opens the back of the small U-Haul truck. "Just a few things," she'd said. "You'll barely notice me." That's when I should have gotten suspicious. She's not the type of person anyone could fail to notice. Everything about her is loud; always has been.

Now, looking in the back of the van, I realize what I should have known from the get-go: her stuff is loud too, and there's a lot of it. She obviously doesn't subscribe to the Marie Kondo philosophy of only keeping things that bring you joy; either that, or she must be drowning in joy.

There's everything in the van that you'd expect to go in a bedroom: a bed frame and mattress, a bureau, and a bedside table. All of that's fine, obviously. What worries me are the dozens of other boxes, along with three rolled-up rugs, multiple lamps, and several frames wrapped in layers of bubble wrap. Is she going to put those things out in the living room? I can already tell they're not to my taste. Through the packing material, shades of teal, red, orange, and gold are trying to sear my retinas.

Color has its place, obviously. I use color in the games I design— a pop of bright color can be a statement, a message; it can be beautiful. But the place for it is not in my living room, where I keep a pseudo office in the corner. That's supposed to be the neutral zone. My sister Marnie agreed to that, but Marnie just moved in with her fiancé. If Andy were a Craigslist roommate, then I could comfortably be a dick about it—my house, my rules—but she's my little sister's best friend, has been since they were in first grade, and if I'm a dick to her, I'll be hearing about it.

Still, I can't totally hold it in. "Um, Andy, where's all this shi—stuff supposed to go?"

She looks embarrassed for half a second, and I remember that her grandmother just kicked her out of their house. Although she gave Andy a couple of weeks to move out, Marnie tells me her grandmother has been ignoring her, pretending she really is dead to her, a pronouncement she made after finding out she has an account on OnlyFans. It's a site where people pay for content.

Porn. Porn is what's usually on there.

Andy says she only made videos of her feet for fetishists, and I know she was being truthful because I have a natural curiosity and spent half the night searching for her account after I found out she was on there.

It seems unfair that she's lost her job and her family because of a few videos of her freakishly dexterous feet...and, I'll admit it, a sexy one of her long curly hair brushing her tanned toes. Maybe it was just the mental image of her bending over and—

Anyway. I know better than anyone that life's unfair, there are no guarantees, and everything can change at the drop of a coin.

Like me, here and now.

I was having an uncomplicated year, and suddenly Andy's moving in with me, bringing all of her brightly colored crap with her.

"I can find somewhere else to go," Andy says, surprising me. "You didn't ask for any of this. It's pretty shitty of me to put all of my problems on you. Maybe I can get a storage unit for this stuff. The movers who packed it up were pretty reasonably priced. I can hire them to unload it and then I'll couch surf until I get my shit together."

She's always had a short fuse, and I was expecting her to argue with me. The unexpected vulnerability in her eyes can be the only explanation for what I say next.

"No. I'm happy to have you here, and we'll find room for your things." Because I'm an idiot, I double down. "All of them."

Sweat beads along my brow. What the fuck have I agreed to? And why do I keep agreeing to it?

Andy smiles and surprises me by pulling me into a hug. "Thank you, Drew. You've always been one of the good ones." She's five-eight or five-nine but still half a head shorter than me. The hug puts my nose directly above her glossy black curls. I feel like a pervert for breathing her in, but it smells good, spicy and sweet, and she feels good too. *Too good.*

I release her so quickly, she nearly falls backward. She's wearing sandals, and I see that distinctive rose gold toe ring winking up at me, reminding me of those videos.

Reminding me that I got hard when I watched her hair swaying over her feet, and you're not supposed to get hard when you're looking at your sister's best friend—especially your sister's best friend who's about to move in with you.

"What's going on over here?" Marnie says from behind us. Even though we only just got done moving all of her shit into the house she and her fiancé, Griffin, are renting, she insisted on helping Andy move in today. I'm guessing the kind of help she wants to offer is emotional support because she's about five-two and a buck twenty. She won't be moving the heavy stuff.

We'll need Griffin for that, and my other sister Sinclair's boyfriend, Rafe, who's built like a Transformer. My buddies would have come over to help, but I haven't told them about Andy yet. I'm not sure why, except...

Andy's hot. That's a fact, not an opinion, and I certainly don't intend to do anything about it. Everyone has a type, but she's one of those people who transcend things like type. She's also my sister's best friend, and I don't want my friends over here every five minutes trying to hit on her.

I'll have to tell them, obviously.

Eventually.

"Nothing," I say, taking a big step back. "Nothing at all. We were just looking at all of this shi—" I feel Andy's eyes on me. "All of this lovely stuff Andy brought. Couldn't be happier."

"So why'd you shove me?" Andy asks, putting a hand on her hip.

"There was no shoving. I just forcefully released you," I say. "I was alarmed. Marnie caught me off guard."

Marnie's giving me an *I see right through you* look, and in some ways, I'm sure she does. That's what comes from cohabitating with someone for so long. We lived under the same roof for most of our lives. She's uprooted herself, and it's a change I can feel down to my bones. There have been a lot of changes lately, and it feels like the life I had—the one I was perfectly comfortable with—has been slipping out of my grip.

"Change is good," Marnie told me the other day. "Change is growth."

She's not altogether wrong. There have been good changes lately: our sister, Sinclair, is back in our lives after being swallowed by Hollywood for nearly two decades. She's famous enough that you're nearly guaranteed to get photographed scratching your ass or stuffing your face with a giant pretzel if you go to the mall with her, but she's ours again. And her boyfriend, Rafe, is a great guy. He's a former personal trainer, and we've been working out together. Griffin and Enoch, the fiancé of Marnie's other best friend, usually join us. "Look at you," Marnie teased me when I got back from our first session. "You're expanding your circle. Did it hurt?"

Again, not wrong. My buddies, Burke, Danny, and Shane, and I spend the majority of our time together. We have our weekly D&D game, our yearly two-week camping trip, and when we want to meet up and drink and complain about shit, we do that together too. We understand each other, and we have the kind of deep bond that's forged when four people have experienced something horrible together. Still, I'm glad my sisters have found men who make them happy, and I'm even more pleased they haven't settled for assholes. Marnie almost married a taint made human last fall, and I busted my ass to make sure it didn't happen.

Griffin pounds me on the back, a little too hard, almost as if he hears my thoughts and is silently thanking me for clearing the way for him. "Let's get to it, man."

So we do.

———

I'm in trouble.

A huge multi-colored rug is on the floor in the living room, covered in splashes of pink, turquoise, gold, and red, as if someone held a paint party for drunk people. I don't know what possessed me, but when Andy bit her lip and said it wouldn't fit in her bedroom, looking on the verge of tears because it had belonged to her mother—her *deceased* mother—I volunteered to put in the living room.

Marnie looked at me with bugged out eyes, correctly assuming that I'd lost my mind, but then admitted she and Griffin could use the neutral rug in their living room.

The good thing about compromise is that I'm able to convince Andy that we shouldn't add brightly colored pictures to the walls in the living room now that the floor is covered in color splotches. Still, there's a brass tea set sitting out on the counter in the kitchen, because there was no room for it in any of the cabinets, and anyway, she *likes* it sitting out.

Andy has also put out what must be half a dozen candles, all with different scents, and a turquoise-painted garage-sale bookcase filled with paperbacks, some of them facing out so the shirtless men are staring at me.

I'm hoping I can get her to hide the man-chest books away in her room, or at least arrange them so none of them are watching me, but I won't try tonight. Her face is drawn and her eyes look glassy. Even though I don't really want her here, I *do* want her to be happy. Comfortable. She's like...

Well, I wouldn't say she's like another sister, but she's important to Marnie, and therefore important to me.

"Are you two staying in tonight?" I ask, glancing at Marnie and Andy, who are huddled together on the couch under a bright throw with a geometric design in purple and turquoise.

It's hers, obviously.

"Yeah, we're going to have a few drinks," Marnie says, "and Sinclair's coming over."

Rafe, who showed up about a half hour after we got started, laughs and grins at them. "That's my girl. Missed the hard part and coming in for the fun." Turning to me, he asks, "You want to grab a drink at the bar, man?"

He means Griffin's bar, Summer Nights. Griffin left a few hours ago to open it, which was fine since Rafe could have moved everything by himself. Possibly with one arm tied behind his back.

"Sure," I say, because I could absolutely use that drink.

"Hey." Andy throws off the blanket. She gets up, and I immediately step back, worried she might be going to go in for another hug and kind of wanting her to do it at the same time. "I don't have a transmissible disease," she says, her tone annoyed.

"Does that mean you have non-transmissible ones?"

She gives my shoulder a nudge. "Shut up and let me thank you again. Some of my best memories from childhood are from this house. It's always been like a second home to me, and you're like another brother. Except less shitty than my brothers." Her brothers who were such dicks to her about the whole OnlyFans thing and only slightly less dickish before that. Tears well in her eyes, and I feel like someone reached into my chest and flicked my heart. "Being here makes me feel like I haven't lost everything."

Then, of course, she hugs me again, her curves pressing into me and the maddening smell of her hair wrapping around me, reminding me that I don't think of her as a sister.

Rafe and I head out to his car—a rust-beaten hunk of junk that my sister must hate that he's kept. I like him better for it. Sinclair's loaded, and some men would use her for her money, but Rafe's not the type to walk around with his hand open, hoping someone slaps some cash into it.

Neither am I. Sinclair keeps trying to buy me expensive shit for the house, but I almost always refuse. There's a fine line—I don't want her to think her money is what I value, and I also don't want to make her feel bad by always saying no.

When we get into the car, Rafe shoots me a look. There's a small smile playing on his face. "You're fucked, buddy."

"Yeah," I say, combing a hand back through my hair. "That rug's pretty ugly, huh? She was getting upset, though, and I don't like seeing women cry. I especially don't like it when Andy cries, because she's not a crier—"

I cut myself off because he's shaking his head. "Not what I meant. You have a thing for her, and she just said she sees you as a brother. What are you going to do about that?"

two

ANDY

"FUCK THOSE FUCKING, SHIT-EATING, DUMB-ASS ASSHOLES!" I shout.

"Did it work?" Sinclair asks. Marnie's sister showed up twenty minutes ago, and because she likes to do everything big, she came with a box of cocktail supplies that she set on the counter in the kitchen. I guess Griffin's been teaching her how to mix drinks, which is good, because that woman's pours used to be so heavy I wasn't even grateful for it.

"No," I say, throwing a throw pillow across the room. I mean, seriously, it's there in the name, folks. Their only reason for existence is so they can be thrown around by pissed-off women. Maybe I'll buy some more of them. "I hate them."

Them being my brothers, Theo and Jack. My mother gave us all Anglican names—Theodore, Jack, Andrea—much to my grandmother's distaste. We're only a fourth Puerto Rican, my mother would tell her, and *Abuela* would snap back that it was the only part that mattered.

She might be right. I barely remember my grandfather, other than that he was quiet and severe. He's probably the one who taught my mom that her heritage didn't matter, because despite having

Spanish ancestry, he was adamant that my grandmother speak to Mom in English rather than Spanish. *Abuela* must have been more accommodating back then, because she only spoke to Mom in Spanish when he wasn't around. Theo, Jack, and I have learned bits and pieces, usually from being cursed out by our grandmother. Then there's my dad. He didn't marry my mom, despite years of hints, direct requests, and three children. Nor did he stick around to teach us anything, so clearly the half our DNA that came from him is flawed.

Maybe the three of us are programmed to be bad at relationships. With each other, and with other people. Hell, it's not a bad theory. My longest relationship only lasted for six weeks, and that last week was a boring-as-hell test I gave myself to see if I could make it.

I couldn't.

My friends tease me about having a three-week rule, because I usually cut a guy loose after three weeks. Marnie claims it's because I date beautiful, stupid men.

She's probably right, but what can I say? I have a taste for big biceps, muscular thighs, and pretty eyes.

I guess that means I'm kind of shitty, so maybe I shouldn't be mad at my brothers for being shitty too. But I *am* mad. I'm mad enough that I want to put a curse on them or ask Nicole and Damien, our private investigator friends, to break into their house and load up malware on all their devices and fill their shampoo bottles with Nair. (Yeah, they got the good Ruiz hair, too, those jerks.) If you think those aren't the kinds of things private investigators would do, then you haven't met *these* private investigators.

But I'm getting ahead of myself.

Here's what went down. I saw something on the news about OnlyFans and how some content creators were able to make thousands without doing anything *really* revealing. My grandmother and I needed the money. She'd inherited my mother's house, which seems like a pretty shit exchange given that she also inherited two kids under the age of eighteen and a dickish new adult, and the house is a bit of a dump. In the same week, I was told we needed new windows, new paint, and to do something about the constant flooding in the basement. I didn't really listen to the long description of what needed to be done, because my mind was fixed on the thousand-dollar price tag.

At the time, I was a daycare teacher. Daycare teachers don't make jack shit. And before you say, "but, Andy, didn't you do it for the kids," I'll admit that while I *did* enjoy the kids—some of them—they weren't exactly handing out tips. Good will alone wasn't going to stop that house from falling down around us.

So I did my research on OnlyFans, and it didn't take me long to find my niche—I've always had nice feet. I used to go to a male pedicurist who'd give me these really thorough pedicures and non-stop compliments. Which was nice until he started asking me for photos of my feet. So I started an account, posting only photos and videos of my feet, occasionally with my hair sweeping over them because my hair is my other best feature—long and dark and so curly it tangles if I look at it wrong.

I figured I was in the clear. Who the hell could ID me based on my feet and hair?

The head of the daycare, that's who.

Apparently, he'd taken as much notice of my feet as that one pedicurist. Because he recognized my rose-gold toe ring and my arch, which he called distinctive, as much as my long, black hair. He fired me on the spot, although from the way he kept eyeballing my feet as he did it, I have a feeling he was hoping I'd offer to negotiate.

Hell to the no. I don't negotiate with terrorists or perverts.

So I left the job and told my grandmother that I'd quit because I couldn't stand the spoiled little kids anymore. A lie because, while they were all spoiled, most of them were too young to have been ruined by it yet.

I didn't post any new content on the account. Not because I was ashamed of what I'd done—I really *do* have kick-ass feet—but because I started worrying about what *Abuela* would think, and, to my misfortune, she's one of maybe five people whose opinion matters.

Turns out my asshole big brother, Theo, who's never thought much of anyone but himself and *especially* thinks poorly of me, knows the director of the daycare center. They got to talking over drinks, and he told Theo the whole thing and showed him the videos. Theo knew it was me, obviously; we share DNA.

And he told our middle brother, Jack.

And then they both showed it to my grandmother.

She immediately declared I was dead to her. Apparently, it's one thing to sway your booty in your own home and use men to scratch and itch and quite another to put yourself online for strange men to ogle.

So, yeah, my brothers suck.

Abuela does, too, I guess, but she's also slowly dying from heart disease. She's in hospice care, and I—in addition to the nurses who stop by the house—am the one who usually takes care of her. Still, she threw me out. I don't blame her as much as you might think. She's always had very strict views on who should do what, where, and when—and I've shattered plenty of them. For her, this was one foot too far.

I'm hoping she'll get over it if I give her enough space.

I'm hoping we'll get back on good terms before she dies.

I'm hoping the nurse Medicaid is paying for will actually take care of her, and listen to her, and watch telenovelas with her, like I always have.

I'm hoping my brothers develop gangrene of the dick.

I'm tempted to text Theo and tell him that if he'd only fixed the house like we'd asked him to, I would never have had to resort to such desperate measures. But before this went down, we'd only ever texted about *Abuela*'s care.

So now, here I am. In the Jones's house, where I probably spent as much time as I did at my own place when I was growing up.

It still feels surreal to see my stuff mixed up with Drew's—my gorgeous, colorful rug on the floor and his boring prints on the walls. Seriously, one of them is a paper bag in a frame. If there's some modern art significance, I don't see it.

"There are other exercises we can try," Sinclair says, and I feel a pang of remorse. Truthfully, I used to dislike Marnie and Drew's sister. Part of it was reflexive dislike—she's famous and gorgeous, and I'm inclined to think most famous, gorgeous people are assholes. I mean, it's not necessarily their fault. If I were famous and gorgeous, I'd probably become an asshole too. It's like the price you pay for living the high life. The rest of the dislike was from the dismissive way she used to treat Marnie and Drew, but I've come to realize their mother is largely to blame for that. She basically groomed Sinclair to be an actress ever since she was a little girl. But Sinclair's finally broken free of her, and she's pretty awesome, it turns out. Like right now. She was invited to a hoity-toity fundraiser tonight, and instead, she chose to be here with us, trying to help me channel my rage by shouting obscenities at my brothers and throwing pillows. Apparently, this is the sort of thing she does to prepare for roles.

"Nah, it's okay," I tell her, patting her arm. "I think I'm just gonna get a drink."

"I'll mix us those cocktails," she says brightly, getting to her feet.

"Her drinks really are much less lethal than they used to be," Marnie tells me when she notices my scrunched nose. "Promise."

"So you promise it won't taste like rubbing alcohol? I realize all alcohol is basically poison, but a person shouldn't feel like they're being poisoned."

Marnie lifts a hand and waves it from side to side. "50-50."

I huff a laugh. "It's too bad that Grace is in New York. She'll regret missing the 50-50 cocktails." Our friend and her fiancé will be spending the next month in New York City. His nephew got into a summer photography program taught by a pretty well-known photographer, and they decided to make the trip with him.

Sinclair comes over with a silver tray—probably real silver, knowing her—with four surprisingly appealing cocktails on it. They're a bright berry color, with lime slices on the rims.

I'm about to ask who the fourth is for, or if she had the correct expectation that I would want to double fist tonight, but she says, "You told me raspberry margaritas were your favorite. I figured out how to make them. It took me a couple of hours last night, and Rafe and his dad and I got really drunk, but—"

"Hold up," I say, but not before taking one of the drinks and setting it on a coaster. "Rafe's dad's still living with you?" It blows my mind that a starlet like her has been sharing a roof with Reggie O'Dooley, an older man who spends the majority of his time at Griffin's bar spouting stories that people only half listen to.

She sighs. "He's leaving next week. I'm actually going to miss him. A little. I mean, the lack of privacy isn't ideal."

Marnie takes her drink off the tray, and Sinclair sets the tray down on the coffee table before choosing one of the glasses.

Marnie lifts her glass up, and we both tap ours to hers. "To new beginnings," she says pointedly to me.

I take a sip, finding it surprisingly delightful. "So," I say, looking at the fourth glass. "Who's that for?"

Someone knocks on the door at exactly that moment, as if they'd been waiting for their cue, and Marnie jumps up to answer it in a way that suggests she knew we'd be having company.

Did they get me a male stripper? I wouldn't say no to a Chippendale.

Hell, maybe he could be my next three-week guy.

But it's Nicole who bursts through the door, her pink pixie cut messy, her studded leather tank top paired with track pants strangely cool.

"I heard there was a party, and you didn't invite me," she says to me, clucking her tongue. A smile plays on her face as her eyes dart from the rug to my bookshelf, pausing on several scented candles. "Drew has got to hate this shit. *Fan*-tastic."

"He was very polite about making space for me, I'll have you know," I tell her. But even as I say it, I have to admit she's probably right. Drew *must* hate my shit. I'm taking advantage of him, and I don't like it. But he's one of the few people in my life that I know I can rely on. If it's late, and I need someone to give me a ride, I've always known I could text or call him, and he'd either come himself or send one of his buddies. He's reliable. He's like a ship in a tossing storm.

Except maybe I'm the storm.

Nicole grabs the drink on the tray, takes a long sip, then asks, "This for me?" Which kind of seems beside the point after she's sucked down a third of it.

"Yes," Marnie says. "Take a seat."

She does, and I ask, "Is this some kind of intervention?"

"Not an intervention, no," Marnie says, "but Nicole *did* mention that you haven't given her and Damien anything to do. It's been two weeks."

"Seriously?" I say, waving around the room. "I've been a little busy, in case you hadn't noticed. Besides, Nicole's the one who guilted Drew into letting me stay here."

Nicole grins and nods as she lowers into the armchair across form us, as if she's holding court. "It's true, I did do that."

She and Damien run the Fairy Godmother Agency, named as such because while they do real detective work for money, they also have a charitable sideline—they choose one sad-sack woman at a time to help with a life makeover. Not just with P.I. stuff, with anything she needs. It's their way of giving back, I guess.

They helped Marnie find a fake boyfriend and track down the asshole who leaked an embarrassing video of her; they helped Grace try to get revenge on Enoch for being a tool, and when she decided his tool was a-okay with her, they put her shitty boss in the hot seat; they helped Sinclair ID the person who was stalking her *and* tanked the reputation of an actor who'd taken advantage of her when she was way too young. Oh, and they're the ones who found her Rafe, who was her live-in bodyguard before he became her boyfriend.

So why, you may be wondering, have I not unleashed these hellhounds made human on my shitty brothers?

I guess I'm just used to handling my own business, to taking the fight to the people who deserve it rather than handing it off to someone else. Letting Nicole and Damien deal with my shit would feel like quitting. It would feel like admitting I can't handle it myself.

The thing is...

I *can't* handle it myself.

I've tried. The only thing I've done so far was to sign both of my brothers up for natural male enhancement reading material. And while it's *very* satisfying to imagine Theo's much younger fiancée finding that pamphlet in the mail, it's not satisfying enough. Sending them glitter bombs and gummy dicks didn't do it for me either. There's still a restlessness inside me. An uneasiness. A feeling that there are wrongs to be righted.

"I don't like..." I clear my throat, frustrated. "I should be able to take care of this myself."

Marnie gives me a knowing look. "You try handling *everything* yourself."

"What about a job?" Nicole says. "You still jobless?"

"Yes," I say through my teeth. It's not for lack of trying. While just about every restaurant in town is looking for staff, none of them appear eager to hire me. Admittedly, I don't want to work at a restaurant, but money is money, however you earn it.

"Well, that's easy," Nicole says.

"No, it's not," I respond, pouting and knowing it. "If it were easy, I'd already have a job."

"You do now." She sets the drink down on the table, purposefully avoiding a coaster. Something tells me Drew's going to zero in on that the sweat outline of that cup like a bloodhound. It's not that he's nitpicky and neat, really—Marnie's told me that he sometimes goes an unreasonable amount of time without doing the laundry—but he's observant. So while he may be the kind of guy you can rely on to pick you up at two in the morning when you stink of gin and can't stop giggling, he's also the kind of guy who might give you shit about making a ring on his coffee table. Probably more to give you hell than because he actually cares. In a weird way, it's one of the things I appreciate about him. If he had too many good qualities, he'd be obnoxious.

"What do you mean, *I do now*?" I ask, glancing from Nicole to Marnie and Sinclair to see if either of them might know what the hell she's talking about. Marnie obviously knows something—her cheeks are pink in that *I know some shit, but I'm not supposed to say anything* way; it's impossible to tell with Sinclair, but then again, she's been an actress since she was a toddler. She's good at hiding things.

"Just what I said," Nicole says, shaking her head slightly. "And here I thought you were smart."

"Presume I am. How would I interpret what you just said?"

"I'm giving you a job. You work for me."

I sit up a bit straighter, suddenly feeling more cheerful. "For real?"

"Did I stutter?"

I look straight at her and say, "My rate is thirty dollars per hour."

She reaches out a hand for a shake. I give her a good one.

"Good," she says with a grin. "I would have paid you twice that."

three

DREW

"YOU'VE GOT to show her you're a man," Reggie says, belching loudly as he lowers his glass to the bar. His beard is especially bushy today, and I have a sudden mental image of a squirrel popping out of it. "Try working out in the apartment. That's what got Sinclair hot and bothered for my boy. She told me so."

Rafe just smirks at his father, slowly shaking his head in fond aggravation. The lighting in the bar is low, and it smells faintly of spilled beer, although not in an unpleasant way. There's a murmuring of conversation that makes for pleasant background noise.

"For the purposes of this conversation, let's assume I don't want to hear anything remotely sexual about either of my sisters," I say as I play with the glass in front of me. "In fact, I'm comfortable with making that a blanket assumption."

Reggie lifts his hands. "Just trying to help, bub. I can tell you need someone to play with the old bait and tackle."

I'm flustered enough that I nearly tip my beer over, but I catch it in time.

"See what I'm talking about?" Reggie says conversationally. "You're all tensed up. You need to let those swimmers do their business, even if it's just into a rubber. You get too many of them backed up, and it's bad for the system."

"I don't... I've had plenty of people play with my..."

Dammit. I don't even know what I'm saying right now.

"How long has it been, man?" Griffin says from behind the bar. He grabs my glass without asking and refills it. Good. I have a feeling I'm going to need it to get through this conversation.

"There've been a few...you know...one-night stands since Lilah."

"You and Lilah broke up over a year ago," he says, lifting his eyebrows.

"Only one-night stands, huh?" Reggie says. "They didn't want to come back for more? If you need a little advice about making them hot between the sheets, I can give you some pointers. The ladies used to call me Reggie the Dinosaur."

"Dad, I'm pretty sure that wasn't a compliment on your sexual prowess," Rafe says with a surprisingly straight face.

"Don't you bet on it," Reggie rebuts. "I had one lady tell me I ate her out like I was a Tyrannosaurus Rex."

I choke a little, even though I don't have anything in my mouth. The guy who was sitting next to me gets up and leaves, heading farther down the bar.

"I don't need any advice on how to have sex, Reggie," I finally manage. "They weren't one-night stands because I was bad in bed. It's—"

"He wasn't over Lilah breaking things off," Griffin suggests.

I can understand why he'd think so. Lilah and I would've gotten married if she'd had her say.

"No, you got this all wrong," Rafe says, glancing first at Griffin and then at me. "Our boy's got it worse than we thought. He already had a thing for Andy."

"I didn't."

Not yet.

Or at least I wasn't aware of it yet.

I think of her long dark curls cascading over her sun-tanned feet, that little ring winking up at me. I've never had a thing for feet. Other people's feet are disgusting, better kept tucked into their shoes. They're meant for conveyance, for bringing a body from one place to another. But then I saw that damn video, and it made me realize things I had no business realizing.

"We're going to help you with this," Griffin says.

Reggie agrees much too enthusiastically. "I'm gonna let you borrow my copy of the *Kama Sutra*. Now, I know what you're going to think, but it's just frosting between the pages. I was looking at it when I had this big box of donuts, and—

"I'm not borrowing your copy of the *Kama Sutra*, man. I told you it's not a problem with—" I almost say *my bait and tackle*, but I bite my tongue in time. "Anyway. I don't want anything to happen with Andy. She's like a sister to Marnie, and besides, she's staying with me. I won't do anything to make her uncomfortable. She's had enough shit happen to her—she doesn't need me letting her down too."

"And that, my friend, is exactly why you shouldn't give up," Griffin says emphatically. "You care about her. She deserves to be with someone who cares about her."

I squirm on my stool, uncomfortable. They're getting me all wrong. I might care about Andy, I might want her, but that doesn't mean anything can or should happen between us. Not that she'd ever go for me anyway. She—

"Can I get a drink down here?" a woman calls out from a few stools down. Griffin waves in acknowledgement but stays put.

"Andy thinks I'm boring," I say. Then, because there's something to be said for honesty, "Fuck, from her perspective, I *am* boring. There's no way a woman like her would be interested in someone like me. I like things to be comfortable. Easy. She's—"

Trouble, but in a way that makes you want more.

"Can you leave the boring guy alone and come take my order?" the woman calls out.

Griffin shakes his head slightly, his mouth quirked in a smile, then reaches over the bar to clap me on the shoulder before walking away.

"You don't like your boring life half as much as you think you do," Rafe says knowingly.

I'm suddenly annoyed with him. Where does he get off telling me what I do and don't like? First, he had to have his say about Andy, and now this.

"Are you my self-appointed therapist?"

"Maybe I should be," he says good-naturedly. "If I were, I'd point out that if you were so into your comfortable, easy life, then you wouldn't have such a hard-on for someone like Andy."

His words cling to me like the seed pods from a burdock plant. For some reason, I find myself thinking of Lilah. She was an accountant like my father, and she made these really impressive spreadsheets to help keep herself—and the people in her life—organized. They were color coordinated and everything. She made one for Marnie and me so we could evenly share the chores in the house after our dad died. (We ignored it.) She made one for me so I could keep my ideas organized for work. (I ignored it.)

She made one to schedule our sex life.

I *tried* to ignore it.

"You know, Lilah made really nice spreadsheets," I find myself saying. "Top notch. They were supposed to make everything more streamlined."

"You broke up with her, didn't you?" he says, his eyes sparkling as he shifts toward me on his stool. It creaks in disagreement, and I wouldn't be surprised if it shattered. I'm a tall guy, but Rafe's tall and wide—a beast—the kind of person who could break chairs just by sitting on them. "Griffin seems to think she broke things off, so

I'm guessing you told people it was mutual, but he's wrong. You did."

Hell, maybe he really should be my therapist. He's seeing through me like cellophane tonight.

Everything should have felt right with Lilah—she was sexy and smart, and life always felt organized with her. Under control. *Safe.* She kept me—and herself—on track. But we had a conversation about our future one night, and she followed up the next morning by presenting me with a spreadsheet tallying up what we should spend on our wedding. I felt like I was in a business meeting, and it made me twitchy in a way that surprised me. I thought about it for two days. I even made my own damn list. Then Marnie told me she was sick of me sitting around brooding, and backed me into going bowling with her and her friends. What she didn't mention was that it was glow stick night. I rolled my eyes at her when we walked in and then asked Andy if this was her bright idea.

"Obviously," she said. "I'm full of bright ideas."

Then she snapped glow sticks together into a crown and set it on top of her curls. "I hereby declare myself the Queen of Bright Ideas."

She made another and set it on top of my head. "The court jester."

"I'm grateful for the confirmation that you think I'm hilarious, but no thanks," I said, pocketing it.

It glowed from inside my pocket, and she told me my balls were on fire.

Hell, it was fun. We wore glow sticks and drank Jell-O shots and danced in the dark when they shut off the lights at midnight. I didn't want to be anywhere else. I certainly didn't want Lilah to be there. And that decided it. If I had more fun hanging out with my sister and her friends than with my girlfriend, then something wasn't right in my relationship.

So when Lilah came over for breakfast the next day, I sat her down and told her no.

"No to a big wedding?" She'd pursed her lips and tucked a loose strand of hair into her bun. "We could elope, although I won't go to Vegas, Andrew. It's *dirty*. I know someone who caught herpes from a toilet seat at one of the casinos."

"I don't think you can get herpes that way."

"You tell that to her open sores," she said, sniffing.

I was tempted to ask her if she'd seen the open sores, but there was no point in getting in an argument about it. So I cleared my throat. "I think we need to break up, Lilah," I said. "I care about you, but there's something..."

Missing.

The most disorganized thing she ever did was to dump my dirty laundry into the toilet and then scrape *loser* into the side of my car. The penmanship was, of course, good, the word *very* readable.

I left it there. It's a reminder, although what the lesson is supposed to be, I'm less sure.

Somehow, Marnie slept through all of it, and when she asked me about the "loser" engraving later on, I pretended it was the result of a bet I'd lost with my friends.

"Okay, yeah, you're right," I say. "But it was because she made a spreadsheet for our sex life. Everyone has their limits."

"You sure you don't need some lessons, friend?" Reggie says, stroking his beard thoughtfully. "Because that's not the kind of thing a woman would do if you're steaming it up between the sheets."

I shake my head, more amused than annoyed. "She was just like that. She literally had a spreadsheet for everything." Turning to Rafe, I nod. "So, yeah, in a way you're right. I guess I don't want life to be too boring. But I don't have it bad for Andy like you're thinking. I just... She's hot. I've noticed for years, but that doesn't mean I feel inclined to do anything about it. And not just because she's my sister's friend. She's...an agent of chaos. I don't need that in my life."

He studies me for a long moment, then twists his mouth to the side and leans closer on his stool, the seat creaking. "I'm telling you this as a friend, Drew, that might be exactly what you need."

"What about her books, man?" Griffin says, returning to his spot behind the bar and resuming the conversation as if he hadn't left. "Marnie tells me she's into romance books. Why don't you try reading one of them? It'd give you something to talk about."

"They all have half-naked men on the covers. I don't want to read about some guy's rigid sword or cucumber or whatever euphemism they use."

Reggie snorts. "But you'd also get to read about the woman's quivering pudding, son."

"I don't want to read about any of it," I say. "I'd rather keep food and sex separate."

"Maybe you really *do* have a limited imagination," Rafe says, smirking.

"Romance books aren't like that anymore," Griffin says. Then shrugs. "Most of them, at least. They use the proper words for things."

Reggie helpfully spouts off a few.

"So, what?" I ask, feeling sweat gathering under my collar. "Are you telling me she reads porn?"

How many times have I seen Andy curled up on the couch in my house, a paperback book or her kindle clutched in her hand, reading with a rapt expression next to Marnie? I can see her now, biting her lip, maybe twisting a lock of her impossible hair. Was she reading graphic sex while she did that? The thought's more alluring than I'd like it to be, and I know I'll never be able to see her reading again without wondering what's in front of her.

Thanks a lot, Griffin.

"Yes," Griffin says, with a wicked grin. "People always appreciate it when you pay attention to the things they like and keep an open mind. If you're *very* lucky, she might even want to act out the scenes with you."

"Damn it, you're talking about my sister, aren't you? Do you have any bleach behind the counter I can pour into my ears?"

He looks amused, because of course he does—it's not *his* sister who's being discussed. "Speaking of...does Marnie know about any of this, man? Because if she does, she hasn't said anything to me."

"No," I say, feeling my ears burning. "And you're not going to tell her either." I shoot an accusatory look at Rafe. "Or Sinclair."

They both lift their hands. "Don't worry," Rafe says with a slight smile. "I've been told I don't gossip nearly enough. Just make sure you don't let anyone get my dad drunk."

"He has a point," Reggie says, lifting his glass. "I do get a little chatty when I've had one too many." He says this as if he couldn't talk the ear off an elephant without drinking a single drop of alcohol.

Fantastic.

four

DREW

RAFE DROPS me back at the house. Before I got out of the car, he shoots me a look and says, "We're going to help you, man."

"Yeah," I say, unfastening my seat belt. "That's what I'm afraid of."

Marnie and Sinclair must have cleared out, because there are no cars in the driveway other than my dark blue Subaru Outback, the neatly scraped *loser* in the side greeting me home, and Andy's old station wagon.

There's a feeling of anticipation tingling inside of me, because I know she's inside. It's twined with uneasiness, because usually going home is a comfortable thing—it's the place where I can unwind, somewhere I know no real demands are going to be made of me. But it's become unfamiliar to me, an unknown quantity.

When I walk in, the combined smell of the scented candles attempts to smother me. Damn, I really need to convince her to narrow it down to one scent.

The lights are off, but the television is on the screensaver, a massive, glowing bear casting light on Andy, who's splayed on the couch, her long hair spilling off one end, her legs tucked under the bright throw blanket, which is also spilling over the side of the couch. One of her throw pillows is wedged under her head. Something warm unfurls inside of my chest. I might not be crazy about the rug, or the tea set, or the books…but I like seeing her there. I go to her without really meaning to and pull up that blanket so it's covering more of her.

She makes a low sound in her throat and snuggles in deeper.

Then her eyes snap open, and she punches me in the balls, her aim so accurate it's like she has a homing beacon.

"Jesus Christ," I shout, bending over, sharp pain radiating throughout my body and pooling in my midsection. It feels like I'm about to puke. Or drop to the floor and play dead like a possum. "What the fuck did you do that for?"

Her eyes widen to wakefulness, and she sits up, her hair splaying around her shoulders. "Oh shit. I'm sorry, Drew. I was disoriented. I thought I was at my grandmother's house, and some dude had broken in and… Can I get you an ice pack?"

I don't answer. I'm too busy sinking into the part of the couch she vacated, but she gets up and hurries over to the refrigerator.

When she comes back, she has a bag of frozen peas.

"Really?" I choke out.

"It's appropriate!" she says, thrusting it at me. "They're little balls."

"Glad you're finding humor in the situation," I say with a groan, taking the bag and pressing it against my crotch, because in that moment I have no chill.

"Sorry, sorry. Gallows humor." She perches on the arm of the couch and watches me, her expression suddenly nervous. "Do you already regret having me here?"

"Right now? Yes."

She laughs, a husky sound that would probably be doing things to my dick if I didn't still feel like I'd been slammed with a sledgehammer.

"Not right now," she says after a moment. "I meant before I hit you in the balls."

"No, I don't regret it," I reply with a sigh. "But can we please, for the love of God, stick with one flavor of scented candle?"

Her lips twitch into an almost smile. "They're not flavors, Drew, you can't eat them."

There's something perverse about me because I find myself thinking of quivering pudding and sex and food. I *really* need to go to bed, though I can already tell it'll be a long time before I get any sleep.

"One flavor," I repeat stodgily. "It smells like a candle factory. To be clear, that's a bad thing."

"What about vanilla spice?" she says, lifting her eyebrows. There's a wicked glint in her eyes and, God help me, I like it.

"I can tell you're leading into a joke about me being vanilla," I say, "but I'm too wrecked to object. Vanilla spice it is."

I get up, groaning a little more, and then carry the peas back into the kitchen.

"Please tell me you're not putting your crotch peas back in the freezer," she says.

I wasn't intending to, but now I'm feeling contrary. "Why not?" I ask, turning to her, still feeling a twinge of pain from my crotch. "It's not like I stuffed them into my boxer briefs."

"Boxer briefs? I had you down as a tighty-whiteys type."

"Believe it or not, I know enough about women to understand that's an insult." I gaze at her as I toss the peas into the trash, and her slight smile makes me smile back.

"I'd never." She's saying she'd never insult me—not that she'd never want to see what's in my boxer briefs, but that's what it feels like. I remind myself that whatever my new friends have to say about the matter, I shouldn't want her *that way*. It's better like this —being friends but not in each other's business. The way we've been for years, more or less. We've hung out countless times, but always with the buffer of Marnie and other people.

Then I notice that her eyes look puffy and slightly red in the low lighting. God help me.

"Hey, are you all right?" I ask. "I know this has been—"

"Sure, yeah. I'm fine," she says, her guard going up, not that I'm surprised. She prides herself on being tough. Always has.

"Okay, tough guy," I say, giving her a nod. If her walls make her feel safe, I'm not going to attack them. "I'm going to bed to clutch my aching balls while I cry myself to sleep."

That gets a laugh out of her. I grab a glass of water from the kitchen, then pause and get another for her. She looks surprised when I walk over to the table to hand it over.

"You didn't need to do that, Drew," she says.

"No shit, but I can do something nice for you without having Nicole corner me into it." I pause, then tell her honestly, "You should know that I would have offered you a place to stay even if she hadn't taken it upon herself to offer for me."

She takes the cup of water from me, her fingers grazing mine, and I feel a jolt from her touch that I try not to show. Her eyes are light brown, fringed with deep black lashes, and they've always been expressive—like you could fall into her moods if you weren't careful, because they're swimming on the surface. It's happened to me before. I defy anyone not to feel joyful—or sad—when she does.

"Thank you for that," she says. "Now you can go clutch your balls like a baby." Her lips lift up. "But I *did* want to tell you that I got a job."

I glance down at her feet before I can stop myself.

"Not that kind of a job, pervert."

"Yeah, *I'm* the pervert," I mutter, thinking of those books that apparently talk about something other than jiggling puddings.

"Aren't you going to ask me what the job is?"

I realize we're still standing close together, close enough to touch, but I don't move back. Neither does she, but probably only because she doesn't notice or care.

"Well, what is it?" I ask. "It's too late in the night for dramatic pauses."

"Nicole and Damien are hiring me to work for them," she says, beaming with the news. "She said I could work toward becoming a licensed P.I. if I want."

"And do you want to?" I ask, suddenly uncomfortable. P.I. work can be dangerous, and Nicole and Damien probably offend half a dozen different people before breakfast. Working for them definitely isn't a safe choice, but the choice also isn't mine to make, and Andy definitely isn't the type to opt for comfort over excitement.

"Yeah," she says. "I'm excited, except..."

"You're worried it might be dangerous," I blurt.

She looks taken aback. "Uh, no. The possibility didn't even cross my mind."

Of course it didn't.

"Maybe I just don't want to get fired from my third job in three months." She lifts the water to her lips and takes a sip. I don't want to, but I track the movement as she presses her full lips to the glass. It's like I'm more aware of her now that the guys have called me on my attraction.

Goddammit. I was plenty aware of her before.

"I'm pretty sure they wouldn't fire you," I say, forcing myself to look away. "Nicole seems really into the whole fairy godmother thing, and firing someone wouldn't exactly give them a karmic boost."

"Yeah, I guess you're right," she says. "On the plus side, this means I can start paying you rent earlier than I thought."

I'm already shaking my head. She needs to save up her money, not hand it over to me. My father owned this house, free and clear, before he died—which means I'm only paying taxes, plus the money I'm going to transfer to Marnie each month to pay off her half.

There's no reason for Andy to pony up what little cash she has. "I don't want you to do that. Buy some groceries if you want." A corner of my mouth hitches up. "Or some pedicure shit."

"I don't want to be a freeloader."

She says it like it's a dirty word, and to her, I know it is. "You're protecting me from being in this house alone. Do you know what it's like being alone in a house this size and hearing the floor creak? I sleep with a baseball bat beside my bed. Your room's the first one down the hallway. So now I can sleep the sleep of someone who knows they'd be attacked second."

We're across the hall from each other, neither of us first or second, but I got what I wanted. She's laughing again, and I feel like a cat that's found a patch of sunlight, because *I* did that. "I'm glad I can protect you, Drew, but for real, let me contribute something."

"Groceries. Or buy some power tools if you think that's sexist."

She laughs harder, but I can tell her heart's not in it anymore. There's a little crease in her brow.

"What's wrong?" I ask, concerned. "Are you...homesick?"

She heaves a sigh. "I'm worried about my grandmother. I know she did a bad thing, pushing me out, but she's stuck relying on my brothers now, and you've heard enough of me bitching to Marnie to know they're self-involved jerks. Especially Theo."

She's opening up more than I thought she would, more than I can remember her ever doing with me.

"I'm sorry, Andy. Those assholes haven't been bothering you, have they?" I'm bristling, and I know it. I already want to track them down and have a word with them about the shit they've pulled on her.

"No," she says. Then, more emphatically, "No. Don't worry about me, Drew. You don't need to worry about me. I know you've got plenty of your own stuff to worry about."

But she says it like she knows that I don't. She's right, I guess. I've avoided having the kind of life I have to worry about overly much. I've done it purposefully, because what happened after college made me *want* that kind of life—even if I'm starting to wonder if Rafe is right and it's not enough.

She takes a step back, nods, then says, "I'm going to bed." With that, she walks off toward the stairs, her shapely ass swaying beneath her sweatpants. I don't move until she's out of sight, and then I walk over to the turquoise bookshelf and choose the book that looks like it's gotten the most action. Maybe it'll help me understand her.

ANDY

IT'S MONDAY MORNING.

It feels weird waking up in Drew's house, knowing he's inside too, doing...

Well, hell, I don't know what he does in his spare time. I feel like I *should* know, but I guess I've always taken him for granted. *He's Drew, and he's there when Marnie or I need him. He's Drew, and I like messing with him, and he likes messing with me. He's Drew, and he's safe.* That's a shitty attitude, and I promise myself I'll improve upon it. He was so sweet to me yesterday, even after I busted him in the balls for the crime of walking into his own house.

It sounds stupid, but I was choking back tears when he gave me that glass of water. I couldn't remember the last time someone other than Marnie or Grace had done something like that for me—gotten me something not because I'd asked for it but because they recognized I needed it.

I check my phone for a message from Nicole, but I'm not surprised there isn't one. It's seven o'clock, and Nicole's never struck me as an early riser—more like the kind of person who never went to bed in the first place. I know because that's how I'd naturally be, when I'm not required to report early to a daycare and take care of a bunch of other people's kids.

I slide the phone into the pocket of my sweats and head out my bedroom door, humming, but my gaze finds Drew's door and sticks. Maybe I'll ask him if he likes pancakes. I mean, what sane person doesn't? It would be a nice gesture to make the man breakfast. He *did* give me a place to live. Then I'll go through the candles and give all the non-vanilla-spice ones away. Or I can store them in my closet so we can swap them out periodically.

I knock lightly on his door. He hollers something I don't process, other than the last two words—*come in*. His voice is strained, and worry pricks at me. Shit, did I punch him so hard in the balls he suffered a rupture? That happened to a guy Sinclair struck in the balls, although that dude definitely deserved it.

I swing the door open, and for a second I'm frozen. Drew's sitting up on the bed, naked other than a pair of athletic shorts he has shoved down, his slightly wavy brown hair mussed, his eyes wide with shock, his hand wrapped around his cock. His *enormous* cock. A paperback book is sitting beside him, facedown on the bed.

Wait...

"Is that my book?" I ask before I can think better of it.

"Andy, what the fuck?" he shouts, grabbing a blanket from the foot of the bed and pulling it up, but it doesn't do anything to hide that monster tenting it, or his chest and arms, which are more defined than I remember them. Apparently those workouts he's been doing with Rafe have stuck.

Holy shit.

I feel a surprising wash of heat that settles between my legs.

"Get out!" he shouts again, and this time his words don't fail to register.

Yes, the thing to do when you walk in on someone masturbating is to leave—unless you want to join in. And I definitely can't do that. I about-face and leave the room.

As I head downstairs, my mind stays fixed on Drew, on the sight of his hand wrapped around his dick. Is he going to finish?

It feels strange going about my business now that I know what he's up to. I can't deny that thought turns me on as I bustle around the kitchen, following the directions on my phone to make pancake batter. While I'm down here measuring flour, he's probably pumping his hand up and down that bad boy, his face straining as he—

What the fuck is *wrong* with me?

I've known Drew since I was six and a half years old. He's Marnie's brother, for God's sake. I can't let the revelation that he has nice cock send me down a bad path. He's untouchable. And I don't *want* to touch him.

At least I don't think I do. My mind feels like a pretzel, wrapped around the memory of Drew's hand moving up and down, the muscles bunching and releasing as he pleasures himself.

It takes him a long time to come down. Long enough that I've finished the pancakes and set the table. I'm not sure why, because I've never been the bashful type, but my heart starts racing when I finally hear him on the stairs, then I burst out laughing when he comes into view.

It's summer—a balmy day in late June, or so my phone app tells me—but he's got on a long-sleeve shirt with a short-sleeve shirt over it, paired with sweatpants, like he's overcompensating for me seeing him naked by overdressing. It's funny is all. Even funnier when his cheeks start burning.

"Jesus, Andy." He scratches the back of his neck. "You don't need to laugh."

"I'm sorry," I say, bending over the table, my hands fixed on the edge. I notice him noticing, and I feel another flash of heat that I cover up with more laughter. "It's just...you were really going at it. Did you finish? Should I give you a round of applause?"

"I told you not to come in," he grumbles. He glances at the door, like he's considering fleeing his own house.

Right. This *is* his house. I was supposed to be thanking him, not making him regret he was ever born.

"You don't have anything to be embarrassed about," I tell him. "Everyone does it. I do too. We should figure out a code word, or maybe we can put socks on our door handles like they do in college."

His blush burns brighter. It's...cute.

"Besides, you're packing some serious heat, my friend. If anything, you should be proud."

"Let's never talk about this again," he says, sitting down at the table and serving himself a couple of pancakes with a fork. He pours syrup over them.

I settle into the seat opposite him and do the same. Part of me wants to ask if he worked up an appetite, but he's obviously embarrassed and doesn't want me to harp on this—even if I *do* enjoy teasing him. The thing to do is to let it go. Except...

I need to know something first.

"Were you reading that book? Was that what did it? Because there's this one scene at the beginning, where she's getting it on with the two dudes, and he's going at her from the front while the other guy takes the back door—"

"Andy. Shit." He looks away. "I'm sorry. Obviously, I'll get you a new copy. I just... I didn't realize you were reading books *like that.*"

"Yeah, this situation is a lot like that bag of peas you had to throw away last night," I say. "You can keep the book." I wink at him, mostly to watch him squirm. "You obviously like it too."

He nearly chokes on the bite of pancake he just took.

"Ohhhkay," he says, lifting the plate. "I'm gonna go upstairs now. Don't wait up."

"It's morning!" I nearly hop out of my chair. "Don't hide in your room. It's like I said, it's completely normal and not weird at all. In fact, I'm glad we're comfortable enough with each other to have this conversation." Except we're obviously not, or *he's* obviously not. And it's probably not completely normal that I keep thinking about his dick. It was shocking, is all. *Unexpected*. I've never really seen Drew in a sexual light—he's just *Drew*, like he has a category all to himself in my mind.

And now he's Drew with the big cock, who likes jerking off to the same scenes that make me grab for my vibrator.

"Yeah, I've got to get ready for work. And, for the record, I am actually very uncomfortable with this conversation," he says. "If we could forget that it ever happened, that would be for the best. And, please, for the love of God, don't say anything to my sisters."

I lift a hand to my chest as if I'm doing the pledge of allegiance. "Scout's honor."

"Thank you," he says, nodding. "Now, I'm going upstairs to put on more clothes. Maybe a chastity belt."

A smile sneaks out of me. "To keep you safe from yourself?"

"It's you who worries me, Ruiz," he says with a teasing grin. "You're the take-no-prisoners type."

"Probably wise," I say, sitting back down. I cut off a big bite of pancakes. "Although I guess I mustn't have socked you that hard in the balls after all."

He's shaking his head ruefully as he walks away with his plate of breakfast, but he looks back at me before he heads up the stairs. "Hey, just so you know, my buddies are coming over for a game night on Wednesday. Seven o'clock."

"Oh, cool," I say. "I kick ass at board games."

He nudges the bottom stair with his foot. "It's kind of a four-person game we're playing."

"Oh," I say, feeling a swell of self-consciousness. I guess he wouldn't want me to join—I can't expect him to include me in things just because I'm here. He has his life; I have mine. They've intersected in the past, but that doesn't mean he wants to suddenly be my bestie.

"It's not like that," he says, setting the plate on the end cap of the banister to balance it. "You wouldn't want to. We have this long-running D&D campaign."

"You're still playing Dungeons & Dragons?" I ask. I know he and his pals used to play it in middle school and high school. On a couple of occasions, Marnie and I spied on them, because we figured they might be doing something interesting.

He scowls at me. "You don't need to act like it's a kid thing," he says. "Plenty of adults play it."

I lift my hands. "Didn't mean it like that. Besides, no one could confuse you for a kid."

I didn't mean to put the insinuation behind my words, but I can't deny it's there.

"Going upstairs now," he says, starting to climb.

I'm not sure what possesses me, since I'm not exactly the Dungeons & Dragons type, but I ask, "Can I watch?"

He drops the plate, then swears a blue streak when it cracks and pancakes and syrup fly everywhere.

I grab a napkin and hurry over to help him.

He takes one look at it and then bursts out laughing. "What're you going to do with that?"

"So I'm shit at cleaning," I say, laughing too, since the mess is obviously not going to be fixed by one napkin that's not even wet. "You were going to find out eventually." I go to pick up one of the shards of the plate, but he stops me with a hand at my wrist.

"I'll do it," he says, "I don't want you to hurt yourself."

"Do you take me for a shrinking violet?" I ask, lifting my eyebrows. "Because if you do, I've really done something wrong."

"No, Ruiz," he says as he shakes his head slightly and smirks. "I don't think anyone could mistake you for that. But it's my mess, and I don't need anyone else cleaning up my messes."

"I could say the same," I tell him, pointedly picking up a piece of the plate, "but here I am with you, and one could argue you're cleaning up *my* messes."

"Nah," he says as he picks up more of the broken plate. "I'm just giving you a boost. That's what friends do."

His eyes are on mine, and I feel warmth gather inside of me. "A friend would let me watch their D&D game."

"Oh," he says, as if surprised. "That's what... You seriously want to watch us play D&D?"

"What'd you think I wanted to watch?" I ask, still holding that shard of the broken plate. Then it hits me, and I can't help but grin. "Well, it *was* quite the show, but you obviously didn't want a peanut gallery."

He's flushing slightly, but he doesn't look away. "Who says I want one for D&D? Something tells me you're not going to sit there silently drinking a beer."

"I prefer margaritas."

"Then I hope you know how to make them."

"I do," I say, smiling. "Does that mean I can come?" I'm not sure why I'm making such a big deal out of this, but I really do want to see what it's all about. It's clearly important to him. Besides, I've met his buddies before in passing, but I don't really know them. I should, if I'm going to be living here.

"Make margaritas and you're a shoe-in."

I'd prop a hand on my hip, but there's that shard of plate to consider. "So the woman needs to make the refreshments?" Although I'm teasing, there's an edge of seriousness in there too. My mother had always doted on Theo and Jack—and she'd encouraged me to do the same, even though Theo was an entitled dick who'd eventually taught Jack to follow in his footsteps.

"Nah," Drew says. "I'm going to make the dragon dip."

"Is that a thing?" I ask, strangely excited.

"Oh, it's a thing," he says with a grin. And for a moment there, looking at his slightly wavy hair and that grin, his white teeth flashing at me, all I can think about is that I've known Drew nearly my entire life, but there's so much more I'd like to know about him.

And if my mind summons that image again, of his hand on his dick, that's between me and my subconscious.

ANDY

NICOLE DOESN'T CALL ME, it turns out. She just shows up at the house at half past twelve, several hours after Drew left for work. I've been puttering around, putting more of my stuff away and dealing with the over-candling situation. Plus, I *may* have peeked into Drew's room to see if the book was still splayed open on the bed. Since it was, I did the obvious thing and checked to see where he'd stopped reading —yup, it was the threesome scene. And I *may* have stopped back into my room for self-care—although I'm not a heathen and locked the door—but that's only because it's been a while since I got any.

When I let Nicole in, she steps into the house, a cloth garment bag in hand. It's so full it looks like a stuffed animal. She promptly crinkles her nose and says, "Why does it smell so basic in here?"

"Vanilla spice," I say, lifting a candle from the kitchen counter. "I've decided it's Drew's scent."

She gives a wicked laugh, then inclines her head toward her shoulder, cracking it. "Good call."

"Do you want to sit down?"

"Do I *look* like I want to sit down?"

"You look like you had a long night," I say. Because she does—

there are dark circles under her eyes, and her short pink hair is mussed.

"I did," she agrees. Sighing, she slings the garment bag over the side table in the foyer, knocking over a few framed photos. The one in the back flies onto the floor with a clink of breaking glass. "Oops," she says in an unrepentant tone. "Hope that was a photo of their mother."

The Jones family matriarch is a narcissistic nut job. So, yeah, I hope it's a picture of her too. But when I bend to retrieve it, picking it up, I see Drew and four other dudes posed in front of a mountain trailhead—Craggy Gardens. They're young, early twenties maybe. Drew was scrawnier then, in that stage where he let his hair grow out for several months before chopping it when someone told him he looked like a Jonas brother. I recognize three of his buddies, but not the fourth. There's a fissure down the middle of the glass that looks foreboding and tells me I'll be heading to Michaels later to get him a new frame. Even if he had this photo hidden in the back, where no one can see it, thus making it a pointless display, I can't just leave it broken.

"Huh, who's this guy?" Nicole asks, pointing to the one person I don't recognize. He's got a James Dean thing going on, with a sexy glower that doesn't match the enthusiastic grins of the rest of the group. "Looks like he got the short straw in gym class and got paired up with a bunch of nerds. Well..." She pauses, then taps another of the guys. I think his name is Kirk or something like that. "That guy doesn't look like a nerd either. Two short straws."

"Drew's not a nerd," I snap. Then, propelled by some impulse I don't fully understand, other than that my mind's been on it all morning, I add, "I'll have you know, he has a huge dick."

She lifts her eyebrows and then whistles. "I gotta hand it to you, you work fast. I appreciate the hustle." Then she lifts her fist to me, presumably for a bump.

I don't give it to her. "It's not like that," I insist, annoyed. "I walked in on him jerking off."

My mind jumps to that image of him.

"Wanted to check out the goods before making a decision," she says, nodding. "I get it."

"It was a mistake," I snap, then add, "but he's not a nerd."

"He can be a good-looking nerd with a big cock, you know," she says, walking into the kitchen and helping herself to a cup, which she fills with water. She's apparently as familiar with these cabinets as I am. Then again, she's like me—the kind of woman who's used to helping herself to what she wants. "Those things aren't mutually exclusive," she continues, turning back toward me with a speculative expression. "Besides, I'll shank you if you tell anyone I said so, but you shouldn't assume being a nerd is a *bad* thing. He's a smart, scruffy dude who likes video games and those movies with dumb space shit and doesn't care about clothes. *Nerd*." She shrugs. "But Griffin likes that stuff too, and Marnie seems like a satisfied woman."

"I'm not *interested* in Drew," I say emphatically, setting the broken frame on the table and following her into the kitchen. "He just so happened to be in a compromising position when I walked into the room. It happens."

"Uh-huh, sure," she says, winking at me. "Your secret's safe with me."

Fuck, it probably isn't, is it?

"Don't tell anyone," I insist, giving her the same look I gave four-year-old Jason Steward a few months ago after he whipped it out and peed all over the wall to see if he could make the shape of his name. The J was surprisingly convincing. "He'll be pissed. And then I'll be pissed. He was super embarrassed."

She takes a long sip of water, studying me over the glass, then sets it aside. "Sounds like he doesn't have much to be embarrassed about, if you know what I'm saying."

"No, he really doesn't," I agree, smiling despite myself. I'm kind of glad I have someone to talk to about this, even if it can't be Marnie (for obvious reasons) or Grace (because it's not the kind of news you break to your friend over the phone). "It was kind of shocking, if I'm being honest."

She shrugs. "It's the stealthy ones who catch you off guard. I mean, you look at Damien, and you think, big dick." Another shrug. "You'd be right. I'm a *very* satisfied woman. But Drew doesn't have obvious BDE." She gives me a speculative look. "Maybe he just needs a woman to ride him right."

"Not it," I say, lifting my hands. But I can't deny my palms feel slightly sweaty. It's just that image from this morning. I need to figure out how to banish it from my brain. "So what's with the garment bag?"

"Well, I'm so glad you asked," she says with a sharp grin. "You're going to spend the day dressed as a banana. You spent the morning looking at one, so it should be right up your alley."

"Is there a reason for this, beyond humiliation?" I ask, putting a hand on my hip and leaning against the wall in the entrance to the kitchen.

She finishes her water before answering me. "Thirty dollars an hour," she says, although there's more amusement than attitude in her tone. "You'll be watching a man who has a meeting in an apartment over a smoothie shop."

"I'm going undercover?" I ask, getting amped up. I mean, the most exciting thing that happened at the daycare was when the kids got in line to sing their ABCs at a "pageant" I'd made the arrangements for, and they all started projectile vomiting on their parents, who'd gathered across from them for the show.

Nicole gives me a wry look. "If that makes it more palatable to you, yes. There's a camera tucked into the suit. I'll show you how to use it. But don't interact with this dude."

"Is he dangerous?" I ask, remembering what Drew asked me last night.

She snorts. "Not unless you're a box of staples. He's been accused of reselling office supplies."

That takes some of the wind out of my sails. Still, it's better than getting puked on.

"Was it at least a *lot* of office supplies?" I ask.

seven

DREW

The Last Dungeon on the Right chat, WhatsApp

Long story, but Marnie's friend Andy is going to be living with me for a while. I invited her to watch us play D&D tonight. Anyone have a problem with that?

Burke: You mean hot Andy? Hell, yeah, she can join us. She can join us every week.

Shane: Sure, I don't care. As long as you don't forget the snacks. Last time you forgot the snacks.

Danny: I don't know, man. Is she going to ask a lot of questions? I want to actually play tonight.

Burke: You need to get laid.

Danny: I had high hopes for my character getting laid. Hence my hesitation.

Burke: Drew's Dungeon Master. Not gonna happen. He doesn't get laid, no one gets laid. And now he's got Andy living with him. His balls must be Carolina blue.

45

I TAP my pen on the side of my desk, then drop it. Probably because my hands are slick with sweat. I knew Burke was going to say something. He's always been a ladies' man, and I'm not going to sit by while he tries to play footsie with my roommate under the kitchen table. No way in hell will I let him disrespect her like that.

> Hands off Andy, Burke. I don't want you flirting with her. She's off-limits.

> Burke: Maybe for you, bro. Marnie's not my sister, and Andy's not YOUR sister.

> OFF. LIMITS.

I pause, then add:

> FINNEAS.

Now, I know how this sounds, and I certainly won't be telling Andy about it, but when Burke, Danny, Shane, and I were kids, we developed a fantasy language for one of our long-running D&D campaigns. *Finneas* was a magical word—an oath of friendship that could only be invoked once in a blue moon. If you called *finneas*, your friends had damn well better listen to you.

> Shane: Well, shit. You better listen to him, Burke. The last time finneas was ignored, Leonard disappeared.

I feel a twinge of guilt. Or grief. Of responsibility. I'm glad Shane can joke about it. You should be able to joke about the screwed-up things that've happened to you, if at all possible. But for me it'll always feel like scratching at a scab—satisfying for only about ten seconds before it starts to hurt. Then again, what happened to our friend wasn't Danny's fault; it was mine.

Burke: Message received. Sorry, Drew. Didn't
realize you had a thing for her.

I'm about to type back that I don't, but I guess that would be a lie, or at least half of one, and I've promised myself not to knowingly lie to the people I care about. My mother's an accomplished liar, and she's also a shitty person who causes problems. So less lying, fewer problems.

Yeah, there are snacks, Shane. Maybe try not to
shove them all into your face at once this time.

Shane: It was a bet.

Danny: It was stupid. We all thought it was stupid.
Even Burke, and it was his bet.

Burke: Can I bring a woman next week?

If you can find someone to take pity on you, sure.

Danny: I don't like where this is going.

Burke: Yeah, because you know you won't find
anyone who'll take pity on you.

I cast my phone aside, trying not to feel twitchy about the whole thing. It's been a little weird with Andy over the last couple of days, for obvious reasons.

She might think that scene in the book made me jerk off, but it didn't. Sure, it was a lot hotter than I thought it would be, but what made me hard was the thought of Andy reading it, of it making her hot, of her reaching down beneath her panty line and touching herself. That thought took over my brain, and I knew I needed to do something about it before I saw her, because otherwise I'd be walking downstairs with a hard-on she was bound to notice.

But the lock on my door was busted, and I hadn't made the time to fix it—a mistake I've since dealt with.

I told myself I wouldn't avoid her after she walked in on me with my dick in my hand, her book propped open beside me, but it would be easier to follow through with that pledge if she'd stop *talking about it*. And if I hadn't seen a flash of something that wasn't disgust in her eyes before she turned and left the other morning. And if she didn't like showering at night—and *I* didn't have to walk past the closed bathroom door, hearing the pounding water and imagining it raining down on her glorious curves, her long hair wet and plastered to her breasts.

Maybe Danny's not the only one who needs to get laid.

I'm running my hands through my hair, cursing under my breath, when my boss pokes his head into the room.

"Drew!"

"Yup, that's still my name," I mutter, pushing out my chair slightly. "What's up?"

"I'm guessing you saw that *BuzzFeed* article about the game?" he asks with a bit too much self-satisfaction. "Great lead-in to the launch, huh?"

I fight a cringe. My old boss was my mentor—a man who believed in doing things the right way, however long it took, and taught me to do the same. But doing things the right way isn't exactly quick, so the dumbasses in charge pushed him into early retirement and gave the job to Ryan, who's twenty-four. He's been talking up the game we're working on—yet another first-person shooter game, this one with clown zombies—as if the launch is right around the corner.

The launch is *not* right around the corner, unless he wants to make a game out of all the bugs players can find. Right now, if the MC's not careful, they might find themselves stuck in between their bed and the wall with no possible escape. Unless they enjoy existential dilemmas, that's not going to get us great press, but again, try convincing Ryan of that. I can guarantee he'd spout a bunch of bullshit about can-do attitudes.

My friends and I have been working on a game of our own for a few years now—something we've put together in our free time. Danny's the coder, and I'm the designer. Burke and Shane aren't as involved, but they've both helped with the story. We're calling it *Survival of the Fittest*—and, yes, there are plenty of survival games out there too.

But this one is special.

Danny says we're done. Burke says we're done. Shane says we're done.

But I keep dragging my feet. The fire needs to be brighter and more realistic, the grass should look like less of a unit and more like individual strands...

Besides, who's going to back it? I'd thought about presenting it to my old boss, but I'm glad I held back. Because *this guy* would be in charge of it.

"Yup," I say. "Fan-tastic."

He frowns at me, his brow giving an impressive furrow. "Is something wrong, Drew?"

"Nope," I say. "Everything is exactly the way it's supposed to be."

A fucking mess. Call it karma, if you will.

———

"I'm so excited," Andy says, bright-eyed, as we wait downstairs for the guys to arrive. We're sitting opposite each other at the dining room table after preparing the dip and drinks.

"About the dragon dip?" I say, nodding to the bowl between us. "You should be. But if your excitement is about watching someone else's D&D campaign, I'd suggest managing your expectations."

"I *did* think there'd be a cool game board or a plastic dragon or something."

"Nah," I say, even though Danny does have figurines he painted for each of our roles. Something tells me she wouldn't find that impressive. "This is all we need." I gesture to the notepad and pen, the seven-sided dice.

"So it's about imagination." She throws her hair over her shoulder. The casual way she does that—like it's nothing—has always struck me. Like she doesn't realize she has the most beautiful hair of any woman, anywhere. "Like my books."

"I'd argue that they don't leave much up to the imagination," I mutter.

Thankfully, she changes the subject. "I'm sure I'll enjoy watching and learning. I mean, I've spent the last few days watching people. I'm getting good at it." From the look on her face, she absolutely intended to make another reference to what happened on Monday, and blood makes the ill-advised journey to my dick, which has no use for it right now. I clear my throat and shift in my chair.

"You getting a cold?"

"I just needed to clear my throat. You know, Marnie told me you really fill out that banana suit."

She lunges for the chip bowl, presumably to lob a chip at me, then shrugs and dips it into the dragon dip instead.

"Hey, that's for the game."

"You should have thought about that when you teased me about the banana suit."

It's my turn to lift my eyebrows. She's been teasing me about something so much worse than a giant yellow suit that conceals everything except for her face and that hair, which can't be contained by anything. Then again, maybe she wants me to complain about that.

"So, what do you think of the dip?"

She looks at me, and the admiration in her eyes just might be my undoing, even if it's only for my dragon dip. "*You* made this?"

"Are you accusing me of being one of those people who buys things and shifts them to different containers? No, I don't like taking credit for other people's work."

"Judgmental, much?" She does another hair toss, and my dick reminds me it's both there and interested. "I'd like to see the game you're working on sometime. I've only seen bits and pieces on your screen."

"The clown zombies or the other one?"

"Obviously not the clown zombies. Marnie told me about the game you put together with your friends."

"It's not finished," I object. "I don't like showing people things when they're not done."

"Looked pretty finished to me."

"It's the details that need work."

"For someone who doesn't know how to do laundry to save his life, you can be such an anal perfectionist," she says, grabbing another chip. I don't try to stop her. I know a losing battle when I see one.

Still, for some reason, I say, "No, I'd just prefer not to brag about something that's not finished. When it's done, I'll do all the bragging. You won't be able to stand me." I pause. "It's going to be incredible if we do it right. Better than ten dragon dips."

"I don't know about that. This is delicious. Spicy and sweet and tomatoey."

"Tomatoey's not a word."

She gives me an arch look. "I'm not a writer. I'll leave that to Grace. But if you ask me, this dip might be your biggest accomplishment in life."

"I've helped create an entire world, but by all means, congratulate me on the dragon dip."

"Well"—she crosses her legs—"you let me try the dragon dip, but I haven't seen the world you created. I can only act on what I know."

"I see what you're doing," I say, leaning a little closer because I can't help myself. She's like the sun during an eclipse—everyone tells you not to look with your bare eye, but it's hard to resist when all you want to do is lean close and take a look at something so rare and beautiful you're never going to forget it. And since you'll probably burn your retinas, you'll *really* never be able to forget it.

"Does that mean it's working?" she asks, arching her brows as she takes another chip and dips it.

There's a knock at the door that tells me the guys have arrived.

I get up, and Andy does the same. "Are they going to be wearing costumes?" she asks as she trails me to the door. "I figured you'd wear costumes like when you went to that comic thing with Marnie."

It was a *Star Wars* fan event, and we'd all dressed up at Griffin's request. He'd wanted to make it a real experience for Marnie, because that's where he'd proposed. It wasn't the kind of request I could turn down, even though I made the mistake of dressing like Darth Vader in June and sweating my balls off.

"No costumes, Banana Girl," I say. "But if you choose to put on your banana suit, no one will object."

"Very funny," she says, socking my arm. She does it playfully, or at least she probably thinks it's playful, but everything about Andy is forceful. It makes me smile to myself as I open the door.

My buddies carpooled together, like usual, since Burke and Danny live together and Shane's just down the street from them. It makes sense to save the gas money and street space. It strikes me that all of us have lived in the same places since college. Danny, Shane, and I attended UNCA, right here in town, while Burke's parents insisted he was destined for better things and sent him to Duke. I guess that probably says something about us.

"Hey, guys," Andy says, all confidence as they stream in. Danny looks like a college kid again—a college kid who feels awkward around the hottest girl in class.

Hell, I get it.

Burke, of course, is in his glory, grinning at Andy, even though he promised not to flirt with her.

"We heard you took pity on our buddy here," he says, clapping me on the back. "Moved in with him to keep him from muttering to himself while he jerks off sadly on the couch."

"What the hell, man?" I ask, praying to all the gods ever imagined that Andy doesn't offer up the information that reality isn't too different from his imagined scenario.

She doesn't, but she shoots me a knowing smirk. "Do I need to launder the couch, *Andrew*?"

"No," I say, bumping Burke with my elbow, hard.

"Just messing with you," he says.

"Hilarious."

I do introductions, or reintroductions, since they've all seen each other before, and we head toward the dining room. Except Danny takes one look at the side table by the door and announces, "Your frame's broken."

"Huh?" I ask, then spot it at the back. It's a photo of the four of us and Leonard, taken a week before he disappeared. It's in the back, because I can't stand to look at it every day—and also because I can't bring myself to put it away. It would feel like a betrayal. Especially since he brought it to me the day he left, frame and all. He wasn't exactly a thoughtful-gestures kind of guy, so it stuck with me that he'd gone to the effort of buying—or possibly stealing—a frame. It also made me feel like more of an asshole after everything went down.

"How'd that happen?" I ask out loud, feeling a chill down my back. I don't believe in ghosts, but I've been giving some thought to karma and how it probably doesn't look too kindly on me.

"Shit," Andy says, putting her weight on one foot and leaning to the side. We're all gathered around the side table like mourners at a funeral, another thought that gives me a shiver. "I'm sorry. Nicole broke it the other day. I've been meaning to replace the frame, but I forgot. I'll fix it this weekend."

Relief wells inside me, because at least there's a reasonable explanation. The relief fizzles out when Shane picks up the photo. "I didn't notice you had this out here," he says. "Man, we were so young."

A corner of Burke's mouth hikes up as he studies it over his shoulder. "You still had braces, Danny."

Danny shrugs stoically. "That's what happens when your parents are too cheap to pay for an orthodontist and you have to wait until you can afford it yourself. You wouldn't know, Burke."

No, because Burke's family's rich, and he had a job lined up before he finished elementary school, let alone college. Burke just grunts. It's true—he doesn't know what it's like to struggle in that way. But I know his life is a struggle in different ways.

"Who's the guy in the corner?" Andy asks. "You guys still hang out with him?"

There's a collective flinch.

"What," she asks with a laugh, "did he kill your dragon or something?"

"There are no dragons in this campaign," I say, which isn't really an answer.

"Well, *that's* a disappointment," she says. Then she motions to the photo again to let me know she's not done. Of course she's not done.

I'm the one who finally answers her. "That's Leonard. He's dead."

ANDY

WELL, shit. I walked right into that one.

No one says anything for a while, then Shane sets the photo down, lifts an imaginary drink in a toast, and says, "Gone but not forgotten, buddy."

To my surprise, Burke looks away, his mouth set in a hard line. Then again, maybe he's doing that stoic thing guys do. Stiff upper lip and all that bullshit.

"I think we need some real drinks," I say, because hell, do we ever. The others nod, and we head over to the dining room table, where the guys literally attack the dragon dip, not that I can blame them. It's pretty damn delicious. I pour everyone a margarita—also delicious, obviously—and after we have drinks, the atmosphere lightens. Still, the guys are all a little twitchy, as if I unleashed something by asking about their friend. My mind keeps pinging back to that photo—all of these men, dark haired and tall and hot in a stealthy way, as gangly guys not long out of boyhood.

Like any normal human being, I'm consumed by curiosity. Who was this Leonard? How did he die? Why didn't I know about any of this before tonight? Then again, even though Marnie and Drew are close, she doesn't typically hang out with him and his buddies, and the only kind of hiking she likes to do is to an ice cream shop at the crest of a hill. So maybe she doesn't have the kind of intel I'm looking for.

But I know better than to kamikaze the evening by asking uncomfortable questions. I'll have to do that later, after everyone leaves. If I know anything about men, it's that they don't like talking about things that make them feel vulnerable, especially in front of other men. After my mother died, my brothers never once said anything else about her, not even in passing. Then again, it's well-documented that they're emotionally stunted assholes, so they're probably not a great metric for anything.

I feel a stab of worry for *Abuela*. I've been texting her once a day, but she hasn't answered. She made it very clear she didn't want to hear from me, and yet...

"Let's play," Danny says. "I have a feeling I'm gonna get lucky tonight."

Burke's bright blue eyes sparkle in amusement. "Only in the game."

Danny rolls his eyes but doesn't seem all that annoyed.

It turns out Drew is wrong—it *is* pretty damn interesting to sit through someone else's game. Mostly because Drew himself is the Dungeon Master. Yes, I *absolutely* plan to give him shit about the name, but he's a good storyteller—imaginative—and I like the way he makes the game come alive. I can't help but get into it, and everyone except for Danny bursts out laughing when I shout, "Oh shit," after he tells them there's a monster on their tail.

Drew grins at me, and in that moment, looking at him with his face lit up like that, his hair a little messy, I feel like someone punched me in the chest. In a good way, but in a bad way too. Because he's *Drew*, and living here is messing with my head a little. I hadn't expected that at all. I tell myself it's only because of what I saw the other day. I haven't meant to keep bringing it up—I know it embarrasses him—but I can't stop thinking about it.

After we finish playing, the guys hang out for a while and shoot the shit.

"I like all the stuff you brought here, Andy," Burke says, looking around with a slight smile. "You really busted apart Drew's neutral zone."

"Neutral zone?" I ask, surprised.

"Yeah," Shane says, popping a chip with dragon dip into his mouth. "Get him drunk, and he'll tell you all about it. He has this theory that he's most creative when everything around him is neutral."

"It's fine," Drew says, his tone clearly annoyed. "I like it. The rug's great. Everyone wants random splashes of color everywhere. Why wouldn't they? I've always wanted to live in a Jackson Pollock painting."

Danny snorts. "If the neutral zone worked, you'd be ready to roll out the game."

"It worked," Drew says tightly. "But now it no longer exists."

"Oh, so it's my fault that you haven't finished your game?" I ask, annoyed.

"I didn't say that." He swears. "The game is basically finished anyway."

"Exactly," Danny says, glaring at him. "But you're going to drag your damn feet until it celebrates its tenth birthday."

"Anyway, the rug is great," Burke says.

"Thank you, Burke," I tell him, because I'm annoyed. If Drew had such a problem with my shit, he should have said so. I could have stuck the rug in the basement or something, but now it's under all of the furniture, and moving it will be a production.

"You're welcome, Andy."

Then, because I'd been wondering, I ask him, "Is Burke your last name?"

"How'd you guess?" he asks, his mouth tipping up. He has a sexy smile, all white teeth and swagger. I'll bet he's used it to charm the panties off plenty of women, but it does nothing for me. Maybe I've just *been there, done that* with too many charming men. Burke's probably not a bad guy—Drew's a good one, and they're close friends—but most of the guys who spout charm like it's carbon dioxide are full of shit, and your electronic friend can give you better orgasms.

I tap my temple. "I think the big thoughts."

"His parents own Burke Realty," Danny says. "He's Lucas Burke the fourth, so he's a Junior-Junior-Junior. They own half of Asheville."

"It's a fraction of that," Burke says with the kind of humble-brag a person can only achieve when they're worth a shit-ton of money.

"So why don't we call you Junior Cubed?" I ask with a smile. "It has a certain ring to it."

"You can call me anything you'd like," Burke says. But then he glances at Drew, and his easy smile falls. Probably because Drew looks like he wants to add blood spatter to the carpet's color scheme.

Interesting. Did Drew warn him off me or something? The thought is an obnoxious one, because I'm more than capable of protecting myself unless I don't much feel like being protected.

"Oh-kay, Junior Cubed, but I wouldn't go around making that offer. If you do, you're going to find someone who wants to call you Shitbag one of these days, and there's no way that wouldn't catch on."

Everyone laughs, and Burke's smile feels more genuine this time. He gives me a two-fingered salute instead of the one-fingered salute I probably deserve. "I'll keep that in mind."

After everyone leaves, I refill my drink and Drew's, and we sit back down at the table across from each other, the dip and chips and dice still out.

"So," he says with a faint smile, "let me have it."

"What do you think I'm going to say?" I ask, mock-offended. "You think I'm going to make fun of you for liking dragons? If anything, I'm disappointed by the lack of dragons. It makes the name of the dip, and the game, feel misleading. Although the battle was pretty cool."

He looks pleased, and I watch as he wipes condensation off the side of his glass. His fingers are long and tapered. Strong.

My head summons what's become a familiar image.

"You have nice hands," I say.

Oops. Maybe I've had too much to drink. That's the thing about margaritas—they're delicious and refreshing in a way that lures you into drinking three of them before you realize the first is gone. Except I can't deny what I said is true; they *are* nice, and I *have* been thinking about them.

"You have nice feet," he says, smirking a little this time.

"You totally watched my OnlyFans videos, didn't you?"

"Wouldn't *you* have watched them in my position?"

"Nah, only if they were of your hands doing things. I'm not into other people's feet." I reach forward and tap him on the nose. Or at least I meant to. I hit his cheek instead.

"You sure like talking about things we're not supposed to talk about," he says.

He's looking at me with intense focus, his eyes an almost reddish-brown, so soulful and pretty. Almost too pretty for a man. But his *face* is manly, his jaw strong and always covered in dark stubble, no matter what the hour, his nose with a slight bump in it—in a way that made me want to run my finger down it just now. His eyebrows are darker than his hair, and—

Why does my mind keep going there?

I sit back in my chair. "Your friends are nice."

His expression changes slightly, his jaw clenching. "Yeah, Burke's pretty charming when he wants to be."

"I saw that weird look between the two of you. Did you warn him off me or something?" I ask, any wisp of a filter I might have had banished beneath the weight of too much tequila. "Because that's unnecessary. I can take care of myself."

"Oh, you've made *that* perfectly clear," he says, pushing the margarita away. He gets up and starts carrying things into the kitchen. The bowl nearly empty of chips, the dregs of the dragon dip. I stay sitting, because he's the one in a huff, not me.

"Why do you say that like it's a bad thing?" I ask when he gets back.

He grabs the back of the chair he'd been sitting in and leans against it. "It's not a bad thing, Andy. It's just..."

"Were you *jealous* of Burke?" I ask, because I'm honestly curious. Because I'm tipsy. Because part of me wants...

"Why the hell would I be jealous of him?" he asks tightly.

It's a good question, but I feel something sink inside of me, because I guess part of me wanted him to be. Which is bullshit. I'm not the type of woman who wants two men to fistfight over me. I mean, I'll pick whichever guy I want, and my decision will not be based on the outcome of some macho man-fest. If they want to give each other bruises and bask in testosterone, I guess that's their business.

"I don't know," I say, retreating from the topic. "Maybe because he gets to be the Bard, and you're the Dungeon Master. I mean, if you were into BDSM, that would be a pretty sick title, but—"

"How do you know I'm not?"

"Are you?" I ask, my eyes bugging out.

"No," he says harshly, just the slightest hint of a smile on his mouth. "And I'm not into gangbangs either, or whatever was going on in that book of yours. Sorry to disappoint."

"You were into it the other morning," I challenge.

"Nope, that wasn't it," he says, and my blood starts pumping harder through my veins. Is he saying—

I cut off the thought.

"Well, I'm not into having them in real life either. Just because you like reading about dragons and watching space cowboys or whatever, doesn't mean you want to be one."

He smiles back. "Speak for yourself. I'd love to be a space cowboy. Or have a dragon." He rubs a hand over his forehead then, as if I've wearied him, and announces, "I'm going up to bed."

"Wait," I say. "There's something I wanted to ask you about. The guy in the picture."

"Leonard," he says, swallowing.

"Leonard," I agree. "What happened to him?"

"Those are bad memories, Andy," he says, rubbing that strong jaw of his. "I don't want to go there."

"I'm just curious," I tell him. "I know what it's like to lose someone too early."

"I know you do," he says softly, his voice wrapping around me like a hug. He knows my mother died young, when I was a teenager, and my grandmother practically raised me. He knows she's dying now and won't speak to me. When he sighs and sinks into his chair across from me, it feels like a victory. "You must be worried about your grandmother."

"I am," I say. It's my turn to look away, to pick at the side of the table. "She's not answering my texts, not that I'm surprised. She thinks I'm unsalvageable. Like my father."

"She's wrong, obviously," he says without hesitation. "But she's also old. Old people get stuck in their ways sometimes. We'll probably be like that when we're old too. I'm guessing it's one of the only perks." Silence sits between us for a second. Then he shocks the hell out of me by asking, "Do you want me to look in on her?"

I look across the table at him, taking him in. "You'd do that for me?"

"Of course," he says, and there's no hesitation, no hitch in his voice. Nothing to indicate he'd be doing it against his will or inclination. "I'll go this weekend." He lifts his eyebrows. "Maybe I'll take Burke. He's good at impressing women."

"Nah," I say. "He's probably a nice guy down deep, but he comes across as one of those dudes *Abuela* always say is ten pounds of shit in a five-pound bag. She'd see right through him."

That gets a laugh out of him, and I'm pleased to have lightened his mood and reassured him that—

I'm not really sure of what. But of something.

"Thank you," I say, pressing a palm to my chest. "For everything. This means a lot to me."

"You're welcome," he says lightly. "I'm happy to do it."

"Now, about Leonard..."

He actually smiles slightly, even though he obviously isn't pleased that I'm pushing. "You don't let things go, do you?"

"Never. Your sister could have told you as much."

"She has. But I've observed it myself." He pauses, and for a moment, I'm certain he's not going to tell me. Then he says, "We met him after college. Hell, you probably saw him a couple of times in passing. He was funny as hell, but he liked to get into trouble. I used to bail him out sometimes, I guess. Burke too. He actually worked for Burke's parents—buying up real estate for them to renovate. Burke and I were closest to him, but we all hung out together. Went on camping trips. Played D&D. Got drunk and pulled stupid pranks."

"Like what?" I ask, perking up. "I require details."

"Nah, I'm not going to give you anything else to use against me."

I nod, because that's fair. "Proceed."

He heaves a sigh, sounding so tired, so *done*, I feel guilty for pressing him. "He went camping by himself one weekend, and he never came back. They found his pack in the woods, by the river. The authorities decided he must have gone swimming and drowned in the water. They were pretty certain of it. He wouldn't have been able to survive without his supplies. His wallet was in there...his water."

"Holy shit," I say, fascinated and horrified. "And they never found his body?"

He flinches. "No."

"Ho-*ly* shit," I repeat. "Why didn't I know about this?"

"You and Marnie were in college. She knows, but..."

Thinking back, I remember her telling me that one of Drew's friends had died. It happened our senior year, I think. We were both sad about it because he was young, and we raised a shot in his honor. But she didn't give me the full backstory.

He picks at his cuticles. "I was supposed to go with him that weekend. We had a disagreement, and I canceled. He shouldn't have gone on his own. We never go on our own."

"Oh, Drew," I say, reaching across the table and grabbing his hand.

He gives me a crooked smile as he turns his hand and squeezes mine. "It's okay. It's not like I pushed him into the river, but I guess it felt like it at the time."

"It's not your fault."

"I know." He squeezes my hand again and then lets it go. "But he wouldn't be dead if I'd gone with him the way I should have. That's true too."

And with that, he gets up from his chair and goes upstairs, leaving me with the rest of my final margarita, which I will now definitely finish, because again, and I can't say this too often or too loudly, holy shit.

It strikes me then that I have a more important purpose with the Fairy Godmother Agency than dressing as a banana and catching dimwits stealing office supplies—I have to give Drew closure.

nine

ANDY

"NO," Nicole says, sounding bored. She picks up a shrimp from the serving platter and pops it into her mouth. "Damn, these are good. I wish I had the recipe...and any desire to cook."

"Just no?" I ask. "You don't want to hear more?"

I'm at an end-of-week lunch with Nicole and Damien—a bonus, Nicole said, for helping them nab the supply thief. Yesterday, I got a photo of him with a box of notepads and pens cracked open, the logo clearly visible, which was the smoking gun they'd wanted, I guess. I asked them how he'd managed to get away with it for so long, and Nicole gave me a flat look and said, "He didn't get away with it. He's so bad at being a thief that a woman in a banana costume foiled his plan." She paused, then added, "To be honest, you didn't even need to wear the banana suit, Damien and I just thought it would be funny."

I gritted my teeth together, because I wanted to stay on their good side, and told them the story about Leonard—what little I knew, anyway. After my talk with Drew on Wednesday night, I'd looked him up and found a few articles from the *Asheville Gazette*. *Local Man Missing. Local Man Presumed Dead. Local Man Wins Hot Dog Eating Contest.*

That last one was a different Leonard Ashford, but I read the whole two-page article before I figured that part out.

I'd asked Marnie about him too. She'd blown out a breath and said, "Yeah, that whole thing really screwed Drew up. I don't know if it's such a good idea to poke into it, Andy. It'll bring all of those memories back to the surface. It was really hard for him to forgive himself for not going into the woods with Leonard."

And yet, here I am poking. Because I don't think he's forgiven himself, not fully. It's there in the way he advocates for other people, hard, but not really for himself. It's there in the way that he's designed a game that Marnie says is mind-blowing, but he's working for a man who genuinely thinks zombie clowns will be the next big thing in gaming. It's there in his hesitation to take chances.

He needs to know what happened to Leonard. Which means I need to find out. He's not just Marnie's brother—he's my friend. He's someone who's stuck out his neck for me, and I'm damn well going to do the same for him.

"You've got to understand, Andy," Damien says calmly, "this guy disappeared over eight years ago. No one has heard from him. His supplies were found. His wallet. Sounds like we know what happened to him."

"What if we can...I don't know...locate his body?"

Nicole snorts. "Good luck with that. What are you going to do, travel up and down the river with a fishing net? Hire a psychic?" She shrugs, inclining her head. "Actually, that could be fun. If you want to do the psychic thing, let me know."

"What about talking to the people he knew? Isn't that what you do?"

"Haven't you already done that?" Damien asks, not unkindly. "You said Drew and his buddies are convinced he's dead. Marnie too. They've gotten as much closure as they're likely to find."

It's not good enough. Because I saw the look on Drew's face before he climbed up the stairs the other night. I noticed the way he removed the framed photo from the side table before I could fix it, tucking it into the drawer. The situation is unresolved for him. It's a sentence that has no punctuation mark at the end. He requires a resolution, and life has robbed it from him. I'm going to steal it back.

"Their one friend had a shady look when they were talking about Leonard."

"Well, there you go," Nicole says, popping another shrimp. "You solved the case. That dude clearly held him under the water. Want me to call Officer Nutman?"

Damien snorts. I do not. Officer Nutman is a police officer who badly mishandled Sinclair's case when she was being stalked, and now he's receiving a commendation for having identified and arrested the perpetrators, despite having done nothing but read them their Miranda rights.

"I'm going to talk to Burke," I say stubbornly.

"You do that," Nicole says. "Now, can we talk about how you're avoiding your own problems so you can solve Drew's imagined problem?"

"It's not an imagined problem," I object with a scowl. "This is a real issue for him, and he's been very supportive of me." Then, because there are only two shrimp left, and Nicole's clearly on a mission to devour all of them, I grab the rest and shove them into my mouth. Why give her the satisfaction?

They really are delicious, though, and I let my enjoyment show just to mess with her.

"You're an asshole, but I admire you for it," she says, almost making me choke. "So here's what we're going to do. You are going to go talk to the murderer friend, and if you find something interesting, and Damien and I *agree* that it's interesting, then we'll help you. Agreed?"

"Yes," I say. "You won't regret it."

"No," Nicole says, "because nothing is going to come of it."

Damien angles his head toward me. "You should be prepared for that possibility. We've tried to solve cold cases before, just for fun, and it's usually a waste of time."

"That's what you do for fun?" I ask, intrigued. Can I do that if I become a P.I.? It sounds a hell of a lot better than wiping noses and changing diapers, even though I do miss some of the little terrors.

"Correction: it's *one of* the things we do for fun," Nicole says. "We're also working our way through the *A-Z Kama Sutra* for the fifth time. Speaking of which, how's Drew's dick doing?"

Damien chuckles to himself and pulls a server aside, asking for more of the shrimp. He's always doing things like that for her. It makes me think of the way Drew brought me that glass of water on my first night in the house. Or how he helped me squeeze limes for the margaritas when it took way longer than I thought it would. That thought only makes me more determined to be a good friend to him.

"I wouldn't know," I ask, the words coming out a little more aggressive than they needed to. It's just... I'm pretty sure he's been avoiding me. He didn't want to go over to Marnie and Griffin's with me last night, instead opting for a movie night with Rafe and Sinclair. And he hasn't been coming down to the kitchen for breakfast before leaving for work. I mean, maybe he's been hightailing it to the office because he suddenly has a thing for zombie clowns, but I'm guessing no one has a thing for zombie clowns.

"You might want to get on that. Literally," Nicole says. "I didn't guilt him into letting you live in that house for nothing." She wags a finger at me. "I see something there. He needs someone to fuck up his life, and I like you for it."

"You think I'm going to fuck up his life?" I ask, offended.

"In a good way." She rolls her eyes. "If ever I've met someone whose life needed to be fucked up, it's that guy. He's let himself get boring. Give him another few years and he'll have a stapler collection." She lights up like a slot machine with three bananas. "Hey, you think he'd agree to go by Andy too? That'd make it easy for everyone, you know? They'd only have one name to learn."

"I'm not going to have sex with him," I say. "He's my best friend's brother. That's not how things are between us." I think I mean it. A week ago, I would have definitely meant it. We've teased each other for years, but in the past it always felt safe. The other night, though...

It was *different*. Still, there's no denying a few essential facts.

Fact One. I live with Drew now. Do *not* have sex with someone you live with unless you live with them *because* you are having sex with them.

Fact Two. He's not my type. I mean, sure, when I was a teenager, I *may* have had a bit of a crush on him, but that was before I started watching my brother's muscle videos and discovered there were men who had arms the circumference of tree trunks.

What can I say? I'm an arm woman.

The thing is, Drew's arms are actually pretty nice. They're not tree trunks, but they're defined and strong. Tan from hiking. Actually, the other day I found myself staring at his forearms when he was typing on his computer. So fact two is less of a fact, I guess, than an observation. The men I've dated have been different from him.

The men I've dated have also sucked, so there's that.

Which brings us to Fact Three, which is the most important fact —as girthy as Drew's dick. He's Marnie's brother. If it doesn't work out—and it probably wouldn't—things would get weird. I can't let them get weird. Marnie's like a sister, and Drew's more important to me than any other man. We may not have hung out outside of Marnie before I moved into the house, but I've always known I could rely on him. In fact, he's the only man I've *ever* known I could rely on.

I can't lose either of them. I *can't*. It already feels like I've lost everything, but if I lose them, I really will have lost everything.

"I've known him since I was six," I blurt.

Nicole cackles. "When you put it that way, it does sound pervy. I still think it's going to happen. Damien, what do you think?"

"Are we going to make a wager?" he asks, his eyes sparkling. He pulls her chair closer as if it—and she—weigh nothing, and wraps an arm around her. "I'll bet on Andy getting it on with Leonard."

"So you think he's still alive?" she asks. "Interesting."

"Never said I wanted to win," he tells her with a lazy smirk. He's an obscenely good-looking man, but I don't feel any pull toward him other than the obvious pull of someone with charisma. Probably that's because Nicole is legitimately terrifying, and I can only imagine what she'd do to anyone who dared hit on her man. She tugs him close by the collar and kisses him.

"Good God, get a room."

"We have one," Nicole says, her eyes widening as she sees a server walk over with the new plate of shrimp. "We're pulling surveillance on someone at a hotel. And it's a good thing, because I am going to jump this man's dick so hard."

"I can honestly say this is the weirdest meeting I've ever had with an employer."

"Just wait," Damien says, laughing. "This is nothing."

ten

DREW

"SHE KEEPS TALKING about how big your dick is?" Rafe asks, giving me a look. It's Friday night, and we worked out together before heading over to the bar to join his dad. Griffin has another bartender working, but he's busy and hasn't been able to come over to talk to us yet. Andy's running around doing undisclosed errands for Damien and Nicole, and Sinclair's treating Marnie to a last-minute spa night.

"Well, yeah. I wish she'd stop talking about it. She's driving me crazy." The other night, after the guys left, I had to hold the top of that chair until my knuckles turned white, because I wanted to kiss her. I wanted to pick her up and carry her to my room and show her that I could fuck her better than both guys on page sixty-three of that infernal book. It would take some doing to best their acrobatics, but I could do it if I put my mind to it. I've always been good at the things I set my mind to, and I can't deny it anymore—that woman has become a fixation for me. Not just in this last week, but for some time.

I've been avoiding her since Wednesday night, because it's hard to be around her without thinking about winding her long hair around my hand and kissing her. About spreading her legs and burying my head between them. The other night, black spots were pulsing in front of my eyes when Burke tried to charm her. I've never been so pissed at him before, and he didn't even do anything wrong. He was being himself—a harmless flirt. A dumbass. He'd texted me later that night to apologize, but I still felt pissed. Even now, thinking about it, I'm upset.

I've also avoided her because I *know* her. When my sister made up a prom date in high school, Andy made the dude a fake page on Facebook to help her convince people it was true. People figured it out anyway, but the teasing stopped when Andy punched a guy for making fun of my sister. Another time, when some dickweed told Marnie she looked like Sinclair if she'd been put in the wash too many times, Andy threw a piece of dirty laundry at him every day for a week. She doesn't give things up. She's not a quitter.

Which means she's going to keep poking around about Leonard.

I'd rather she left that particular stone unturned.

"Huh," Reggie says, giving me a look similar to the one Rafe gave me. He strokes his long beard contemplatively, like he might find the answers to all the questions of the universe in there. "You didn't strike me as someone who'd have a big dick."

"Jesus, Dad." Rafe nudges him with his shoulder. "Why'd you have to go and say a thing like that?"

"What? I'm just being honest. Drew wants me to be honest, right, buddy?"

"Not really," I say.

Griffin comes over at this ill-chosen time, and I'm not at all shocked when he asks us what we're talking about and Reggie answers, "Drew's dick."

"I guess Andy's impressed with what he's packing," Rafe adds with a smirk. "Should we get him a congratulatory drink?"

God, why do I spend time with these people?

Griffin laughs so hard his shoulders shake.

"Yeah, thanks for that, Griff."

"It's because he doesn't come off as someone with a big dick, right?" Reggie says. "I would have pegged him for a six-incher, max. Why is that, I wonder?" He studies me for a moment, as if the shape of my ears or the color of my hair might tell him why he thought I had a small-to-average dick despite being six-foot-three.

"I know," he says, snapping his fingers.

"Do tell," I say dryly. I actually *want* him to tell me. If there's something about me that's making me come off as a person with a small-to-average dick, I guess I should know.

"You're not aggressive enough," he says. "You're a good-looking dude—"

Rafe is silently laughing beside him, and Griffin is not-so-silently laughing behind the bar.

"He is!" Reggie says before continuing. "You are. But if you're looking to impress a woman like that, you need to exude pheromones."

"What, like stop using deodorant?" I ask, not because I have any intention of doing such thing, but because he's entertaining as hell and I don't want him to stop.

"Yes," he says emphatically. "And growl at her. Women like it when men growl at them."

"You want me to *growl* at her?" I ask. "Like I'm some kind of rabid dog?"

"Wolf," Reggie corrects.

It's ludicrous, but at the same time, I remember one of the heroes growling in that book I took from Andy. It did make the female character hot and bothered, so maybe he's not entirely full of shit.

"What other pearls of wisdom do you have for him, Dad?" Rafe asks with clear enjoyment.

Griffin swears as someone calls for him farther down the bar. "I really regret having to work tonight," he mutters as he strolls away.

Reggie continues studying me, then nods, agreeing with himself. "Grow a beard."

"Like yours?" I ask, alarmed. I might get sick of shaving, but I'm a few years away from a Santa Claus beard, I hope.

"No, like that handsome devil's." He points down the bar at Griffin. "The beard helped him get with a hot little ticket. Maybe it'll work for you too."

"You do remember Marnie's my sister, right?"

He shrugs, a chagrined expression on his face. "Might have gotten a little carried away."

Yeah, just a little.

"You know, he's right," Rafe says, studying me. "You'd look good with a beard."

"Oh, for fuck's sake," I say. "I didn't ask for a fashion consultation. And since when do you think about things like that?"

"It's your other sister's influence," he says with a gruff laugh. "You can blame her. Look, on the plus side, you have Andy thinking about your dick. That's good. I'll bet you anything she never gave it a passing thought before she walked in on you the other day."

"Thanks."

"Like you've said, she's known you nearly her whole life. She's used to looking at you a certain way. She needed something to reset that for her."

Like those videos of Andy reset it for me, I guess. I can't deny I like the thought of her seeing me in a different way. And the other night, for a moment, it felt like maybe she did. But it would still be stupid as hell to make a move on her. If she rejected me, I'd have to live with a woman I want who's made it clear she doesn't want me. And if she didn't, I'd have to explain all of this to Marnie. And if things ended badly, I'd have to keep seeing Andy, all the time.

I have a feeling she'd drive me even crazier if I knew what it felt like to kiss her, to wrap my hand in her hair, to sink deep inside of her. Even the thought makes me half hard, which is another sign this is nuts. Although maybe the fact that I'm considering listening to any of Reggie's advice should be enough of one.

She makes me lose control entirely.

"It's like I said," I tell Rafe, glancing at Reggie so he knows I'm talking to him too. "I don't actually want anything to happen with her. I just need to figure out a way to stop wanting her."

Rafe snorts. "Good luck with that. Didn't work out so well for me with your sister. It took less than a week of living with her for me to cave. You think you can stop wanting her when she's walking around that house, always there, swaying her ass and talking about your dick?"

I heave out a sigh, because the man's right. Trying not to want Andy is like trying to force the sun not to rise. That particular Pandora's box is open, and there's no closing it.

I acknowledge as much, and Reggie perks up. "Who's this Pandora? If you get some of her box, that might be enough to help you hold off."

I start, "It's—"

Rafe claps him on the back. "It's okay, Dad. Good suggestion." He winks at me. "He's not wrong, you know. If you get some of Pandora's box, you might not be so desperate to jump into Andy's."

He's right. Dating someone else might help me put a lid on what I'm feeling. But wouldn't it be wrong to pursue anyone else, knowing how I feel about Andy?

I rub my throat, which feels raw. "Yeah, I'll consider it."

"Want me to set you up with someone?"

I give him a hard look. "Are you volunteering my sister for that duty?"

"No, man, I know people too. I can set you up. Say the word."

I take a gulp of my drink, which does nothing to settle the feeling in my throat.

"I'll let you know," I say.

He gives a solemn nod. Reggie's brow creases. "But what about Pandora? Sounded like you had a real good thing going."

"Sometimes things just don't work out the way you want them to," I tell him. Or maybe I'm telling myself. I incline my head toward Rafe. "You busy tomorrow morning?"

"I'm not taking you out on a date, buddy. Spa days are Sinclair's thing."

"No shit. I wanted to check on Andy's grandmother for her." I look around, then add, "I figured you could help me intimidate her brothers if they're around."

"They're pricks, huh?"

"Yes," I say, feeling a pulsing anger that runs much deeper than my irritation at Burke. "And I'm going to have a hard time not losing my shit on them."

"Want me to come?" Reggie offers, running a hand over his beard. "Back in the day, they used to call me Reggie the Ham Sandwich because—"

"No," Rafe and I say at the same time.

—————

Andy's on the couch when I get home, drinking a beer. One of *my* beers. It's something Leonard would have done, which I'm only thinking about because he's at the forefront of my mind again—a place he hasn't occupied for a while. He was a little bit like Andy, actually. Both of them the kind of people who can't be contained.

If things were normal between Andy and me, I'd probably give her shit for taking the beer, even though I'm happy for her to drink my beer, sit on my couch, check out my dick.

Yeah, it took my brain all of five seconds to go there, which doesn't bode well for my ability to not think about her that way.

"Hey," she says, getting to her feet. She's wearing sweatpants that would look dumpy on the majority of people, but they only bring attention to the swell of her ass, and her hair is back in a bun it's already escaping.

"Sit down, Ruiz," I say. "You looked comfortable."

She seems uncertain for a second, which is damn near incredible, then says, "Want to join me?"

She's watching a painful reality TV show—some dating monstrosity that's filmed in Highland Hills—but hell yes, I want to join her. I grab a beer and settle down beside her.

"So, who do we hate?" I ask, then point to a dead-eyed blond guy on the screen. "It's him, isn't it? I can tell from the way the camera's focusing in on him."

"Got it all figured out, huh?" She gives me side-eye. "I'll have you know that he just told her he likes her, exactly as she is. So he's basically the perfect man, not that you'd know anything about that."

"Or he's just derivative enough to steal his lines from old movies. I'm surprised you watch this shi—"

I cut myself short, because I'm acting like a guy who got friend zoned years ago, which is exactly what I am.

Isn't that what I want to be?

No, but it's what I need.

"I mean...watch whatever you want," I finish awkwardly.

She looks at me like she wants to check my temperature. "You okay?"

Not really.

"I mean, don't watch the *Star Wars* prequels, because they don't exist in this house, but other than that." I wave at the screen, where a bunch of dudes are trying to make a cake. "But this is great. Perfect. Nothing I like better than to watch a bunch of dudes fail. It makes me feel manly."

"Glad something does."

I nudge her with my shoulder and instantly regret it, because the warm press of her seems to radiate through my entire body. Maybe that's why I say something stupid. "Reggie told me I look like someone with a small-to-average dick."

She laughs, her whole body moving with it, and it hits me that this is one of the things that's always drawn me to her. She's so damn alive. Every bit of her. It comes off her like heat from a stove, and maybe part of me wants to be warmed by it.

"You want me to call him up and tell him he's wrong?" she asks.

"Maybe. Feel free to exaggerate."

"Won't need to," she says with a bawdy wink.

"I feel violated," I tell her, even as my dick twitches to life. I pull a throw blanket over my lap because I don't want to stop watching this terrible show with her.

After it's over, she turns the TV off and gives me a long look, then says, "You loved it," and starts cackling at the expression on my face.

"Did you purposefully turn that on just to mess with me?" I ask, grinning because I can't help myself.

"No, I genuinely like trashy TV. You're just lucky I wasn't watching *Los Hermanos Que Amo*. My grandmother and I can't get enough of that show."

Her expression slips, and I nudge her shoulder again, leaving it pressed against her this time. She lowers her head to it, leaning into me, and a feeling of protectiveness washes over me as I breath in the scent of her hair. It would probably piss her off if I told her. She'd definitely tell me she doesn't need anyone to be protective of her, and she'd be right. Andrea Ruiz is a goddamn force of nature.

Doesn't matter. I still want to punch her brothers in the face—with Rafe as backup, because honestly, I've seen pictures and they're built like Transformers too. I want to talk her grandmother around to being a decent person for what little time she has left on this planet. In short, I want to make things better for Andy, because being around her makes *me* feel better. I like the way she sees me—as a good man, a reliable one—and I hope that one day I'll be able to see myself that way again too.

"I'm going to talk to her, Andy," I say. "I'll try to make her see reason."

I can feel her smiling rather than see it. "I wouldn't be surprised if she runs you off with a rubber spatula." Her voices hitches a little before she recovers. "Not that she's doing much running these days."

"I bet she'd be perfectly terrifying waving it from a chair," I say. "She's picked you up from this house back in the day. I remember."

"You don't have to go," she says, lifting her head so she's looking at me, so close her breath is warm against my face.

"I know. But I'm going to. You couldn't keep me from going. Unless you cemented the door shut or something. That might do it."

Her smile is weak, nothing like the way she beams when she's happy about something, or her wicked smirk when she's up to no good. "I bet you'd annoy it until it crumbled."

"I *am* good at that."

Then she surprises me by laying her head down on my shoulder again and nestling in. "You know, wearing a banana suit is surprisingly tiring," she says, making me laugh. My heart rate kicks up a notch.

"It can't be more tiring than running around after a bunch of kids who still shit their pants."

"Touché." She edges closer, ever so slightly, her side pressing into mine, her hair tickling my skin, and my heart races along a little faster.

"Well, it's more interesting than my job. Today, my boss brought in a photo of his mother-in-law and asked me to make one of the clown zombies look like her."

"Did you?" she asks, laughing a little, her body moving against mine in a tantalizing way.

"Sure. There's a chance she'll see it and he'll get in trouble. I can't not be a part of that."

She glances up at me. "If you don't like it, why don't you quit? You're really good at what you do."

"How do you know?" I ask. "You don't strike me as the gamer type."

"I've played a couple of the games you've designed before," she says quietly. "Your design work is awesome. I took a bunch of screenshots so I could show people and brag about you."

"You did?" I ask, my heart feeling warm and full. I like the thought of Andy being proud of me, of her telling other people about me like I'm someone special to her.

"Now, the last thing *I* want to do is sit on my ass in front of a computer for hours, hence my difficulty with staying employed, but I still found it impressive."

"No," I say, nudging her, "you'd rather sit around and read one of those porn books."

"Seems to me that's an interest we share," she says with a smirk.

We're in dangerous territory again. For a moment, I waver between two decisions—two paths—but I take us back. "So what'd Nicole and Damien have you doing tonight?"

She laughs, the air blowing up one of her curls. I want to catch it in my hand. I don't. "I picked up takeout for them. But next week I get to trail a couple of cheaters. The gold standard for P.I. work, according to Nicole."

I don't like the idea of her taking photos of a man who might try to chase her down. I know my concern won't be welcome, but I still ask, "Did they teach you self-defense too?"

She gives me a wry look. "You think they needed to?"

"No, I guess not. But do you have pepper spray?"

"I grew up on the wrong side of Patton. Of course I have pepper spray."

That makes me feel better. A little. But I can tell there's something she's not telling me. She's holding something back. Something to do with me.

That's when it hits me. I sit up straighter, feeling a pang of regret when I displace her head and can no longer feel the brush of her soft curls against my skin. "Andy, you didn't tell them about Leonard, did you? It's a closed case. He was declared dead."

Her mouth purses to one side. "Well, I did mention it, but they weren't interested."

I'm relieved. I'm...disappointed. Sometimes being a person is strange; it never ceases to amaze me that I can feel so many conflicting emotions in the same moment. The same way I simultaneously want to pull Andy into my lap and push her away and stomp upstairs like a kid having a tantrum.

"Of course they're not interested," I say woodenly. "He's dead."

Because of me.

I still think it sometimes, even though I don't want to, even though I spent years in therapy trying not to believe it.

"It wasn't your fault," she says, staring into me.

"And it's not your fault your grandmother's pushing you away. I'm going to go see her in the morning, but you need to know that I'm one hundred percent on your side. You didn't do anything wrong." I lift my eyebrows, my lips tilting up too. "This is me officially admitting I saw the videos. All of them." Because I'm an idiot, I add, "Several times. You did nothing wrong."

"I know," she says slowly, drawing out the words. There's a startled expression in her eyes, and she leans in slightly, her breath warm against my cheek. There are a few freckles across the bridge of her nose, almost invisible.

There's a moment when I could kiss her—and maybe she wants me to—but the moment ends, and I get up off the couch. "Goodnight, Andy."

When I get up to my room, I pace for ten minutes.

Then I jerk off, thinking about Andy reading that book, her hand sliding down to touch herself, her hips rising and falling as she thrusts with her fingers. I think about what might have happened if

I'd done what I wanted to just now—what my whole body was straining to do—and slid her onto my lap and kissed her.

I think about going down there and telling her that I've always thought she's beautiful, but for the last few years, it's been harder not to notice, and after I watched those videos it became impossible.

I think about what she said the other day. *"Being here makes me feel like I haven't lost my family."* And I know that even if I'm willing to take the risk for myself, I can't do it for her sake. I can't make her feel like she's going to lose another person. I won't.

Then I text Rafe.

> Yeah, what the hell. Set me up with someone. Tomorrow night?

He replies quicker than I was expecting.

> You've got it. Can I tell her you're packing heat?

> Fuck off.

He responds with a winky face.

Really, I should stop talking to my sisters' boyfriends.

DREW

"YOU THINK HER BROTHERS ARE HERE?" Rafe asks, cracking his knuckles as I park on the road outside of Andy's grandmother's house. The purple paint is peeling off the wood siding, giving us a peek at the white lead-based paint beneath, and the windows look like they'd collapse if you dared to breathe on them.

It's about nine o'clock on Saturday morning. Andy wasn't up when I left the house, or maybe she just hadn't left her room yet. Maybe, knowing what I was intending to do this morning, she didn't feel up to seeing me.

"Doubt it. They're obviously doing the bare minimum," I say, already pissed. "Theo's a financial advisor, so I know he has money. He should be taking care of his family. If he stops by, I'm going to tell him so."

He snorts and gets out of the car. I get out too, making sure to lock it. "This guy's made it pretty clear he doesn't give two shits about his family. So what should I expect here? Are we going to get stuff thrown at us?"

I have an image of Andy's little old grandmother coming at us with a wooden spoon and other utensils. Well, if that happens, at least I'd have a story that would make Andy laugh, I guess.

"God, I hope not."

"What if we give the old broad a heart attack?" he asks, eying the door as we walk toward it on a path lined with overgrown plants.

I pause partway down the path. "Wait, you think that could happen?"

He gives it a second's thought, then shrugs. "Probably not."

I consider that for a moment, but turning back is not a possibility. I told Andy I was going to do this for her, and I'm damn well going to do it. "Let's just try not to startle her. She does have a heart condition."

He snorts. "We're two six-foot-plus men showing up at her door early in the morning. I think we're going to startle her."

"She knows me," I say, except that's not necessarily true. I remember her because she's Andy's grandmother, but she doesn't have any real reason to remember me. I'm Andy's best friend's brother—part of the scenery, as far she's concerned.

"Let's hope, buddy, because I don't want to get clocked in the head with a cast iron skillet. I've already had one head injury too many."

"You're supposed to be my muscle."

"Against a little old woman?"

"The brothers," I tell him. Looking around, though, I don't see any cars in the drive except for a Toyota Corolla that's probably as old as I am. I'm willing to bet it hasn't moved from its current spot for at least six months, maybe a year. "But if they do come over, and things get violent, I want first go at them. Only step in if it looks like they're going to kill me."

"You're more brave than you are practical when it comes to shit like that," he says with a shake of his head.

"And you're different?"

"I'm bigger." He smirks, and I start walking down the path again.

We reach the door a few seconds later, and I pull in a deep breath and knock. The knocker looks like a new addition, heavy and gold, and the door itself has been freshly painted. I have an image of Andy setting down a drop cloth and painting it, nailing on that knocker. I'm sure she did it. I wish she'd asked for help. I wish I'd known things had gotten this bad.

But I don't have long to dwell on it because the door swings open. It's done so quickly, so officiously, that for a second, I worry we really are about to get our brains bashed in with a cast iron skillet, but Andy's grandmother doesn't look physically capable of violence. She's lost about twenty pounds since the last time I saw her, which was, admittedly, over a decade ago, and has the hollow-eyed appearance of someone who's had a lot of sleepless nights. Still, her hair is a glossy salt and pepper, shorter but with the same texture as Andy's.

"Who are you?" she asks, her gaze pinging from me to Rafe and then back.

He gives me a smug glance as if to say, *She remembers you, huh?*

"Hello, Mrs. Ruiz," I say, putting out a hand. She ignores it, and I feign an interest in the doorjamb. "I'm Andrew Jones, Marnie's brother."

Her expression shifts, and she reaches out for something to steady herself. I instinctively grab her arm. "Andy," she chokes out. "Is she okay?"

My first thought is, *Oh, shit. I really am going to give this woman a heart attack.*

My second thought is, *Why does she care?*

"She's great!" I say, overcorrecting. "Actually, she was worried about you, and I offered to check on you. Can we come in?"

Her gaze shifts to Rafe, hardening. "Who is he?"

"I'm his bodyguard," he says. "He expressed some concern about getting his ass kicked by Andy's brothers. I go where the money is."

Thanks a lot, Rafe. I give him a dirty look, then turn back toward her. "Sorry, Mrs. Ruiz. This is my sister's..." Well, shit. If she doesn't like Andy showing her feet on the internet, she might not be the sort of person who believes in living together before marriage. "Boyfriend," I finish, stumbling over the word. His eyes twinkle with amusement, and I am absolutely going to figure out a way to get back at him. "He has a misplaced sense of humor."

"Yes, *very* misplaced." She opens the door wider. Pointing to me, she says, "You come in. The funny man waits outside."

So maybe I won't need to get back at him after all. She may be sick, but she's capable of some perfectly good takedowns. Giving Rafe a smirk, I follow her inside. She shuts the door behind me, then locks it for good measure. I don't know if she's keeping me in or Rafe out, but I feel a little on edge.

"You'll have tea," she says.

"Oh, no thank you." The last thing I want is for her to have to wait on me. I doubt she could even carry the tea set out into the living room.

"Wasn't a question. Sit." She points to a clawed sofa that looks like it was recently reupholstered. My mind summons Andy, because it must have been her. I don't want to be pissed at a little old woman who's on the last stretch of her life, but I am. It's obvious Andy's poured her heart and soul into making this place nice for her grandmother and herself. She doesn't deserve to be treated like shit for the methods she used to make that happen.

"I don't want tea," I insist. "I'd like to know if a nurse has been coming around. I don't see anyone here."

She lifts her eyebrows. It's hard to tell whether she respects me for standing up to her, or if I'm about to get pushed out onto the porch with the funny man. But after a beat, she says, "She's here once a day."

"Is that enough?" I don't think we're on warm enough terms for me to tell her she looks like shit.

"For now," she says primly.

"And do your grandsons visit with you?"

She laughs, reaching for the back of the couch to steady her. "You think I want those worthless *pendejos* spending time here? No. I won't let them through the door. When they come, they stay on the porch like your friend. Theo won't be going through my things while I'm still alive. Let him try to come like a cockroach once I'm gone. Jack too."

Confusion twists around my brain like rubber bands, but I'm still pissed. Now that I've spent a few minutes in the house, I'm seeing signs of Andy everywhere, from the colorful prints on the walls, burning my retinas, to the plentitude of candles, all with different scents, of course. Where the fuck did she get all those candles and still have so many to bring to my house? Did she buy them in bulk?

"If you don't like them, then why the hell did you kick Andy out of the house for them?"

She gives me a death look, and I realize I swore.

"Sorry for the language."

She studies me for a moment before nodding firmly. "Andy is staying with you and Marnie?"

Well, shit. I'm not about to tell her that Andy and I are living there alone, without any chaperones. The word chaperone feels misplaced since she's thirty and I'm thirty-four, but I have a feeling Mrs. Ruiz would expect one.

"Yes, she's staying at our house." True. Marnie is still half owner—will be until I buy her out.

She gives another nod, this one pleased. "That's good. That's very good. I knew I could count on Marnie to be a good girl and let her stay. The boys didn't know where she was going."

"What the fu—what is going on here, Mrs. Ruiz?" I ask, frustrated. "You were worried about Andy when I showed up at your door, and you're glad she has somewhere to stay. So why did you kick her out, and why aren't you answering her messages? Are you really that offended by feet?"

"Sit down," she says again, and before I can push back, she adds, "*My* feet get tired these days, Andrew. I can't stand for long."

So I sit next to her on the sofa Andy almost certainly reupholstered, feeling like an ass for making her uncomfortable.

"To answer your question, no, I do not care about her feet." She smiles slightly, and I see a whisper of the young woman she must have been. "I've been told I have nice feet too, although not for many years, as you can imagine."

"Then what—"

"Andy has spent years taking care of me. She has done what she can to keep this heap of wood and brick from falling apart, but she is a young woman. Beautiful. She should be enjoying her youth, not spending it watching her grandmother *and* her house die. No, *mijo*. She needed to leave before things got bad. My granddaughter and I both watched her mother die, and it broke our hearts. I won't let it happen again with me. It could go on for months."

I feel like I did when Andy socked me in the nuts. This is... unexpected.

"With all due respect, Mrs. Ruiz, that's a shitty plan." She lifts her eyebrows, and I shake my head. "Not going to apologize for that one. Do you have any idea how devastated she is?"

"She's told you this?" she asks, cocking her head.

"No, of course not. You've met her, haven't you?"

She laughs, pressing a hand over her heart, but hopefully not for heart-attack related reasons. "Yes. I'm not surprised."

"But I know her, and she's *devastated*. You could end all of that with one word."

"This is for the best, Andrew," she says quietly, shaking her head. "You can visit me and let me know if she's well. You can tell her that I'm not dead yet."

"You may not want her to have to watch you die, but she wants to be there for you. I think she needs it."

"She'll know after it's done," Mrs. Ruiz declares, as if she's speaking of something other than her own death. "She'll know how much I've always loved her. Those fool boys will get what is coming to them too. *Nothing*."

I get up from the couch and start pacing. Pausing, I glance at her, but she hasn't budged, and the look in her eyes says she's not going to budge.

"I'm sorry, but I have to tell her," I say. "I'm going to."

She lifts her eyebrows again. "If you do, I will tell her you were lying. I will say I haven't seen you since you were a scrawny young boy." Her lips tilt into a mischievous smile, this one speaking entirely of Andy. "You've grown up nicely."

"You can't just let her worry!" I want to tear out my hair. I want to throw a scented candle. I want to fix this for Andy. But I can tell from this woman's demeanor that she means exactly what she said. She really would lie to Andy, hurting her again. Maybe making Andy distrust me in the process.

"You care for my granddaughter," she says, eying me speculatively.

"Of course I do." The words almost come out as a snarl. "You're not acting like *you* do."

"I do more than anything," she replies, holding her hands in her lap. "Sometimes we need to do what we know is best for the people we love, whether they can see it or not."

"I'm not letting this go."

"No, I don't imagine you will," she says with another slow smile. "When you come back, you can tell me how Andy is doing."

I gesture to the house. "What about your grandsons? They're not going to do anything to fix the house?"

"They don't care for anyone but themselves," she scoffs. "Especially the older one."

"It needs repairs," I persist.

"It's stood for a hundred years, *mijo*. It'll stand a little longer. There'll be some money when I'm gone. Life insurance. Andy can fix it then." A scowl slips into place. "Better that than for her to shake the gifts God gave her for some dirty old men."

"I'm coming back with some friends," I tell her.

"Is this a threat?" she asks with bemusement.

"No, God no," I say, running my hands through my hair, probably making it messier. It's a habit Marnie always calls me on, but that's never done anything to dissuade it. "They'll help me. My buddy Burke flips houses for fun. He's replaced windows in old places before, and I know how to paint..."

"You want to fix my house?" she asks in disbelief. Then her brow creases. "Why?"

"Because you're not letting Andy take care of you. Your grandsons aren't trying. Someone needs to."

Her perusal of me is longer this time, and then she gives a final nod. "You can go now, Andrew. But yes, you may come back. You've given me a lot of comfort today."

Well, that makes one of us.

———

"What am I going to do?" I ask Rafe in the car. I'm driving him back to the penthouse apartment he's sharing with Sinclair and, for another few days, his dad. My sister has already informed me that they're having a housewarming party next weekend to celebrate their cohabitation. Andy was invited too, of course.

"Is it because Reggie's leaving?" I'd asked her the other night. "It is, isn't it?"

She'd responded that I was just sour because he'd thought I had a small dick. Fantastic. Now, Rafe and Reggie have my sister talking about my dick.

He rubs his chin before sharing his thoughts. "You can't tell her yet. You've got to convince the old broad to do the right thing herself."

"She's just as stubborn as Andy. Maybe more so."

He chuckles, giving me a sideways glance. "Then, I will repeat, you're fucked, buddy."

"Thanks for that."

"On the plus side, I'll help you paint. But don't tell Sinclair. If she finds out I've been using a ladder after my head injury, she's never going to let me hear the end of it."

I nod, grateful. "Thanks. I still don't feel good about Mrs. Ruiz being so isolated in that house. I'm going to see if I can find some people who might be willing to spend time with her."

"You know," he says, "funny you should say that. My friend Shauna lives with her grandparents, and they'd talk the ear off anyone. They don't live too far from here. I'm sure she'd be willing to swing by with them. You'd better give Grandma a warning, though. She looked like she was having serious thoughts about that cast iron skillet when she locked me out on the porch."

"Thanks, man," I say, feeling better. A plan is coming together, and even if the plan I like best is Mrs. Ruiz telling Andy what's going on—now, without delay—I can work with this. I've already texted Burke to give him a heads-up that I'm going to stop by after dropping Rafe off so we can shoot the shit about the windows. Mrs. Ruiz let me take some photos of them, and she even let Rafe measure them with a soft tape measure she uses for sewing, though she gave him side-eye the entire time.

"You spend enough time there, you'll soften her up," Rafe says, nudging my shoulder. "You're good at wearing people into submission. Your sister is too. It's like the Jones family superpower."

"Thanks for that," I say dryly. I park in the private lot attached to the apartments, expecting him to get out, but he sits for a second, eyeing the door to the building.

"What's wrong? Did you piss Sinclair off? Or is it your dad you're avoiding, because I can actually—"

"Neither of them," he says. "Although I'm obviously counting the days until my dad moves out. You coming to the party next weekend?"

"Yeah, of course. I wouldn't miss it."

"Good. Sinclair's going a little over the top."

"Which means a lot," I say with a grin. "Tell me there's not a theme."

"Not a theme so much as a literal cauldron she bought for punch. Don't ask. Seriously, it's best if no one questions it. But that's not what I wanted to talk to you about." He looks a little nervous suddenly, which is frankly novel. I don't think I've ever seen him look anything but entirely sure of himself. "I've already talked to your aunt, and I'm going to talk to Marnie about it tonight."

"Um...okay." I can't think of any earthly reason why he'd confide in my aunt before me. I mean, my aunt *is* sort of dating his father. I say sort of because they're polyamorous—which is something real, obviously, but I'll be damned if I understand it. I mean, the slightest hint of flirting between Burke and Andy was enough to piss me off, and we're not even together.

"I'm going to ask your sister to marry me," he blurts. "I was hoping I could get your blessing."

A huge grin splits my face. "Holy shit, man. You had me thinking you had cancer or something. That's awesome."

"So, I have your blessing?" he asks. "I feel like a bit of an ass asking a movie star to marry me, especially since I had to ask my dad for the ring, but she's the kind of woman who wants to be asked rather than do the asking."

"Don't be an idiot. She loves you. The rest of us..." I give him a sidelong grin. "Put up with you." Then I detach my seat belt and lean over to give the hunk of steel a hug. "Fuck, man, I love you. You're helping me with this whole debacle with Andy and her grandmother and—"

And me being in lust with her. Andy, that is. Not her grandmother.

"Of course I am," he says, hugging me back—but carefully, because he knows he can crush nine people out of ten like a tin can. Then he pulls back, smiling at me. "We're gonna get this sorted out. I'm going to ask Sinclair next week, after the party."

"Thanks for telling me. I needed some good news."

He detaches his seat belt, then snaps his fingers. "And here's some more. I got that date lined up for you."

It takes me half a second to catch up, because I'd honestly forgotten about our discussion yesterday. My mind's been on Andy and the problem of her grandmother—and then on his news. The reminder puts a knot in my throat, but I'm the one who asked for his help. I'd be an ass to renege if he's already made the arrangements.

"Who's it with?" I ask.

"Shauna," he says, nudging my shoulder. "She of the elderly grandparents. She's the second-best person I know. And you're in the top ten, at least, so I figure it'll work out great."

"Uh-huh, thanks," I say, my mind working hard. I've met Shauna. She's hot, with short hair dyed bright purple, brown eyes, and a quick wit. I should be excited about this news, because he didn't just set me up with some random bimbo he met in his gym days. Shauna is his best friend. She's the whole package.

But somehow that makes me feel worse.

"I told her you'd meet her at Steak Haus at seven thirty. Make me proud, brother." He pounds me on the back a little too hard, then gets out and disappears into the apartment building, leaving me with a sense of uneasiness as I start the car and make my way to Burke's.

twelve

ANDY

I HEARD Drew rustling around in the morning, but I didn't leave my room.

Last night was...surprising.

There was a moment there, on the couch, with his shoulder pressed against mine, his heat wrapping around me like a comfortable blanket fresh out of the dryer, when I felt the kind of contentment only lazy cats usually feel. Then there was his reaction to me saying I'd played some of his video games. I mean, of course I'd checked them out. If you have a friend who's a writer, like Grace, you read the damn book. If you have a friend who's a video game designer, you bite the bullet and check out his games. But he gave me this look that suggested I'd given him a gift—one he wouldn't be in a hurry to return to the store.

But I ruined everything for myself by having an errant thought that can only be explained by the sight of his dick last week. Because it occurred to me that the only thing that would make our cozy scene better would be if he'd slide me onto his lap and slowly start fucking me while the show kept playing, and neither of us would acknowledge it was happening. Actually, the thought and image were so intrusive that I was uncomfortably turned on by the time I

93

got up to my room, and I needed to take care of my needs with my vibrator if I wanted to get any sleep whatsoever.

So, yeah, I didn't want to see him before he left for my grandmother's house. Partly because I was worried those thoughts would kick back in, and partly because I figured he might take one look at me and know I was up to no good.

After he left, I ate a quick breakfast of some of Drew's toaster pastries—*thank you, Drew*—and then looked around until I found what I needed. I'm slaying this spying shit! Admittedly, it was pretty easy since he has an address book sitting on the corner of his desk under a couple of well-thumbed paperbacks—not romances, unfortunately.

Drew doesn't seem like the kind of guy who'd keep an address book, but it's a product Marnie designed for her Etsy business, and he's nothing if not a good brother. It takes me all of two seconds to find Lucas Burke III's address. Yes, he wrote it in there that way, presumably because he found it funny.

I probably shouldn't use the information I just stole, but I'm doing this to help Drew. If I manage to find anything of interest this weekend, Nicole and Damien will help me, and I obviously need their help. This is my Hail Mary.

The nice thing to do would be to text Burke a heads-up using the number that's *also* in the handy-dandy address book, but I've watched enough crime dramas with my grandmother to know that you shouldn't warn people you're coming when you're in the middle of the investigation. I mean, if the dude with all those office supplies had known the woman in the banana suit actually worked for a couple of private investigators, something tells me he would have found another path to his rendezvous point.

So I get dressed in a black T-shirt and cut-offs and head over to Burke's downtown apartment, located in a fancy loft building that reminds me of Sinclair's old place. Street parking's a bitch, but I'm not about to pay, so I find a spot a few blocks away and walk. When I get to the front door of the building, a thirty-something guy is leaving—jackpot!—and I theatrically feel around for a key that doesn't exist before slipping through the door he's holding for me.

Man, they really need to beef up their security.

"Thank you so much!" I prattle. "I can't believe I locked myself out."

I use the elevator to get up to Burke's floor, then make my way to his unit. Standing outside, I don't allow myself second thoughts before knocking.

"Hold on," someone calls from behind the door and then Burke opens it, his expression comically surprised. His black hair is wet from a shower or a really gnarly fit of night sweats, and he has sharp blue eyes, the color almost aggressively bright. He's wearing a pair of gray weather-inappropriate sweatpants and a T-shirt with a Burke Realty logo on it. I'm guessing that's his father's business, from which he gets the big bucks to afford a place like this.

"Surprise," I say on impulse, spreading my arms out wide. "Can I come in, Junior Cubed? I need to talk to you about something."

Burke, who struck me the other night as the kind of charmer who's used to getting a woman's pants off and asking questions later, seems at a loss for words. He opens his mouth, shuts it, then finally says, "It's great to see you, Andy, but what are you doing here?" He hasn't stepped back or invited me in, and I look past him to suggest he should get moving on that.

He takes the bait, stepping in and saying, "Sorry, I'm being rude. Come on in."

"Nice place you've got here."

Understatement. It's fantastic, with a view over Walnut Street, tons of natural lighting, and honeyed hardwood floors. The furniture is modern, but not so modern it looks uncomfortable.

"Take a seat," he says, still coming off as flustered. "Can I get you anything? Water? Coffee?"

"Coffee, absolutely," I say. "Can't have too much coffee."

I sit on the black couch, which is surprisingly comfortable. He heads into the adjoining room and, no kidding, comes back with two cups of coffee on a tray with a small carafe of cream and a bowl with sugar cubes. After setting it on the coffee table, he sits on a papasan chair about as far away from my perch on the couch as humanly possible. Who *is* this guy? The other day, he came off as an affable flirt, but today he's acting like I'm an STI made human.

"So?" he asks. "What's up?" They're relaxed words, but *he's* not relaxed. The other night, he acted like a man who knows he's attractive and wears it proudly. Today, he looks like someone shoved a stick up his ass.

"Is Danny here?" I remember him saying they lived together, and I suspect he's not going to be as open if his buddy is sitting in the other room, liable to walk out at any minute.

"No," he says slowly, eyeing me. "He went out for a bike ride with Shane."

"Good. I mean, not good that he's gone, but there *is* something I wanted to talk to you about privately—"

"Andy, I'm gonna have to stop you right there," he says, wincing as if he's in physical pain.

"What's your *problem*?" I blurt, because I've never been good at controlling my reactions. I mean, admittedly, I did just show up on his doorstep, but it's not *that* weird. I live with one of his friends. For all he knows, I'm planning a surprise party.

He swears under his breath, then says, "Look, you're one of the sexiest women I've ever met, no joke, but it's never going to happen. Drew's my best friend, and—"

I burst out laughing, because suddenly I can see all of this from his point of view. I barged into this apartment, made sure his roommate wasn't home, and told him I had something private to discuss. He probably figured I was going to rip my shirt off and start a strip tease.

"Oh, shit. That's not why I'm here. I'm sorry, but I'm not interested in you like that. Not even a little." His expression shifts from surprised to sulky in half a second, making me laugh harder. "Don't take it personally, I'm just—"

Actually, I don't know how to finish that sentence. Normally, I'd be all about taking a ride on that pogo stick. Then my mind boomerangs back to his last words. *"Drew's my best friend, and..."*

"But what does Drew have to do with it?" I ask. "You said he's the reason you'd—"

"I just meant it would get awkward if things didn't work out," he answers, a little too quickly. Then, "No offense, but if that's not why you're here, why *are* you here?"

"I want to talk to you about Leonard."

He looks even more shocked than he did when I showed up at his door ten minutes ago. Man, I just keep on surprising this guy. If only I had a trick scarf to pull out of my pocket. "Why do you want to talk about Leonard?"

"Drew blames himself for what happened. He needs closure."

"So you're...?"

"I'm looking into what happened to Leonard," I finish. "I have a couple of friends who are private investigators, and they said they'd help me out if I find anything interesting."

"You don't think he's dead?" he asks, tilting his head. His reaction is noteworthy, because he doesn't seem shocked by the idea— more by the fact that I'm the one who had it.

"Oh, I don't know." I make a flippant gesture with my hand, then remember we're talking about the possible death of one of Burke's friends and settle the hand in my lap. "Probably. But I was thinking there might be more to his disappearance. You know, something that might make Drew feel less responsible."

"He'll feel responsible no matter what you find out," he says darkly. "That's just the kind of guy he is. He thinks it's on him to protect everyone around him."

"What about you?" I ask, tilting my head. "Are you that kind of person?"

"You think I played some part in this?" he asks, looking annoyed or maybe pissed. I mean, fair enough. I crashed his Saturday morning, insulted his manhood, then insinuated he might be involved in his friend's death. There I go, pulling an Andy—plowing into a situation with the grace of a monster truck.

"No." I lift my hands. "But you acted a little funny when the guys started talking about him the other night. It made me think you might know something you didn't tell everyone else."

He picks up his coffee, takes a sip.

"You said you have a couple of private investigators who might be interested in looking into this?"

"If I have anything interesting to give them." Wink, wink, nudge, nudge.

"Okay." He nods a few times too many, then sets the coffee back down on the table. "This probably isn't a big deal, but Leonard borrowed some money from me before he disappeared."

"How much money?" I ask, leaning forward.

"Sixty-five large," he says.

Well, that is *very* interesting.

"Why'd you lend him that much scratch?" I ask.

He swears, looks down at his coffee again. "He'd been doing some work for my parents' company, and they fired him. So I offered to do a flip with him."

"Um. I assume you don't mean a backflip?"

He gives me a small smile. "Flip a house. It's what I do for fun."

The words feel barbed, though he didn't mean them that way. It's just that home improvement was never about "fun" for me; it was about survival. It was about learning to rip out the vanity in the bathroom and put in a new one because mold was creeping out from behind it like the mustache on an overwatered Chia Pet. It was about saving for months to buy paint for the exterior of the house and never getting around to using it because my grandmother kicked me out.

"So why'd you pay him instead of a broker?"

He smirks wider this time. "Because I'm an idiot? He said he had a bead on a property. Super cheap, but we needed to act immediately and make a cash buy. He showed me all the photos, and we even did a drive by. I was going to put down the initial investment and take a larger share of the profits."

"When did this happen?"

"A few days before he disappeared. I told the cops, obviously, but I didn't tell the rest of the guys. I didn't want to make it sound like I was getting on Leonard's case or implying he'd pulled a runner."

"Did he?" I ask, lifting my eyebrows. Because, good Christ, it's really starting to sound like it. Can I tell Nicole *I told you so*? Because I really want to.

"I don't know," he says. "Maybe. Or maybe the guy who was selling decided he'd keep the money after Leonard died. Who could call him on it? I wasn't in on the negotiations."

"Do you know anything else that could help?" I ask. "Like where he used to live?"

"Sure, but you don't want to go around there."

"Why not?"

"It's not safe."

"Maybe I like to live dangerously."

His eyes sparkle, a bit of his charm creeping back in. "So I've gathered. But I think it would be a waste of your time. His old neighbors are long gone, and he didn't like them much. Are you really going to follow up on this?"

"Drew's doing me a huge favor. I want to give him one in return."

He studies me for a second, then says, "Look, Drew wouldn't like me saying so, but he kind of...warned us off flirting with you. He made it pretty clear that—"

He's interrupted by a knock on the door, which is unfortunate, because I really *do* want to know what he was about to say.

"Just a sec," he says, rising to answer it.

I know it's him before I hear his voice. I can tell from the way Burke goes rigid again, as if someone just shoved that stick back up his ass. Because he just got done telling me that Drew didn't want him flirting with me, and he's probably thinking he'll be in for a hell of an explanation.

"Hey, man," Drew says, mostly hidden by Burke, who's tried to stretch out to make himself bigger than the door—a task that would be daunting for most people but which he can very nearly manage. "Did you get my texts? I wanted to talk to you about the windows." Then he looks past Burke's shoulder, maybe because he possesses the same sixth sense for me that I have for him, and I can see a flash of his face—the jaw hardening, those amber eyes as pissed as a cat thrown into a full bathtub.

"Oh," he says to Burke, "I see you have *company*." There's no mistaking his tone. He pushes past Burke and stalks into the apartment, his gaze on me, hot and holding. It feels like there's no one else but us in the apartment, like Burke and all of his pretty things have faded away. "So *this* is why I didn't see you this morning."

It takes a second for his meaning to register and then I gasp and leap to my feet.

"Are you insinuating that I spent the night here? You think I watched that show with you, waited until you went upstairs, then snuck over here for a booty call?"

He watches me for a second and then swallows, my eyes tracking his Adam's apple.

"Well, did you?"

"No," I snap. "I'm not interested in Junior Cubed. But if I were, that would be between him and me. You don't get to dictate who I spend time with, Drew. You're not *actually* my brother."

His gaze holds mine for a long moment before he swallows again and says, "You need to make up your mind, Andy. Last week you told me I *was* like your brother."

He sounds pissed about that too, and my heart starts beating faster in my chest. Not because I'm afraid of him; I know without a doubt that he would never intentionally hurt me. My body's reacting to the way he's looking at me, with those tortured, beautiful eyes. My mind blinks back to last night, to sitting with him on the couch, our sides pressed together, and I can't help but wonder what would have happened if I'd edged onto his lap.

"She just showed up fifteen minutes ago," Burke says, breaking the spell. I give myself a mental shake. "Swear to Christ," he continues. "I didn't invite her."

Gee, thanks for throwing me under the bus.

Still...when he's right, he's right.

"I wanted to get you a thank you present for letting me move in," I tell Drew. "I figured Burke might have some ideas. He seems like a big spender."

I'm not ready to tell him about Leonard yet. I don't want to disappoint him if Nicole and Damien deem my information insufficient of their interest. I also don't want him to tell me to stop digging. This search for information has given me something to focus on, and I desperately need that right now. It's giving me a sense of purpose that stops my mind from hanging out in dark places.

"So you snooped through my things to find his address?" he asks flatly. "Or did he give it to you?"

Burke lifts both hands. "I swear—"

"Yeah, that's exactly what I did. It's not like I had to sift through your most cherished belongings," I say, cutting him off. "You have an address book. That should be open to anyone who lives in your house. Public property, if you will."

"Why Burke?" he presses, his mouth in a hard, displeased line. His tone is accusatory. "Why not Danny or Shane?"

I roll my eyes and put a hand on my hip. "Danny and Burke both live here. Duh. Two for the price of one."

"That's not why you came here," Drew says, but he takes a step back. "But it's fine if you don't want to tell me. You're right. It's none of my business. I didn't tell you I have a date tonight, so there's no reason for me to expect you to tell me if you're interested in someone."

Something in my chest twists, like someone just took a couple of turns with a wine opener. He has a date? With whom?

He looks away from me then, his gaze shifting to Burke.

"I'm sorry, man." Burke scratches the back of his neck. "It really isn't what it looks like."

"Like I said. None of my business. We'll talk about the windows later."

Then he turns around without another word and leaves, shutting the door a little too forcefully behind him.

"What windows?" Burke whispers to himself.

But my mind is still caught up on that other thing...

"I didn't tell you I have a date tonight."

thirteen

DREW

MY BLOOD IS TOO hot in my veins, my skin too tight across my body.

I get back home, change into workout clothes, and go for a long run. It doesn't help.

I return home and take a long, cold shower. It doesn't help.

I have a group call with my sisters, and they talk about living with their partners. Marnie ends with a joke about me and Andy living together, making it clear that she's never, in a million years, imagined that there could ever be something between us. That *definitely* doesn't help.

I keep seeing Andy sitting on that couch, cozy in my best friend's apartment, wearing lounge clothes as if she'd been there all night.

I believe her, mostly. I don't think anything has happened between them yet. What troubles me is my own reaction. She was right. She's not mine to control or dictate, and I wouldn't want to try. I like her as wild and uncontrollable as her hair.

She'll probably date someone while she's living in my house. I have to accept that, no matter how much it makes my skin crawl, but I can't put up with it if it's with my best friend.

After I get out of the shower, I finally check my phone. There's a missed call from Burke, plus a couple of texts.

> Nothing happened, Drew. I'd never break your trust like that.

> I saw your texts from earlier, and of course I'll help with Mrs. Ruiz's windows.

There's suddenly a knot in my throat, because I believe Burke too. He may be a self-confessed manwhore, but he's a good guy—the kind of friend who'd give you the shirt off his back and five from his drawer. I happen to know he's never collected a dollar of rent from Danny. Our friend didn't come from money or have the kind of parents he'd want to live with post college.

Of course, Danny would never accept something he sees as charity, so Burke gives him work to do in exchange for rent—things like setting up and maintaining the website for his house-flipping side hustle. He could do it himself without breaking a sweat. Danny probably isn't unaware of that, but I know he appreciates the ruse.

> Thanks, man. I'm sorry I reacted like that. I wasn't expecting to see her there.

> You and me both.

Three little dots appear, disappear, return.
Then he writes:

> You should tell her how you feel.

I set the phone down and sigh.
It pings again, and when I pick it up, I swear at him. Good-naturedly, of course.

> You didn't need to pretend you have a date.

WTF? I DO have a date.

There's only room for one manwhore in this group.

Who, Danny?

Very funny.

Come with me to Mrs. Ruiz's house tomorrow? I want to get started this week.

Done.

I return the phone to my dresser. There's the sound of rustling downstairs, and my pulse picks up. Either it's Andy returning home, or someone is breaking in. Either way, it's an occasion for a spike in blood pressure.

I get dressed in a short-sleeved, button-down checkered shirt and some jeans, then head downstairs. I can see her in the opening to the kitchen, drinking from the jug of orange juice, still dressed in those cut-offs that hug her ass.

"Caught you," I say, and she nearly drops the juice.

"Sorry." She caps it and sticks it back in the fridge.

"Isn't that like if I'd kept those peas?" I ask, coming to a stop in the opening between the dining room and kitchen.

"Nope. Those were touching your junk."

I'm an idiot, a lost cause, because I find myself saying, "So it's okay if our mouths touch the same place?"

She shuts the fridge, staring at me, her hair loose around her shoulders and back. "Only the orange juice will know."

"I'm sorry," I blurt. "I was out of line earlier. Way out of line." My throat constricts before I manage to let the next words out. "It's none of my business if you and Burke are interested—"

"We're not," she snaps. "Why would you assume that anyway? You think I can't keep it in my pants? That if I'm in a guy's apartment it automatically means we're having sex? I mean, obviously that's not true because I'm living in your house, and *we're* not fucking."

It feels like a jab. She's also right.

Unfortunately.

"I've never thought that of you." I pause, because she looks unconvinced, and add, "You asked me the other day if I was jealous of Burke. I guess I am, sometimes."

"Why?"

"You mean it's not enough that he's rich and successful?" I swallow, then decide *what the hell, I've gone this far.* "Women don't torment him. They like to play with him instead."

She gives me a slow smile that I feel in every last molecule. "You haven't met the right kind of woman then. Because it's no fun if you don't do both."

My chest sizzles with the look she's giving me, with the implication, and I take a step forward in spite of myself. It's hard not to feel drawn in by her, like a fish with a hook embedded in its mouth.

Her gaze lowers to my feet before inching back up. "*That's* what you're wearing for your date? You're lucky I live here, because you're gonna need some help."

Her words try to douse the fire in my chest, but it's a persistent bastard and doesn't go out easily.

"I don't need a fashion consultant."

"You mean you don't want one," she says, opening the pantry and surveying my ingredients, plus a few things she must have bought. "I'm going to make empanadas tonight."

"Trying to get me to stay?"

Maybe it's a challenge, although I'm not exactly sure who I'm challenging, Andy or me.

She meets my eyes, a slightly startled look on her face. "No, Drew, you should go. I'm happy for you. I mean, hell, the last person I remember you seriously dating was that spreadsheet woman. You deserve to have a little fun."

The words stab into me. Maybe they were meant to. Maybe she realized what was going through my head earlier and is trying to set me straight. Then it occurs to me that she's probably been waiting all day to hear something about her grandmother, and I've been a withholding dick, putting my needs before hers.

"I saw your grandmother," I say carefully, because I don't want to make a mess of things. Rafe's right. The best approach is to work on Mrs. Ruiz slowly, to get her to trust me. "She's okay, Andy. She looks—"

Gaunt. Old. Tired.

"Tough as nails. I'm pretty sure they've named hurricanes after her."

A weak smile lifts her lips, and she drifts across the kitchen toward me, coming to a stop a couple of feet away. "She'd certainly like to think so, anyway. Were Theo and Jack there?" Her brow knits. "Did they give you any trouble?"

"No, they weren't around." I smile at her. "But Rafe came with me as backup just in case, and your grandmother wasn't impressed with him."

She barks out a laugh. "What'd she do?"

"She made him wait out on the porch."

"Classic move. She did that to my prom date. Actually, come to think of it, he kind of looked like Rafe."

I'll bet he did. He probably didn't wear checkered shirts either. But this isn't about me, so I hold her gaze, avoiding the temptation to ask for more than she wants to give me. Still, she needs comfort, and that's one thing I can give her. I reach out and squeeze her hand, trying not to feel the jolt that instantly shakes me. "She's going to come around, Andy. I know it."

I want to tell her everything. I'm aching to. But I don't have a single doubt that Mrs. Ruiz would do as she threatened. If I earn her trust, if I make her understand what Andy's going through, then I can't imagine she'll persist. She must want to see her granddaughter every bit as much as Andy wants to see her.

"Sure." She squeezes my hand, too, and then releases it, leaving me with a hole inside my chest. "You have fun tonight, Drew."

So I go. But I wear the damn checkered shirt.

"Nice shirt," Shauna says when the host brings her back to our table, where I'm already seated. I showed fifteen minutes early because I didn't want to hang out in the kitchen with Andy after she told me to go. So I've sat here trying to make origami out of my napkin and not give in to the sadness pulling at me. "I love the pattern."

So there, Andy. Of course, I shouldn't still be thinking about Andy on my date, but I think about her every other place. Might as well be consistent.

"Thanks," I say, "I like your…"

I'm not exactly sure what she's wearing. It looks like an apron, actually, and it's covered with smudge marks.

She laughs. "Oh, shit. I forgot to take that off, didn't I?" She removes it, stuffing it into the big tote bag she brought with her. Under it, she has on a green vintage shirt and denim skirt. It looks good on her, especially in contrast to her purple hair, but I can't bring myself to care. "Sorry. I was at my workshop before I came here, and sometimes I forget the time when I'm working."

Shauna's a clay artist and a personal trainer—the latter to help support the former.

"Happens to me too, but it would be harder not to notice if I were walking around with a computer in front of my face."

"Yeah," she says with a grin, "Rafe told me you were a game designer. That's pretty rad. What're you working on?"

"Zombie clowns," I say glumly.

"No shit." She seems kind of overjoyed by it, her face lighting up and a dimple popping out in her cheek.

"Yes shit, sadly."

"Is there any upside to that? Knowing that you're going to give people psychological trauma?"

Despite my mood, I laugh, and I end up telling her about the game I'm working on for fun, the one that might actually be worth a damn. And she reciprocates by telling me about her art.

We order drinks and then food. Shauna's fun and easy to talk to. After the food arrives, it seems entirely natural for me to start talking about Andy. Shauna *did* just tell me a story about her roommates, after all, and while she lives with her grandparents, a roommate's a roommate, right?

"The whole house smells like a Starbucks that only makes crème frappucinos, but I guess she did narrow it down to one scent at least."

"Here's the question," she says after finishing a bite of her lobster mac and cheese. "Do you *like* crème frappucinos?"

I laugh. "I feel like I shouldn't answer that question."

"What, don't you think it's *manly* to like crème frappucinos?"

"I'm pretty sure it's not. I definitely wouldn't order one in front of Andy."

She purses her lips and nods. "So you want her to think you're manly?"

"I wouldn't put it like that, exactly," I say. "But I wouldn't mind if she remembered I was a man." I grab a fry.

Her face lights up with humor. "Rafe told me she walked in on you choking the chicken. She probably knows you're a man."

I almost choke on the fry but manage to get it down with a big gulp of beer. "You know, I've decided never to speak to my sisters' boyfriends again. It might make family events awkward, but a surprising amount of information can be conveyed by hand gestures."

"You'd know," she says with an easy grin.

"Very funny. It would be worth it because it would ensure that nothing like this ever happens again."

She waves this off. "It's not his fault. I made him tell me."

"You made him tell you about my dick?" I ask incredulously. "Is that your barometer for whether you want to go on a date with someone?"

"Maybe it should be," she teases, then says, "No, he seemed amused by something involving you, and I couldn't stand not knowing what it was. It became this whole thing. He made me guess, and I finally guessed right."

"How long did it take?"

She grins, her nose crinkling slightly. A little crystal winks at me from her piercing. "Not that long, surprisingly. My mind is a filthy place."

It's a sexy-as-hell thing for a woman to say. I wish it made me feel something, but she might as well have made a comment about the weather.

It makes me lose my appetite. To be honest, it feels like I'm doing something wrong by being here. Like I'm being unfaithful to Andy, even though we're not together and she encouraged me to go on this date. I mean, for all I know, she has a thriving sex life that takes place entirely outside of my house, but here I am, out on a date with a funny, beautiful woman and feeling drawn back home to a woman who doesn't want me.

At times, I've felt certain that she no longer sees me as an old shirt hanging in her closet—comfortable, but not the kind you put on for good times. But isn't it possible that's just in my head? All I can know for sure is what she's told me, and *go on your date and have fun* isn't exactly an encouraging sign.

I sigh and push my food away.

"Shauna, I'm—"

"In love with your roommate?" she asks with a wry expression.

"I wouldn't go that far," I say, rubbing the bridge of my nose. "But it's fair to say I'm hung up on her."

"Don't sell yourself short, Drew. It's always best to be honest, even when it's a bitch to try." She takes a big bite of her food.

"I'm sorry for wasting your time," I say, feeling like an ass. Possibly even a dumbass. "You're incredible."

"Yeah, yeah, it's not you, it's me," she says, waving a hand. "I've heard it all, and I've got the T-shirt. Anyway, I'm going to be brutally honest with you; remember what I said about honesty? Rafe told me you were a great guy, and I thought you were hot when we met a couple of months back, but he *did* mention you probably have a thing for your sister's friend. He said, and I quote, 'He needs to go out with the most stupendous human being on the planet, because if he doesn't hit it off with you, then he'll know he has it bad.' That's him saying that, not me."

"You expect me to believe he used the word stupendous?" And then, because I'm a guy, I add, "You think I'm hot?" I try not to sound pleased with myself, because even if I'm not interested in Shauna, she's definitely the kind of woman whose attention is gratifying. If my head weren't full of Andy, I *would* be interested.

"You're definitely hot. And maybe Rafe didn't exactly use that word, but you get the picture. Anyway, yes, I'm sorry to say that you are diagnosed as being very much hung up on this woman. What are you going to do about it?"

"Nothing."

She gives me a dubious look, then shrugs and takes another bite of her food. When she finishes, she says, "Hot people are usually stupid. You seemed smart with all the game design shit, but what do I know?"

I run a hand through my hair, because the "date" part of the date is apparently over, so who cares if my hair's messy? "It's complicated with Andy."

"Because you live together?"

"She told me just last week I'm like a brother to her."

"Did she mean it?" she asks. "People say a lot of shit they don't mean."

"I'm not going to risk hurting her. Her brothers turned their backs on her, and her grandmother has this crazy notion that she can save her heartache by refusing to let her take care of her while she's dying. What Andy needs now is my support, not for me to make a move."

Then, in the eternal wisdom of women, she says, "That's fair, but what makes you think you can't do both?"

"Without complicating things?"

"Oh, it's already complicated," she says. "You flew the coop on that one."

"I think I'm screwed," I tell her honestly. "I mean, she knew I was coming out with you, and she encouraged me to go. Hell, she even wanted to pick out my outfit. If she's not interested, I'd be an ass to make things uncomfortable for her."

I don't mention that she's got some weird thing going on with my best friend.

She shrugs. "Maybe. People do some messed-up things, though. I mean, I agreed to be a bridesmaid for my ex-boyfriend's wedding."

"He asked you to be a bridesmaid?" I ask incredulously. "Wouldn't his fiancée be the one to decide?"

She gives me a wry look. "Sure. She was my friend."

"Ouch."

"Exactly."

We talk for a little while longer, this time about Rafe and Sinclair, since it turns out she's in the know about their soon-to-be engagement, too, then about the possibility of her grandparents visiting Mrs. Ruiz. They're game as long as she doesn't shoot them for showing up on her porch. I assure her that if she didn't shoot Rafe and me, they're probably safe, and besides, I'll give her a heads-up. Then we part as friends.

"Good luck, Drew," Shauna says after I walk her to her car, a sporty little red hatchback. "Something tells me you're going to need it."

With those less-than-promising last words ringing in my ears, I head home.

When I open the door, the smell of beef empanadas overpowers the Starbucks scent for once. My appetite returns, because I can't think of anything better than eating empanadas with Andy on the couch and watching that horrific show of hers. Something steels inside of me, and I tell myself that Shauna's right. I can be straight with Andy and tell her how I feel without putting pressure on her. But there's a note waiting for me on the dining room table, underneath a plate of empanadas.

Don't wait up, champ. Hope you're about to share these with your hot date, you hunka, hunka burning love. She'll need stamina to deal with what you're packing.

Her car is in the driveway.

That means someone picked her up. I don't believe it was Burke —he wouldn't pull a move like that—but it doesn't matter, because the one person it definitely wasn't is me.

I go straight to the alcohol, which is now stored in a dumb bar shaped like the globe—something Andy was "amazed" to find by the side of the road, because she couldn't conceive of anyone not wanting it. I grab the bottle of whiskey and the plate of empanadas and, because I'm a masochist, I watch *Matchmaking Small Town America* as I slowly get wasted alone.

ANDY

"IS IT ALWAYS THIS BORING?" I ask, fidgeting in my seat.

"It isn't boring with Damien," Nicole says pointedly. "Only one person needs to watch, so he could have had his head in my lap this very second. But no, you just had to come along. *'Oh, Nicole, my life is so pathetic, there's nothing I'd rather do on a Saturday night than hang out outside someone's house while a cheating asshole gets his dick wet.'*"

"I didn't say it like that," I object.

Actually, I'd asked her to get coffee or a drink so I could fill her in on the Leonard situation. She'd refused because she and Damien were about to go on a stakeout—taking over for a contractor who couldn't stay out past nine. I mentioned that I'd never been on a stakeout, and weren't they supposed to be training me? So Nicole gave the sigh of a teenager whose life is being ruined and offered to bring me with her instead of Damien.

That's where we are now, parked across the street from a little yellow house with a bright green door, watching that door like it's a giraffe waiting to give birth and we're a zoo cam.

When I agreed to this scenario, it seemed like a banner idea. I figured I could unload the Leonard situation on her while she was stuck in the car with me, unable to leave. Of course, it took me all of five minutes to tell her what I'd learned, and that was four hours ago. On the plus side, she *did* admit it was "not totally worthless" and said she'd talk to Damien about next steps—if they were inclined to take any.

I also didn't hate the idea of clearing out of the house for the night. Grace is still in New York with Enoch, and Marnie and Sinclair are out on a double date. They offered to let me crash, but is there anything more depressing than crashing someone else's double date? I would generally avoid a double date like a plague, even if I were part of one of the couples, but it's *them*, dammit, and they're going to have fun. I'm suddenly feeling desperately single—and not in an empowering way. I've watched my two best friends fall in love, and to be honest, it wasn't the horror show I'd thought it might be. They didn't lose themselves. They didn't start buying matching Tupperware sets and molding their personalities to fit the other person. They're still them, but they're happier.

Growing up, I watched my mother fall in love with men who broke her heart. She was a nurse, so there were doctors. *Married* doctors. And there were patients too—like the man who came in with a bullet wound and left with her number. And I watched her give my brothers everything, treating them as if they were golden gods—the best cuts of meat at dinner, the most pocket money, the choice of what we'd watch together at night.

But I watched my grandmother too. *She* never let men take advantage of her. Or at least she didn't anymore.

When I was twelve, I walked in on *Abuela* and a younger man going at it athletically on top of the dryer. I asked her about it later, and she told me that she'd had one great love—my grandfather— but even though she'd loved him with all her heart, he'd been a taker, and each day, he'd taken another piece of her, until it felt like there was nothing left. Since then, she'd been finding those pieces and restoring them to herself.

"I see the same thing with your mother," she'd said, making

the sign of the cross on her chest like a woman who hadn't just had sex on top of a dryer. Then again, she's a woman of contradictions, my grandmother. "Every day, she gives more pieces of herself to those boys, to the men who come in and out of this house. What is left?"

She was right. I saw it happening, more and more, every day. The way my mom looked drained after a long day. The stoop in her shoulders. And then she got sick, and where were all of those men then?

My grandmother and I took care of her, but Theo only came by when he wanted something, and Jack's visits were haphazard and unplanned, and neither of them offered to really help.

The thing is...

Not all men are like that. Griffin's not. Enoch's not. Rafe's not.

Drew's not.

"Aren't you supposed to find me a boyfriend?" I ask Nicole conversationally. "You found Griffin for Marnie, and you terrorized Enoch until he hooked up with Grace. You even found Rafe for Sinclair. Where's my hot dude?"

She yawns theatrically. "I already told you. My money's on Drew. I got him to take you in. That was the first step."

"He said he would have offered even if you hadn't pushed him into it."

"Probably," she says with a disinterested shrug, her gaze settling on the door we're watching. Nothing continues to happen. "I mean, the dude *did* pay that asshole not to marry Marnie a while back. He's got some kind of good guy complex going on."

"Or maybe he's just a good guy," I snap back.

Her gaze flicks to me, interest kindling in her eyes. "Oh, *real*-ly? You've been thinking about his schlong, haven't you?"

Yes.

"No." I fold my arms, displeased with her, because somehow this all feels like her fault. "He looked in on my grandmother for me this morning." I can practically hear her thinking *good guy complex.* "I didn't even have to ask."

She looks positively smug. "Don't you think he should have some more self-interest? Do something for himself for no other reason than that he wants to?"

I tighten my arms across my chest. "Well, he's off having dinner with some bimbo, so how about that?"

Shit. I hadn't meant to say that.

"A bimbo, huh?" she asks, giving me a searching look. "You've met her, then?"

"No," I admit.

"So she's a bimbo because you don't want her to go out with him, not because she's a good-time gal who likes to get her freak on?"

"I didn't say I didn't want her to go out with him," I say stiffly. "In fact, I *encouraged* him to go. It's like you said, he needs to do more for himself."

She releases a puff of air and settles back in the seat, her eyes on the door again as if she's completely lost interest in me. "Well, that was stupid."

"You're kind of a shitty fairy godmother."

Without looking at me, she lifts up her thumb. "Got her a place to live." Her pointer finger. "Gave her a job." She tucks her thumb and pointer finger down and gives me the middle finger. "Practically gift-wrapped her a hot nerd with a monster cock." She turns to look at me, cocking her head. "Who's the asshole now? If you encouraged him to go out with someone else, you have no one to blame but yourself."

"I'm not into him like that," I insist, even as my mind rewinds to the way he looked at me this morning, after he saw me in Burke's apartment. For a minute there, I thought he was going to pick me up and sling me over his shoulder like a caveman claiming his woman. For a minute there, I wanted him to.

Nicole snorts. "Yes, it's completely natural to get jealous of men you're not interested in. Totally normal. Nothing suspicious about that at all."

"He seemed a little upset this morning," I say slowly, "when he found me at his friend's place. He thought I was there for a hookup." I don't know why the hell I'm confiding in her—a mirror would be more sympathetic, because at least I'd be vibing with myself—other than that I don't want Marnie to know that things are weird between Drew and me. Because that might make things weird between her and me, and I couldn't take that.

At the same time, have I *already* made things weird? I've asked her to hang out over the last week or so. Called and texted less too. It's not just because of this strange tension with Drew... She's engaged and living with her fiancé, doing her dream job. Samesies with Grace. I, on the other hand, am working part-time for a couple of private investigators who had me running around in a banana suit all week for their amusement, feeling a strange compulsion to kiss a man I've known for most of my life. And all of it is encompassed by an aching sadness that I can't fix—a problem without a solution—because I know my grandmother is dying, and if she gets her way, I might not even be able to say goodbye.

In short, I am a mess.

I don't like being the one who's the mess. I'm the one with the solutions. The one who runs in to crack someone in the balls. The one who makes stands.

Maybe that's why I've got it in my head that I can solve Leonard's disappearance. I want to believe I can fix something, for somebody, and Marnie and Grace are already living the life fantastic. Drew might lead a comfortable existence, with a job he's had since college and a house he's had since forever, but inside he's a mess too. And if I can fix this for him, then—

I don't know.

Nicole pats my hand, but from the way she does it, it's obvious she comforts people about as often as a one-year-old uses the potty. "You're realizing you made a mistake. I'd say it happens to the best of us, but let's be honest, I don't make a lot of them."

"You picked me," I point out.

"Not really," she objects. "Sinclair did."

That's their thing—they let the last person they fairy godmothered pick their next charity case. I'm still surprised Sinclair chose me, mostly because—until recently—I've never gone out of my way to be nice to her. What can I say? It took a while for me to get over the grudge I held about her being mean to Marnie back in the day. I guess it's a character flaw to hold grudges, but it's kept me strong, so I'll keep it.

"How long does it take to fuck someone?" I ask forlornly, looking at the door. The color is probably seared into my retinas.

"You know, I'm impressed," Nicole says. "He doesn't look like the sort of dude who'd have it in him. I mean, yes, he's pompous looking. *Obviously*. But I feel like a lot of guys who either don't have it or can't use it have this undeserved air of self-satisfaction. I mean, would you have guessed he could get his freak on for this long? Maybe he's got some of those blue pills. I've heard a guy with some of those in his system can go for *hours*."

"What are you talking about?" I ask, annoyed. "I don't even know what this guy looks like. He was already inside when we took over for your contractor."

"Oh, yeah," she says with a knowing smirk. "That's right."

"O-kay. Are you going to tell me who we're tracking?"

"A cheating asshole," she says. "Need I say more?"

"Yes," I tell her, reaching for the canister of trail mix sitting in the divider between the seats. She grabs for it before I can get it and takes out a handful of M&Ms before returning the container. Now, the rest of the candy is all the way at the bottom, leaving nothing but a bunch of salty raisins and peanuts within reach. "You're such a tool."

"At least I'm not a *fool*. I'd rather be a tool any day. You don't see me setting my husband up with other women."

"I didn't set Drew up with anyone," I say bitterly. "He arranged this himself."

"Huh, didn't know *he* had it in him either." She pops a few of the M&Ms. "Maybe you got him all hot and bothered when you walked in on him the other day, and he had to get a nut off."

I grit my teeth against the image in my head—of Drew walking in through the door with a woman draped over him. Maybe they'll feed each other my empanadas and then fuck on my colorful rug. It's his right, obviously. It's his house. I just...

I wish I hadn't left that note, practically daring him to have sex with his date.

"You are *not* a good friend."

"Nope. Never claimed to be otherwise."

A sullen minute passes, my mood worsening with every M&M Nicole crunches into, especially since I'm bored enough to try snacking on the rest. Then she says, "Ah-ha," and pulls her camera out of the footwell of her seat. Sure enough, the green door has finally opened, and my mouth drops open as I watch my brother Theo emerge from it. A dark-haired woman who is not his fiancée is all over him, and as Nicole clicks away, the woman gives him an open-mouthed kiss that makes me want to vomit salted raisins all over the car.

I mouth *"what the shit?"* at her as they close the door, and Theo leads the way to a minivan that's clearly hers—he drives a Range Rover, the pretentious prick.

Nicole gets several more photos as he helps her into her seat unnecessarily, grabbing a feel of her ass, then gets into the driver's seat and drives away.

Then I turn to look at her.

"What's that you were saying about me being a shit fairy godmother?" she asks pointedly, fluttering her lashes. "I accept apologies in M&Ms and goldfish, just don't get any of the pretzel ones. I mean, vom."

"Y-you made me...beg to come with you," I say haltingly, my mind working overtime.

"Yeah, it was kind of fun listening to you beg," she says with an amused smile. "I was going to tell you that you had to come, but you called me first."

"I think I might be in love with you."

"I get that a lot."

ANDY

WHEN NICOLE DROPS ME OFF, Drew's car is in the driveway. There aren't any other cars around the house, other than mine, but that's no guarantee he's alone. His date could have ridden with him.

"Remember what I said," Nicole tells me from the car window.

"What part?"

"Better to be a tool than a fool."

Then she drives off, hitting a garden gnome that Marnie left too close to the road and smashing it. It probably goes without saying that she doesn't slow down.

Feeling an uncharacteristic burst of nerves, I get rid of the ruined garden gnome—RIP, Gnomeo—then walk slowly up the driveway. The lights are on in the front room, so someone's up. Will they be sitting on the couch, cuddled together under a blanket the way Drew and I were just last night? I'll have to pretend it doesn't bother me, obviously, even if it costs me a piece of myself, because he really does deserve to have a good time with this anonymous woman if that's what he wants.

He deserves everything.

But when I open the door, all but holding my breath, he's the only one I see on the couch, cuddled up on his side with his feet tucked in because he's too tall to comfortably fit. There's a half empty bottle of whiskey next to him, and the TV is running. It's some kind of infomercial, the sort of thing that only plays in those hours that can neither really be called night or morning. My heart is a mushy mess of relief, aggravation at said relief, and affront—because surely his date must have done something awful for him to be in such a state, and how *dare* she?

I close the door and walk over to him. He smells like a bar, but he looks adorable, his long body curled up, his eyelashes brushing his cheeks, his hair rumpled from sleep. I trace the lines of his eyebrows, unable to stop myself, as a deep, cloying fondness washes through me. I want to protect him from whatever happened tonight. I want to take care of him. That thought arrests me a little, because isn't that how it probably started for my mother?

But from what I remember of my father, he never took care of anyone—only sucked in the care given to him like he was a black hole, then left after he'd had enough of it. Nicole was right about one thing: Drew's a good guy. He deserves to have people look after him the way he looks after them.

So I go to the kitchen and get him a big glass of water, then retrieve a bottle of Tylenol from the bathroom.

His eyes flutter open, and he groans.

"What time is it?"

"Fabgadget time," I say, waving to the TV, where a very enthusiastic blond woman—Megan Fabulous, according to her name tag—is telling us about how the Fabgadget has changed her life by giving her the ability to slice, shred, smash, season, and cook with one handy dandy device that looks as big as an instant pot and probably takes up half her kitchen counter.

"It's pretty impressive," he says with a hiccup. "You'll be relieved to know they make them in five different colors. The red is aggressively bright. You'd love it."

"You were actually watching this?" I ask with a frown. "I figured it switched to infomercials after you fell asleep."

"It did. But you try watching this woman talk about the Fabama-jig's ability to season while it shreds without waking up. I thought she was going to orgasm for the camera."

"How could you watch it if you were asleep?" I ask before I realize that he's obviously still drunk. "Here." I push the water and Tylenol toward him. "You'll thank me later."

"Your car's been here all night," he says darkly. "Where were you?"

"Nicole picked me up."

Something softens on his face, and I realize that he must have thought I was out with a man, maybe even his friend. I'm annoyed by the presumption, especially since he's the one who went out on a date, but he clearly had a hard night. "Bad date?"

"Something like that." He shakes two Tylenol onto his palm and lifts his head from the pillow just enough to dry-swallow them, his Adam's apple bobbing, before chasing them down with some water. He sets the cup back down, his hand a little wobbly.

"Want me to fight her for you?"

The corners of his mouth lift as he relaxes back into the pillow. "No. She's nice."

"So you weren't attracted to her?"

"I wouldn't say that."

And suddenly I feel like I did that one time I went to a manicurist and she stabbed the inside of my fingernail hard enough that a line of blood was visible through the nail.

"So what was the problem?" When he doesn't answer right away, I snap my fingers. "I know. Did she tell you the *Star Wars* prequels were her favorite movies?" I'm teasing, but part of me wants to know what went down. I can't deny I'm relieved to have walked in on this scene—Drew with a hangover in the making—

rather than him snuggled up with his mystery woman, the two of them with their hands all over each other.

"Yes, Andy," he says, sounding exhausted. "That's exactly what it was." He pauses, then says, "Why don't you go up to bed? It's late."

"What about you?"

"I'm going to keep watching this infomercial until I wake up with a hangover."

"Sounds like fun."

He gives me a half-smile. "It won't be. I'd go upstairs if I were you."

That's what I should do. That's what I had every intention of doing a few minutes ago, but he looks so cozy curled up on the couch, and I can't deny that I want to soak up his comfort. So I find myself saying, "Scoot over, the couch is big enough for the two of us, and I really want to see that red Fabgadget."

His gaze takes me in, warm and lingering. "No, you don't. You can't handle the red Fabgadget."

I put my hand on my hip. "Don't you tell me what I can and can't handle, Andrew Jones. Besides, don't you want to know what happened with Nicole?"

"Maybe," he says, his eyes dipping to my hip and following the curve of it. I shift on my feet because suddenly I'm feeling a little hot and bothered. "Maybe not," he continues. "That woman scares me, and I don't feel like less of a man for admitting it."

He starts to sit up, sighing theatrically, but I shake my head. "No, I want to lie down too."

His pupils dilate, his eyes boring into me. "With me?"

"If I must," I say, but my nerves dance as I watch him lie back down and push into the back of the couch to give me room. I feel self-conscious as I lower onto the cushions next to him, but only for a second, because he immediately wraps an arm around me. It feels so good to lie here like this, with him, that my eyes feel hot. I'm not a woman who likes to cuddle usually, or at least I'm not a woman who lets men cuddle. It's vulnerable to want this kind of affection—vulnerable to give it too. But I've needed this, I realize. I've needed someone to hold me. To lie to me and tell me that everything's going to be okay. Even if it's not true.

"Story time," Drew says next to my ear. His hand is draped across my hip, the warmth of him washing through me. His breath is hot against my ear. "What'd she do?"

"Well"—I lean back against him—"we did a stakeout. Guess who's cheating on his fiancée?"

"I'm seriously hoping it's not Griffin or Rafe," he says, "because I'm pretty sure I couldn't beat up either of them, but I'd have to try."

I turn in his grip and look at him, our faces only inches apart, and suddenly every part of me—every last atom—is on high alert, because my whole world has become his face—so familiar, yet not. I've never seen it this close up before. There's a tiny mole next to his right eye, little more than freckle, and the smallest of indents in his chin. "You *would* try, wouldn't you?" I say, thinking again about Nicole and what she called his "good guy syndrome."

"Of course," he says, his voice husky. "It's up to me to defend my sisters' honor."

I give his chest a little shove, which isn't easy since he's inches away. "That's chauvinistic."

"Absolutely. So who was dipping his dick where it didn't belong?"

"Theo."

His expression darkens. "No offense, but your brothers remind me of Thing One and Thing Two in Dr. Seuss. They're a couple of real assholes."

"On a Dr. Seuss kick, huh?" I say, feeling my mouth lifting into a smile.

One of my curls tumbles over my shoulder and he picks up the end between his fingers, playing with it.

"I'm just trying to speak your language. You were a daycare teacher up until a couple of months ago."

"We both know how that went."

"What, did you trip a kid? Spike someone's milk?" His smile stretches wider. "Or are you talking about those videos?"

"You know I was. At least I purposefully filmed myself. I'd prefer to get myself into trouble than to have someone else get me into trouble."

"Of course you would," he says, still playing with the end of my curl. My throat suddenly feels too narrow, my skin too tight. "What are you going to do about it? Are you going to show the photos to your grandmother?"

"And let her go to her grave knowing at least two of her grandchildren are perverts?" I joke. Shaking my head, I say, "She's actually not as much of a prude as you're probably thinking, but I don't think anything good would come of it. I'd prefer for things to stay civil with them in case she needs anything. Besides, the person who needs to know is his fiancée. Nicole's going to make sure she gets the photos."

There's a pause where we're looking at each other but not speaking. It seems to last for minutes but is probably thirty seconds long at most. "You don't have to feel guilty about it, Andy," he says, releasing my curl. He smells like whiskey but not in a bad way. It makes me want to get drunk off him. "She should know what she's getting herself into."

Until he said that, I hadn't realized I *was* feeling guilty. He's right, though, and I feel seen in a way that I'm not altogether sure I like. I turn back around, because I can't bear to look into his eyes right now. "Uh, here she goes," I say, waving at the TV. "Are you ready to see the seasoning power of the Fabgadget? I mean, could anyone ever be ready?"

He doesn't answer. He just puts his arm around me and holds me. I don't say anything either as a few tears escape my eyes. I mean, if you're going to cry while watching an infomercial for the Fabgadget, it's best if no one knows about it.

After a few minutes, I blurt, "You really think she's going to come around, Drew?"

"Yeah, Andy," he says, his voice soft in my ear. His hand is making maddening circles on my hip. I'm not even sure he realizes he's doing it, but it feels fantastic, and if I draw attention to it, he might stop. "I do. She's not perfect, but she loves you."

I laugh a little, even though it's not funny. "I thought I was the imperfect one."

"You're perfect to me," he says, and more tears well in my eyes, because I *believe* him. No man has ever made me feel that way before. I've always been too abrasive, too bossy, too unhinged, too independent. I want to tell Drew that he's perfect to me too. That he's the best man I know, and maybe the only man I fully trust. But if I break that wall down, then no amount of drywall will fix it. And if the bricks crumble, he might realize all of those things everyone else has. Or maybe *I'll* realize that *he* isn't as good as he seems, like desserts in the window of a bakery that look like a dream but taste like canned air.

Worst of all, I would have to keep seeing him, unless Marnie and I fall apart, something I can't bear to consider, and each time I'd be hit with the knowledge that everything would have been fine if I'd just left him alone.

Neither of us says anything for a long time and then, as the Fabgadget lady gives us her best "O" face, I can hear his breathing even out behind me.

I haven't said anything, because I didn't want him to get embarrassed. I haven't said anything, because I didn't want him to move, but his hard cock has been digging into me where he's spooning my butt.

I let myself lie there for a few minutes longer. Then I go upstairs and crank out my trusty vibrator.

ANDY

WHEN I WAKE UP, Drew is gone. Not just off the couch gone, but out of the house gone. It's impressive, because seven hours ago, he looked like he was in for the kind of hangover that only couch time and questionable raw egg concoctions could soothe. It's also disappointing. I tell myself it's just because I was hoping to subtly talk to him about Leonard, but I know bullshit when I hear it, even when it's from my own psyche.

There's a note on the coffee table, written in a sleepy scrawl that makes me grin.

Did you know the Fabgadget can also be used to grind coffee? Sorry for being a drunken idiot last night. I hope I didn't say anything stupid. Pray for me while I'm out all day with a pounding headache.

I sigh, because I really will be thinking about him all day, wondering where he is and what he's doing. The date obviously went poorly, so he won't be out with the same woman. Maybe he's with Burke and his other buddies.

I eat breakfast, drink some more orange juice from the carton, thinking of Drew's lips pressed to the same places, and then go up to my bedroom to get dressed.

When I check my phone, I nearly drop it on the bed. There's a text from my old boss, the owner of the daycare.

> Did you send this to my wife, you cunt? You've ruined my life.

It's accompanied by a screenshot of what looks to be a private credit card statement, from which the chump wasn't smart enough to block out his numbers. There are several charges highlighted in yellow, and on the top is scrawled:

Some men don't think it's cheating when they're just watching girls strip for the camera. What do YOU think? Either way, it's a hell of a way for him to spend YOUR nest egg. ;-).

The charges are all from OnlyFans. Some sites use fake names to keep their users' habits anonymous, but not them.

Damn, Nicole's been busy.

I probably shouldn't answer—higher road, and all of that, plus I could probably sue his ass for harassment. At the same time, I'm not the type to take my problems to a lawyer, and I don't want this asshole to think I'm afraid of him, not even for a minute.

I respond:

> No, but I really wish I had. Eat shit, and have a blessed day. Send your wife my way. I'll help her find a real man.

His response comes rapid-fire:

I don't believe you. You're behind this.

I don't care. You're a tool.

I text Nicole next:

You took down my old boss? What else do you have in the pipeline, you crazy genius? Is Thing Two up on next on your list?

I snort, realizing I've referred to my brother in Seussian terms because of Drew, but I decide not to correct it. Something tells me she'll know exactly who I'm talking about.

She doesn't respond right away, probably because she's sleeping or banging Damien. I feel a twinge of something, loneliness, maybe, because most of the people I know are with someone, and I'm here by myself, *waiting*. It makes me itchy to do something to prove to myself that I'm alive. Usually, when I feel this way, I might drop by the gym in latex and try to pick up a guy for some fun, or grab my phone and swipe right, but I don't feel an itch to do that right now. Part of me wants to drive by my grandmother's house, maybe get a glimpse of her, but I don't trust myself. I'll want to go in, and if she turns me away at the door, it'll tear my heart into bloody pieces. Maybe I'm a coward, but I send her another message instead. Easier for her to ignore me that way; easier for me to pretend that maybe she didn't see it. Then I vacuum the house and respond to several texts in my best friends' thread with Marnie, Grace, and Sinclair.

Marnie, Sinclair, and I are having a girls' outing tonight, which is good, but tonight feels pretty damn far away. So I pull out a smutty romance.

The story pulls me in, but an intrusive thought keeps surfacing: maybe I should leave this out. Maybe Drew will pick it up, and...

Finally, Nicole responds.

> Damien and I are taking you to breakfast. You ready?

> It's two o'clock.

> What, did you want me to be cute and call it brunch? Dream on.

Fair.

> OK, I'll be ready.

They pick me up half an hour later, and Nicole grins at me as I get in the car. "Baby's first stakeout. You should have seen the look on her face, Damien. It was classic."

"I *did* see the look on her face," he says wryly. "You took a picture."

"Still, it was one of those *you had to be there* situations."

"Not to interrupt your little moment, but where are we going?" I ask.

"Bear's Buns." Nicole makes a face. "I know. That name. But the owners always give me a table in the back because they know I like to cause trouble."

Also fair.

Before long, we're parked in the back corner of Bear's Buns with coffee for me and coffee and breakfast sandwiches for them.

"So," I say. "What do you have planned for Jack?"

Nicole makes a face and takes a bite of her sandwich.

"What she means to say," Damien tells me with dancing eyes, always amused by his wife, "is that your middle brother is a little boring. Still, I'm guessing he's pissed some people off. Like maybe you?" He studies me as he asks the question.

"Including me." I rub my chest, feeling a tightness in my heart. Because there was a time when Jack used to be precious to me.

Theo was always cold—he was born with one foot out the door, my grandmother once told me. I don't know about that, but he was always ashamed of our little purple house, of living with two women and no father. He'd started searching for ways to prove himself. Coming home with bruises he wouldn't let anyone fuss over. Stealing the cash my mother hid in her cookie jar, which she *kept* hiding in her cookie jar even after he started taking it. She wanted to support him, and he wouldn't just take it from her hand, only steal it. Then he got himself a rich friend, who got him a rich-friend opportunity—an internship at a local financial management company. That, in turn, led to a scholarship. I read the essay he wrote for the application, because we only had one computer growing up, shared by all of us. It went something like this: poor boy who grew up on the wrong side of the tracks supports his entire family after his father leaves. It made me laugh so much I snorted my drink.

After he graduated college, he came back and got a job at said financial management company. He told my mother, who was dying from breast cancer at the time, that he'd succeeded with no help from her. He'd insisted we were losers, bad bets, *anchors*, and he was done with us. He'd mostly meant it, but occasionally he'd invite Mom to some PR event to make himself look good, or introduce her to a girlfriend so he could brag about his upward mobility. She'd always gone, right up until the end. *Abuela* was not so accommodating.

Jack, though? Jack loved me once. But he made some dumb decisions that got him kicked out of school, and even though he earned his GED, he wasn't exactly an appealing prospect for colleges. When Theo offered him a job, he'd have been a fool not to take it. None of us are fools, so he works with our brother now. He's his yes man. His apologist.

Theo can go screw himself. Preferably with an implement that makes it uncomfortable. It's Jack's betrayal that stings. I might understand why he decided to take the cozy offer he was given, but I resent him for throwing me and *Abuela* out to do it.

"I stole some of his mail," Nicole says flippantly, as if it's not a federal offense. "And he gets a natural history magazine. Seriously. The horrific part is that he must have purposefully subscribed to it. He's going to be a hard nut to crack."

"I'll talk to him," Damien offers. "See what I can get."

"No offense, Damien. Jack's way more easygoing than Theo, but he's still a Ruiz. He's not just going to give you a laundry list of his sins. He'd fuck you up just for asking." That's all of us—always spoiling for a fight. Struggling to come out ahead.

Nicole snorts. "As if that's possible."

Damien gives me a smile that should be devastating. "I'm going to be a bit more circumspect than that." He gives Nicole a teasing nudge with his shoulder. "I'm used to getting difficult people to *want* to offer up personal information."

"You know I didn't make it easy on you," she says with a sidelong look.

That should-be-devastating grin turns on her, and it's clear she *does* find it devastating. I'm not sure Nicole ever looks soft, but there's a warmth in her eyes that's close to it. "I never said I wanted it easy," he says.

"Whoa," I say, lifting my hands. "How long have you two been married, anyway? Because you've got definite honeymoon vibes going on, and I've known you for at least six months."

"Five years," Damien says, giving her another nudge and wrapping his arm around her.

"Damn, are you serious?"

"Serious as the grave." Nicole gives me a pointed look. "If you find the person who gets your crazy, you lock that shit down. There aren't that many men in the world who will let you be who you are without trying to change you or own you."

My mind darts to Drew. *"You're perfect to me."*

He was drunk, though, and even if he meant it...

I'm no good at keeping people, at least when it comes to romance, and I can't risk losing him and Marnie forever. *I can't.*

I clear my throat. "Well, if you're all hot and bothered about me and Drew, then I'm guessing you're going to help with the Leonard thing?"

They exchange a look, and suddenly my throat feels thick for a different reason.

"Nah," Nicole says. "Like I said, we're your fairy godmothers, not Drew's, and you're only looking into this to avoid your own shit. It would be immoral of us to encourage that."

My eyebrows wing up. "Immoral?" I hiss. "You just said you stole my brother's mail."

"Yes, and saving someone from that history magazine should be classified a public service."

"We didn't say you couldn't keep looking into it," Damien says pointedly, rubbing his eyebrow. There's a small scar slicing through it, and I wonder how he came by it. I'm guessing it wasn't a cooking accident. "Or that we won't give you pointers."

"So what's your first pointer?" I ask.

Nicole makes a sound of aggravation. "You're like a dog with a bone, and not the good kind of bone."

"Thank you," I say, while Damien snorts out something that sounds like, "Takes one to know one."

"Why'd he get fired?" Nicole pauses to eat a piece of egg that had fallen out of her sandwich and onto the wrapper. "What'd his neighbors think of him? Did he have any other debt?"

"I can see if my buddy on the force will show me the police report," Damien offers, which lifts my spirits a little. That'll help, knowing who they talked to, what they did.

"We agreed we wouldn't be helping her," Nicole says, leaning into him. He still has his arm lazily looped around her, in the way of someone who knows he doesn't have to stake his territory—it's known—but he tightens it, and there's a smirk on her face as she finishes her sandwich.

"Don't think this means you won't be doing other work," Nicole tells me. "Your brother's not the only cheating asshole out there."

"Did you deliver the photos to her?" I ask, my heart beating a hard rhythm in my chest.

She gives a slight nod, her eyes fixed on me. "But they don't all leave, Andy."

"I know."

"For all we know, she won't even confront him about it. But the woman he's messing around with *does* happen to be his boss's daughter—his married daughter, I might add—so we have that in our back pocket. They rented out that house just so they have somewhere to get their freak on." She gives me a long, scrutinizing look that sees right through me. "What do you say, Andy? How badly do you want to ruin your brother?"

I can't swallow anymore. My throat has stopped working. My heart feels like it's ceased to function. Theo is a cruel man. Probably a bad man. I don't have many good memories of him, but he's in so *many* of my memories. And part of me understands him—the urge to escape, the urge to prove himself, the urge to become untouchable. Not literally. Clearly, he's gotten *plenty* of touching. But untouchable to anyone who'd want to destroy him.

Like we could do. With the click of a mouse.

"Not yet," I say through a tight throat. "Let's see how the thing with his fiancée plays out."

She gives me a *your funeral* look, and I tell them about the texts from the director of the daycare.

"Have you told Drew?" Damien asks, his attention sharpening.

"Why?"

"You'll want to be on the lookout in case this guy comes around."

"I'm not scared of him," I scoff, because I'm not. He might talk big over the phone, but he wouldn't give me any trouble in person.

Nothing beyond trying to talk down to me—and failing, because no way would I let someone talk smack to me without talking back.

Maybe that sounds naïve, but I'm used to judging whether or not a man will give me a hard time. That little purple house is in the kind of neighborhood where you learn those things. Or at least it used to be.

"Even so," Damien says with a nod. "He should know about this...and about Theo too. There's a chance your brother will tie the photos back to you."

"He won't," I say bitterly. "He doesn't think enough of me."

"Not even if his friend calls him up about those messages?"

"Why would he?"

Nicole gives me an incredulous look. "It didn't seem strange to you that your sexy, hotshot brother with the good job is suddenly pals with the tubby director of a second-rate daycare?"

Oh. *Oh.*

"You think he was keeping an eye on me?" Except that's not quite right. If he were concerned about me, he wouldn't have jumped on the first opportunity to fuck me over. "So, he was trying to, what, find damning information to use against me? But why go to the effort?"

"You're right," Nicole says, looking at me. "You know, your grandmother's house might need a lot of work, but it's a 1920s house, and the land it's sitting on is worth a good bit of money. Besides, we already know your brother likes to get it on with a little strange. They're renting that house, but if he had your grandmother's place, he wouldn't need to go to the trouble. He might want somewhere to carry on his extracurricular activities. I'm guessing that's his game." She shrugs. "Or he could just be the kind of man who ruins people for the fun of it. For the thrill of knowing he can."

She lifts one brow higher than the other, cocking her head, her pink hair shining brightly under the overhead lights. "Change your mind about releasing that information to his boss yet?"

"I'll think about it," I say numbly. Because my world feels a little more off its axis. I wasn't under the misapprehension that Theo gave a shit about me, but I never would have thought him capable of something this calculated. Maybe the signs have been there all along, and I just didn't want to believe it.

I rub my chest with my thumb in slow circles. "It was pretty easy for you to figure all of this shit out."

Nicole gives a self-satisfied nod.

"I'll bet you could figure out what happened with Leonard in a single afternoon."

This gets me a laugh, although I couldn't say whether it's an amused one. "See, Damien? Dog, bone. How about this, Andy? We'll help you...*if* you can get Drew on board. He'll need to be a part of it."

"You don't need to blackmail me into spending time with him," I say, rolling my eyes. "We live in the same house."

"But I'm guessing I do need to blackmail you into being honest with him," she replies pointedly.

Well, shit, she might be right.

seventeen

DREW

"SO IT WENT THAT WELL, HUH?" Burke says when he comes down from his apartment. I got out of the car to wait for him, because there's a slight breeze today—surprising for this time of year—and it feels fantastic.

"What do you mean?" Obviously, I know what he means. I'm a mess, barely human. Still, I'm better off than I was this morning, before I poured myself a huge travel mug of coffee and drove to Craggy Gardens for a quick hike. Something in me needed to see the sun reach its full height over the mountains. Maybe I was hoping it would shed light on what it is I'm doing—and what I should be doing instead.

Sleeping was the only answer that the came to mind, which wasn't particularly helpful since I'd already filled myself up with so much caffeine that I probably won't be able to sleep for the next two days. So I decided to pick up Burke so we could drive over to Mrs. Ruiz's house to get a more accurate measurement for the windows.

At least I can do something good over there.

"Your date," Burke says, snapping my tired brain back into half attention. "You look like shit, man."

"Thank you." Despite being dressed in a white T-shirt and work pants, holding a toolbox, he still looks like he just stepped out of a damn Brooks Brothers catalog. Then again, he always looks like that, and I can hardly resent him for being put together when I'm wearing an old *Star Wars* T-shirt and ripped jeans, feeling like the Crypt Keeper from that old show.

The only thing I resent him for is Andy noticing him.

Maybe noticing him.

I still don't know why she was over here yesterday, and the not knowing is eating at me, particularly after last night. Lying next to her, having the curves of her ass pressed up against me, her soft hair captured against my chest, was the sweetest torture I've ever experienced. I want it to happen again every night—and never again, because now it's the only thing I can think about.

I don't know what possessed her to lie down next to me. I don't know if it meant anything. All I know is that she left.

Besides, the situation hasn't changed. She's still in a vulnerable spot, and I can't let her think she's only important to me because I'm attracted to her. I can't drive her away from the last place she has to call home just because I want her in a way that I've never wanted a woman.

"Sorry," Burke says, wincing. We get into the car, and he stows his toolbox in the back seat. Neither of us says anything as I start driving, and there's a strange tension in the car. It's not usually like that with us, and I don't care for it.

"You're wondering why she was at my place yesterday," he finally says.

"You didn't phrase that as a question."

"No"—he gives me a sidelong glance—"because I can tell you are. She obviously didn't want me to tell you, but I've been thinking about this all night."

A laugh escapes me. "You look like you spent the night sipping champagne on Junior's yacht."

"We live seven hours from the ocean, dipshit," he says good-naturedly.

"All I'm saying is that sleepless nights affect you differently than they do me."

"I think that might be the whiskey you stink of."

"Shit, is Mrs. Ruiz going to notice?"

"Probably." A small smile lifts his lips. "You got any coffee left in that thermos? Spill some on your shirt. Pretend you had an accident in the car. You'll look like a slob—more of a slob—but it should help with the smell."

Sighing, I pull over on the side of the road. Then I reach for the thermos and step out of the car. Is there anything sadder than purposefully pouring coffee on yourself? Maybe. But it sure feels pathetic as hell.

I get back in and sponge at the mess on my shirt with a couple of paper towels.

"I liked this shirt," I complain.

Burke smirks at me. "I didn't make the suggestion just because of the smell." He pauses, then adds. "Look, you're my friend, and there's something you deserve to know."

There's an instant tightness in my chest. He told me nothing had happened between him and Andy, and I believed him. Still do. He wouldn't lie about something like that. But maybe she made a pass at him. Maybe he *wanted* something to happen, but he held back because he's a good friend and we have a code. If that's the case, then the adult thing to do would be to give him my blessing, but—

"She wants to find out what happened with Leonard."

"What?" I ask, completely thrown. I mean, I knew Andy was interested in what had happened with Leonard, but I'd honestly stopped thinking about it over the last day or so. My mind is so full of *her*, there's not much space for anything else.

But why the hell would she come to Burke to talk about Leonard? Why not just talk to me?

Then it hits me. Andy's not paying me rent. When she offered, I'd told her to save her money, and she'd demurred. She never demurs.

This is her way of paying me back, of making sure she doesn't owe a debt. It sticks in my throat, because I'd *liked* that she was letting me do something for her.

"I guess…" My attention reverts to Burke, whose presence I'd almost forgotten. He pauses. Clears his throat. "I guess she figured I knew something about him because of the way I reacted when we all saw that photo the other night. She wanted to ask me about it. She thinks you need some closure, man. I figure she's got that right."

"I have closure," I say bitterly. "He's dead. That's the most extreme form of closure a person can get."

"But we don't really know what happened," he argues, studying me. "She's got some private investigator friends—"

"Yeah, I know all about them. Andy's just trying to pay me back for letting her stay at the house. She doesn't like owing people. I thought…"

Never mind. I don't want to tell him what I let myself think.

"I paid Leonard a lot of money," Burke says, avoiding my gaze. "My parents had just canned him, so I felt like I owed him something, and he came to me with this opportunity. He wanted to buy a flip house with me, for cash, but after he disappeared, they never found the money, and the guy who owned the house said he'd never met Leonard."

"What?" I ask. I probably sound like a broken record, but seriously, what the hell? "Why the fuck didn't you say anything before now?"

He swears, runs a hand through his hair. "I told the police, man. I didn't want to tell you guys because I figured it would sound like I was accusing him of something. The cops still think he drowned. There's every chance the guy who owned the house took the money and figured he could get away with it."

"I get it," I say slowly. He's right, I might have interpreted it differently back then, steeped in guilt as I was. "Do you have any idea why your parents fired him?"

He shrugs. "A bit. But you know we're not exactly close."

I do. They're the kind of parents who took a very personal interest in his grades and extracurricular activities, but not out of any sort of fondness. He was their investment, and they intended to collect one day.

"They said he kept coming in late," he continues. "Obviously, part of that was true, but it sounded like a bullshit reason for firing someone who was so good at buying up properties."

Time had been a fluid concept for Leonard. He was so constantly late that we'd started telling him to show up half an hour before the rest of us would be there.

Burke rubs his forehead, as if discussing this causes him physical pain. It doesn't feel all that great for me either. "Besides, all of this went down around the time the Newton building collapsed. It was a PR shitstorm, and it didn't feel like a good time to start interrogating them."

"I remember." Everyone in Asheville probably did. It's not every day a building up and collapses, but it had been built too close to a sinkhole, and the contractors had cut corners with the framing. A few people had died, several more had been injured, and Burke's parents had been involved by virtue of having paid for it. "I'll tell her to stand down, man."

"Are you sure you want to do that?" he asks.

Yes. No. I don't know. I'm in over my head, which is hardly a unique sensation lately. Andy makes me lose my mind—along with any sense of what's left, right, or all around me.

"She doesn't have to do anything to pay me back for letting her live at the house," I finally say. "I'm happy to have her there." I don't add that I *want* her there, that her colorful things have actually started to grow on me, because they're an extension of her.

"Who says she's trying to pay you back?" he asks, cocking his head. "Seems to me she genuinely wants to help."

"I know her. I'm sure it at least figures into her thinking."

"And how about you?" he asks. "Why are you so bent on helping her grandmother?"

"She's an old woman, living alone. Isn't that reason enough?"

"Sure, but we both know you're doing it for Andy. And why were you so hardline about asking us to stay away from her? You know we're all good guys. Yes, even me." He's staring at me intently, his eyes boring into me. Burke's easygoing until he's not.

"You know why."

He lifts his eyebrows, eyes still fixed on mine. "Yeah, and maybe she should know too."

"We'll see about that."

He lets it rest, and I drive the rest of the way to the house in silence. When we get there, Mrs. Ruiz takes one look at me and insists I change into one of Theo's T-shirts despite my suggestion that I get started on the painting today. I try to object, but she argues that if I'm sloppy enough to wear soiled clothing, even for painting, only a fool would let me paint her house. I'm not sure about the logic, but my head hurts. So I change.

Burke says it's going to take him a while to get the windows measured, and I don't want to sit around talking to Mrs. Ruiz, who has a distinctly disapproving look on her face that suggests she smells the whiskey, so I call in Rafe, who has painting experience of a different kind, being that he's an artist. After he gets done laughing at me for being such a dumbass with Shauna, he gives me a reason to be glad I called him. I was just going to go at it with the paint, but he says we need to clean up what's on there before we slap something new on top of it. He also agrees to come with some drop clothes.

Everything else we'll need looks to be here already.

Because Andy made damn sure of it.

It feels wrong that she's not working alongside us, but I know better than to push Mrs. Ruiz yet. She's letting us stay and help, and I get the sense that's a big deal for her. The fact that we showed will help her trust us—even more so when we come back. Then I can push her about Andy.

Preferably when I smell less and am wearing acceptable clothing.

Rafe brings Reggie along, which turns out to be a good thing, because Mrs. Ruiz has all the marks of a micromanager. She agrees that Rafe can help as long as he stays out of the house, and we get the prep work started. It's a big job, bigger than the two of us and Burke, once he finishes the measurements, so we text the other guys. Danny and Shane are out of commission, but Griffin finds a substitute bartender so he can come. Meanwhile, Reggie's inside talking Mrs. Ruiz's ear off about God only knows what. I'd be more worried about that, except I don't want her to fuss about the mess we're making.

"Am I going to have to lie to my fiancée about this?" Griffin asks after a while, giving me a searching look.

I can't in good conscience tell him yes, especially since my sister deserves better than some asshole who's going to happily lie to her, so I shake my head. "I'll talk to her. Tonight. Or you can."

He cocks his head as he keeps working, scraping at the places where the paint has started to bubble and peel. "They're all getting together at a bar tonight. Marnie, Andy, and Sinclair. Didn't you know?"

"Andy didn't say," I tell him, feeling like he's scraping something inside of my head. Of course she didn't tell me; we're not together. She doesn't owe me any explanations.

I'm in a bad mood for the rest of the afternoon, but I try to keep it to myself.

Finally, Rafe declares the house adequately prepped, which

would be fantastic if I didn't have to spend my Monday working on zombie clowns.

"I'll get it started," he says, pounding me on the back.

"I can help," Griffin offers. "I don't open the bar until early afternoon. It'll do me good to get some fresh air in the morning."

Painting in the hot, baking sun?

They're doing it for me, and I'm doing it for Andy, and if I said any of that out loud, I'm pretty sure Rafe would call it the powerful gut-punch of kumbaya.

"I've got nothing for you," Burke says with a grin. "You know I have to go to work, but I'm at your mercy next weekend, and I'll put in the order for the windows tonight. I get a pretty good discount, so don't worry about reimbursing me. We want to make sure to keep the weather out for Mrs. Ruiz."

What he means is that he has a multi-million-dollar trust fund, and this is the kind of thing he likes to use it for. I already know he won't accept no for an answer.

I feel like a real shithead for subjecting my friends to the mood I've been in all day, hangover notwithstanding. "You don't need to do that."

"Which one of us?" Burke jokes.

"Any of you."

"Yeah, buddy," Rafe says. "We know. But we're doing it all the same. Besides, it's been a while since anyone's hated me as much as Mrs. Ruiz. Your sister would tell you I take it as a personal challenge. She'd be right."

"Let me buy a round of drinks." Truthfully, the last thing I want to do is drink tonight, but today's been hot as hell, sweaty, and buying them something cold to wash it down is the least I can do. Besides, they said my sisters and Andy are having a drinks thing, and I don't want to be in the house alone.

It's a stupid thought. I used to *like* being alone in the house. Hell, when it was my dad, Marnie, and me all living there, we used to crave it. Being alone at home was like having someone *give* you the Holy Grail, no searching required. But I know the house would feel empty in a bad way tonight, like something essential had been carved from its core. It felt like that after my dad died.

The thought scares me a little. Andy's only been at the house for a week, and already I feel like she's a necessary part of it. That it will feel less like home without her. It makes me wonder how long these feelings have been festering inside of me, and whether it's been longer than the last couple of months. If Andrea Ruiz has had her place inside of me for years.

"I think the polite thing to do would be to say no," Rafe says, giving me another of those great claps on the back, "but throw in a pizza, and I'm game."

"Two pizzas," Burke says.

"Done."

I go in to get my dirty shirt, and Reggie and Mrs. Ruiz are having an animated conversation on the couch. At least he's not trying to show her why he's called Reggie the Dinosaur.

"I'm going to go get changed into my other shirt," I announce, to which Mrs. Ruiz immediately shakes her head. "I tried to wash it, but the stain kept. I had to throw it out."

"You threw out my shirt?" I ask, trying not to sound upset. I've had that shirt for over ten years. My father got it for me, and he's gone now, beyond the point of being able to give anyone anything.

"There were holes in it. Other stains." She makes a face that suggests it would be unthinkable for me to want such a thing. Even so...

"That's okay," I tell her. "I still want it."

"I threw it in the trash," she says, giving me a pointed look.

"Which trashcan?"

"You would rescue something that's been ruined?"

"I like it," I say flatly. "I want it."

I half expect her to throw me out and say I'm not welcome back, but she gives me a look that almost reads as respect.

"Okay. I'll get it for you."

She leaves to retrieve it, and Reggie gives me a nod. "We heading out?"

"I'm going to bring everyone out for a round of drinks," I say, because hell, he's been doing us a service too. "Any idea where we can go that's not Griff's place?"

As laidback as Griffin is, I suspect he won't want to hang out at his own bar on the one night he's not working.

"We're going to another bar?" he asks, crestfallen, as he gets to his feet.

I guess I'll have to ask someone else.

Mrs. Ruiz returns with the shirt, crisply folded. It looks completely clean, so if it was in a trashcan, it was sitting on top of laundry fluff. I don't see any evidence of a stain.

"You said it was stained." I didn't mean for the words to come out accusatory.

"Right there," she says pointing to a fleck of discoloration.

I grab the shirt, worried she'll change her mind and run for the kitchen shears, and tell her that Rafe and Griffin will be coming tomorrow to start the painting.

"You won't be there?"

"He has to work," Reggie says, wrapping an arm around my shoulders. "He's not much of a bragger, this one, but he's the lead designer for *Heads Will Roll*. Zombie clowns."

I'd love to tell him to stop helping me. Mrs. Ruiz looks predictably unimpressed. "This is what you do with your free time, *mijo*?"

"No," I say, disentangling myself from Reggie. "This is what I do with my work time. In my free time, I'm designing a different game. It's an outdoors simulator. A survival game."

"So you do this instead of going outside," she asks, as if I'm an idiot.

"I do it because I love going outside."

She gives a nod, though it's still obvious she thinks my life's work is meaningless. I don't hold a grudge. I'm certainly no heart surgeon, and the only thing *Heads Will Roll* is likely to do for people is wake them up with anxiety dreams. I guess my game is meant to do the opposite and *soothe* anxiety. When I can't sleep at night, it's usually because my head won't stop returning to the mistakes I've made. Like when I told Leonard to go by himself on that hike. Or the time I urged Sinclair to stop coming home from Hollywood because she always made Marnie cry. It wasn't until later that I realized my mother was probably behind that, like she was behind so many of Sinclair's decisions back then. It's in those moments that I want to find the kind of peace that's natural to me outdoors.

I earn a slight nod from Mrs. Ruiz. "Will these boys expect me to feed them tomorrow?"

"No, that's okay," I say. "I'll order a pizza for them at lunchtime."

She glares at me. "I'm more than capable of feeding them."

"You remind me of Andy," I blurt.

She nods again, but a look of pain crosses her eyes, and I know in that moment that I'm going to get there. I'm going to convince her that the only thing Andy needs is her.

eighteen

DREW

"WHY ARE you wearing my brother's shirt?"

Goddammit. I should have known better than to let Rafe choose the bar, especially after leaving him outside to conspire with Griffin and Burke. The décor is a bit...well, "extra" is the word Burke would use for it, and I don't miss the way he smirks at the glitter on the walls or the decorations, which look like they were made by someone with an addiction to watching five-minute craft videos on the internet; bowls made of Starburst wrappers, picture frames made of popsicle sticks, that kind of thing. But he didn't get a chance to snicker, and I didn't get a chance to comment on it. Because we got no more than a few feet inside before I saw them—Marnie, Andy, and Sinclair sitting at four-top table.

Answering recognition sparked on their faces, and they got to their feet. Sinclair was the first to speak, beaming at Rafe. "You know how I feel about stalkers..."

Leave it to them to make an inside joke out of my sister's stalker.

Then Andy's eyes caught on me and held.

Dammit, I knew I should have changed in the car. The stain on my *Star Wars* shirt had to be two millimeters in diameter, tops, but

Mrs. Ruiz has the ability to scare the spit out of a man, and I had a feeling she'd know if I put it back on.

That's when she said it. "Why are you wearing my brother's shirt?"

Rafe gives me a "good luck, buddy" look, which is disturbingly similar to his "you're fucked, buddy" look, and starts scooting chairs up to the table, which probably isn't going to work out that well since we're all tall men with the exception of Reggie, who's a *broad* man.

"Long story. You want to talk?" I ask Andy, my tone a little confrontational. I guess I'm still a little upset that she didn't try talking to me about Leonard again before going to my friend. Call me crazy, but we live together. It seems like the kind of thing she could have mentioned over cereal or sandwiched in between jokes about watching me stroke my dick.

"Yes," she says, then glances around as if realizing that there are several of our best friends gathered around us. My sisters are watching us with interest.

"Let's go order some drinks," I say. "I promised these assholes a round."

"What about us?" Marnie says, and I feel a lurch of having missed her. We've texted back and forth, and I met her for lunch the other day, but it's not the same as seeing someone constantly. I've missed her. "Can we be assholes if it'll get us free drinks?"

"You were included under the asshole umbrella." I walk over and give her a hug, then I hug Sinclair too. That leaves only Andy unhugged, though, and there's a feeling of *should I or shouldn't I?* that seems to have invaded even the simplest interactions with her. But she looks delectable in a red sundress with bright blue flowers all over it, her hair loose around her shoulders, and I have a need to feel her against me that's almost powerful enough to be called a hunger. I'm pulling her to me before I can question it further—or wonder why I'm questioning it at all. I've hugged her before, plenty of times. When did it start to mean something?

I still don't have answers for that. I only know that it feels right to have her in my arms.

She's the one who pulls away, and for a second she just looks at me, almost as if she's never seen me before. Then she says, "Yes, let's go order these assholes some emasculating drinks."

"I think everything on the menu is probably emasculating," I say as we walk toward the bar.

"So why are you wearing my brother's shirt?" she repeats, giving me a sidelong look that thrums through me. God, she's so beautiful. It's like a constant ache. A scab that won't heal.

"It's not actually that long of a story. Your grandmother made me." She pulls me to a stop at the bar, though we're at the very edge, probably too far to catch the bartender's notice anytime soon, because it appears this monstrosity of a place is actually quite popular. There are people all around us in outfits that can best be described as "looks." Eighties looks. Nineties looks. And God, when did the nineties become the kind of blast from the past that it could be described as a look?'

"This place makes me feel old," I blurt.

"You *are* old."

"I'm only four years older than you."

She lifts her eyebrows, then pointedly looks at Theo's shirt.

"Like I said, your grandmother made me. I stopped by to check on her and take care of a few things around the house, and she took a dislike to my *Star Wars* shirt. She almost threw it out. It was only out of sheer tenacity that I got it back."

"You already went back there?" she asks in obvious shock.

"Well, yeah," I say, rubbing my shoulder. I don't like the way she's looking at me, like she feels she has something to be grateful for again. If gratitude and a sense of debt over my invitation to stay at the house was what sent her on this Leonard bender, what will more gratitude do? Will she insist on designing the zombie clowns for me?

Will she make more of those videos to raise money for rent?

A hot shiver rolls through me, heightening my awareness of her, of the glints of gold in her eyes, the curve of her hip where I had my hand last night, the way her hair is long enough that it brushes the rise of her ass.

"You did chores for her?"

"Just a couple of small things," I say, downplaying it. "You're right. The place is a bit rundown."

She swears under her breath. "So my brothers haven't done shit?"

"Like I said, her nurse has been coming around. I saw her earlier, so I know your grandmother wasn't just telling me what I wanted to hear. But I got the sense your grandmother doesn't want your brothers around." I take her arms, because I can see this isn't soothing her. "I'm working on her, Andy. It's helping."

I expect her to pull away, but she doesn't. Neither do I. Her arms are warm beneath my touch, her skin soft, and I start moving my hands slightly, just because I want to feel more of it.

"Thank you," she says adamantly, and something like disappointment trickles through me. I pull my hands away and stick them in my pockets, because that's the only way I can be sure I'll keep them to myself.

"You don't need to keep thanking me."

"I know. You do this stuff because you're a nice guy. I get it."

That's not exactly true. I'm not the kind of person who goes around offering other people my coffee, leaving little tchotchkes around in plastic bags that are just as likely to become trash as treasure, or telling strangers to have a nice day. Nor am I the kind of person who does massive favors for people I don't care about. But I don't correct her on it. If that's what she wants to think, let her think it. That'll be written in my obituary, maybe. Andrew Jones, nice guy.

If that doesn't sound like the friend zone, I don't know what does.

"I hear you've been asking around about Leonard."

She glances back at the table and gives a death scowl to Burke, who doesn't notice her. If he did, he'd probably just wave, knowing him.

"He's my best friend," I tell her. "Like you and Marnie. He wouldn't keep something like that from me."

It's not supposed to be an accusation, although I *am* hurt that she kept it from me. Then again, I suppose I haven't been the picture of forthrightness about the situation with her grandmother.

"It doesn't matter," she says flippantly, as if it's no big deal that she's decided to singlehandedly solve a disappearance that was solved eight years ago.

"It doesn't matter?" I repeat. "What part?"

"I was going to talk to you about it anyway. I'm guessing he told you about the money."

I give a slow nod, my mind churning.

"Well, I told Nicole and Damien too, and they changed their minds. They're willing to look into it, but only if we both do it with them."

I'm taken aback by this for several reasons. One, I'm no private investigator. Two, I'm not interested in poking around in a personal matter that's painful for me. Three, she sounds excited about it—and like she thinks I should be excited about it too.

"No," I say. "Now let's get these people some drinks."

"No?" she says, tossing her hair, a sure sign I'm in trouble.

"No, Andy. I told you. The police already know what happened." But even as I say it, I feel a prickle of misgiving, of *maybe*. Because what Burke told me earlier about the flip house threw me for a loop. I push the thought down. "I know you're doing this because you think you owe me, but you don't owe me shit. I *want* you to stay at the house."

She grabs my arm, her touch burning into me, as if she's claiming with it. It's a stupid thought, but that doesn't stop me from feeling heartened by it.

"It's not because I think I owe you, you idiot. You need closure, and we have a couple of people who are basically magicians helping us out. Why wouldn't we look into it with them?"

I could put her off. I probably *should* put her off. But all of my old thoughts and feelings about Leonard are already stirring to the surface like angry bees. I'm going to get stung anyway. Might as well see if there's anything to it. Plus, there's that seductive *we* she used, like the two of us are a unit, a team.

"I think this would be good for you, Drew. Even if we don't find out anything useful, you'll know you gave it every effort. Won't that give you peace of mind?"

I don't believe anything good will come of poking around. Maybe my memories of Leonard will just get tarnished. He can be an asshole and still dead. But it occurs to me that it's a chance to spend more time with Andy. I'll also be giving her a distraction that she must desperately need if she's digging this far down to get it. I'm pathetic—truly and deeply—because I'm not going to turn that down.

"Okay," I say.

"Okay?" she asks, joy flooding her with an exuberance that has every molecule in her jumping. God help me, I like pleasing her like this.

"Sure. But, for the record, I think it's a bad call, Ruiz, and we'll almost certainly regret it."

"You can do all the regretting." She takes a step toward the larger stretch of bar, presumably to see about those drinks, then hangs back, looking at me, her eyes shining with surviving joy but also curiosity. "What happened that day, Drew?"

"You mean when Leonard left?"

She nods.

"You probably think it was some big thing, but it wasn't. It was a lot of little things, stupid things, and it never occurred to me until later that it might be a big deal."

A corner of her mouth lifts. "That's what a lot of mistakes feel like."

"It's like I said. I was supposed to go with him." I swallow, feeling an old numbness steal over me. He'd invoked *finneas* a couple of days earlier, after he got fired, but no one ponied up until I offered to go camping with him. "I woke up in a shit mood, with a headache, and the weather was overcast. It wasn't a good day for camping. When he came over, he got on my case for not having packed yet. He talked a lot of shit, actually, saying I was the kind of person who skated through life and he was sick of picking up my slack. That kind of thing. Which was pretty rich considering he was the one who always caused trouble and had just lost his job. I told him we all knew he wasn't even into hiking, that he only went on trips with us because he was afraid of missing out. He was always complaining when we were outside, about the bugs, sleeping under tarps. Everything. So he said he was going to prove to me that he was ten times the outdoorsman of any of us, and he stomped off. I figured I'd give him time to cool down, but I guess he went off by himself."

"Shit," she says.

"Shit," I agree.

Then she shocks me by pulling me into another hug. "You didn't do anything wrong," she says into my ear. "And we're going to carve away at this dead-ass case until you realize that."

"You like wasting time, huh?" I ask, leaning my head in slightly. She's tucked into me, nestled against my chest, her head on my shoulder. It's a sentimental thought, but it feels like she belongs there, that maybe we've been leading up to this moment for years.

"If you ask Theo, he'll tell you I like nothing better."

She's the one who pulls away, and the loss of her hurts.

"He's not someone I'd consider much of an authority on you," I tell her.

"No?"

"No. What happened with his fiancée?"

"I don't know yet. But Nicole and Damien have something else on him. I think I could get him fired if I wanted."

"Do you want?"

She worries her lip. "He's my brother."

"You don't choose who you're related to."

"No, but you have the best family in the world. It's easy for you to say."

I give her an arch look. "You've met my mother. By the time I was five, she'd told me five hundred times that having me was the biggest mistake of her life. You know, I have it on good authority that getting pregnant with me was what stopped her from being the movie star instead of Sinclair. She never would have married my dad if he hadn't knocked her up."

Andy winces. "Okay, fine, you win."

"It's not a competition, and if it were, it wouldn't be the kind anyone would want to win. Now, what do you say? Should we get these assholes drinks?"

She holds my gaze for a long moment. "Thank you for helping my grandmother...and me."

"So you *are* doing this to pay me back," I tease.

"No," she says, her eyes sparkling, "but I *did* order you a little something as a thank you."

"Oh yeah? Is it a book with a bare-chested man on the cover?"

"Wouldn't you like that?" Neither of us says anything for a moment, our words hanging between us, then she adds, "I left out a book I think you'll enjoy."

Is she suggesting she *wants* me to fuck my hand?

There are other things I'd prefer to do with my dick, but then again, our situation hasn't changed, and my sisters are across the bar, probably wondering why we're having a ten-minute discussion when we're supposed to be buying everyone drinks.

Still, I'm not totally in control right now, with her looking at me like that, her eyes bright under the bar lighting, her head tipped up to me, her face a challenge. It makes the want swell into need. "So you liked what you saw?" I say, my voice coming out strange.

"What wasn't there to like?" she says. I can't be imagining the flirtatious edge to the words. They're a challenge of their own, but I'd be foolish to read too deeply into that, because everything this woman does is a challenge.

"It's been messing with my head," I admit. "You seeing me like that. I've been thinking things I have no business thinking."

"Me too," she says.

That's when I know...

The feelings I have for her have become too big to be restrained. It took that image of her hair swaying over her feet to make me realize what I'd already been experiencing—the pull to look at her a little longer than was socially acceptable, to sit near her when she came over for dinner, the need to make her laugh. To make sure she was safe, at all costs.

For Marnie, I used to tell myself. *You want that for Marnie.* And that's true, but I also want Andy for myself. I don't know the exact minute it started—all I know is that I'm already in the middle of it, and I don't think it's ever going to end.

And the way she's looking at me...her words. Maybe there's hope.

Then, it's like a switch has been flipped, because she shakes out her hair, one of the curls smacking me in the face, and offers me her elbow. "What's a little light pornography between friends? Let's get those drinks, huh?"

Disappointment forms a sucking pit in my gut. She's purposefully reeling us back from the abyss, setting a boundary, and I can't be the one who breaks it. But I'm angry—at her, at myself—and about as sexually frustrated as a man can be while still drawing breath.

"Yeah," I say, "let's." I thread my elbow through hers, admitting, "The arm-in-arm thing makes me feel like a tool."

My tone is light-hearted, but I'm not feeling it. I can barely even summon the energy to pretend otherwise.

"Because you *are* a tool."

We're back on familiar ground, but right now, safe, familiar, and expected don't sound so good anymore. I can't pull off the pretense of it. I don't want to anymore.

nineteen

ANDY

"SO, give us the scoop. What's going on with our brother?" Marnie says, giving me a sharp-eyed look over her drink. It's Thursday night, and we're at Summer Nights, Griffin's bar, with Sinclair. Grace is still in New York—damn Enoch and his adorable nephew—but it's our monthly book club meeting, so we called her up on Face-Time, propping the phone up against the side of the table in the booth. She's in her hotel room and can barely hear anything we're saying, but it's reassuring to see her face and hear her voice.

None of us read the book this time—I'm not even sure what it was, to be honest—but that's never been what book club is about.

"I'm easing Drew into liking color," I say. "One gaudy tchotchke at a time."

"It's not that he doesn't like color," Marnie says with a grin. "He had this whole thing about the living room being a neutral zone, but hell, I think it's good for him. It's like exposure therapy."

"He *exposed* himself?" Grace asks with wide eyes, leaning closer as if it'll help her hear better. "To whom? Andy?"

Well, I guess he kind of did expose himself, but I'm not about to tell them. I made a promise to Drew, and the least I can do is keep it.

"*Exposure therapy,*" Marnie says slowly, leaning toward the phone as if Grace is an elderly relative who can be made to understand if she speaks slowly and clearly enough.

I leave them to it, my mind churning. Drew and I have our first outing with Nicole and Damien tomorrow night. I'm not sure what to expect, but I'm looking forward to it, partly because I'll get to spend time with Drew. I haven't seen much of him this week. He works during the day, and I've been taking later shifts, tailing a shifty character with Nicole. Still, that doesn't totally explain my near-complete lack of Drew sightings. He usually stays up at least a couple of nights a week to work on his game. Last week, I came down to the kitchen for a glass of water, and he was sitting at his desk in the dark with his headphones on. It gave me a jump scare, which in turn gave him a jump scare, and we probably collectively scared the hell out of a bug or mouse. So I get the sense that he's been avoiding me. I know I won't see him tonight either—he's at Burke and Danny's place for their D&D game, which got pushed to Thursday for some reason.

I didn't score an invite to this one.

The only time we've really spent together was on Tuesday night, when he walked in on me looking up prognoses for hospice patients with the same condition as my grandmother.

It's not the first time I'd done it, so I knew the news wouldn't be good. The hour glass is running down. Will I get to say goodbye? She's a surly woman, as tough as week-old steak, and despite everything, I love her more than I love color.

I had tears in my eyes when Drew got home, and I wiped them away so viciously it hurt. He saw, though. He always seems to see.

"I got you some ice cream," he said, bypassing the freezer and grabbing a spoon from the drawer. He brought over the pint and handed it to me. "I noticed you were out."

Something in my heart burst, because it felt like too much—being noticed by him that way, him anticipating needs I didn't even know I had.

But all I got out was an inadequate "Thank you," my tone a little clipped, because I didn't like that he'd caught me crying.

His eyes strayed to the screen before darting back to me. "She's stubborn as hell, but she loves you, Andy. More than anything, I think. And she knows you love her."

"Because you've told her, I suppose," I said, not wanting to sound confrontational but sounding it just the same.

"Because she knows."

And then he squeezed my shoulder and left me there with the ice cream I didn't feel I deserved from him.

Something shifted between Drew and me at the bar on Sunday night, but maybe it shifted in the wrong direction. I guess that's my doing. We both admitted that something had changed between us after I saw him with his big cock in his hand, but then I pulled an Andy and pushed him away.

Because in that moment I felt the sand shifting beneath my feet. I knew I could have leaned in, and he would have kissed me, and *everything* would have changed. Because kissing him wouldn't be like kissing anyone else. Kissing him would matter.

"*Well?*" Marnie turns back to me, having either gotten the idea across to Grace or given up entirely.

"Drew and I are good," I say. I think about the way it felt to lie in front of him the other night, his body plastered against mine, his breath in my ear, every part of me touching every part of him. I clear my throat. "We've been getting along pretty well, although he did get really pissy with me the other night for cleaning his desk and moving some of his shit around."

Marnie clucks her tongue. "Oh, he wouldn't like that. He's very particular about the disorder he has going on there."

"Yeah, you're telling me," I say, blowing out a breath that sends one of my curls flying. "He's checked in on my grandmother a couple of times for me." I've already told Marnie, Sinclair, and Grace about the Leonard thing; Marnie's unconvinced it's a good idea, but

Sinclair said she knows how much unfinished business could eat at you. Grace asked who Leonard was, then told us she was going to need an intensive Q and A session when she gets back from New York.

Marnie and Sinclair exchange a look, then Sinclair says, "You know, Rafe set him up with his friend Shauna last weekend."

I try not to look overly interested by this news. "Oh? I guess it didn't go too great, huh? He got drunk on the couch that night, and when I came home, he was watching infomercials."

Marnie makes a face. "I don't know, because he refuses to talk about it other than to say they're not a good fit. Which sucks, because Shauna is so cool, and I figured they'd be perfect for each other. She's an artist, and he's sort of an artist, too, you know? *And* she's a gamer."

Sinclair shrugs. "Yeah, Shauna's awesome, but sometimes you're drawn to people who are different than you. Maybe they're too alike." She traces the rim of her glass. "You know, I'm pretty sure he was the one who called it. Rafe said she was kind of into him."

Relief unfurls inside of me, like stepping into a soft rain shower after working in a hot kitchen. Yeah, I've had a whole battery of odd jobs.

Am I an asshole for hoping he held back because of me?

"Seriously?" Marnie asks. "Dumbass. I'm going to have to give him hell for that. Maybe he's going through an early midlife crisis. I grabbed coffee with him yesterday, and he looks like he's trying to grow a beard." Turning to me with an amused smile, she says, "Why didn't you tell me? That's obviously the kind of update I need in my life."

"It looks okay," I say, my tone a little sullen.

It looks better than okay. It's not really a beard, more like a very heavy five o'clock shadow, and it makes him look edgier. So does the mood he's been carrying around, though I wish he'd table it and hang out with me again.

"I saw the way he hugged you the other night." She tilts her head, studying me, and for a second I'm sure she knows everything —the way my pulse kicks up a little quicker whenever he walks into the room or I hear his voice, the craving I feel for his simple touches, and the longing I have for that room just across from mine. Then her mouth twists to the side, and she says, "I think he might have a thing for you. You'd let him down easy, wouldn't you? I mean, I don't think he'd say or do anything to make you uncomfortable, he's too much of a good guy for that, but if anything happens, be gentle."

It's an entreaty. A *heartfelt* entreaty.

For a second, I'm stunned. Marnie usually sees so much. How come she can't see this?

"What makes you think I'd let him down at all?" I ask, implying through my intonation that it's a joke.

"He's not your usual type," she says, lifting her shoulders in a shrug.

"So what's my usual type?"

"More muscly and macho. A little..." She's laughing and trying to pretend she's not.

"What?" I say, both annoyed and entertained.

"A little, well, dumb. I don't think you've ever dated anyone who's as smart as you."

"Are you saying Drew's too smart for me?" I ask, now more annoyed than entertained. Drew *is* smart. Last week, when he was still hanging out with me, we watched an episode of *Jeopardy!* I'd seen with my grandmother before, and he knew all of the answers. I'd actually watched it before, and I still didn't remember.

"Who's dating Drew?" Grace asks from the phone, her voice barely filtering up to me. Sinclair's just watching and listening.

"*No*," Marnie says to me, ignoring Grace's question. "Definitely not. It's just...you don't usually go for the more intellectual types. The guys you date are nice, usually, but there's something conversationally lacking, and—"

I mime digging a hole. "And you continue to dig it deeper and deeper."

She laughs, and I join in, even though I'm not sure I'm actually amused.

"We're not always drawn to people who are just like us, though," Sinclair says, watching me. There's a look in her eyes that makes me wonder if she's caught on more than Marnie. Sinclair's a good observer—something about being an actress, maybe. She picks up on people's tones and expressions.

"Sure," Marnie says. "And I guess it can be argued that Griffin, the very best of fiancés, is nothing like the guys I used to date. So, how about it, Andy? Want to marry my brother? I'll even throw in a stationery pack. Make it really nice dowry."

There's a twinge of something inside of me—anger or defensiveness, maybe—and I snap, "I don't think he'd appreciate us joking around about this."

Her eyes go wide with confusion, but after a second she nods, her hair moving with the motion. "Yeah, you're right. Sorry, I got a bit carried away."

I should apologize, but I don't want to. I'm pissed. I'm not really sure what I'm pissed about, just that I am.

My eyes lower to the propped-up phone, where Grace is hovering with a confused look on her face, then I see the door open behind her, and Enoch comes in. They kiss, and he lifts her off her feet and twirls her, and my heart hurts. I'm angry and lonely and *wanting*.

———

I didn't see Drew last night or this morning. I'm pacing the living room, stepping from colorful splash to colorful splash, wondering if he's actually going to come back. I guess he stayed at the office late, or maybe he went out for drinks with a co-worker.

Maybe he decided to give Shauna a second chance after I blew him off at the bar last Sunday, a thought that makes me prickle even though it would be no less than I deserve. I've been hot and cold, a tease. I haven't meant to act that way—I'd promised myself to keep my distance, to be no more than the friend by association I've always been, but I keep feeling drawn in by him.

The present I ordered for him last weekend just came in.

I got it for him to say I'm sorry.

I got it for him because I want to show him how much he's always meant to me—and how he means more to me every day.

Finally, I hear his car in the drive, then the door opens, and he steps inside.

"Hey," I say, taking a step toward him.

"Hey," he says with a nod, as if I'm a co-worker he's only barely on first-name basis with, and then moves past me and goes directly upstairs. His presence is gruff and forceful, underplayed by the slight curl in his brown hair, the irrepressible warmth of his eyes.

"Is this your way of telling me you're not coming?" I shout up the stairs.

"I need to change," he calls back.

Five minutes later, he comes back in his *Star Wars* T-shirt, the one that my grandmother tried to throw away. Maybe it's his way of telling me the Ruiz women don't control him, but it reads differently to me—because it reminds me that he helped my grandmother, something else he didn't need to do for me.

"So are we doing this thing, Ruiz?" he says, lifting his eyebrows, the darker brown, almost black, standing out. For a second, it feels like he's asking me something else, but his rueful glance at the window suggests he's talking about Nicole and Damien.

So instead I tell him, "They're picking us up. But the present I ordered for you finally arrived."

A corner of his mouth lifts. "Still trying to pay me back?"

"Maybe you should open it before you tell me I shouldn't have," I say, challenging him. "Then at least you'll have two reasons to say so."

"Fair point."

Excitement jumps through me as I head behind the kitchen counter to retrieve the wrapped present. I come back around and set it down on the counter with a thunk.

"Holy shit," he says, sounding slightly alarmed. "It's enormous."

"Yes, it would have to be. Then again, you know all about enormous things." He gives me a look that tells me to shut up, or maybe to stop tormenting him if I'm not going to please him as well. "I'm not much of a gift wrapper."

That's an understatement. I used some Christmas paper I found in the closet of their spare room. Only there wasn't enough of it, so I used a catalogue to make up the difference.

"I like it," he says as he crosses the floor to me, his presence washing over me. "It feels more authentic this way."

"Yes," I say, nudging his shoulder. "The Ruiz experience. Is it trash or is it treasure? Who knows?"

His face creases into a frown. "Don't talk about yourself like that."

"You saw where I grew up." I shrug. "It's no big deal, Drew. You need to be able to joke about the hard shit if you want to make it feel lighter."

"It *is* a big deal," he insists. "Your grandmother is a badass, and you're fucking amazing. Don't think I haven't noticed the work you've put in at her house. It must have been you. And, knowing you, no one taught you how to do that shit. You taught yourself."

My heart throbs painfully, because if he noticed, he's the only one. No, not the only one—my grandmother appreciated the work I put in, but Theo sure as shit didn't care.

"Open the box," I say, nudging his shoulder with mine again. This time I let it linger, because I want him to know that he's special to me too—in a way that goes far beyond gratitude.

He picks up the box, a big hand on either side. Shakes it. The look on his face, of a little boy at Christmas, is so endearing, I feel a twist in my chest. I'm so anxious for him to open it I'm on edge. I feel a sense of glee that wants to burst forth.

He rips open the paper, and a huge smile crosses his face as he reveals a box emblazoned with a photo of the red Fabgadget in all of its glory.

"How'd you know?" he says, turning to me with a devastating smile. "Was it the second time the informercial came on or the third that gave you the clue?"

"You seemed really excited about its ability to grind coffee. I had to make sure you got to try it. You think it really works?"

"It's going to take up two-thirds of our counter space," he says playfully, setting the box down. "It had better work." Then he takes a step toward me, closing the space between us, and pulls me to his chest. I let myself breathe him in. This time, he's the one who pulls away.

"Still, I would have gotten plenty of use out of the book." His eyes are sparkling with amusement—he's teasing, but there's an edge to it. We're slipping back into that game we've been playing without meaning to. The *will they* or *won't they*.

"*Drew*."

His gaze sharpens, and he looks down at me, his eyes flitting ever so briefly down to my lips. The feeling of longing I've been carrying around sharpens and forms teeth. My heart starts pounding in my chest, and it feels like my entire person is teetering between agony and ecstasy, between the start of something and the end of everything. I can't take this risk with him—but I can't not take it either.

"I shouldn't have ended our conversation on Sunday like that," I say through numb lips. "I... Things have been changing for me, living here. The way I see you, I mean. Have they been changing for you?"

Of course, that's when a car pulls up outside, and Nicole, never the soul of patience, lays on the horn three times. It always feels like I'm running out of time lately, like there aren't enough grains in the hourglass.

He reaches out and takes my hand, and that simple touch is enough to send liquid fire through my veins. His eyes bore into mine.

"Only a little." There's no time for me to feel devastated, because he finishes, "because I already had it bad for you."

I'm the one who closes the distance between us, grabbing the shoulders of his old shirt, bringing him down to me as I lift my head to him. He's looking at me the whole time, a mixture of wonder and joy in his eyes. He lowers his mouth to meet mine, and a sound of need escapes me at the hard press of his lips. He devours me as he backs me up toward the kitchen counter, forceful in a way that surprises and delights me. Desire pulses through me, hot shivers coursing from where we're kissing feverishly, trying to get closer, to take more, to show each other all of the things we've been hiding just out of sight.

His mouth against mine feels like a revelation, his hands, a promise as they skate over my skin, finding the curve of my breast before continuing on down my side.

I pull away slightly, but only to say, "Don't be a gentleman. I want them everywhere. I want *you* everywhere."

He swears under his breath and then says, "You want my hands on you, Andy?"

His voice is low and almost hoarse, and it radiates through me.

"*Yes.*"

He pushes me up against the counter, his lips traveling down the side of my neck, trailing heat as he palms my breasts and then flips up my dress.

Of course, that's when the door bursts open.

I push him away, but not soon enough.

twenty

DREW

"YOU KNOW, people might stop barging in on your private moments if you'd learn to lock your door," Nicole says conversationally.

It takes a moment for her meaning to register, because my senses are full of Andy; her taste, the fruity mint of that gum she always chews, the way her soft skin felt beneath my fingers as she tipped her head up to me in a question I was goddamn determined to answer. It's a mindfuck, going from that to the assault of Nicole at the door and Andy's hands pushing me away rather than finally, *finally* pulling me toward her.

Not the kind of awakening a man would like to have. My whole body is pounding with the need to take her upstairs. To show her how good it can be between us. To do to her the things I've been actively fantasizing about for weeks—and thinking about for much longer.

"Can we do this another time?" I ask Nicole, clearing my throat. "We're a little..."

"Busy?" Nicole says with bemusement. "So I can see. I must say, I'm pleased as hell about this turn of events. I enjoy being right whenever possible." Turning to Andy, she asks, "Was it the beard? Reggie felt sure the beard would do it."

Goddammit, Reggie.

"You grew a beard because Reggie told you to?" Andy asks me, her eyes dancing with merriment. She's definitely going to give me shit about this for a long time. "And the guys all know about…"

I expect her to end with "us," but instead she chooses, "this." Not the word choice I would have preferred, but hell, I'm ten million times happier than I was this morning. If I'm in deeper than she is, it's no less than I expected.

"Griffin and Rafe could tell I was interested," I say. "And Reggie's at the bar constantly. He doesn't know how not to be there. Trust me when I say I did not ask for advice, nor did I encourage them in any way whatsoever."

I choose not to mention that Marnie asked me to meet her for coffee the other day, because Griffin had, with my blessing, told her about what he was doing at Mrs. Ruiz's house.

She'd looked concerned for me. "You have feelings for her, don't you?" she'd asked.

My *no comment* was interpreted as a yes, and she fretted with her mug of coffee. "I understand why, obviously. She's Andy. But…"

"You don't think I'm good enough for her," I blurted.

"What?" she asked, horrified. "No. You're, like, the best person I know."

"I'm telling Griffin you said so," I said with a small smile.

"Uh-huh. But that's not what I meant. What I meant was…she isn't serious with guys usually. I just don't want you to get hurt. Or for things to get weird."

She hadn't told me anything I didn't already know, but it stuck with me. It stuck with me enough that I'd doubled down on my stay-away-from-Andy plan. But there's only so long you can stay away from the people you love when they literally live in the same house. Sit in the same chairs. Watch the same TV. There were signs of her everywhere, ghosts of her scent, a strand of curly hair that I wrapped around my finger before throwing it away...

And now I sound like a weirdo.

Maybe I *am* a weirdo. These feelings have made me into one.

Nicole laughs, jarring me. "Well, it definitely encourages Reggie when you listen to his advice." She taps her temple. "You'll want to keep that in mind for the future."

"Maybe I just forgot to shave," I object.

"Did you?" Andy asks.

She still looks amused, and maybe even a little pleased, which is why I admit, "Yes, I listened to Reggie. Feel free to mock me for the rest of my life. At least I didn't growl at you. He suggested that too."

"Too bad," she says with a sexy-as-hell grin.

Nicole, who's been ignoring my *please, for the love of God leave* looks, claps her hands, then darts a pointed glance at me. "We've got places to be, so maybe you should take care of your...situation, and we can be off?"

Her words prompt Andy to look at the bulge in my pants, which only makes my "situation" worse, especially since she licks her lips —lips that are slightly swollen because of me.

"Jesus," I say, grabbing the heavy Fabgadget box off the counter and sticking it in front of my dick. Which isn't fantastic, because I do it too quickly, and the thing feels like a steel tank.

"Look, this is no time to play Dick in the Box, Drew," Nicole says, ignoring my wince. "Although I've heard what's in that box is impressive. We have plans."

I nearly drop the Fabgadget, and now Andy's laughing hysterically, her whole body bobbing with it.

"You told her?" I ask.

She laughs harder. "Sorry," she gets out between gusts of laughter. "You said I couldn't tell Marnie. I had to tell someone."

"Fantastic," I say, annoyed but slightly amused. "Well, at least my problem's going to take care of itself."

"Good!" Nicole says. "Let's go."

"Do you want to do this?" I ask Andy, still holding the box for the moment. I don't need Nicole checking out the size of my package. "We can let the Leonard thing go. I think we probably should."

"We're going," she insists, her expression fierce. "You need this."

If she says so. Right now, I'm just going because she's going, simple as that.

Andy's lips creep up into a smile as I set down the Fabgadget.

"Let me have it, Ruiz," I say, reaching for her hand. "What dumbass thing have I done now?" The easiness with which she gives her hand to me is a miracle I don't take for granted, and warmth blossoms in my chest. After last Sunday, I'd figured I was all out of chances with Andy—that she'd set the line between us, and it was my job to stay on my side. I've kept busy, and so have Griffin and Rafe, bless them. The little purple house is freshly painted, inside and out, and we replaced a couple of "trick" steps as Mrs. Ruiz called them. She'd horrified us by admitting that she's been stepping around them. Rafe brought up the good point of whether she should be climbing stairs at all—and promptly got banished outside again. Shauna's come through, too, and when I stopped by tonight to check in, she and her grandparents were eating dinner with Mrs. Ruiz. She'd cooked for them, because she refuses to stay off her feet for long—*"I'll be dead soon enough, Andrew. I'll do plenty of sitting then"*— and even though she didn't look good, she seemed content. I would have taken a photo for Andy, except if Mrs. Ruiz had caught me, I'm pretty sure I'd have been relegated to the porch like Rafe.

Before I left them to talk amongst themselves, I pulled Mrs. Ruiz aside and asked if we could chat over the weekend.

"You're going to push me about talking to Andy, I suppose," she said, her eyes glinting.

"And you're going to want to say no," I agreed. "But we're both going to go through the motions anyway, and I'm going to tell you why."

She tilted her head in accession, silently conveying, *I'll listen, fool boy, but I'm not going to like it*, and I told her about finding Andy in tears the other day, looking up information on the internet.

She scowled. "No one should look up health information on the internet."

It was a valid argument, but she was also missing the point, and I told her so. "Andy never cries." Then, because might as well go big or go home, I asked, "Whose feelings are you sparing here, your own or hers?"

Her expression firmed, but to my surprise, she didn't kick me out on my ass. "Sunday," she said. "We'll talk Sunday. Come at eight-thirty."

I could have objected that eight-thirty was an obscene hour for a weekend meeting, but I figured she was challenging me, and if so, I was damn well going to meet that challenge. I planned on coming by to work on the windows anyway. Might as well get an early start.

I plan on laying it on thick, because this farce has gone on long enough.

"You haven't done any dumbass things," Andy says, bringing me back to earth, "but maybe a genius one. I think you just figured out a new use for the Fabgadget. We should call into the infomercial to let them know."

A corner of my mouth lifts, and just like that, I feel lighter. More willing to roll with the craziness of whatever Nicole and Damien have in store for us. "It would be a public service."

"Okay, quit flirting, kids," Nicole says. "Chop-chop." She grins. "Hey, is this what it feels like to be a daycare teacher?"

"Yeah, basically," Andy says. "Except we'd be throwing rocks at each other."

"Can we play grab-ass instead?" I ask.

"Tone it down, Romeo," Nicole says. "Normally, I'd be all about the grab-ass, but we've got people to see and lives to screw up."

Andy puts on some high-heeled sandals that do all kinds of

things for her legs, and I slide on an old pair of Toms with fraying at the toe.

Once we're outside, Andy squeezes my hand and drops it. Nicole bombs on ahead as I pause to lock the door.

"Was that weird?" I ask Andy, giving her a sidelong glance. "Holding your hand, I mean."

"Yes," she says, playing with the hem of her dress. It's red, her favorite color, with a slight fringe on the bottom. I'd like to see it in a pool on the floor. "But good weird."

I glance at the road, and Nicole's already well on her way to the car.

"You know, we could make a break for it," I say, edging closer and stooping to kiss the curve of Andy's neck.

She grabs the back of my head to hold me there, for just a moment, my lips moving across her soft skin, and then sighs and releases me. "She'd catch us. She's scrappy like that. Besides, I think this is good, Drew. They wouldn't be helping if they didn't think there was any point. They're not time wasters."

"I know you've convinced yourself this is unfinished business for me, but I'm good. I don't need this." I can already see the argument brewing in her. It's as obvious as an informercial. "Go ahead, tell me why I'm wrong."

"Your game," she says. "Why haven't you done anything with it?"

"It's not ready."

"It *looks* ready. Danny seemed to think it was ready the other day. Burke too, when I asked him about it."

"Have you been texting him?" I ask, my tone coming out sharp.

She rolls her eyes. "What does it matter? I thought I made it pretty clear whose cock I want to jump."

A curse slides out of me. "Maybe the coding side of the game is finished, but the design isn't done. The fire isn't realistic enough."

She purses her lips as if she thinks I've made her point.

"What does my fake-looking fire have to do with Leonard?" I ask, annoyed even though I'd rather not be. "I'm sure you have some connection in mind."

"You don't take chances on yourself. You don't think you deserve to succeed. You still blame yourself."

I lift my eyebrows, and she surprises me by reaching up and tracing them.

"Don't try to distract me by grooming me," I say, capturing her hand and lowering it. "You just called me a coward."

"I did not," she says, her tone affronted. "No one could call you a coward. If anyone caused trouble for Marnie or Sinclair, you'd go after them without a second thought."

"Add yourself to that list."

Something gleams in her eyes. "That was almost a growl," she says, taking a slight step toward me.

"Damn right."

"And it was sexy as hell, so I guess Reggie knows what he's talking about after all."

"Don't distract me with your devil-woman talk. You were giving me a lecture."

"What I meant is that you don't take chances on yourself; for other people, you'd move mountains. You've told yourself your contribution to the game isn't good enough, because you don't trust your own judgment. Or worth."

"If that's true, then what am I doing with you?" It's a challenge, but she's the woman who loves challenges. "Isn't this the definition of a risk?"

"For *me*," she says, suddenly looking sad. "There's no real risk for you. But if it doesn't work out, you could kick me out of the house. Tell Marnie you don't want to see me anymore."

I release her hand as if it burned me. "You think I'd do that?"

"No, not really," she mutters, glancing off toward the car, where Nicole is probably making crude and impatient gestures.

I take her shoulders in my hands. "Look at me, Andy."

She does, her eyes a little defiant. "Now you get to tell me where to look?"

"Yes. I need you to know I would never do that. *Never*. If this doesn't work out, even though I hope to God it does, because I've never wanted something so much in my life, I would move before I told you to leave. Or I'd find you somewhere better to stay. And I would never, ever tell Marnie I didn't want to see you, or that she couldn't bring you somewhere because I was coming. You need to know I wouldn't *do* that."

The look in her eyes softens. "I *do* know. It's just...this is hard for me." She gives me a half smile, her gaze combing down my body and lingering on my pants. "Looked like it was hard for you back there too."

Leave it to her to make my blood boil for two very different reasons within the space of a few minutes. I let my hands wander, smoothing down her shoulders and arms and bringing her close. "Damn straight. I want to be alone with you, Ruiz. I want to do more things to you than a Fabgadget has functions."

She looks up at me, her eyes full of mischief. Lifting her hand to my chin, she traces the line of my jaw, feeling the beard I grew for her. "That thing has, like, ten different modes, Drew. Do *you*?"

"Yes. Would you like to test them all?"

"*Thoroughly*," she says, her eyes sparkling as she passes her fingers across my lips.

I kiss them, feeling like I must be having a dream, because an hour ago, I felt like my luck had all run out, and here Andy is, talking about testing my modes.

"Lovebirds!" Nicole shouts, loudly enough to be heard in West Asheville. "Time's a wasting."

I'm still halfway hoping Andy will give up the ghost, possibly literally in this case, but she lifts up onto her toes and gives me a quick but hard kiss—a burst of heat, of her—and then heads toward the car. Is it any surprise that I follow her?

I disagree that my reluctance to pull the trigger on *Survival of the Fittest* has a damn thing to do with Leonard, but Andy has it in her head that this is something I need, and I'll be goddamned if I disappoint her.

I'd probably follow this woman into hell, but let's be honest, this is an outing with Nicole and Damien, so I might be doing exactly that.

twenty-one

ANDU

"UM, why are we parked outside Burke and Danny's apartment?" Drew says, looking first at me and then, since I'm obviously just as confused as he is, shifting his focus to Nicole and Damien.

"Burke's coming with us," Nicole says. "He's going to be part of our shenanigans."

"Does he know this? He's not the kind of guy to stay in on a Friday night."

It's a valid question. We don't even know where we're going yet. We asked them, obviously, and Nicole insisted on keeping it a surprise. Drew muttered that it wasn't going to be a fun surprise for anyone other than her, and I think he has that right.

On the one hand, I wish I'd taken him up on his offer and run from Nicole. We could be making out in a park somewhere, hidden in the trees, our bodies wrapped around each other...

On the other hand, there's an icy feeling inside of me, down deep, that questions whether this is a mistake. I meant what I said to Drew—I trust him. I know he wouldn't intentionally hurt me or cast me out, but I've already shaken up his life, and we've barely even begun this thing. How long will his tolerance last?

I also can't stop thinking of Marnie, the other night, telling me to let her brother down easy, as if she couldn't imagine a world where I wouldn't hurt him.

"Yup," Nicole says, bored. "I went to the trouble of introducing myself. But you should probably go up and get him."

"Isn't this what phones were made for?" he grumbles.

But he tries to make the call, and Burke doesn't pick up—so he heads upstairs.

Damien glances back at me as I watch Drew go, and I can feel my heart thumping around in my chest, as if it's a scared animal caught in my ribcage.

"He's a weak man," he says.

For a second I'm arrested with shock. Then righteous indignation kicks in, hot and consuming. "No, he's not. He stands up for the people he cares about, there's nothing weak about that. He's the strongest, most supportive person I know."

Damien and Nicole exchange a look and then he bursts out laughing, which does nothing to make me less pissed off.

"You're a dick," I snap. "Where do you get off judging him?"

Nicole gives me a look that's half impressed and half pissed—as if she admires me for daring to insult her husband in front of her but isn't exactly happy about it.

"I'm not talking about Drew," Damien says through his laughter, and I realize my mistake. He's been talking to my brother this week, to Jack.

"Oh." My voice sounds small, because I've been waiting for this news, but now that I'm on the cusp of getting it, I'm not so sure I want it.

"But it sounds like he's frustrated with Theo."

"How'd you get him to talk?" I ask.

"When someone wants to talk, all you have to do is let them."

It's a bullshit answer, because even if Jack had a guilty conscience to unload, he'd probably be more circumspect to let it all out to a stranger. Then again, maybe it's easier to tell a stranger.

Maybe we were both wired that way, him and me, to look strong at all costs but to feel things just as much as the next person. When my mother was dying, I got on the city bus one day and just rode from stop to stop without getting off. An older woman asked me what was wrong, and I started crying. She ushered me out at the next stop, bought me a hot chocolate, and I told her everything.

I wasn't sure why, but when I told her I had no idea why I was blubbering to a stranger, she said that we'd both been exactly where we needed to be at exactly the right time.

I never saw her again, but I've always remembered her.

Maybe Damien was Jack's right-person-at-the-right-time stranger.

"Theo's got his nuts in his fist," Damien continues, colorfully. "He faked his credentials to get Jack the job, and he could take it away just as easily. Make it look like your brother is the liar."

"Jack told you all of this?" I ask in disbelief.

He laughs. "No, that part was easy enough to find out on my own."

Nicole taps her chin. "What do you think will happen if you pull the plug on Theo's job? You think he'll blame your brother? *That* could be interesting. All it would take is one little picture for it all to come tumbling down. I notice his fiancée hasn't left him."

I'd noticed too, dammit. Or at least she hadn't taken the excessive photos of her heart-shaped diamond ring—*vom*—down from Facebook.

Nicole's dangling something tasty over my head with a string, but something's holding me back. I don't know what, exactly, but I don't like doing it this way, underhanded. If I'm going to fuck someone over, I'd like to do it loud and proud, where they can see me.

I say as much, and Nicole tuts her tongue. "Not a very sound mentality for a P.I."

She's right. It's just...

"This is personal. It's different."

"Only if you have a thing for getting in trouble," Damien argues. "If you don't, it's best to take the covert approach."

"Sure, but I'm not ready."

"Keep in mind that they're the ones who did this to themselves," Nicole says. "All you'd be doing is broadcasting the truth. Your brother is screwing his boss's daughter. Truth. Your other brother let him lie so he'd get his job. Truth. If they turn against each other, because Jack assumes Theo's behind this, or just because he doesn't want to be the only domino to fall, that's *their business*."

"It might do Jack good not to be under your brother's thumb," Damien adds. "He's not totally worthless. Just...weak."

"Besides, if I had a sister or brother, I'd make damn sure they weren't able to get away with this kind of shit. It's not good for a person to think there won't be consequences for their actions. Theo's probably just going to go through the rest of his life being an asshole, no matter what you do, but maybe not. Maybe he just needs the right kick in the ass at the right time to get himself together. You'll never know if you don't try."

Damien gives her a significant look, and she smirks at him.

They're right. I know they're right, but at the same time—

The knowledge comes to me with a jolt. I don't want to break their lives apart like that because I'm afraid they'll find out I'm behind it. I'm going to lose my grandmother forever—the kind of loss you can't come back from—and they're going to be the only family I have left.

Except they stopped acting like family a long time ago.

Drew and Burke emerge from the apartment building, and I push to the far side of the back seat to give them room. Drew opens the door and smirks at me. "Does this mean I'm riding in the middle?"

He's over six feet tall, so I start to scooch over, taking pity on him, but he shakes his head and piles in. "I don't mind crowding you, Ruiz."

I can't help but wonder if it's because he doesn't want me riding next to Burke. But I don't mind Drew crowding me either—it's a relief, actually. Having his side pressed to me, seeing his long legs folded up like a pretzel. Hearing his voice. It's soothing the bees under my skin.

Burke nods to me, and I nod back. He looks slightly dazed, like he's not quite sure how he came to be here, in this car, in this situation. Fair enough. We still don't know where we're going either.

When the door closes behind Burke, Nicole claps her hands and says, "Fantastic, let's get this show on the road."

"What exactly is this show?" Burke asks slowly. "You're the P.I.s, right? That's what you said on the phone."

"Yes," she says, glancing back at him. "And look at you! Aren't you a tall drink of diet soda."

It sounds like an insult, although with her there's no knowing.

"Where are we going?" I chime in as Damien pulls out of the parking space.

She leans farther back in her seat, her face glowing and her pink hair all askew. "We're going to a person who's going to be able to tell us everything."

———

"You've got to be kidding me," Burke mutters, although I'm pretty sure that Damien and Nicole are dead serious.

They brought us to a psychic—and not a legit-looking one either. The storefront is in a little strip mall, next to an abandoned restaurant with a "C" health and safety rating in the window. The glass door has a paper sign attached to the inside reading "Josie, the Great and Powerful." The twinkle lights tracing the border of the glass kind of underplay the impact, but they *are* pretty. Blackout curtains cover all of the windows.

Nicole glances at us, still packed into the back seat like sardines. "What better way to commune with a dead man than through a psychic?" She must be a sadist because she cackles to truly drive home the fact that we've wasted our night.

"Can we leave?" Burke asks, directing the question at Drew.

"Nope," Damien says. "My car. My rules. You can try calling an Uber, but it'll take at least fifteen minutes for one to get to this part of town. Might as well go in and see what Josie has to say. I have no doubt it'll be interesting."

Burke turns to Drew. Drew turns to me. "I'll let you decide," he says, "but I reserve the right to bring this up at every possible opportunity for at least a month."

"Fair," I say, grazing my knuckles against his leg as a silent promise that I'm going to make this worth his while. I don't know why I don't want to leave, other than that I've committed to seeing this thing through. He might have told me he doesn't need this, that his belief in himself wasn't knocked by what happened with Leonard, but I see what I see. Besides, I won't deny that it's one hell of a distraction. "We're going in."

Burke groans as he opens the car door and gets out. "I had a date with a really hot girl tonight."

"And now you're hanging out with several hot people," Nicole says as the rest of us pile out. "Boo-fucking-hoo."

He gives her a look that suggests he's not used to being razzed by strangers.

"That's her way," I tell him. "You'll get used to her."

"Let's just get this over with," Drew mumbles, placing his hand at the small of my back. Heat radiates from his hand, and I remember what it felt like when he kissed me. Everything felt uncomplicated and *good*. After this, I wish we could go back to the house and lock ourselves in for a week. Put up a sign on the door that says we're closed for visitors.

Burke's gaze traces the movement, and there's a glimmer of understanding in his eyes. When Nicole says, "Let's go, campers," he walks forward without putting up more of a fight.

It occurs to me that Drew and I are going to need to tell other people about this thing between us. It's not a simple thing—deciding you have "feelings" for someone you've known this long. Other people are going to find out. They're going to be invested in the outcome, one way or another. They're going to have *opinions*.

My mind's buzzing with bees again as we reach the door. It opens just before we can knock, which would be a pretty funny trick if a woman hadn't been waiting at the door. She's wearing wire-rimmed glasses and has long black hair that hangs loose down her back. She's wearing some kind of black kaftan dress decorated with silver thread, but there's nothing particularly otherworldly about her other than her distant gaze. "You're three minutes late for the séance."

Behind her, I can see a round table with several chairs tucked up to it, a few fat, black candles in the middle with a canister of grocery store salt. The whole store smells like patchouli and pot. There's a guy with curly hair sitting behind a counter next to the door, reading a non-fiction paperback about World War II that seems like an almost laughable mismatch with this scene, but he only glances up from it once to nod before returning his attention to whatever riveting thing happened almost a century ago.

Burke swears under his breath.

"Séance?" I hiss, glancing at Nicole. "What if Leonard's not dead?"

"Twenty-five percent off," says the woman in glasses—Josie, I'm guessing. "But I might still be able to get information about him from my spirit network."

I continue to study Nicole, who feigns a look of innocence. What the hell is she playing at anyway? Because there's *got* to be an angle —I've learned there's always an angle with her.

"How long will this take?" Burke asks, glancing at Damien. If she says it'll be more than fifteen minutes, I suspect he'll take his chances with Uber.

"Ten minutes," she says. Then, giving us a look that suggests we're putting her out, she says, "*If* you follow directions."

I guess we're not great at doing that, because it's another five minutes before we're all situated at the table, Burke and Drew sitting opposite each other because Josie insists there must be a balance, and they're the two who knew him.

Burke looks like he regrets getting up this morning. Maybe the last several mornings, actually, because even though he's as composed as ever, he looks like he's been losing sleep. Could it be because of Leonard? I don't think it's a guilty conscience, per se. He seemed like he was being straight with me last weekend. And if he had done something shady, I doubt he'd be so cooperative. Truthfully, I want to think the best of him because he's Drew's friend, if for no other reason, so maybe I'm not the best judge.

Drew is obviously just doing this for me, and I'm doing it because...well, I guess I'm interested in seeing where Nicole's going with this.

Josie mutters something under her breath that sounds like a chant until I recognize it as lyrics from a Clash song. Again, this is obviously bullshit, but Nicole wouldn't put us through it for no reason at all, would she?

"I will be the conduit for the spirit," Josie announces. Then she lights the candle and picks up the container of salt and promptly throws some at Burke.

"Hey," he exclaims, flinching away from the table. "What the hell? That got in my eye."

"Your energy is wrong," she says.

My interest is piqued, because she's right about that part at least. Something is up with him.

"And it'll be less wrong if I can't see?" he asks bitterly, rubbing at his eyes.

"Oh, don't be a baby," Nicole comments as she grabs a piece of gum from her purse.

He's obviously on the verge of leaving, but something keeps his ass in his seat. Maybe the fact that Josie, hack though she obviously is, saw something in him. Or maybe he's just anxious to know what really happened to Leonard, and he figures it can't hurt to sit through this little production if it makes Nicole and Damien more willing to help us.

"Envision Leonard," she says, ignoring Burke entirely. "Bring him up in your mind's eye—the more powerful the vision, the better it will work."

She sits in her chair and bows her head, staring into the flames of the black candles.

Several seconds pass this way, and it feels more awkward than cosmically meaningful, especially since the only pictures I've seen of Leonard are that one Drew tucked away, plus a couple I found online. Then she looks up at us, her pupils dilated, and says, "I can't locate him, but I see something."

Drew mutters something along the lines of, "Of course you do." I squeeze his knee under the table.

"Money," she says.

Burke jolts a little in his seat, probably thinking about the sixty-five grand he gave his friend to buy the house.

"That's pretty generic," he says in challenge.

"A lot of money. Given to him by..."

I expect her to point at Burke dramatically. Maybe accuse him of offing Leonard in the library with a candlestick like we're playing an acted-out version of Clue. But she surprises me by humming under her breath, the Clash again, then saying, "An older couple. The woman has blond hair. Brown Eyes. The man has white hair...ever since he was thirty. Blue eyes."

Burke looks like he's going to shit himself, although I have no idea why. Shouldn't he be happy to be out of the hot seat?

"There's a document too." She waves a hand, her eyes getting a far-off look. "Some legal bullshit."

"What *kind* of legal bullshit?" Drew asks.

"That's not how the vision works," she snaps.

Burke looks like he *did* shit himself, and is now sitting in it. "Is he dead?" he asks, intense. "Can you see that?"

Nicole tuts her tongue. "For a bunch of non-believers, you sure seem invested now."

That's when it all clicks into place. She *knows* all of this already. She knows because she told this woman what to say. While I've seen her multiple times this week, it was never before five p.m. I figured she was sleeping in late, but for all I know she's been busy—looking into Leonard.

For some reason, she set this scene up for Burke. I meet her gaze, and she must see that knowledge in my eyes, because she winks.

My mind whirrs through what Josie said. Those people...are they his *parents*, the great and mighty Burkes? The agreement would be a non-disclosure agreement, something about keeping his mouth shut. Burke told me he got fired, but maybe that was never the real story. Maybe Leonard knew something, and they shut him up.

Permanently?

Because most of the people you pay off pop back up again eventually, and no one's seen or heard from him.

"I can't tell," Josie says, "but I don't sense his spirit."

Nicole laughs. "I see what you're doing." She puts two fingers to her eyes, then points them at Josie. "You just don't want to give us that discount."

Josie's expression is affronted. "How dare you question my professionalism."

"Did you see anything else?" Burke asks, leaning over the table a little.

"No." She bends forward and blows out the candles, sending a plume of smoke directly in Burke's face.

To my surprise, he doesn't so much as flinch.

I glance over at the front desk, where the curly-haired man yawns and turns a page. He's seen some shit.

"You can all go," Josie says, glancing over to the door. A cat clock hangs there, the tail moving hypnotically. "We're having a dinner date at the restaurant next door."

It looks like it's permanently closed and should be. But if she were a real psychic, she'd already know that.

twenty-two

DREW

AT FIRST, Burke's quiet in the car. I'm quiet in the car. Andy's quiet in the car.

I'm the one who breaks the silence. "What *was* that?"

"A test," Nicole says. She glances into the back seat. "A test for Burke. You really didn't know, did you?"

"Didn't know *what*?" he asks, but he obviously knows what she's talking about. We both do. Most of the details Josie shared were vague and half-assed, but I only know one man besides Steve Martin whose hair went white at thirty, and it's Lucas Burke the Third, or as Andy would probably call him, Burke Squared. It only made him seem more intimidating when we were kids.

"You fed that woman information," I accuse, glaring at Nicole. The séance felt like some sort of half-assed dinner theater because that's exactly what it was.

"Fun, wasn't it?" she asks, chipper. "Josie's an old...well..." Her mouth twists to the side. "I wouldn't call her a friend. Acquaintance, maybe, or co-conspirator."

"I'm supposed to be your employee," Andy says with a pointed look at Nicole. "Why didn't you warn me about this? You're supposed to tell me things."

"I'm your boss," Nicole counters. "*You're* supposed to listen."

Andy taps her ear. "Speak up, boss."

"What do *you* think this is about, Lucas Burke the Third?" Nicole asks, her gaze on Burke.

"The Newton building." He still looks pale, like he did after the night he learned that you should start with tequila, not end with it. "I thought about it the other day after Andy asked me about Leonard. I couldn't remember if it happened before he disappeared or after. But I checked at the office yesterday, and it was before."

"You think he knew something about the building collapse?" I ask, jolted by this.

"Yeah," he says, nodding. "I think maybe he did." He swallows. "The contractors got blamed, and that one guy, the structural engineer, went to jail. They said he was drinking on the job."

"Seems like your parents would pay a lot of money to keep something like that quiet," Nicole comments blandly. "Maybe even make a few well-placed threats. It wouldn't be the first time they've stooped to it."

My gaze darts to Burke, who looks sick. "It wouldn't?" he mutters.

"That's what first put us on to the idea, but we've found other evidence pointing to it. We tracked down an old neighbor who remembers seeing them at Leonard's apartment around then. Do your parents seem like the kind of people who'd visit a neighborhood like that?"

He shakes his head solemnly. "They said they fired him for coming in late too many times."

"Not news they'd deliver in person, surely," Damien says, his eyes on the windshield.

"No," Burke agrees.

"And then there's the NDA."

"You found it?" I ask, surprised.

"Yes," Nicole says, "but it's intentionally vague. All it says is that he can't speak about Burke Enterprises, the Burke family, or anything else juicy or God will smite him. I'm paraphrasing here."

Obviously.

"So why would they have fired him if they gave him a payoff?" I ask.

"Are you sure they did?" Nicole glances back again. "Or did he stop showing up to work? Maybe they asked him to quit, or maybe he stopped going because the negotiations fell through."

Burke lowers his head into his palms, kneading it as if that might make the world make sense again. When he looks up, I notice his eyes are bloodshot. "I don't know," he admits. "He told me he got fired, but he could have lied to cover this up. Maybe he roped me into the flip house plan to get one more payout from the all-mighty Burkes." He says it bitterly, not that I blame him. His whole life, he's been used. By his parents for prestige. By classmates. By women.

"Would they have hurt him?" Nicole asks.

Well, shit.

"I don't think so," Burke says quietly.

"You don't *want* to think so," Damien says.

"No," he agrees, sounding miserable. "I don't."

Andy puts a hand on my leg, pulling it toward her. "Slant them toward me," she whispers. "It'll be less uncomfortable."

They were digging into the center console, and I didn't even realize it; my mind's a mess of overcooked spaghetti. "Andy..."

She takes my hand, weaving her fingers through mine. Her hold anchors me. "I'm here with you. We're going to work through this together."

"And here I thought you were going to tell me that you were right for saying something was off about what happened to Leonard."

"Oh, I was definitely right," she says, squeezing my hand. "But there'll be plenty of time to lord it over you later."

It occurs to me that Burke doesn't have anyone to anchor him, and I grab his shoulder. Squeeze it. "It's going to be all right, man."

He gives a fierce nod. "Yeah. You're right."

"We won't tell the other guys until we have something solid."

"Thanks, Drew."

We get to Burke's place, and Damien parks outside. He looks back at my friend. "Seems to me you have some work to do," he tells him. "Can you get into the offices over the weekend?"

"Yes," Burke says flatly.

"You might not know what to look for, so we'll go with you. You have Nicole's number?"

He nods, then leaves the car. I'm desperate to go home with Andy. I don't even care if we watch three hours of the Fabgadget infomercial while waiting for the device that's going to swallow our kitchen to cook us homemade bread, or whatever the hell it's supposed to do. But I can't leave Burke like this. I squeeze Andy's hand, then say, "Don't let them leave without me," and slide out into the night. It's balmy and warm. Then again, the weather has never been very considerate about matching my moods.

I call Burke's name, but he doesn't turn around, and when I rush forward and touch his arm, he flinches as if I hit him.

"What's up?" he asks.

"Do you need company tonight?" I ask.

He shoots an incredulous look at the car. I see a glimpse of Andy in the backseat—her dark curls over that red dress. "You like Andy. Seems like something's finally happening. And you want to stay *here*?"

"I'm in love with her," I blurt, my heart beating faster as I say the words. They feel right, and I don't regret them. "I don't think she's there yet, but it seems like she's willing to give me a shot."

"So what are you doing out here, dumbass?" he says with a smirk.

"I'm in love with her, but you're my best friend, and you just got buried in a heap of shit. If you need me, I'm staying."

He's already shaking his head. "No way. You go on home. Danny's probably here. I'll play a game with him to keep my mind off things." His gaze goes distant. "Do you think Leonard might be alive?"

"It's a possibility," I say slowly, although I'm not sure I believe it. "Even if he took a payoff from your parents, he could have still drowned in the woods."

Or they could have hurt him, although I see no point in saying so. He looks broken enough without hearing those words.

He nods. "I know. But if they did this...any of it...they're not going to get away with it."

I believe him, because he's the kind of guy who'd burn his own world to protect a friend, even if that friend turned out to be a different sort of person than he'd thought.

"Talk tomorrow?"

"Yes." He pats me on the back. "Go make me proud."

"And you say I'm the weird one."

He smiles—a genuine smile—and then I watch him stalk into the building. There's purpose in his walk.

I'm still worried about him—about this whole FUBAR mess—but there's not much I can do about it tonight. And I don't think he's in any danger if he goes poking around. Even if his parents are worse than we ever imagined, they wouldn't hurt their only son.

———

When we get back to the house, Andy and I get out, and Nicole rolls down the window. I'm tempted to walk up the drive without asking what she wants, because I've had just about enough of her for one night, but I pause for just long enough to get hit between the eyes with a three-strip of condoms. She's leaning over Damien, who doesn't seem displeased to have his woman draped over him.

Fair.

"Wrap it up," she shouts.

Then they ride off before I can do more than pocket the strip.

"You're saving them?" Andy asks, her lips tipping up. She seems pleased, which is all it takes for my cock to get half hard. I lean in to kiss her.

"Why not? This saves me from going upstairs."

She gives me a weighing look. "I thought you might want to talk about what happened with Burke."

"I'm a good multitasker." Then, because I don't want to be glib about this—about her—I add, "I need you, Andy. That's all I need right now."

She holds my gaze and nods, then reaches into my pocket, a look of mischief in her eyes. "Shouldn't we check whether they're *ex*-tra big?"

"Why should we have to check?" I ask, lifting my eyebrows. "Seems to me Nicole knows everything."

She snags them from my pocket, then squeals when I pick her up and hoist her over my shoulder, walking toward the door.

"What if the neighbors see?" she asks, laughing now, the condoms clutched in her hand.

"Then they'll know that they should be exquisitely jealous."

"Aren't I heavy?"

"Nope, I've been lifting with Rafe and the guys to be prepared for just such an occasion."

I fumble for my key one-handed, my other hand on Andy's ass, and I feel lighter than I have any reason to, all things considered. Or maybe not. Because I might be in the middle of some dark shit, but I'm also a man who's in love. I was hopelessly in love not too long ago, and now I'm hopefully in love, and if that's not a reason to feel good, I don't know what is.

"You're going to drop me," she squeals as I throw the door open.

"Don't question my manliness." I slam the door with my foot.

"I would *never*," she says as I walk over to the couch and set her down. Her gaze lowers to my jeans. "You look very manly. Every last inch of you."

"I'll let you touch it if you ask nicely," I say with a grin. "Sounds like you've been talking about it all over town."

"Don't get your ego out of check," she says. "I've only told half the town. The other half is still unaware of your above-average dick."

"Above average, huh?" I say, reaching forward and tracing her full bottom lip. I like the way she's looking at me—leaning forward slightly, anticipation and warmth in her eyes, her lips parted. "You really do like to talk me up, don't you?"

She takes my finger into her mouth, and I hiss, because having her suck on my finger makes me think about having her lips on my dick. Not that I needed help thinking about that.

She pulls away slightly, eyes on me. "I don't like to talk about things outside of my personal experience. So maybe it's time for you to take your pants off."

"Not yet," I say, getting to my knees beside her. I lean forward and kiss her, burying my hand into the mass of hair at the back of her head to take it deeper. She opens for me, and her tongue duels with mine because there's not a damn thing she does that doesn't come off as a competition. It feels so damn good, kissing this woman. I could die here and die happy. Well, mostly happy. I pull back. "I want to bury my head between your legs until you scream."

She swears, then says, "You know, I had this sort of fantasy the other night."

"Tell me about it," I say, reaching under her dress for her panties. She lifts herself a little so I can slide them off, and I do, hooking them around her heels and sticking them in my pocket.

"You perv," she says, her voice breathy.

"You bet," I say. "Now, push your legs open for me and tell me about your fantasy."

She hikes up the bottom of her dress and spreads her legs, and I'm so damn hard that I can barely think, since there can be no more than a few drops of blood left for basic brain function. I touch her, because I need to, and she's so wet for me. A groan escapes me because it's almost too much—to be able to touch her, taste her. I thrust a finger into her slowly, savoring the feel of her and the way she leans forward to take me deeper, and then I curl my fingers around and rub her clit with the heel of my hand, rocking against it. "Tell me," I say, my voice low and barely recognizable to my own ears.

"We were watching that dating show," she says, her breath hitching. Lowering my head to her thighs, I kiss the soft, hot skin there, making my way inward.

"*Matchmaking Small Town America*," I supply, the words a soft breath against her skin. Then I run my tongue over where she's wet for me and take her clit in my mouth, sucking. Her hand finds my hair and latches on, her grip activating the nerve endings.

"Y-yeah," she says through her panting. I love hearing the way her voice hitches, the way I'm affecting her. I love the way she tastes and feels against me—better than in all the fantasies I've had. "We were sitting next to each other, our sides pressed together." I can feel her quivering around my hand as I keep working her with my mouth, and my dick is urging me to slam into her. "And I was thinking...ah..." Her fingers flex around my hair, pulling it, and it hurts in a way that thrills me because Andy's losing control. I'm making her do that. It makes me feel like a god. "That it would be really hot if you just pulled me onto your lap and...ah...started fucking me. Without saying anything about it."

The thought drives me to a fever pitch, especially since it proves I haven't been suffering alone in this—that she's been right there with me since at least last week. I suck harder, fucking her with my fingers. She pushes into them, panting, her hand with a punishing grip on my hair, and then says, "Drew, I'm going to come. I'm going to—" And I look up as I keep working her, because she's thrown her head back, her lips slightly open, her magnificent hair splayed all over the couch, her head back, her eyes slightly closed, and I can't believe it. I can't believe that we're here, like this. That I get to have her. It's pointless to say I'm hers. I've *been* hers. Hers to toy with, hers to keep. Hers to throw away, too, if that's what she wants.

When I'm sure she's done, I kiss her clit and sit up on my knees so I can bury my head in her neck and kiss her there. Taking in the scents of her perfume and her hair too, because I want to memorize all of her scents, all of her looks, and especially this one.

"God," I say into her ear, "you're so damn beautiful."

She kisses the side of my head, then pulls me away forcefully, making me smile, and kisses me hard.

"That beard feels good on my thighs," she says when she pulls away. "Maybe I'll buy Reggie a beer."

"Please, for the love of God don't tell him why you're buying it," I say, lifting the hem of her dress. She helps me pull it over her head, leaving her only in a black mesh bra that allows me to see her nipples. "Hell, I don't know what the point of it is if it's see-through, but I like it."

"Maybe *that's* the point," she says as I lean in and take her nipple in my mouth through the mesh. She sucks in a breath, but then she's tugging at my jeans, and hell, I have no intention of stopping her. "Get them off, now. Your shoes too. They're ridiculous."

"Only if you leave *your* shoes on."

"I can be persuaded," she says with a smile.

I toe off my slip-on shoes, then take off my jeans, hopping in place to get them off.

"Your shirt, too," she says, watching me.

"You don't want to have sex with a man wearing a *Star Wars* shirt?"

"Not for the first time, no." She picks up the strip of condoms, my eyes tracking them like they're a magnet. "But you can wear it when you fuck me on the couch later. We *will* be watching more *Matchmaking* reruns."

I'm not about to argue. I'd watch ten hours of infomercials if she was sitting next to me. Twenty, if she was writhing in my lap. "Where am I going to fuck you this time?" I ask.

She's getting up, her legs long and sexy in those heels. "Follow me...once you ditch the shirt."

I've never pulled off a shirt quicker.

I follow her up the stairs in a daze, because she looks like a goddess in those shoes, her bare ass swaying in front of me, her hair nearly down to it, and the packet of condoms dangling from her hand. She stalks into my bedroom like that, then turns to face me in the doorway. My brain might have permanently relocated with my dick.

"Go ahead," she says, glancing down at it. "Give it a good pump for old time's sake. That's why we're starting in here."

I almost laugh. Almost. But I stare into her eyes as I reach down and grab my dick, pump my hand up and down. Her eyes dilate.

"You liked it that much, huh?" I ask, stalking forward.

"Yes," she says. "*Yes*. It was a real eye opener."

I gather her in my arms and lift her up, and she wraps her legs around my waist, my dick captured between her and my body, and it's torturous bliss.

"You know why I was doing it?"

"I've read the book. I told you, that scene did things for me too."

"And I told you it wasn't the book," I say, walking into the room with her. "It was *you*. The thought of you reading that and touching yourself."

She's staring at me with a look I can't untangle, and I don't have enough brainpower right now to give it a real go.

"Throw me onto the bed, Andrew."

I do, suppressing the instant worry that I might have hurt her, because she doesn't look hurt. She looks like she's having a good time and would like to continue having one. In fact, she's already tearing off the first in the row of condoms.

"We're going to use them all, obviously," she says, climbing over to the side of the bed. "You accepted the challenge when you caught them."

I take another two steps toward the mattress. "I'm not about to object to that."

I hiss out a breath as she reaches for my dick and strokes it, waiting for me on her knees. She hums deep in her throat and then tears open the condom package and rolls it onto me. "I can't wait anymore. I need you inside me."

Good, because I honestly can't think of anything I've ever wanted this much. I climb onto the bed and kiss her, pushing her back into the mattress.

"Now," she says.

"You're pushy," I say, then kiss her jaw and her neck as I reach down to line myself up.

"Now," she says, urgent.

I press into her, but it takes a few strokes to get all the way in. The pressure is exquisite, the need for self-control paramount.

"Oh my God," she says, wrapping her legs around my hips. She still has those heels on, and they dig into the bottom of my back, the slight pain enhancing the pleasure. I look into her eyes and kiss her deeply as I start moving inside her, stroking nearly all the way out before I thrust back in, her legs at my back urging me on.

"You're driving me crazy," she breathes into my ear, digging her feet in again.

"That's the idea." I'm driving myself crazy too. The only brain left to me—my dick—is urging me to take it faster, harder. But I don't want to hurt her, and I don't want to come too quickly. There's already the tugging sensation that tells me I'm close.

"And it feels fucking phenomenal," she says, pausing to bite my ear lobe. "But I'm going to need you to fuck me so hard we break this bed."

That's not the kind of thing a woman needs to tell you twice.

twenty-three

ANDY

DREW DRIVES into me deep and hard, the whole bed shaking, my body quaking from it, and it feels so, so good. "Yes, like that," I say. "Just like that." Then, because I'm a talker, and he's staring into my eyes while he fucks me, making me feel vulnerable in a way I don't like, I ask, "What have *you* been fantasizing about?"

"Is this your way of telling me you miss playing show and tell?" he grunts, thrusting into me again in that body-shaking way.

"*Yes.*"

"Okay." He pulls out, my body instantly objecting to the loss. "Get on your knees and hold on to the headboard for me, Andy." His eyes are shining, his dick jutting out, and he's so handsome that for a second all I can do is look at him and marvel that I didn't see him this way until I moved in here. That I might have gone my whole life without knowing what it is to be taken by Andrew Jones. To be his sole focus.

"You want me on my knees?" I say, doing it, and then a sigh escapes me when he gathers my long hair in his fist.

"Yes," he murmurs, his hot body pressing over mine, and then he enters me with a single thrust, tugging my hair while he does. A rush of heat shivers through me from my scalp down to my toes as he keeps working me like that, his other hand moving over my body like a free agent, stopping to play with my nipples through the translucent bra before caressing down my side and reaching for my clit. My body is completely under his control, my hands on the headboard, and the sensations are so hot, so all-encompassing, that I feel another orgasm shaking through me as he tugs my hair back, revealing my neck for him, and kisses me in the sensitive spot behind my ear. His big dick is hitting all the right spots inside of me, his hand helping me along, and the feeling of him tugging my hair back like that—it's the unholy trifecta.

"Drew, I'm coming."

"Thank God," he breathes out, and I can tell he's been holding on by a thread. And I like that I can drive him crazy, that I can make it hard for him to hold back. It drives me higher, harder, and I feel myself tumbling down the edge of a feeling that's so fierce it almost has teeth. Because I can't remember ever coming this hard. I've always liked sex—sought it out for the thrill of it—but it's never felt like this before. He's right behind me, his gasp in my ear as I feel him come.

He pulls out and kisses the side of my face, then turns me and holds me to his chest, cradling me like I'm something precious. There's sweat beading his brow, and I trace it with a finger, prompting him to smile. "You worked me hard, Ruiz."

"Damn straight. That's one out of three."

He kisses me softly, sweetly, and I feel those tears again, the ones that have been trying to come out for weeks.

"Don't you have to wash up?" I ask, needing a minute to get a hold of myself.

"In a second," he says. "I need to hold you."

His arms feel so firm around me, like he's not just holding me but protecting me from the world, and it's a dangerous thought, an insidious thought—the kind that might creep into a woman and make her do stupid things.

"Well, if you're not going to claim the bathroom, then I am," I say, getting up. There's a flash of hurt in his eyes, and I feel like a dick for having caused it, but I need a minute to myself. I need to remember how to breathe.

I use the bathroom and then look in the mirror. "Get it together, Andy."

My reflection doesn't respond. I find myself thinking of what he said—*"It wasn't the book, it was you."*

And then there's the way he refused even a token payment for the room I'm staying in. I've schemed ways to get him the money; sticking cash in the pocket of his jeans, or sending him Venmo transfers with service lines saying things like *for services rendered* or *thanks for last night, stud.* But I haven't done it yet. Something's held me back. Maybe because of the way he looked when he said it, like he'd be disappointed if I didn't accept his offer.

I don't want to need him.

A voice inside of me says I already did.

I don't want him to need *me.* Because I can already feel myself wanting to give things to him—pieces of myself that I might never get back. Maybe this is how it starts.

When I come out of the bathroom, Drew's not in his room. Probably because there are two bathrooms in this house, one upstairs and one down, and he didn't want to sit around with a full condom on his dick. Again, I feel like I've done something wrong, but I don't know how to process it—or how to process what I'm feeling, other than to know that I'm somehow both happy and afraid.

I grab a T-shirt from his drawer, another old *Star Wars* one, and a pair of underwear from my bedroom and head downstairs.

He walks over from the vicinity of the kitchen, and a slow smile crosses his face as he gets closer. He has the *Star Wars* shirt on again, but with a pair of boxer shorts this time. His hair is a mess from my hands, and he's so adorable it's painful. "Now I *know* you're trying to drive me crazy," he says.

I laugh despite myself. "So this is what does it for you, Drew? An oversized *Star Wars* shirt?"

"On you, yes." Reaching me, he leans in for a kiss, as casually as if this is something we've been doing for years, not hours. Happiness sparks inside of me, refusing to be doused. "I'm making us some dinner. I'll tell you right now to manage your expectations, though."

"What?" I say, putting a hand on my hip. "You're not making me empanadas?"

"Eggs and toast, and there's a fifty percent chance they'll get burned. Maybe seventy-five if you keep looking at me like that."

"Is this your way of asking me to cook?" I ask, amused.

"No," he replies, his expression surprisingly serious. "I wanted to do something for you."

I could respond that making someone burnt eggs can't be classified as a favor, but there's something earnest about him, and there's a burning sensation in my throat, as if all those tears I've held back have backed up and become a flood—barely held back. So I settle for, "Thank you. Let's go into the kitchen to ensure a minimal amount of burning."

We do, but the huge Fabgadget box looms on the kitchen counter. I wave to it. "Come on. We have to experiment."

He laughs. "You think it makes eggs?"

"What doesn't it do? We need to take it out and find out."

"Okay," he tells me, "but we're doing this together. I'm not going through Informercial Hell alone."

Turns out it does make eggs. Poorly. They're somehow both undercooked and overcooked at the same time.

Drew makes a face as he picks at the overdone part. We're sitting next to each other at the dining room table, our feet touching under it, and even though the food sucks and we're dressed like teenage boys at a sleepover—minus the pants—I think it's maybe the best date I've ever had. "You know," he says, rubbing my foot with his. "I'm going to call in and tell Megan Fabulous that she lied to me."

"Megan Fabulous?" I ask, dropping my fork.

He theatrically widens his eyes. "Wait, you think she lied about her name too? Damn. Now I feel like everything in my life is a lie."

I start laughing, but I'm caught short by the reminder that some things in his life are a lie—or might be.

"How are you doing with everything? The stuff with Leonard, I mean. That must have been shocking."

"We don't need to talk about that right now," he says, his expression sobering. "We have this amazing feast to enjoy."

"Now, *you're* lying. Are you worried about Burke? I mean, let's be honest, if Leonard's dead, Burke's parents made him disappear. Now, that's shocking and pretty sucky for Burke, but you had nothing to do with it."

"I'm not going to let myself off the hook that easily, Andy," he says, pushing his plate back. Of course, it might be because the eggs are gross and not because he lost his appetite.

I lift my eyebrows. "But you said you don't feel guilty about what happened anymore."

"I know what I said." He sighs and swipes a hand through his hair, only making it messier. "Maybe you were right about that too."

"Ah-ha, he admits it," I say, but I can't muster up any enthusiasm about it. "Are you worried about Burke?" I repeat.

"Terrified," he says. "But he's going to be okay."

He says it like he's challenging anyone who might want to make it otherwise. That's the thing about Drew—he's laidback about most things, but mess with anyone he loves, or his desk, it turns out, and a fire lights inside of him. It's one of the things I love about him.

Not that I'm in love with him. I just...

I clear my throat. "Yes, and so will you."

His gaze pins me. "And so will you."

"Are we doing that thing where we repeat each other's phrases to make them sound more profound? Because it's giving me acid flashbacks of the *I know what you are but what am I* game from daycare."

"Deflecting with humor," he says, then startles a laugh out of me when he lifts his hand for a high five.

I give it to him, our hands smacking together, and then he captures my hand and pulls me to him, gathering me onto his lap. It feels so good, I feel tears in my eyes again. His warmth is surrounding me, pulling me in, his arms wrapping me up in the kind of hug that I'll remember—the kind that gives you comfort for months instead of moments.

"You're going to be better than okay," he says in my ear. "Whatever you decide to do about your brothers. About *anything*. Because you're the strongest person I know. You're so damn strong that you can't help but make other people stronger just by being you."

A couple of tears fall, but he knows me well enough not to acknowledge it or try to wipe them away. He just keeps holding me like that, his breath on my neck, his arms around me.

"I like that you see me that way," I say at last. "But I'm not sure it's true." My voice is shaking, but he doesn't comment on that either, he just moves his hands up and down on my arms, soothing me.

"It's true."

"Why don't I *feel* strong, then?" I ask, turning my head to look at him. His face is so dear to me, so familiar and not. So handsome, his eyes kind and warm and *loving*.

Marnie has always made me feel like I found a place where I could belong. But so has Drew. He wasn't one of those kids who was an asshole to his little sister and her friends. He was always sweet to her and nice to me. I think he found me amusing when I was a kid, because even then I was convinced I could kick the world in the ass. But he was four years older than us, and the first meaningful conversation I had with him without anyone else around was when I was in high school. Fourteen or fifteen. Marnie had made up a fake prom date with a senior to impress her sister, which was a bold move, because back then it wasn't very easy to impress Sinclair. I'd helped back up the ruse, and when it came to light, I'd had words with a few people to protect my friend.

Words and, on one occasion, a fist.

Old Chase Montgomery hadn't thought a woman would hit him.

Chasey had gotten it wrong.

I'd been suspended, of course.

Drew was in college at the time, but he went to UNCA and lived at home. At the time, I figured it was because he was a homebody, like Marnie always said, but later I figured he did it for the same reason I stayed with my grandmother. To help without seeming like he was helping. To be there for the family who wanted him.

The next time I saw Drew after the fight, he made a point of talking to me when Marnie was in the bathroom. "I know I can count on you to bring the muscle, Ruiz," he'd said with a grin. "You and me, we won't let anyone hurt her, will we?"

And he'd given me a high five, just like now, the contact from his hand radiating through me. I think that's when I got a crush on him. It didn't last long, because I was a teenager, and shit like that never sticks for long when you're a kid.

It didn't last long, because my mother was dying, and Theo had already let the door slam behind him.

It didn't last long, because back then I'd needed Marnie and her home and her family more than I needed Drew to smile at me.

But maybe it never entirely died, because Drew has always been special to me. Different than other guys.

That also makes him more dangerous.

Of course, he doesn't know what's going on in my head. "Strong isn't something you feel; strong is something you do." Then he laughs at little, ducking his head almost shyly. On reflex, I reach out and lift his jaw. "Shit, I basically just quoted *Star Wars*, didn't I? You sure you want to get it on with a nerd?"

I shift in his lap, straddling him on the chair, our faces inches apart, and the look in his eyes changes.

"Don't you dare talk badly about yourself," I say. "*Ever.*" Then, because this is all starting to feel too real, I add, "That's my job."

"Talk away, Ruiz," he says with a smile, his hand reaching under the baggy shirt to cup my hip, hot against my skin. His hands are large and capable, and I'm desperate for them to be all over me again, for him to quiet the voice in my head. "But I'd prefer it if you'd act."

"Does this mean we're going to use condom number two?" I say, rocking against his growing hardness.

He closes his eyes as if in pain—or very, very profuse pleasure—and says, "Hell, I really hope so."

———

It's late, and we're on the couch together, tucked up against each other on a blanket, Drew's arm around me. I feel content. I also feel like there are ants under my skin, lurking and waiting to eat me alive.

"Hey," he says, playing with a long piece of my hair, "what should we get Rafe and Sinclair for their housewarming party tomorrow? I wasn't going to get them anything, but Marnie told me I was being an idiot, and she's usually right about that kind of thing." Laughter rumbles from his chest, then he says, "We could get them a Fabgadget. Then again, that's not something you should do to a person you love." He gives me a sidelong grin. "We could always pick out a candle. You *do* have a thing for them. They could have their own signature scent like we do."

But I don't smile back because his words have brought those ants to the surface.

The party.

We.

He's going to expect us to go together, as a couple.

Part of me feels gooey inside at the thought—at the knowledge that he wants me in that way, because Andrew Jones is the best man I know. The best man there is. I've known that for a long time. I've put him on a pedestal, to be honest. He was the kind of man I could safely admire—the proof that not all men would take and take until you were spent and broken. But to keep him there on that pedestal I couldn't think of him *like that.* That's changed, obviously, and if we go to that party together, Marnie will know.

She acted like she couldn't fathom that I'd be interested in Drew.

"Let him down easy."

She's going to think I'll break his heart.

Maybe she'll pull away from me because of it. And what if this does go badly and I *do* hurt him?

I might lose both of them forever...

"I'm not ready for everyone to know," I say, pulling back slightly to look at him.

His eyes widen with a hurt look, and every part of me hates myself. "*Oh.*"

"I don't think it's a good idea for us to tell them yet, you know, before we know if it means something."

The hurt on his face vanishes, which might have been a relief if his entire expression hadn't shuttered.

"I see," he says flatly. "You're okay with fucking me, but only if it's our little secret."

"I didn't say it like that," I say, defensive. "Don't put words in my mouth."

"But you can put lies into mine?" He swears, getting up, and my heart lurches in my chest, because I'm the one who put distance between us. I did that, even if it was the last thing I wanted. "I don't like lying to my sisters. We promised we were going to tell each other the truth. That's important to me. Besides, Rafe and Griffin already know I'm interested."

"I know," I say. "But I'm only asking you to keep everything else to yourself for now. Until—"

He turns to me, his eyes flashing. "Yeah, I heard you. Until we know *if* it means something. Message received."

"It's only been one night," I snap, getting to my feet. "Aren't I allowed to be a little uncertain?"

One corner of his mouth tips up, but he's not the least bit amused. "Maybe it's only been one night for you."

My heart feels like it's swelling and contracting at the same time. I feel like my lungs can't get enough air, like everything is topsy turvy.

"We're having fun. Can't we take this one day at a time?"

"I thought we were doing more than having fun," he says, swallowing. "I thought we were starting something. But you're right, I didn't ask." He takes a step toward me, his eyes lit with an entreaty. "So this is me asking. Do you want to be with me, Andrea Ruiz? Because there's no question in my mind that I want to be with you."

Yes. *Yes.*

But my heart is pounding in a flight or fight response at the thought of Marnie knowing, of her disapproving. Of that look on her face.

"Let him down easy."

"I'm just asking for some time, Drew," I say through numb lips. "I don't think that's unreasonable. We can hang out at the house. Figure out the rest as we go along."

His face closes down again, a tiny furrow forming in his brow. "So you want to keep everything the way it was but fuck occasionally. Got it."

"Is there anything so wrong with that?" I ask, even though I know it's a stupid thing to say. Worse, I know I don't mean it.

"Who am I to complain?" he says, but his tone is cold. "You can fuck me whenever you want, Andy. If I feel something more, that's my own problem. Goodnight."

He walks off, leaving me standing there next to the couch. "Drew," I call, but I don't know what else to say, and I don't follow him.

When his door shuts behind him, I sit down on the couch and hug myself, but it doesn't feel the same as when he did it. I feel so desperately cold and alone. I tell myself that it's better like this—that we can't just jump in the deep end and pretend we don't need to breathe—but I don't really believe it.

I take out my phone, meaning to text Marnie, to tell her, but I can't get past the first word.

I can't lose her.

Because a little voice in my head whispers that I might already be losing him.

I text my grandmother instead.

Me: *Abuela, I miss you. Please let me come see you.*

DREW

IT'S EIGHT A.M., and I've gotten maybe two hours of sleep all night. I can still taste her. I can still feel her around me. The shape of her is imprinted on me, and I already know no one else will do. She doesn't feel the same way about me. I have to accept there's a chance she never will. As of last night, she was still interested in sleeping with me, which is one hell of a perk. But I know it'll never be enough for me, not with Andy, and I'm guessing that kind of arrangement wouldn't go on indefinitely.

Maybe I'll become a monk. Can monks masturbate? Use the computer?

I don't think I've ever heard of a monk video game designer.

Okay, maybe I don't want to be a monk. But I could give Andy the house. Burke might want to clear out of town after this mess with Leonard is over, because I know he meant it when he said he'd make his parents pay if they covered something up.

That thought makes my heart race. I've known the Burkes since I was a kid, and it's hard to imagine them capable of murder and a cover up. Then again, the reason I struggle to imagine it is because they're people who never wanted to get their hands dirty—with cooking, cleaning, gardening, you name it—not because they're too virtuous to have done awful things. My mother's a complete asshole, but I'd still be thrown if I found out she was a murderer. Burke must be in a mind storm.

I check my phone—no messages—then text him.

> You up, man?

Never slept.

> You still going to the office with Nicole and Damien later? Want me to come?

Hell, yes. I was hoping you'd ask. Come by in half an hour?

> I wouldn't say I'm looking forward to it, but yes.

That makes two of us.

Those three little dots appear, fluctuating. Finally, he asks,

What happened with Andy?

> I don't know what's going on with us. But I considered becoming a monk for about five minutes before I texted you.

That good, huh? Sorry, man. I hope it works out.

I tap my finger against the side of the phone.

> Yeah, me too.

I head downstairs to make some coffee.

The TV's on, and Andy's sitting under a pile of blankets on the couch, a huge travel cup of coffee in her hand. It's bright red, of course. She's still wearing the *Star Wars* T-shirt from last night. I can report that it's also still hot.

She meets my gaze, but I can't tell what she's thinking. My heart feels strangled. At the same time, she's here and that's something. "I made coffee," she tells me.

"Thank God," I say, heading into the kitchen to get some. "Tell me you didn't use the Fabgadget to grind it.

"Of course I did."

I pour some for myself, doctor it with cream, then head into the living room. I think for half a second before sitting beside her, close enough that we're touching. She instantly leans into me.

"I'm sorry," she whispers.

I set the coffee down, spotting the last condom on the table, and wrap my arm around her.

"You're sorry, but you still don't want to tell anyone."

She doesn't say anything, which really says it all.

Then I look at the screen and see what's playing—*Matchmaking Small Town America*.

"Are you watching this on streaming?" I ask, surprised.

"Missing Megan Fabulous?" she asks.

"Obviously." But my mind is working. I'm not an idiot. She told me her fantasy yesterday, and now she's sitting on the couch with this show playing, a throw blanket over her lap. Maybe it's a peace offering, but I can't help but make a more bitter interpretation— she's showing me what use she has for me.

Still. I'm not about to turn her down. I lean forward to get a sip of my coffee and grab the condom.

She watches me do it, and I see a glint of something in her eyes. It's enough to make my dick come to life—because I want her. I'll always want her.

Leaning back into the cushions, I reach for her and pull her onto my lap. She sighs and rocks back against me. I rock forward, and for a minute we just sit like that, pretending to watch the show as the single men are paraded out to meet the star. Or at least *I'm* pretending—my awareness is completely on her. On her scent, on the feeling of her hair against my shirt, on the curve of her ass in my lap.

I reach beneath the blanket and slide my hand under the elastic waistband of her underwear. I start playing with her, holding back a hiss when I feel how wet she is for me, how much she wants this. Neither of us acknowledge it as I slide my fingers into her.

"These guys are dumbasses," I say, my voice ragged as one of the contestants introduces himself with a slogan, rhyming lawyer with voyeur.

"Yeah," she responds, moving with my fingers. "He's the worst. Wait until—ah—you see the veterinarian who's afraid of dogs."

"You've seen this episode before?"

"Obviously," she says, grinding back against my dick. "I wouldn't want to miss anything."

I slide her underwear off and keep playing with her as the next asshole introduces himself.

By then, I'm so hard I can't take it anymore, so I slide her down next to me so I can take off my boxers and put on the condom. Andy's gaze is still on the screen, but I can feel her watching me from her peripheral vision, her hot regard seeping into me. I pick her up, and she reaches back to help guide me in. I hold her by the hips, easing her down slowly—the sweetest torture I can imagine—so she can adjust to me. A gasp escapes me when I'm all the way inside, because it's deeper from this angle.

"Oh my God," she whispers, almost like she didn't mean to, and then she starts grinding back against me as I thrust up into her. I keep one hand on her hip and let the other wander under her shirt to find her breasts, then down to her clit to make sure she's getting everything she needs from me. The blanket is tented over us, and someone on the TV is talking about RV camping, but every molecule in my body is attuned to every molecule in hers, to the feeling of her moving up and down on my dick.

Little sounds are escaping her, weaving around me, and I need to grind my teeth to keep from coming too soon. I want to give it all to her—everything she wants.

"That guy's the villain, huh?" I say as a blond dude with a shit-eating grin struts onto the screen. I bring both of my hands to her hips, lifting her and then slamming into her hard, and she leans her head back, making another of those sounds that I want to swallow. But I don't kiss her. She grinds down, taking me deeper, panting.

I lift her up again. "How'd...ah...you know?"

"It's the music," I say, thrusting hard. "They always use dramatic—"

But I can't talk anymore, because I feel her clenching around me, and I find her clit with my fingers again, needing to bring her all the way there. Needing to make her remember this. She grinds down again, taking me deeper, even as she clenches against me, her eyes squeezed shut with the sensation, her head thrown back, and I come hard, her name escaping my lips.

"Oh my God," she says, leaning back into me, my dick still buried inside of her. Her hands reach back to caress my face, my hair, and the feeling of longing inside of me is so strong it hurts. She leans back to kiss me, but I turn my face away.

I lift her up gently, then set her down again and go to the bathroom to clean up, stopping to pick up the jeans I left on the floor last night.

When I leave the bathroom, she's still sitting there on the couch, staring at the bathroom door with a look on her face that I can't interpret.

"I've got to go," I say, grabbing my keys from where I dropped them on the floor last night. "I'll see you here before the party."

"What about the candle?" she asks, her eyes going wide.

"I'll pick something up at the store on the way back."

"I'll pay for it."

I'd fight for the right, but I can't find it in myself to care. "Fine. You can Venmo me."

She calls my name before I reach the door. I turn to look at her, my heart seizing in my chest, because she looks undone, her hair down, wearing my *Star Wars* shirt, and if there's a more beautiful sight in the world, I don't want to see it—I'd like this to stay burned in my mind.

"You're mad at me," she says softly.

Yes.

But I can't tell her I'm angry because she doesn't love me. It's not on her to fix the feelings tearing me up inside. I'll need to figure out a way to contain them.

"No. I'll see you later, Andy."

I leave, and she doesn't come after me, not that I expected her to.

I feel like an asshole for leaving like this, but I also don't know how to stay right now, with everything boiling beneath my skin. I can't imagine being out in public with her and pretending she doesn't matter to me. It would feel like the worst kind of lie.

———

"So what exactly are we hoping to find?" I ask Nicole and Damien. "A smoking gun? A signed confession?"

"That would certainly make things easier," Damien says with a wry look. "But people are rarely so considerate in their criminal activities."

We're in Burke's parents' office. They share the front office at Burke Enterprises, overlooking the city. I feel like people are watching us, like they know what we're up to and we're going to get caught. But the security guard let Burke and his "clients" in without a moment's hesitation.

"Let's look on the bright side," Nicole says. "They might have a personnel file on Leonard. That would certainly make things easy on us."

It turns out that they do—there are his employment papers, the vague NDA, and also severance paperwork. That's of interest because he was given a two-million-dollar severance payout.

"Is that the norm around here?" Damien asks, raising his eyebrows. We're all standing around a circular table in the back of the gargantuan office—a little spot for taking meetings. Burke's been in here before for those meetings, and I spare a thought to what it must feel like for him to be in here now, for such a different purpose. He looks like a man who's had his world blown to pieces, and I know from the glimpse I got in the mirror earlier that I look no better. Damien and Nicole look like two people who have gotten plenty of sleep and the kind of sex you don't regret. Right now, regret is my middle name.

The party this afternoon is going to be hell. A hell lined with candles.

"If so, I'm going to get hired by these people just so I can get fired, if you know what I'm saying," Nicole says.

"No," Burke says, his face pinched. "We give good payouts, but that's definitely not the norm. Far from it."

He's probably thinking about that money Leonard got from him too. Two million and sixty-five thousand. It's the kind of money you could run with. Maybe he did run—and got away. Or maybe he only got as far as that river snaking through the woods. Maybe they gave him the money only to recollect it a few weeks later.

"How does this help us?" I ask.

"Well, it seems to confirm they gave him a payout, but I'm guessing only Leonard would tell us what it was for."

"He didn't seem inclined to tell us much of anything," Burke says bitterly. "I guess we didn't know him much at all."

"Maybe you did, and maybe you didn't," Damien says, rapping his knuckles against the desk. I watch as he takes out his phone and photographs the pages of the severance agreement. "People are complicated," he continues. "It would seem that he was more complicated than most."

"This is a dead end, isn't it?" I ask, suddenly exhausted. "Because if he's gone, we'll never know. We can't ask him."

Burke huffs out a laugh. "Too bad we don't know a real psychic."

"Don't discount us just yet," Damien says, tucking the papers back into the file. "We might be done *here*, but we're not done. Let's call a spade a spade. Leonard didn't tell you about this for obvious reasons, Burke."

Burke flinches, then nods. "He didn't know whether I'd be loyal to them."

"But that doesn't mean he didn't tell anyone."

Something in my gut twists, because I'd thought Leonard and I were close, but he didn't tell me either. Or Shane. Or Danny. I say as much.

"But you're all in a group circle jerk," Nicole says.

"What?" Burke asks, horrified.

"He knew you and Burke were best friends," she continues, undaunted. "And that you'd probably gossip over cookies and tea, or Jim Beam and Pop Tarts, or whatever it is you crazy kids like to do. So he didn't tell you four. But that doesn't mean he didn't tell anyone."

"I still don't think my parents would have done anything to hurt him," Burke says, rubbing his chest. "They...they're not nice people, but it's risky to do something like that. I don't think they would have taken the risk."

"Not even if it would save them from looking culpable for the collapse of that building?" Damien asks, studying him. "Because there are murder charges wrapped up in that too. Gross negligence. That's the kind of thing to make an empire fall, Burke. Did this guy have any friends beside you? Any family? Do you know where he came from? Because we haven't been able to find anyone who was related to this guy. I'm ninety percent sure Ashford wasn't the last name he was born with."

"What the hell?" I ask. "Why didn't you mention this before now?"

A corner of his mouth lifts. "For the same reason Leonard didn't spill his heart out to you. We needed to know that Burke was on our side first."

"I am," Burke mutters, then his back steels. "I am. I want to follow through with this. I want to find out what happened. I think I need to."

"What I'm saying is that he would have been easy to wipe out," Damien says, "especially if they knew what we did—that he was a man with layers of secrets, and if they took him out, no one was going to look too hard. Seems to me that he gave them the perfect excuse when he went on that camping trip. Maybe he was even trying to blow town and they caught up with him."

"So you *do* believe he's dead," I say flatly. Despite everything, I wanted to believe there was a chance that he might be around somewhere, even if it meant that he was the kind of asshole who let us believe the worst for years—who let me believe that I'd killed him.

He lifts his gaze to Burke, then shifts it to me. "Sorry, but I do."

"So my parents are murderers," Burke says flatly.

"I don't think they did it personally, no," Damien says.

"But they're probably killers whatever way you look at it, bub," Nicole says, giving him a pat on the back that doesn't look remotely comforting. "Because people died in that collapse. Now, who wants a beer? My treat."

"I need to go buy a scented candle," I say.

"How the fuck is this my life?" Burke asks mournfully, looking out the window.

I don't know why, but I start laughing.

I don't know why, but he joins me.

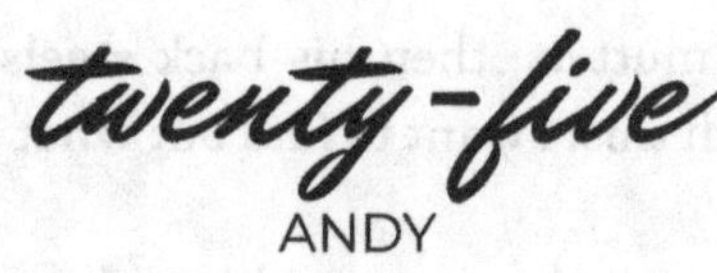

ANDY

AFTER DREW LEAVES, I get dressed and start cleaning the house, because I desperately need something to do. Marnie texted me, asking if I wanted to get coffee before Sinclair's party, but I don't think I can see her without telling her everything, and I wasn't going to tell her everything yet. Wasn't that the point of this fight Drew and I are having? I feel brittle, on the verge of breaking. I'm pissed at him. I'm pissed at myself. I'm—

I open the drawer of the table in the hallway and see that photo with the broken frame. That makes me feel like an asshole, too, because I'd told myself I'd fix it. Of course, Drew tucked it away, so it's sort of his fault—

And there I go again, blaming someone else for something I've done.

I pick at the glass, trying to get it out of the frame so I can throw it away, and I cut my finger. After I spew two dozen curse words, I get a Band-Aid and finish throwing out the loose glass. I look at the photo for a moment—Drew, so young and careless. My heart swells, and I also feel sick, because he certainly didn't look that way this morning. He looked...tortured. And it was because of me. I was supposed to do something nice for him, not make everything worse.

Sighing, I pull the photo out and then I see it, a tiny slip of paper tucked between the photo and the backing. There's a name on it: Roland Finneas. Beneath it, it says: *Just you.*

That's weird.

I mean, maybe Drew tucked it back there for safekeeping or something, but it's not in his handwriting, and I can't think why he'd want a name tucked behind the photo. Or that note. I know all of the guys in the image, and Roland isn't one of them. Honestly, it doesn't even sound like a real name, though it's familiar in some way I can't quite place.

Intuition prickles at me, and I text Drew.

> Did you buy the frame that photo is in?

> I mean, the one of you and Leonard and the guys?

> The candle should be doughnut shop scented or something like that. Rafe always gets your sister doughnuts.

It strikes me that they're probably not the sweetest texts I could send to the guy who fucked my fantasy into me this morning, but then again, he left immediately afterward. Practically without saying a word to me. And when I went to kiss him, he turned away.

Maybe he told himself he was giving me what I wanted, but it felt like a punishment.

I can't help but think it was meant to, which pisses me off, because I was telling him what I needed—space to figure this out, just the two of us—and communication is supposed to be a *good* thing. I wasn't rejecting him. I wouldn't. I may be scared about what's happening, but I care about him deeply. I—

I hate that this morning was the hottest experience of my life and there's a dark cloud hanging over it.

I look up the name on my phone, but nothing comes up. Nothing that's a person, anyway. So Ole Roland is unlisted. Or nonexistent.

The name still sounds fake to me. I do a search on social media too. Nada. Or at least there aren't any direct fits.

Shrugging, I gather my stuff and head off to the store to get a replacement frame. I set the photo out where it was before, because I fixed it and it seems stupid to tuck it away again, and I put the little piece of paper from the back on the refrigerator with a magnet. It's only just past noon, and the housewarming party isn't due to start until eight.

That's eight hours with nothing to fill them.

I sit down with a book, but I keep reading the same page over and over again, thinking about the way Drew looked at me from the door. He said he wasn't mad, but he obviously was, and now I'm mad, although I'm not sure who I'm pissed at. Him? Myself? Marnie, for having an irresistible brother who's annoying and adorable and *everything*?

My phone rings, and I hate myself for how fast I pick it up. It's a number I don't recognize. Usually, I don't answer unknown calls, but it could be from my grandmother's nurse, a thought that makes my heart flutter. I pick it up.

"Hello?"

"Andy?"

I recognize his voice at once. It's Jack, otherwise known as Thing Two. I blocked both his number and Theo's after they torched my life, so he must be using someone else's phone.

"What do you want?" I ask, hating the stab of anguish I feel. My feelings are all so close to the surface, enough that a scratch will bring them welling up like blood. Drew called me strong, but would someone who's strong feel like this?

Would someone who's strong let her brothers walk all over her because she's afraid of losing the last bit of family she has left?

"I wanted to check on you," he says. I can't tell whether he means it. "I've been worried."

My middle brother used to save me the last of the ice cream, and one time he picked a flower for me because I'd skinned my knee. It was a flower from a rich asshole's yard, and we had to go running, but the gesture was sweet all the same. He used to act like he was my brother. There's a terrible temptation to believe he wants to be my brother again, and it infuriates me.

"Worried, Jack? Why would you be *worried?* Because you and Theo convinced *Abuela* to throw me out? Because you knew I didn't have a job or anywhere to live? Where was your worry weeks ago?"

"I knew you'd be okay," he says sheepishly. "You're more like *Abuela* than Mom. Theo shouldn't have done that, though. It was a shit move, and I told him so."

"So why didn't you stop him?" I ask, almost shouting now. Blood is pounding in my ears.

"He could get me fired," he snaps. "They don't know about my record at work. I'd lose everything."

"Did you ever stop to think that you might deserve to?"

There's a pause, and when he speaks again, there's no warmth in his voice. "I should have known better than to expect you to understand. You're always so self-righteous. On your high horse. Queen Andy, who knows better than the rest of us."

I take a second to consider whether that's true, then I hand him his ass. "It's convenient to think so, isn't it, you spineless piece of shit? You're so far up Theo's ass you don't remember what fresh air feels like."

"Where have you been staying?" he blurts, and I get a sense of uneasiness. Why isn't he arguing back? Why does he suddenly want to know where I'm staying?

My mind shifts to Nicole taking those photos. To the texts I received from the director of the daycare. Does Theo think I'm behind all of it? It's obvious the principal's in his pocket, so I'm sure he shared his little theory with my brother.

Is Theo trying to get even?

But what would he do? He's already taken my grandmother from me...

"Still doing his errands? What does he want to do? Spank me? Take away my candy?"

"He wants to talk to you, Andy. We both do. But you've blocked his number."

"And yours," I say, hating myself a little for it. It makes me feel weak. "And yet, here you are, calling me. Why didn't he do it himself?"

"He doesn't like jumping through hoops," he says, sounding annoyed by it, because here he is, jumping through Theo's hoops for him. "I...I think you should call him, Andy. Talk him down."

Our mother always did that—talked Theo through his rages. It obviously didn't do much good.

"Go fuck yourself, Jack," I say, and hang up the phone.

It instantly rings again, but I'm quite happy to have had the last word. I'm not giving it to him. Still, the thought of Theo having it out for me sends a chill down my back. I don't want to be alone right now, especially not in this house.

I text Marnie:

> Can I come over? It's been a shitty day.

> Duh. I've been trying to get you to make a coffee date with me. COME PLAY. Griffin's taking the night off work, but he's there right now. I've been watching a terrible romcom on Zoom with Gracie. Sinclair's off preparing for this party like it's a wedding. We asked you to join us, but you didn't respond.

Huh, I didn't even see that. I'm a mess.

I reply,

> I'm coming, but first there's something I need to do.

I look up the photos Nicole sent me and put them in an email to Theo's boss, whose email address is conveniently located online.

I look for my laptop, since it'll be easier to do what I need to do on a computer, but it refuses to turn on. Fabulous. So I turn on Drew's computer, smiling when I see that he's been working on the fire in the game. It looks like it would burn.

Then I minimize it, set up a dummy email account, and send the photos to Theo's boss without further explanation, because, really, no further explanation is necessary. My brother is an asshole. He was born an asshole, probably. I'll bet he bit my mother every single time he nursed.

I don't feel any remorse when I hit the send button, but it occurs to me that Theo might be more of a problem than I gave him credit for. I'll tell Drew about him tonight.

If he comes back.

He'll come back, dumbass, it's his house, I tell myself. But there's a creeping sense of uneasiness that hugs itself around me. Maybe it's a dangerous game I've been playing. At least I took Damien's advice and did it anonymously, though it's a bit of a tip-off that I pulled the trigger immediately after Jack's call.

Well, shit. Should have thought that one through, Ruiz.

But what's done is done, and I can't bring myself to regret it. Nicole was right—I'm only telling the truth. If they fall into a grave, it's one they dug together.

My phone buzzes, and I see a reply from Drew.

It's a photo of a doughnut-scented candle.

Another message pops up:

Don't worry about replacing the frame.

Well, too late for that.

I send a photo of the picture frame.

He sends back the laughter emoji, and that's that.

227

Fine.

I want to tell him about Jack's call, but it can wait. Theo and Jack obviously don't know where I'm staying, and even if they somehow manage to figure it out, I won't be here.

But I do text Nicole to let her know I've sent the photos.

She responds:

Finally. I knew your inner badass would wake up.
We're out drinking. Want to come?

She sends a photo, and there's a squeezing sensation in my chest because he's there in the photo, laughing, but he didn't say anything. He certainly didn't invite me.

So I respond that I have plans and leave for Marnie's new apartment.

———

I told myself I'd tell Marnie everything if the opportunity arose. But the movie ends, and I can't bring myself to bring it up. Instead, I turn the conversation toward Grace and what's been going on in New York. I do tell them about my brothers, and they're appropriately pissed off and disgusted on my behalf.

"Have you told Drew?" Marnie asks me, looking worried. "He should know about this. Maybe he can set up an alarm system."

"He doesn't need to do that for me," I say, scowling, trying to tell myself that even though she brought him up, this still isn't the opening I was looking for. "He's already done enough. He won't even accept rent money."

Marnie's eyebrows wing up. "Really? So what are you paying him in?" She says this with the confidence of someone who knows me well enough to know I'd have found a way to pay him in something. Or at least that's what I would have done with anyone else. With Drew, it's been seductively easy to accept favors.

"Empanadas and unsolicited advice," I say, my tone a little short. I want to tell her; I can't *bear* to tell her.

"Have you two been arguing?" she asks.

"Something like that, but it's nothing you need to worry about."

"You know," Grace says, beaming at us through the computer screen, "you're going to say it's the romantic in me, but I've always sensed some *will they or won't they* chemistry between you two."

I'm torn between the desire to slam the lid of the laptop shut and draw her into a big hug the next time I see her.

"Drew and Andy?" Marnie asks.

"We have the same name," I say glibly, "it would never work out."

"Different by one letter," Grace points out.

Marnie studies me, her bottom lip pressed slightly farther out than the top. "I don't know," she finally says. "Maybe you have a point. They *are* always bickering. I thought it was kind of like the way Drew and I always bicker, but maybe I was reading the room wrong."

It's probably the perfect opportunity to tell her, and maybe I would have if Drew hadn't walked out on me this morning. It threw me into this tailspin that I hate. I detest that I've spent all day trying to interpret his behavior, trying to figure out how to please him. Isn't this exactly what my grandmother warned me about? Even now, all I can think about is where he is and what he's doing. It's like a sickness.

So I change the subject to Sinclair's party. We segue into a discussion of the made-for-TV movie she's going to be filming soon, at an estate in Asheville, and then what book we should pretend to read for our next book club. It's so good to talk to them, even though Grace is hundreds of miles away, that for a while I almost forget the turbulent feelings pinging through me.

I go home at seven to change.

Drew's sitting at his computer, his headphones on and that damn fire on the screen. A gift bag sits beside him.

I hate the relief that flows through my veins, so I'm already pissed as I stalk in, shutting the door hard behind me.

He doesn't even turn in my direction.

"Hello," I say—or maybe shout—and he flinches so hard he almost falls out of his chair.

He takes his headphones off and presses a hand to his chest. "Jesus Christ, you almost gave me a heart attack. I didn't hear you come in."

Okay, so he's obviously being truthful about that. He puts out a hand as if to reach for me, but then scratches his head.

"Where were you all day?" I ask, hating that it sounds like an accusation.

He lifts his eyebrows. "I was with Burke, Nicole, and Damien. I thought you knew. Nicole said she invited you out for drinks."

"Why didn't *you* invite me?"

An annoyed huff escapes him. "Because I didn't think you'd want to come. You made it clear that you don't want anyone knowing we're involved."

"She already knows."

He gets up, his chair spinning out a little behind him. "Sorry, Ruiz, I'm having trouble keeping up. I guess you're going to have to make a list of who I can and can't tell. Maybe we can make an app so it feels like a game."

"It's not like that." I cross my arms over my chest.

"Then what's it like? Do I only have to lie to my sisters?"

"You're being a jerk."

His eyebrows lift again. "Is this where I get to say *I know what you are but what am I?*"

"You know, I had a really shitty day. I don't need this."

"So did I," he says, running a hand back through his hair. "But you didn't ask me about that. You came in here hot, accusing me of not including you after you told me you don't want me anywhere near you outside of this house."

"Maybe I don't want you near me inside of the house either," I snap.

Hurt radiates across his face, moving outward from his eyes, like a lake after a stone's been skipped through it, and I feel awful. Raw and terrible. Because I finally admitted to myself that my brothers were lost to me and should be. Because I feel Drew slipping away, and even though it's my own doing, it's tearing me up.

Because I want him more than I've ever wanted anyone, and I don't want to want anyone like that.

"Okay," he says, his hands flexing at his sides. "If that's what you want, I'll get out of your way." Then he grabs the candle bag and walks off. I'm staring numbly at his screen, at the fire flickering on it, feeling like it's burning me up inside, when I hear the front door shutting.

Wait. What the fuck? Did he just leave for the party without me? I run to the door and open it, but he's already driving away.

twenty-six
DREW

I DON'T KNOW what I'm doing. I've missed Andy all day. I've wanted to see her, touch her, soak her in. I got that candle just to please her, because I'm pretty damn sure Sinclair isn't going to use it. And when she came in, it felt I'd found something missing. Still. I don't know how to be with her anymore. I wanted to pull her onto my lap, to kiss her. But wouldn't that just make it harder if we have to walk into my sister's party and act like we're nothing to each other but accidental roommates?

Except maybe that's true now. I might not be a player like Burke, but I know that women generally don't approve of being walked out on. It was a shit move. I'm still mad, but I think I'm even more pissed at myself for handling all of this so poorly. It's just...I've never felt like this about anyone. She makes me want to pound my fists in cement—and also get on my knees to worship her. Add in the heavy shit we found today in the office, and I'm not myself. I'm revved up but with nowhere to channel the energy.

I'm a mess.

I park outside of the building and get out, sweating even though today's temperature is cooler than yesterday. I'm a hot mess, and the first thing my sister says when she opens the door to her penthouse apartment is "What's wrong?"

What isn't wrong?

She's decked out in a fancy, silky dress, the kind that could comfortably be called a gown, and it occurs to me that I'm under-dressed. I took a shower and got changed when I got home, but I'm just wearing a white T-shirt and jeans. It didn't occur to me that the party would have a dress code. Just one more thing I've gotten wrong with the women in my life.

I stalk inside and thrust the gift bag at her. "It's a candle. Don't burn the apartment down."

She grabs the bag without looking at it, and I close the door behind me. Without commentary, she sets the bag down on the coffee table and leads me to a cauldron full of some sort of juice that hopefully has a shit ton of alcohol in it. If Rafe hadn't warned me about the cauldron, I probably still wouldn't have asked questions. It honestly feels irrelevant right now.

I start pacing as she fills a glass and then hands it over.

"What's in it?" I ask. *What is it?* would also be a relevant question, but right now all I want to know is whether it's alcoholic.

She lifts her eyebrows. "Do you care?"

I take a gulp. It tastes like a kid's juice box, but there's a burn at the end. Good.

"What the hell happened?" she presses. "You're not yourself."

"I'm not," I admit. My mind shifts to Andy, to the look on her face right before I left the house. She seemed contemptuous, tired of me. Leave it to me to ruin things with the woman of my dreams in a single day. I take another gulp of the drink. "I did something stupid. Maybe several stupid things."

I finish the drink, even though I'm not altogether sure I like it, and go in for a refresh.

"You're kind of concerning me right now," my sister says slowly.

She nods toward the leather couch, and I follow her to it and sit down with the drink. I look around for Rafe, but he must be in the bedroom or office. It hits me that he's planning to propose tonight, and here I am, bringing my baggage over to their party. Dammit. I shouldn't have come. I felt drawn here, though. Part of me needed Sinclair and Marnie tonight. I can't tell them what's going on, at least not all of it, but I can at least be with them. There's some comfort in that.

Maybe Andy needs them too, you dick.

I feel guilty. Ashamed. But those are familiar feelings, and they're almost welcome. I understand them, and there's a comfort in that, especially right now when everything in my life feels out of grasp.

I take another gulp.

"Drew?" Sinclair's staring at me.

"There's some shit going down with Burke and his parents, and now…"

"But the stupid thing you did involves Andy," she says, giving me a sidelong look.

Sinclair used to go out of her way to appear vapid—to smile too broadly, laugh too loudly—but there's nothing vapid about her. She's good at reading people, and it's obvious she's reading me like a book.

I'm her big brother; I'm supposed to take care of her.

That's another duty I've failed at. I let an estrangement form between us because I didn't understand what she was going through with our mother.

Our mom had never taken an interest in me. It took me a while to realize it, but her complete indifference to my existence was the best thing that could have happened to me. Because she used my sister as her Sim—living the life she'd wanted and thought she was owed through Sinclair. Manipulating her into making the same choices she would have made. I should have saved her from that. I failed Sinclair again after she came home to Asheville. She had a stalker, and the asshole attacked her right beneath my nose. If Rafe hadn't been with her, things might have gone down very differently.

I take another gulp of the drink, which is starting to taste pretty damn good. Then I set the cup down and turn to face my sister.

"She—"

The front door is flung open.

My first reaction is to get to my feet and try to get in front of Sinclair, and her flinch says I'm not alone in my fear. It's not like my sister to leave the door unlocked, not after everything she's been through, but she was focused on me.

Then Andy stalks in, and suddenly nothing else exists. She looks like an enraged goddess in a red and orange sundress, her gorgeous hair cascading down her back. I want to go to her. I want to leave.

"You left without me," she accuses.

"I'm sure it was a misunderstanding," my sister says, coming to stand beside me. But she's definitely rolling out her acting skills, because we all know it was no misunderstanding—and also that Andy probably wants to stab me with a kitchen knife.

I hear something behind me, and a quick backward glance tells me it's Rafe. He gives me a short nod, but it's obvious he overheard us and is wondering what I did this time.

I look back and Andy's still staring at me, her eyes full of fire. She points at the candle bag on the table. "Oh, so he took all the credit for the candle?"

"For God's sake," I say, annoyed again. Because who cares about the candle? "I was going to tell her you helped me." I grab my drink off the table and gulp some of it. I know I should talk to her—I *need* to talk to her—but I can't ruin my sister's party, and I also don't know what to say. She set a line in the sand again, as is her right, and I can't stay on my side.

Reggie makes what is probably the most well-timed entrance of his life with my aunt Helen. They're carrying a tower of Tupperware for some damn reason.

There's some back and forth over the Tupperware, but it's a buzz in the background of my mind. I watch as Andy takes a seat by the bar, and she's watching me too—in a way that makes it very clear she won't be climbing into my bed tonight.

Maybe it's better that way. Maybe I'm an idiot, but I don't think I can walk the middle line with her.

"Hey, how'd the beard work out for you, son?" Reggie asks, nudging my arm as he settles onto the couch. My aunt is humming as she goes through the various pieces of Tupperware.

"Have you noticed the way she's looking at me?" I mutter.

He glances across the room, not bothering to be subtle, not that I'd expect otherwise. He grunts and claps me on the shoulder. "Could go either way, buddy. A woman who's worked up like that might just throw you onto a bed and work out her anger in a fun way. Or you could wind up with a knife in your back. Either way, you're going to have an interesting time."

"Thanks, as always," I say with a sigh, fully aware that she could probably hear every word he said. It's a big apartment, but Reggie has a booming voice, and there isn't exactly a crowd yet.

My aunt joins us, planting herself in Reggie's lap, which might have made me uncomfortable if I weren't so used to both of them.

"I've heard about your troubles, dear," she tells me.

Of course she did.

"Have you tried an attraction spell?"

"I don't want to fool her into loving me," I say bitterly.

"You'll want to focus on getting physical before taking the next step," Reggie says. "See if you're sexually on the same page. Because some people have kinks that might not be compatible, you know? This one woman I knew liked the somno-sleep thing. You know. Like Sleeping Beauty. She wanted—"

I down what's left of the drink. All the while, I can feel Andy staring at me with contempt.

Rafe and Sinclair come back over, having carried on a whispered conversation that was probably about me and Andy, and settle onto the loveseat across from us.

"Hey, Dad," Rafe says. "Can you tell us more about working as a set photographer on the set for *Star Wars*? Drew has questions."

He's obviously going for a distraction, not that I blame him, and I'm more than happy to be distracted by this particular topic. When Reggie first told us about having that particular gig, no one believed him, but we'd learned his big fish story was true. I could listen to him talk about it for hours.

Still, I *feel* Andy.

Marnie and Griffin show up, and the turbulent feelings inside of me amp up. I miss my little sister. I want to tell her about everything I've been going through—the way we used to talk to each other—but Andy asked me not to, and she's already so mad at me. So I tell Marnie that Nicole and Damien have found some evidence tying Burke's parents to Leonard's disappearance and leave it at that.

By the time Shauna shows up, I'm feeling the burn of the alcohol more than the sweetness of the fruit juice.

I amble over and give her a hug. She hugs me back and pats me on the back before I pull away.

"Thanks for lending your grandparents to Mrs. Ruiz," I say. "She tolerated them, which means she likes them."

"Oof," she says, releasing me. "What the hell have you been drinking, and where can I get some?"

I point to the cauldron. "It's in a cauldron. I don't think we're supposed to ask why."

"Yeah, you're smashed. I definitely need some of the mystery cauldron drink."

"Rough day?" I ask, scratching the back of my head. There's a weird feeling there, and I when I look across the room, I see Andy glaring at me again. I give her a salute. She shoots me the bird.

"Looks like *you're* having a rough day," Shauna says with a half-smile. "That the roommate you're not in love with?"

"Oh, I'm *definitely* in love with her." I sigh. "Sorry."

"It's okay." She nudges my shoulder. "I think I'll eventually get over our one and only date. You know, twenty years or so from now, after the mourning period is over."

"I don't know," I say. "I think you could get over me in ten years if you set your mind to it."

She laughs again. "Maybe so, but I'm not sure *she* will."

Then she pats me on the back and walks away, presumably to get that drink.

I'm not surprised when Griffin and Rafe pull me out onto the balcony later on. I'm on my fifth or maybe sixth juice box drink. It tastes like nothing at this point. Glorious nothing.

"What the fuck is going on with you?" Rafe asks.

"To the point. I appreciate that."

"Something happened with Andy," Griffin says. "Obviously. But why does she look like she wants to kill you?"

"I think she's upset because I left for the party without her."

Rafe laughs and gives me a *buddy, you fucked up* look, which isn't really an improvement on his *buddy, you're fucked* looks.

"I'm in love with her," I admit. In alcoholic juice boxes, in veritas, I guess. "But if there's going to be anything between us, she says it has to be a secret." I wave the glass through the air and nearly lose a slosh of the good stuff. "Which is kind of dumb, to be honest, since half the people we know already know. It just means I have to keep it from Marnie, who already knows about Mrs. Ruiz's house, so now she thinks I have a hopeless crush on her friend. And I want Andy. I want her so badly, but I don't think I can do it, you know?"

Rafe whistles.

"Have you told her all of this?" Griffin asks, pinning me with a look.

Reggie opens the sliding glass door and joins us. "We talking about the young buck's romance, again? You never did tell me how that beard worked out for you."

Rafe claps him on the back. "You were instrumental in getting him laid, Dad. Now, keep going, Drew."

"No," I say, feeling a cold grip on my chest even though it's warm out here. "No, I haven't told her. Typically, you don't tell someone you love them after they've said they'd like to keep you as a secret until they're sure 'there's something there.'"

"Keep sexing her up, champ," Reggie says, cackling. "You give it to her good enough, she'll want to tell all of her friends. They always do."

I give him a flat look. "Again, Reggie, we're talking about my sisters."

Rafe coughs, or maybe cough-laughs. Then he says, "Look, Drew. I went through something similar with your sister in the beginning. When you love a woman, you want to be open about it. To let everyone know that she's yours and you're hers. That's not the kind of secret you want to keep. So tell her you can't do it, but don't be a dick about it. That kind of attitude isn't going to get you anywhere."

"I know," I say, because do I ever. "I just couldn't..." I trail off, because it suddenly feels like there's a whole sea of things I can't do: tell my boss that no one wants to stare at clown zombies—and if they do, they won't give a shit what their hair looks like; be there for the woman I love in the way she's asking me to be.

Griffin gives me a long look, like he's trying to see my mixed-up thoughts. "You want me to take you home, man? You're not looking steady on your feet."

He's a bartender, so he knows when someone's had one too many. Or several too many.

"You can stay at our place if you want," he continues.

"Imma go say goodbye to Sinclair," I say. Because leaving sounds pretty good right now. "But you don't have to go, Griffin. They invented Uber for drunk assholes. I'll go stay the night at Burke's. He's probably a drunk asshole right now too."

Turning to Rafe, I say, "Good luck man. I'm happy for you...and for me. I don't know how I got lucky enough for my sisters to end up marrying two guys I'm happy to call friends."

"He's definitely drunk," Reggie comments. "That right there is three-sheets-to-the-wind talk."

Meanwhile, Rafe is giving me what could best be called a fondly tolerant look, the reason for which becomes obvious after Griffin says, "Wait a minute...you're asking Sinclair to marry you tonight?"

There I go again.

They let me go without putting up a fight, and I stop by the punch cauldron to refill my drink before finding Sinclair. She instantly pulls me into the hallway.

"Should you be drinking that?" she asks, frowning at my drink.

"It's not that bad," I say. "You've gotten much better at making mixed drinks." Then a hiccup escapes me, and I realize that she was referring to the quantity I've drunk, not the quality of the drink—and also that I am very drunk. I set it down on a table, then realize it's actually a potted plant. Fantastic.

"What happened with Andy?" Sinclair asks.

Then, as if she has a sonar for conversations that aren't supposed to be happening, Marnie walks over from around the corner. "Are you guys talking about what's going on between him and Andy?"

I feel cornered. Trapped. Because I actually *do* want to tell them, but I can't.

"Nothing's going on," I say, making a dismissive gesture, although it probably looks more like I'm warding off attacking birds. "Can you just let it drop? I didn't want her to move in in the first place, and now she's here, and we're dealing with it. So whatever."

I follow it up with a hiccup.

Of course, that's when Andy rounds the corner from the bathroom. Her eyes are glassy, and the possibility that I might have made her cry feels like a stab to the abdomen. "You may come off as sweet and harmless, Andrew Jones, but you're a fucking asshole."

She storms out of the apartment, and I start following her instantly, a magnet drawn to metal, a dying ember drawn to a flame, but I'm most definitely not walking in a straight line. Damn those juice boxes. Damn my big mouth.

"Don't drive!" my sisters yell after me, as if I'm in any condition to think about it.

The elevator's going down by the time I get to it, so I make the questionable decision to stagger down the stairs. I fall down the last two steps and hit my head on the door, the knob clocking me right in the eye, but I shake it off and step out into the balmy night.

"Andy," I shout, catching sight of her getting into her car, a flash of red dress and dark hair.

I feel like Marlon Brandon—or was it Brando?—in that movie, calling for Stella. That's the only part I remember, other than that he was a dick too, so it's probably a good comparison.

"Andy," I call again, but she only hesitates for a second before she drives away.

I sit on the curb, feeling like a dumbass. A waste of space. A mistake. Wouldn't it have been better to have her on her terms if that's the only way I can have her?

I pull up the Uber app, but before I can even find it on my phone —why do I have so many "u" apps?—Damien's car pulls up at the curb.

"Get in," Nicole says, leaning over Damien.

"Are you going to kill me?" I ask, hiccuping.

"No," she answers, "but if you play your cards right, I might give you a hangover cure that'll make you wish you were dead."

"Pass."

"We'll bring you home or wherever you want to go," Damien says, hugging her to his chest. "We were going to stop by to say hey to everyone, but we saw you out here."

"And took pity on you," Nicole adds.

"Do you always feel the need to say something shitty when you're doing something nice?" I ask.

"Yes," Damien answers for her. "Now, get in."

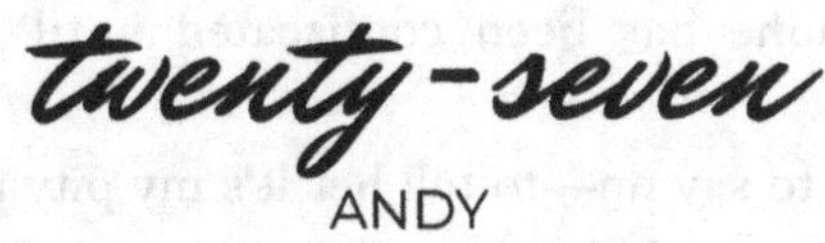

ANDY

I LEFT the party an hour ago—an hour I've spent sobbing on the couch while pretending to myself I'm watching TV. It's all there, all raw. Watching Drew hug Shauna, knowing that she *liked* him and probably still likes him. She's pretty, and I'm guessing *she* wouldn't hesitate to tell people about them. Then, of course, there's my grandmother's refusal to answer my messages and my brothers' dickery. I'm pissed at myself for crying, but in a weird way it feels good—a release of something that's been festering.

I'm roused from my pity party by a knock on the door. For a split second, I'm worried it's the police and something has happened to Drew. He's not dumb enough to drive drunk, especially not *that* drunk, but maybe he, like, stumbled into the road and somebody hit him. What if he had one of those Darwin Award accidents and, like, fell into an open manhole because he was too drunk to distinguish the difference between the pavement and the gaping hole in the ground?

So my heart's beating fast as I look through the peephole. It's Marnie, though, and now my heart is beating fast for a different reason. She's alone, or at least I don't see anyone else with her. Shit. She looks serious, so maybe something *did* happen to him.

I throw the door open. "Is he okay?"

She cocks her head. "Huh?"

"Drew, is he okay?"

Her eyes get wide. "Oh, yes! Shit. I'm sorry. Yes, he's fine. Damien gave him a ride to his friend Burke's place to sleep it off. I'm told his phone has been confiscated until morning. Can I come in?"

I'm tempted to say no—to tell her it's my pity party, thank you very much—but it would be absurd to tell her she's not welcome in the house she owns half of, the house she grew up in and belongs so much more to her than it ever could to me. Except...as I look around, I have to admit that's not totally true. This place has become mine, too, mine and Drew's. Our stuff is mingled together, the neutral zone blasted apart.

He did that for me.

Marnie takes my arm like I'm a kid from the daycare and leads me to the couch. I sit. She sits in the chair next to me, facing me.

"First off, you should know that I've asked Nicole and Damien to keep someone outside to keep an eye on you. I didn't like the thought of you being here alone after that call from Jack, and I'm guessing you didn't tell anyone else about it."

Guilty as charged.

"To be honest, I wasn't even thinking about it, Marnie."

"It's also come to my attention that my brother's in love with you," she says slowly, watching me. "How do you feel about that?"

And, just like that, I start crying again. The only other time I cried this much was after my mom died. I didn't like it then, and I don't like it now.

Marnie doesn't say anything at first. She just climbs onto the couch, kicks off her shoes, and curls up next to me. My mind flashes back to when we were teenagers, sitting exactly like this—on the same couch, even. It was a couple of days after my mom's funeral, and Marnie was comforting me.

Drew found us like that. He brought us ice cream, like he did for me the other day.

The thought only makes me cry harder. He's acted like a dick all day, but that doesn't mean he *is* a dick. He's in pain, and it's mostly because of what I said to him. I made him feel unwanted, and I've felt that way often enough within my own family to know it's an awful sensation. The stupid thing is that it's not remotely true. I want him so much it hurts.

"I...I think I'm in love with him too. I'm sorry. I've tried not to be."

She laughs, then tries to pretend she's not laughing, probably because that's a thing people think you're not supposed to do while someone is crying. But it instantly makes me feel better. "I'm glad you didn't succeed," she says, taking my hand and squeezing it. "You know, when we were kids, I used to daydream that you'd be with Drew, and I'd date Jack, and then we could be sisters all the way."

I shove her with our connected hands. "Goddammit, Marnie. I just stopped crying. What, do you have a thing for my tears?"

"Yes," she jokes. "I want to bottle them to prove to people—including you—that you can cry."

I manage a half smile, then nudge her again. "Man, you used to have shit taste in men if you wanted to get it on with Jack."

She smiles back. "What were my options? Theo's scary."

"If you feel that way, then why'd you tell me to let Drew down easy the other day?"

"Because I didn't think you liked him like that. You hadn't said anything, and you're usually not shy about the people you're dating. In fact, in the past, you could have been accused of offering too much information."

"He's your brother," I say, and then, because that's not a full explanation, "He's different for me." I pause, thinking, then add, "I don't always like it. It makes me feel out of control. You know, my mother always did so much for the men in her life, including my shit brothers, and she never got anything back. My grandmother told me that was what it was like when you loved a man too much."

"No offense, but that's super shitty advice."

A surprised laugh escapes me. "But it's true. I want to do things for him. Not even sexual things. I want to, like, make him food and listen to his problems. It's kind of disgusting."

"But I'm guessing he does things for you too. Hell, you and I do shit for each other all the time. Is that dysfunctional? Just because he's a man doesn't mean he's incapable of being in a give-and-take relationship. I mean, Drew's the best brother I've ever had."

I give her a *he's your only brother* look, and she obviously gets it because she nods and says, "Fair point. But even if I had ten, he'd still be my favorite. He's thoughtful. And kind. And he's the best person you could possibly have in your court. He'd never let someone mess with the people he loves."

She's right.

I know she's right.

"I'm still scared," I admit. "I've never felt this way about anyone. It's a lot."

"It's okay to be scared," she says, nuzzling her head into my shoulder. "*I'm* scared. I mean, hell, I'm getting married. Sinclair too, by the way."

"Wait, what?" I say, turning toward her. "Did I miss that?"

She nods. "But it's okay. They kicked us out immediately after announcing it, and I'm assuming they're having athletic sex right about now."

"I like Rafe," I say. "They're good together."

She gives me a significant look.

"You've never seen Drew and me together."

She gives me a *pointed* look.

"Okay, so you've seen us together roughly a million times over the past several years, but never like that."

"No, but I've thought about this a lot. Grace was right. There's always been...something. I mean, I love him, and he's everything. But he started hanging around whenever you came over. He always wanted to be there, and you didn't seem to mind. Maybe I didn't see it because it was too close to my face. I'm told that's a thing."

"It's like I made you need reading glasses."

"Yes, and you should blame yourself forever for that." She nudges me. "As for being freaked out...being in love is scary. I mean, what if Griffin and I randomly start hating each other one year in? Or maybe he'll start wearing those toe socks. I couldn't possibly be intimate with a man who loves toe socks. And look at Sinclair! She's marrying Rafe despite knowing that he might turn into Reggie one day. That's true love for you." She pauses. "Why didn't you tell me, Andy?"

"I didn't want anything to change with us. I didn't want... If things didn't work out, I didn't want to lose you." *Or him.*

She turns so she's facing me. "You could never lose me, Andy. I'm sorry to report that you're stuck with me. If you break his heart, I'm going to be pissed at you, obviously. He's my brother, and I'm unreasonably fond of him, but you don't get to quit me that easily. I'd forgive you. You're my family, you dum-dum. You're stuck with me, and that's forever."

And goddammit if I don't find more tears inside of me. Apparently there's a never-ending well of them in there, stuck down deep. Because here I was thinking I'd lost my family, but I was wrong.

"I love you," I tell her, hugging her and burying my head into her hair.

"And I love you. So you want to bone my brother, huh? I get it. We're an abnormally hot family."

I laugh, still hugging her. "Do you want to watch terrible movies all night and pretend we're teenagers?"

She pulls away slightly, grinning at me. "Abso-effing-lutely. But I'm telling you here and now, as much as I love you and Drew, I do not want to hear about weird sex things involving my brother. That's a no from me."

"Do I at least get to tell you that he has a super impressive—"

She's covering her ears and loudly humming, and genuine laughter bubbles up in me. I feel so much lighter. So much more joyful. It's only now that I realize how much I was dreading her reaction. I pull her hands off her ears. "Deal. Now, go get the ice cream."

She gets up, and I wipe at my face with my sex blanket, which I have laundered, thank you very much. Still, I fold it up and put it in the basket by the couch, choosing a different one.

Marnie comes out with the pint of ice cream and a couple of spoons, an amused look on her face. "Are Drew and the guys playing one of their games again?"

"D&D, you mean?" I ask, taking a spoon. "Sounds like they've never stopped. They're pretty adorable about it, although don't tell him I said so."

"No, I meant their language," she says as she sets the ice cream down on the side table. "That fantasy language they made up."

I instantly want to razz him about it. When—*if*, I correct—we're on better footing. "They made up a fantasy language?"

"Yeah, but that word on the fridge is the only one I'd recognize. It's their code word. When they say it to each other, they're supposed to all fall in line. Some shit like that. I haven't heard them talk about it for years."

The fridge. That paper.

"What word are you talking about, Marnie?" I ask fervently.

She tilts her head, probably wondering about my sudden enthusiasm for fantasy languages. "Finneas. I think it means truth or something like that..." Her eyes get a far-off look and then she lifts a finger in the air. "Duty."

I'm already taking out my phone and pulling up the search app. There are matches for Roland Duty, not a lot, but some. So maybe...

"I need to call Nicole."

twenty-eight

DREW

MY ALARM BLEEPS at seven thirty, then the phone instantly goes dead. Burke must have put it by my head at some point during the night, because I vaguely remember Nicole taking it away from me and saying something about fairy godmothers not letting their sheep do stupid things. At least the battery lasted long enough so the alarm could remind me that I, in my infinite wisdom, told Mrs. Ruiz I'd talk to her this morning. Obviously I can't miss that, even though I feel like I got run over by a Mack truck, followed by at least three taxi cabs. After I use the bathroom, I look in the mirror and see that at least part of the pain in my head is because I gave myself a black eye running into that door last night. A stupidity tax, if you will. Mrs. Ruiz will undoubtedly have something to say about that. It won't help that I probably smell like fruit punch and grain alcohol. Thank God, Burke had some extra toothbrushes in his bathroom cabinet, because when I got here last night, my tongue was purple. That's something I definitely don't want to have going on in front of her.

I brush my teeth again and splash my face with cold water, as if a little water's going to magically make me feel like I didn't have too much mystery punch less than twelve hours ago.

I keep getting hit with memories from last night. The look in Andy's eyes before she ran off. The sheer stupidity of everything I said and did at the party.

When I leave the bathroom, Burke is already up and making coffee, bless him. Danny stayed out late, so he's probably sleeping, but Burke looks like he's on his second or third sleepless night running.

He whistles at the sight of me. "Looks like someone gave you a shiner."

"I'm probably one of the few people on earth who can say I gave myself one," I say, groaning as I sit on a stool at the kitchen island. The kitchen's pretty modern, sleek and covered in white tiles, and it makes me feel a pang of longing for my house, where the stove is at least two decades old, and the flooring is vinyl, with a pattern that was last popular in the eighties. I wonder if Andy's sitting in it now. I hope to God she's there, because if she left...

I'll never forgive myself if I drove her out by being a dumbass.

I need to get over there and talk to her, but first I have to convince Mrs. Ruiz to talk to Andy. If I can do that for Andy, then maybe she'll forgive me.

Burke places a cup of coffee on the counter in front of me. "God bless you."

"Coffee converted you to religion?" he asks, amused.

"*Coffee* is my religion."

He slides another cup of coffee across the counter to the spot next to me and comes around to sit. We coexist quietly for a moment, both of us soaking in the caffeine and in the fact that we're less miserable, at least a little, because we're together. "Your phone dead?"

I take the brick out of my pocket and flash it at him.

"Nicole asked us to meet this afternoon," he tells me. "Three o'clock at your friend's bar. She says she has information. I guess she's hoping to have more by then."

He doesn't sound particularly excited about it, but then I guess he wouldn't be.

"Where do you see this ending, man?" I ask, turning to face him on my stool.

"Nowhere good." He looks into his cup before meeting my gaze. "Even if they didn't hurt him, they obviously paid him off. There's no way they'd give that kind of severance money to someone unless they had a reason. If they were at fault for what happened to that building, and they covered it up... I can't work there anymore, Drew, and I'm not going to let anyone else work there either. Not unless they know what they're getting into. I'm going to hire Nicole and Damien to keep digging until we have solid proof."

"I wouldn't expect anything less from you."

"Thanks," he says with an almost smile. "I think I needed to hear that. I'm not all about being a Burke right now." He shakes his head mirthlessly. "My father's always going on about the family—doing right by it, leaving behind a legacy—and this is the shit he's been pulling?"

"Look on the bright side," I joke. "Maybe your mom was the mastermind."

"I'll bet they did it together. Well, they'll go down together too. Maybe they can get his and hers prison suits."

"I doubt they'll go to jail," I tell him honestly. People as rich as them don't get put away often, and they have the fanciest lawyers in the state on retainer.

"Unless they hurt Leonard."

"Unless they hurt Leonard and we can prove it," I agree. "Did you ask Nicole why she wanted to meet?"

He laughs humorlessly. "You think that woman offers up any more information than she has a mind to?"

"Point taken."

"Now, tell me what you're going to do about Andy."

I explain my plan about getting Mrs. Ruiz to come around.

"Ask if we can do the windows next week," he says. "I don't think I'm in any shape to get to it today. I'd probably fall off the ladder."

"I was thinking the same thing."

"Good luck, man. That's all I've got to say. But maybe you don't even need to bring her grandmother around. You might just try talking to her. Being straight."

"Yeah," I say with a sigh. "A frighteningly big man told me the same thing last night. I'm going to. But if I can do this for her, I want to. It's been hell watching her be sad about this. I can't fix being an asshole, unfortunately, but I can at least do something good."

He laughs, so at least I'm keeping him cheerful. "You're rarely an asshole."

"I think that's the nicest thing anyone's ever said to me." I take a gulp of coffee, looking off into the distance, then say, "I'm going to tell Andy that I love her. I don't want to mess around without telling Marnie or the other people I care about that we're involved. But if she wants to spend time together platonically so she can become certain about whatever she's uncertain about, then we can do that."

"Better you than me," he says with a little amusement.

"It's terrible," I admit. "But when it's amazing, it's fucking amazing."

"I'll stick to casual relationships." He smirks. "They're just amazing, not fucking amazing, but there's no terrible involved. I've had enough terrible."

I think, but don't say, *That's because you haven't been in love yet. You'll see.* And when it happens, I'll pat him on the back and call him a dumbass, just like Rafe did for me.

———

When I get to the house, Mrs. Ruiz is sitting out on one of the two rocking chairs on the porch. I'm surprised she doesn't have a shotgun angled across her lap, because she's got a serious *get off my lawn* vibe. The house looks fantastic—the purple paint fresh, the weeds removed. Apparently, Shauna and her grandparents helped with that. Her grandfather is a master gardener and, I shit you not, this is the kind of thing he does for fun.

The look of the place gives me a sense of accomplishment. Honestly, most of it wasn't my accomplishment, but I was the ringleader, and that means something.

"You came," she says, as if surprised.

"You asked me to."

She nods as I lower into the other chair.

"Was it Andy who hit you?" she asks.

"Not this time." I reach up to touch the bruise, as if I need the pain to remind me it's there. Or maybe just to remind me that I've been stupid. "But she did deliver a pretty impressive punch to the balls the other night when she thought I was an intruder."

She smiles and gives a slight nod. I'd prefer to interpret her reaction as approval of Andy's ass-kicking skills and not pleasure at the thought of my gut-wrenching pain. "You're here to convince me to speak to Andy."

"Yes."

She turns her chair toward mine, and I do the same. I feel like we're about to fight a duel and I'm only equipped with a water pistol. *And* we're in rocking chairs. So it's the suburban, senior citizen version of a stand-off.

Mrs. Ruiz gives me one of her patented no-nonsense looks. "You love my granddaughter."

I flinch as if slapped. I don't see the point in denying it, especially since I came here planning to tell her the truth anyway. "How'd you know?"

"You came at eight-thirty on a Sunday after getting no sleep." She gestures to my face, which apparently looks a whole lot worse than I realized. "You're a mess, but you arranged for your friends to paint and repair my house and came over after work every single day. This is not something you would do for an old woman who means nothing to you."

"I probably still would have." It's at least partially true. I'm not the kind of person who can walk away from little old ladies in falling down houses. Especially little old ladies who are slowly dying.

"Then there's the way you talk about her. You can't hide things from me, *mijo*. I've been around long enough to have seen everything at least twice. Most things three times."

"I believe you. Which is why I can't understand why you don't see *this*. She needs you. I don't want her to leave my house, but this is where she needs to be." I rock for a second, then add, "That's not easy for me to say."

She sighs heavily, rocking in her chair. "You've made me realize something, you know?"

"And what's that?"

"I don't want her to see me like this, because this isn't the way I wish to be remembered. I wanted her to remember me being strong. But that's an old woman's selfish wish, like how I'd like to meet my end in Puerto Rico."

"So why don't you go there?" I sputter. Her shitty grandson has money, although he's obviously in no hurry to share it. Still, she could sell the house. Use the money to travel. "It's a cheap plane fare. I mean, there'd be some details to work out with the nursing stuff, but it's hardly impossible."

"I've lived in this house for twenty-five years. In the beginning, I told myself I would move on once my daughter got settled again. But her need for me didn't change. After we lost her, my new goal was to leave once Andy got off to school. She and the boys still needed me. I don't know when it happened, but I stayed too long, and everything changed. I became the one who needed Andy. Not those boys, but her? Yes. But I *know* what need does to a person. I know what it did to me."

Her words feel like they're tearing my chest open. I can't help but think of the walls that have been *my* world. I had my reasons for staying too, when most of the other kids I grew up with left. At first it was because my dad needed me. He'd always treated my mother like a rare, exotic bird who'd flown down and graced him with her presence. And if that bird shit on him? Well, he'd been lucky to share space with it. Then she left with Sinclair, and it undid him. He tried not to show Marnie, but I saw the grief clawing away at him. I knew I had to stay until she graduated from high school, but then she did, and I had a free place to live and all of my friends were living close, so why leave? Then Leonard died, and it seemed like a cautionary tale against taking chances—and proof that you have to protect the people you love and keep them close, because God forbid you let them out of your sight.

"Andy would go with you," I say numbly, because I know it's true. She'd drop everything and leave in an instant.

Mrs. Ruiz studies me shrewdly, in a way that makes me think she can tell what I had for breakfast. Coffee. "And you'd let me take her away from you so easily?"

"Hell, yes," I say without hesitation, then bow my head. "Sorry, but I would. She needs you, Mrs. Ruiz. She needs to be able to say goodbye. To make good memories. She doesn't care that you're not as strong as you used to be or whatever it is you're thinking. She just wants to be with you. To love you. I'm serious when I tell you it's been tearing her up inside to be away from you right now. You have some pretty messed-up beliefs, I'm not going to lie to you about that, but I *know* you want what's best for her."

"Yes," she says stubbornly, "I want to free her from her grief."

I rock in my chair for a second, absorbing what she's saying. "There's no freeing a person from their grief. I tried that with my father, after my mother left him. And with Marnie, after our dad died. All you can hope to do is support them through it."

"That's the kind of thing that creates a debt," she says staunchly, giving her chair a rock. "You, Andrew, strike me as the kind of man who has many outstanding debts."

"There are no debts when both people love each other. My dad didn't owe me anything, but he kept paying me back all the same. By being there for me. By giving me half of the house. That's what love is. A back and forth. Sometimes one person needs more, and that's okay."

"But I won't be here to give anything back to her," she says, her eyes shrewd. "*You* will."

A knot forms in my throat. "If she wants me, I'll always be there for her. No debts. Because you're right. I'm in love with your grand-daughter. I think I have been for a while now."

She's still gazing at me, her focus intense. "You felt this way when she was six?"

"Jesus," I say, practically jumping in my seat. "No. Not that long. I'm talking a few months." I think back to Andy in her glowing crown the night of that bowling game. "A few years, at most."

Mrs. Ruiz surprises me by laughing, the laughter lifting her features and making her look more like Andy.

"So Andy's not the only Ruiz who likes laughing at me. Good to know."

"It's her love language," she says, watching me. "Always has been."

My heart expands at that, because how couldn't it?

"You'd wait for her if she went away?"

My mouth lifts in a half smile. "I've waited this long."

"Okay," she says. "I'll talk to her...and so will you. You obviously did something stupid, but you're a good boy. You have my blessing."

"Fantastic. Now, let's hope I can still get hers."

I think she's probably going to say something meaningful, possibly even profound, but a black Range Rover pulls up at the curb, and a big guy with black hair storms out. He looks enough like

Andy that I'd know one of her brothers has finally materialized even if I'd never seen photos of him.

Where's Rafe when you need him?

"Theo," Mrs. Ruiz says, intoning the word as if it's a swear.

Shit. He's the bad one, not that the other one sounds like a milk and cookies type.

"What are you doing here with my grandmother?" the guy says, storming up onto the porch. His gaze pings around, taking in the paint, the overall well-being of a house that had seen better days. "What the fuck is this?"

Confirmation that he hasn't come around all week, though it sounds like he's been busy. "I work for *Extreme Home Makeover*," I deadpan. "Your grandmother was a winner."

I get up and step away from Mrs. Ruiz, because this asshole looks violent, and I don't want her in the line of fire.

"Bullshit," he hisses. "Who is this guy, *Abuela*?"

"More of a grandson to me than you've ever been," she snarls. "I told you to stay away."

She looks fierce as hell, and I have a flash of what Andy will be like in fifty years. I want to be there to see it. I want to be sitting beside her on our porch, rocking. Though preferably not with her brother waving a cane at us.

He ignores her and takes another step toward me. I stand my ground, mentally willing Mrs. Ruiz to go into the house. The last thing she needs is the kind of excitement that might give her a heart attack or mess up her blood pressure.

"Are *you* the one who's fucking with my life?" he asks me.

He's obviously talking about those photos. But the last thing I want is for this guy to realize I know what he's talking about. "Nope. I'm a computer game designer."

"You're a funny guy, huh?" he asks, stalking closer.

"Some people think so. I'd like to think they're right."

"Did you take those photos of me and my girlfriend?" He gestures to the house. "Mess with my grandmother's house?"

He says this as if I damaged it.

"My friends and I helped improve the house, yes."

"Wait." He pokes a finger at me as if I'd been inclined to go anywhere. "I recognize you. You know my slut sister. She put you up to this."

"Don't you fucking call her that," I growl, taking a step toward him. He's bigger than me, but he's also an asshole. I'll gladly take a few punches if it means I get to get one in.

He looks surprised but not particularly alarmed.

"So that's how she got you to help her, huh? You're hardly the first guy she's fucked to get her way, and you're not going to be the last."

"I don't know the first thing about your girlfriend, other than that you're supposed to have a fiancée. Seems to me you're the one who's messing with *my* girlfriend. And this is where you stop."

"Your girlfriend?" He laughs, his eyes as flat as coal. "Is that what she told you?"

I take another step toward him. "That's between me and her. But I won't let you disrespect her. Or your grandmother."

His gaze narrows on my black eye.

"You should see the other guy," I say, edging in on him more.

"So...what? Are you going to hit me?"

"Sure."

"I could end you."

"Probably." I stand my ground, glaring at him, because I kind of *want* him to take a swing at me. It'd give me an excuse to hit him, and even if I only get one punch in, I'd make it good. Still, I'm not going to start a fight out here on Mrs. Ruiz's porch.

"Where's Andy staying?"

I almost laugh. "You think I'm going to tell *you*? It's like I said, you're going to leave her alone. And if your grandmother wants you to stay away from her, then you're going to leave her alone too."

I don't like the implication of why he's asking about Andy. What does he think he's going to do? There's something dangerous about him, unmoored, as if he's realized he's in some deep shit and wants to find someone else to spread it on. Well, it won't be Andy, and it sure as hell won't be Mrs. Ruiz either.

"That bitch got me fired," he says. He wipes a hand across his mouth. "It had to be her."

"Well, something tells me you encouraged her boss to fire her, so I guess all is right in the world."

He lunges at me.

twenty-nine

DREW

I DUCK THEO EASILY, then swing at his face and get a blow in. His body's obviously a steel tank, and I don't trust my odds against steel, but his face is as breakable as anyone's.

His nose is bleeding, maybe broken, but he doesn't even pause before coming at me, getting in a hit to my chest that knocks me back into the wall. This isn't going to go well for me, but I'm not about to make it easy for him.

Then I hear Mrs. Ruiz say, "You leave *now*." I turn to see she *does* have a shotgun, aimed at her grandson.

"*Abuela*?" he asks, disbelief ringing in his tone. Blood is still dribbling from my nose, and my black eye isn't the only bruise I'm going to have. My chest feels like it got hit by a cinderblock.

"You heard me. And if you bother your sister or this boy again, I'll make sure you answer for it."

"They've been—"

"No excuses, Theodore. I heard what you were saying. You're messing around on that girl of yours. Does she know?"

His cheeks are red. "Yes, dammit."

"*Language.*"

To my surprise, he looks chagrined. "She knows. She was going to stay, but now..."

"*Now?*"

"I lost my job."

"And you lay that at your sister's door?"

"It's complicated."

"Was it your boss's wife you were photographed with, by any chance?" I ask. If so, it's less that the situation's complicated and more that he's stupid, but it doesn't seem like a good time to say so.

"*Estupido*," Mrs. Ruiz says, looking like she wants to knock him upside the head with the gun.

"His daughter," he says flatly.

"You get out of here." She points. "You get out of here and you make it right with that girl of yours if you can. You get yourself a different job. You make yourself a life you can be proud of, Theo. Because *look* at yourself. Is this the man you want to be? You don't like your sister, then you stay away from her. You don't think your brother's good enough without making him like yourself? You stay away from him too. I say this to Jack too."

"Sounds like you want me to stay away from everyone," he says, swallowing.

"If this is what you do—charging up onto my porch like a madman, hitting my guests, threatening your own sister...then, yes. I would prefer for you to stay away from everyone until you can control yourself."

He nods slowly, spits at my feet, earning himself a swipe of the gun to his shoulder.

An older man passes on the sidewalk by the house. "Nice morning, Elena," he calls to Mrs. Ruiz. If he thinks it's abnormal that she's holding a gun on her grandson on the porch of her house, next to another man who has a black eye, he doesn't say so.

Maybe it *is* normal for her.

She waves back, still holding the gun with one hand. "Thank your wife for the casserole."

I can feel myself gaping at them.

As soon as the older man disappears out of sight, Mrs. Ruiz turns back to Theo. "Go, now. But you should know I'm not leaving you this house, Theo. I was never going to."

He swears under his breath. "Mama would have left it to me."

"No, she left it to *me*, to do with as I saw fit."

"It should be *bulldozed*," he says. "Condemned. Only the land's worth anything."

"Which is probably why she's not leaving it to you," I mutter. He looks like he's seriously considering going for me again, but he'd need to be a stronger man to withstand the look his grandmother's giving him.

"Leave Andy alone," I tell him for good measure. "She has a lot of friends—friends you obviously pissed off."

"So you're admitting she got me fired."

"No, she didn't do a damn thing," I say. "She seemed to feel some sort of misplaced loyalty to you and your brother. But our friends? Yeah, they probably did take those photos—although, let's be honest, you got yourself fired by being a dumbass. If you think getting fired was bad, wait to see what happens if you keep bothering her. *And* Mrs. Ruiz."

"You threatening me?" he asks.

"Yes, I thought that was clear. Andy is protected. So is Mrs. Ruiz. If anything happens to either of them, you're going to have people knocking at your door, and they're not going to be happy to see you, if you catch my drift."

His jaw flexes, and I'll bet he's fantasizing about hitting me again. His nose has stopped bleeding, but he doesn't look like the polished asshole who stepped out of his expensive car ten minutes ago. "You think I'd hurt my own family?"

"Yes," I say, standing my ground. "I think you're exactly the kind of asshole who would."

Something flashes in his eyes. I'd like to believe it's contrition, but one truth people don't like to admit to is that not everybody's redeemable. I don't owe him the benefit of the doubt, not after he blustered in here talking about Andy the way he did.

He spits at my feet again, earning him another swat with the gun. And then he retreats to the Range Rover and leaves. Suddenly, now that the adrenaline's run out, I'm exhausted. Mrs. Ruiz and I watch him go, side by side.

Finally, she heaves a sigh. "If there's anything to be made of him, he'll need to dig down deep. *Very* deep. But I think we may have just given him a shovel, *mijo*." She shrugs. "Either that, or he'll be an asshole all his life. We've done what we can."

"You said asshole," I say, somewhere between shocked and impressed.

She hits me with a fierce look. "What are you waiting for? Go get our girl and bring her home." Her brow lifts. "But don't disappoint me, Andrew. *You* make things right with her too."

A grin lifts my face because goddammit, *I did it*. I won her over. I mean, she still doesn't know Andy and I have been living in sin, but that's something we can maybe mention after the big reconciliation. First thing's first, though. "Can you maybe put down that gun? We don't want to frighten her off."

———

My heart's pounding as I approach the door to my own house. Marnie's car is in the driveway, which complicates things. I desperately need to talk to Andy, and she doesn't want Marnie to know there's anything between us. Can I ask my sister to leave without seeming like a dick?

I knock and the door almost instantly flies open. Andy's behind it. I have a split second to take in her yoga pants and loose T-shirt, the fact that she's not wearing a bra, because then she's shrieking, "What the fuck?" and yanking me into the house, her hand lifting to my eye.

"Come on, Andy," I say, flinching. "Why'd you poke me in my black eye?"

"Who did this to you?" she asks, pissed. She looks like a Valkyrie, ready to ride into battle on my behalf, and it's sexy as hell. It also soothes my nerves, because if she still wanted me to go screw myself, she probably wouldn't care about the black eye.

"Me," I say, with a half-smile, because it's absurd. "I fell down the stairs and hit a doorknob."

I glance around, seeing no sign of Marnie. "Is Marnie here?" I ask. "I saw her car."

She gets up from the couch, which she must have been lying on, her purse pressed over her face. "Pretend I'm not here," she says, heading for the door. But she pauses when she catches sight of me, the purse falling down and sending tubes of ChapStick, her phone, and half a dozen other things flying to the ground.

"That just got harder," I mutter.

"You expect us to believe a door did that?" she asks. "What'd you do to the door?"

"Very funny," I say, rubbing my chest. Then I wince, because I touched the part that Theo pounded.

Andy's eyes narrow on me, and her hand darts forward and lifts the bottom hem of my shirt.

"For God's sake, you two," Marnie says. "Can't you wait to start undressing each other until *after* I collect my belongings and what's left of my dignity?"

But then Andy hikes my shirt higher, revealing a red spot, the swelling, and the beginnings of what's going to be one hell of a bruise.

"The door do that too?" she asks in a low voice and then

smooths my shirt down, her hand hot through the thin fabric of my shirt. Her eyes are on mine, and it's hard to remember that Marnie is still in the room. But she is, and although I love her, I'd *really* like it if she left, so I stoop to help her collect her things.

The first thing I grab is a bottle of self-warming lube, which I throw on reflex. It hits the wall, which knocks the cap open, and it splashes on the floor.

Fantastic. Now my sister's lube is on the floor.

"Hey," Marnie says, retrieving the lube and sticking it in her bag. "I'm going to need that."

"Don't make my ears bleed," I say as I stand back up next to Andy, so aware of her presence it might as well be burned into me. "You know, I hate to say this now that I know what you've got on the docket, but maybe you should leave, Marnie. Can I say that without being a dick?"

"Just this once." She grabs an escaped tube of ChapStick and sticks in her bag. "Quickly, though, do I need to give Burke a lecture about the meaning of friendship?"

"No," I say. "Not Burke. I'll explain later."

"Okay," she says, retreating. And I can tell she knows. Something inside of me settles, and I let myself hope that it's all going to be all right. Please God, let it be all right.

"Bye," Marnie says, slipping out and shutting the door behind her.

I turn to Andy and reach for her hands. Thank all that's holy, she gives them to me.

"Who hit you?" she asks, still sounding plenty pissed about it.

"Your brother, Theo. But don't worry, I smashed him in the nose. I guess he got fired and took it personally."

The look in her eyes shifts between fury and remorse like one of those pendulum toys. "This is all my fault." She pulls one of her hands free and lifts it to the area by my eyes, staying away from the actual bruise this time.

"No, that one really *was* caused by the door. Apparently, the stuff in the cauldron wasn't actually juice. Who knew?"

"Come with me," she says, dragging me over to the couch. Not that she'd have to put any force into it. I'd follow her anywhere.

Once I'm sitting, she heads into the kitchen and returns with a bag of frozen peas, making me smile. "I'm starting to think this is the only reason anyone buys them."

"Press it to your eye," she says sternly, leaning in.

"I'll take care of that." I take it from her, our fingers passing over each other, because if you're going to have a plastic bag full of frozen pellets on your eye, it's best if you're the one who puts it there.

"Jack called me yesterday," she continues, sitting with her knees tucked into her chest, facing me with her feet pressed against my leg. It feels like we've come full circle in a way—Andy's feet, the bag of peas, *this house*. Hope pulses through me. "He said Theo was trying to find me, and it made me realize that I had to stop trying to placate him. I sent his boss those photos. That's why he was pissed off."

"It's definitely *his* fault," I say, setting the bag aside. "But your grandmother and I set him straight. He won't be bothering you anymore. I warned him that we have friends in low places."

"My grandmother?" she asks in wonder. "I mean, I guess you weren't likely to cross paths with him anywhere else. But what were you doing there at nine in the morning on a Sunday after you drank all of that mystery punch?"

"I made a promise to her...and to you," I say. "That means something to me. You think I'd miss the opportunity to do something for you after the mess I made of everything yesterday? I knew I couldn't make it right, but I had to try."

"*Drew*," she says, tears in her eyes.

I want to kiss her tears away, I want to sink onto my knees and soothe myself with the taste of her, but first I need to tell her everything.

"She wants you to come home, Andy. I don't think she ever gave a shit about the videos. She loves you. She used it as an excuse to push you away because she didn't want you to have to watch her die. I guess she got it into her head that it would be better for you if it went that way, because of what you went through when you lost your mom."

"Oh, *Abuela*. You stubborn asshole." Tears are falling silently down her cheeks.

I squeeze her hand, feeling an old worry pressing on me. "You have to believe me when I say that I've been trying to convince her to tell you the truth for weeks."

"I believe you." She clears her throat. "I'm a lot like her. A hard-headed woman who doesn't let other people change her mind."

I let myself lift my hand to trace her jaw, my fingers brushing her soft curls. "A woman who *knows* her mind. I like that about you, Ruiz. Always have. And even though your grandmother has some pretty dumb ideas, I respect the hell out of her. I messed up yesterday, Andy. I..." My heart feels like it's about to choke me. I wipe away her tears and take her hand again, needing to touch some part of her when I say this. "I'm in love with you. I'm so fucking in love with you. I don't know when it began exactly, except that it started a while ago, and I'm so thick-headed, that I didn't even realize it until I was in deep. So when you said—"

She leans forward and kisses me, her lips soft but fierce, because Andy really is a woman who knows her mind, and there's nothing sedate about her. Nothing simple or easy.

Thank God for that.

thirty

ANDY

WHEN I SAW him at the door, that bruise on his face, the beast inside of me came out to roar. I wanted to destroy whoever'd hurt him—to punch them in the balls or mess with them in more creative ways Nicole would help me with.

He loves me.

I'm screwed-up and difficult, and he still loves me.

I love him too. It frightened me—the things I wanted to do to him, for him. But after talking with Marnie and thinking about everything when I should have been sleeping last night, I realized it's okay to feel that way with Drew, because he absolutely does things for me too. He brings me water and ice cream. He asks about my problems and tries to solve them—just as bossily as I've tried to solve his. We can take care of *each other*.

Right now, I want to consume him. I want to ride his dick until we both come in shouting ecstasy. But there are some things he needs to hear too, and I'm not going to make him wait.

So I settle for straddling his lap, feeling his half-hard dick against me.

"There are some things I need to say too," I tell him, rocking slightly because it feels impossibly good to have him between my legs.

He clears his throat, his Adam's apple bobbing slightly. "I'm not complaining—I'm *definitely* not complaining—but this isn't the best position for us to be in if you want me to listen. I'm having trouble remembering my own name right now."

"You only need to remember mine. Change the 'w' and you're all set." He laughs, and we're so close, just inches between us, that I feel it in my body. "Besides, if you listen, you'll be rewarded." I rock against him again, feeling how hard he is now from just that small movement.

He wraps those big hands around my hips to keep me in place. "Speak now or forever hold your peace."

"I told Marnie about us…"

His eyes brighten, emboldening me to continue. "I…I was hoping there was still an us. I shouldn't have said that to you the other night." My throat feels hot as the words come out. "I knew what happened between us meant something. It meant *a lot.* And I didn't need more time to figure that part out. I was afraid to tell Marnie because I was worried it would change things between us. Me and Marnie. Me and you. I… When I saw you with Shauna at the party, I was so damn jealous."

He laughs. "You know, I think I probably scared her. I don't remember what I said, but it had something to do with the mystery juice." He cocks his head, staring into my eyes. "You don't have anything to be jealous about. We'd only gotten halfway through dinner last weekend before she realized I was in love with you."

My heart catches in my throat because what he's saying casts things in such a different light. When I got home and he was drinking alone on the couch, I'd figured the date had gone badly and he was soothing himself. But he did that because of *me*.

"I'm not used to letting myself rely on other people."

He exercises admirable restraint in not saying *no, shit.*

"I already relied on you. I've *always* relied on you. So when things started changing between us, it felt like too much to put on one person. And I was so scared of losing you. Of losing Marnie too."

He's rubbing my hips in slow circles now, each movement of his hands radiating through me. "I'm yours as long as you want me," he says. "And Marnie would never stop being your friend. Not for anything."

"She reminded me of that," I say, pushing closer, our faces a whisper apart. "Drew...I'm in love with you too." The look of joy on his face fills my heart to bursting. "You've always meant more to me than any other man. But I couldn't let myself think of you that way." I swallow. "I'm going to level with you. All of this scares the shit out of me. You're probably going to need to be patient with me."

"You take as much time as you need," he says, lifting his hand from my hip to my back and pressing me to him. Hugging me. He cringes from the press of me against his bruise, then adjusts me slightly, keeping me close the whole time. That asshole Theo. I have half a mind to drive to his house and confront him. And yet...maybe I don't *have* to fight all of my own battles. Maybe it's okay to let the people who care about me fight some of them for me. Still. I would really, really have loved to watched Drew punch him in the nose.

"Your bruise," I say.

"Five hundred bruises couldn't keep me from touching you." He pulls back slightly to look at me. "Andy, If I have to wait, I will. But I'd rather not wait."

I nearly laugh, because the evidence of what he's saying is there, pressed against me.

"You don't have to wait. I-I need to see *Abuela*."

"Oh, shit," he says. "Yes, let's go." He starts to get up, carrying me with him.

I laugh. "You're going to carry me like this to *Abuela's* house? What are you going to do when we get there? You can't pick up the Fabgadget to hide your hard-on."

"So I'll carry you. No one will catch on."

"Nope, nuh-uh, not going to work for me," I say as he carries me toward the door. "Because if you hold me like this, I'm going to feel compelled to dry hump you, and I'm not dry humping you in front of my grandmother. She might not have been as pissed about the OnlyFans thing as she pretended, but I can guarantee you she was not happy. Dry humping in the street would be a *no* from her."

He laughs as he presses me to the door, my back against the wood, his body hot against mine. "So what do you suggest, Ruiz?"

"In case I was being too subtle," I say, sliding my hands under his shirt, careful to avoid his bruise. "I was suggesting that you fuck me against this door."

His eyes sparkling, he sets me down. "Stay right here. If you leave, I'm going to consider this a very cruel practical joke."

I grab the hem of his shirt to keep him from going anywhere. "No. I'm on birth control, and I'm clean. I need you to take me raw."

"Andy," he says, his eyes soaking me in. "Christ, are you sure?"

"I'm sure."

He buries his hand in my hair, tilting my head up to him, and kisses me hard, even as his other hand flips up the skirt of my dress and pushes down my panties. I slide them the rest of the way down my legs, then reach for his jeans. He lets me unfasten them, his attention fixed on playing with me, his hand between my legs, his palm rubbing against my clit while he curls his fingers up inside of me.

"Now," I say, because I can't wait. "*Now*." Because I'm already on the verge, and I want to tumble over with him this time.

His eyes full of hot intent, he picks me up again and backs me into the door, my legs around his waist and his needy dick captured between us. "You want me to fuck you with this big dick, Ruiz?" he says, a small smile paying on his face. I know he's teasing me for making such a big deal out of it over the past two weeks, but it's still hot.

"Yes, and *hurry*. I want you hard and fast."

He pulls back, holding me to the door, and then adjusts himself. The anticipation is killing me, and when he finally pushes in, I'm already halfway there. It feels so good, so full, so *right*. It feels like coming home—and being fucked against the door when you get there. It's even better like this, with nothing between us.

I wrap my legs tighter around him, wanting to keep him there, wanting to get closer.

He kisses me hard as he thrusts in, my back pressing into the wood of the door. His mouth and his dick and everything about him are filling me up and promising me that I'm not alone—that we have each other. I feel myself cresting that hill when he lifts his lips from mine and buries his head into my neck. "Oh my God, Andy, I'm not going to last."

"Good," I gasp. "Give me one more, Drew. One more is all I need."

He thrusts in hard, and we come together, panting and half clothed, and it's perfect. He kisses my neck and holds me like that for a long moment before pulling out and putting me down.

He's looking at me in a way no one else ever has, and this time I'm not scared. I kiss him and then I pull up his underwear and his pants. Fasten them. He lets me. "I want you to feel me on you," I say. "I want you to go about the rest of your day and know your dick is covered in me."

"Jesus," he says, then weaves his hand into my hair and lifts it up. "Same."

I stoop to pick up my underwear. "What'd you do with my panties the other day, anyway?"

"Wept into them," he says, but there's a small smile tugging at his mouth.

"No, what'd you really do?"

"That's between me and your panties. Shall we go?"

"Don't forget the peas."

"Nope, not putting a bag of peas on my eye in front of your grandmother. She smells weakness from a mile away. By the way, she doesn't know Marnie isn't living here anymore, and I think it's best if we don't mention it to her."

"Okay, go put them in the freezer," I say, laughing, because honestly, he may have a point on both counts. "I'm going to go use the bathroom, and then we can leave."

I'm only in there for half a minute before I hear him calling my name. I wash my hands, my heart thumping, because he sounds like he's in distress. Did one of my brothers show up? I run out into the living room, ready to go for the pepper spray in my purse, but I can see enough of the kitchen to see Drew's in there alone, standing in front of the fridge.

And that's when I remember.

"Andy," he says again, turning to me, his eyes wide. "Where'd you find this?"

The little slip of paper is in his fingers. *Roland Finneas. Just you.*

I take his other hand. "It was in the back of that picture frame."

"Leonard gave it to me," he says, confirming what I'd guessed. "It's...it's his handwriting."

"I guess you haven't been checking your phone?" I ask. I'd texted him about it, and Nicole had sent a group text setting up a meeting.

"It died."

"Nicole asked us to meet her and Damien at Griffin's bar this afternoon. Marnie recognized 'finneas' last night. There aren't any Roland Finneases, but she remembered the word meaning something like duty, and there *are* Roland Dutys. I don't want to get your hopes up, but Nicole thinks there's a chance Leonard's still alive. She figures the message was for you, because Leonard was feeling squirrely about involving Burke."

His eyes are glassy, and my heart twists in my chest. He leans in and kisses me.

"Andy, *you* did this."

"It's no big deal," I hedge. "If he is alive, I didn't raise him from the dead."

"It *is* a big deal. We thought..." He rubs the paper between his fingers. "All along. It was in there all those years. To think..."

"We still don't know," I say, because I can't bear for him to be disappointed about this. There's still a chance that Leonard's gone —either because he really did have an accident or because the Burkes caught up with him.

"Burke... It was looking like his parents did something to keep Leonard quiet."

"Nicole filled us in on what you found," I tell him. "Drew, if I'd known what kind of day you'd had..."

He gives me a chagrined look. "Same. I think we're going to need to pay your brother Jack a visit too. I won't let either of them mess with you."

"I think he was mostly calling to warn me about Theo." I grimace. "Admittedly, if the photos got Theo fired, then there's a pretty good chance that Jack got canned too. He won't like that."

"Sometimes the things we do our damnedest to avoid are pretty good for us." A corner of his mouth lifts. "I finally got it done, Andy."

He must realize I have no clue what he's talking about, because he adds, "The fire."

"Seriously?" I say, more excited about a video game than I ever have been in my life. "I saw it on your screen last night, and I thought it looked pretty damn good. I figured you were just being weirdly anal about it."

He starts laughing, then says through his laughter, "It was the damn rug. All of those red and orange and yellow splotches. I realized there wasn't enough yellow in it."

"This day is really looking up," I say.

"So let's go," he tells me, his expression sobering. "It's time for you to see her."

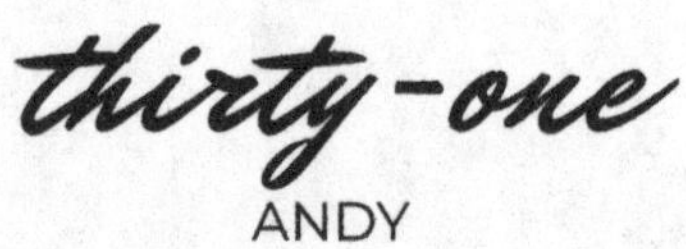

ANDY

I'M nervous as Drew makes the drive. I believe what Drew told me about *Abuela*—my heart needs to, and I know he'd never lie to me about something like that. Even so, the last time I saw her, she sent me away. What if she sends me away again?

And what if she doesn't?

If I move back in with her, I'll have to leave Drew's house.

I glance at him. "You'd be okay with me moving back in with my grandmother?"

"I don't want you to leave, no. I've become begrudgingly fond of your terrible rug and our signature candle scent, but yeah. You need to be with her." He steals a look at me. "I meant what I said, Andy. I'm willing to wait. However long it takes."

"I love you," I say, watching his profile.

He glances at me again, then takes my hand with the one not on the wheel. "I'll never get sick of hearing you say it."

"Good."

It's then he turns the corner, and the little purple house comes into view. Only it doesn't look like the little purple house I left. It's freshly painted, and someone's fixed the steps to the porch.

I turn in my seat, emotion clogging my throat. "I *love* you."

He's grinning as he pulls up to the curb and parks. "No need to go over the top with it, Ruiz. I heard you the first time." He unfastens his seat belt and turns to face me. "In the interest of full disclosure, Griffin and Rafe did most of the actual work, but I'd prefer it if you didn't tell them you love them."

"*You* organized this."

He reaches over to trace the side of my face. "You wanted to take care of her. I did it for you—and her. It's like I said. I respect your grandmother."

I lean in and kiss him. I'm still kissing him, in fact, when a rock hits the window. Drew's the one who jolts back, and I can't help but smile, because I know what he's looking at. My grandmother's always had one hell of an arm.

"You scared of my grandmother?" I ask, then then look out my window, my heart pounding. She's sitting in her rocking chair on the porch. She doesn't look pissed, though. If anything, she looks pleased. She's thinner than when I left, frailer. But the solid strength I've always found in her eyes is still there, even from the distance of twenty to thirty feet. Thank God. *Thank God.* She's still herself, and I'm in love, but *I'm* still myself.

"You know, she threatened your brother with a shotgun a couple of hours ago," Drew says from beside me. "I'd prefer not to piss her off."

"She pulled out the shotgun," I say, turning to grin at him as I pull off my seat belt.

"I had a feeling it wasn't an infrequent occurrence," he says with a snort.

And then we're getting out of the car. I walk for the first few feet before I let myself run. I careen up the porch steps and fall to my knees next to her rocking chair, and I'm crying again, for fuck's sake. She smooths her hand down my hair, and my grandmother, whom I've never seen cry, not once, is crying too. "My Andy," she's saying. "My girl."

I lean in and hug her, careful not to hug too hard, because the last thing I want to do is kill her with my love.

"I've missed you so much, *Abuela*. You wouldn't answer my messages."

Her tears are soaking into the back of my shirt, and I can't be mad at her. I can't. "You've got a good boy, Andy. A good man. He helped me see what a fool I've been. I told myself I was sparing you pain, but I was being a selfish old woman. It was hard-headed of you to make those videos to raise money for the house. I would sooner sell this house than have you debase yourself. But that would never make me turn my back on you. I didn't want you to see me like this. Weak. Helpless."

Laughter tears out of me. "Oh, *Abuela*, you may be dying, but no one would ever mistake you for someone who's weak. Drew just got done telling me that you sent Theo away with a shotgun."

"Sometimes a loud mouth isn't enough to cure stupid."

I pull away, smiling at her, and swipe away my tears. I don't dare touch hers. Drew's standing at the bottom of the steps, giving us our time. He looks like a sentinel, standing there to ensure no one else interrupts our time either. Fondness for him engulfs me.

"Come on up here," I tell him. "The Ruiz woman require your presence."

He looks a little uneasy, as he probably should, given what I'm about to tell my grandmother.

"*Abuela*," I say, standing up and taking his hand. He gives it to me easily. "Drew and I have been living in sin together. Marnie moved in with her fiancé two weeks ago. I love Drew, and I'm lucky enough that he loves me."

She studies us for a second. I'm honestly not sure what I expect her to do, although I'm hoping her fondness for us both will stop her from blowing a gasket. Besides, I know she's not exactly a prude; she's just not into the idea of sharing videos of one's appendages.

"And you wish to stay there?" she asks me.

I glance at him, feeling a pull of longing for the house—our house, it feels like—but I don't hesitate. "No, I want to come home to you. I don't want to miss another minute together."

"So Drew will come here too," *Abuela* says, which truly does shock the hell out of me. "There's plenty of room."

"Drew, you don't have to do that," I say, turning to him. "I know you don't—"

I don't want to say he doesn't leave the house. That's not true. He does plenty of shit, but he's never *lived* anywhere else. It's his safe place. His home.

"You just want me to do more work inside of the house," he says to my grandmother.

He's teasing her, just like he's always done with me, and the look on her face says she loves it.

"Yes," she says flatly, her good humor betrayed by the lines around her eyes. "You and your friends have made yourselves useful. Even the big one. It would be no hardship to have you here."

His gaze moves from her to me and lingers. "I'll do it if you want me to. I'll do it in a heartbeat."

He means it. I can see it in his eyes. His look of determination. And if I had any resistance left—which I don't—it would have melted right then.

"You're one in a million, Andrew Jones."

"Sure," he says, one side of his mouth lifting. "I like those odds. But if we meet another me, I reserve the right to punch him in the face." His gaze pings between us again, and he says, "We'll move here if you'd like, Mrs. Ruiz. But I have a different idea."

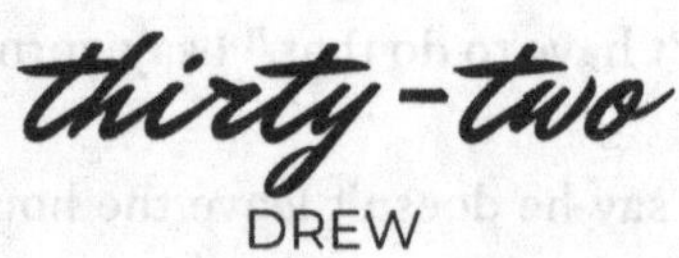

"SO, I haven't found him yet," Nicole says, pausing to take a swig of her beer. We're at Griffin's bar, seated at a table—Andy and me and Burke on one side, Nicole and Damien on the other. Griffin already brought us a round of beers, even though I haven't touched mine.

"But he's not dead?" Burke asks, leaning forward.

I can feel myself doing the same.

Burke somehow looks worse than he did this morning, although I'm guessing I'm not looking great either based on the sideways glances I'm getting. I couldn't give a shit. I feel like I'm on top of the world. Of course, feeling on top of the world hasn't made my black eye vanish.

I've made a few decisions that I never would have contemplated a month ago.

Decision one: I'm quitting my damn job. I have money saved up, despite the whole paying Marnie's shitty ex-fiancé off debacle, and so does Danny. Burke has made it clear he intends to be our financial backer, and it's time to hire the other professionals we need for distribution and marketing so we can launch the game. By ourselves, so we get to do it *our* way.

I've already reached out to my old boss for advice. He might have retired to Boca, but he still has contacts.

Decision two: Andy and I are both going to stay with Mrs. Ruiz, but only for a little while. Because...

Decision three: We're going to bring her to Puerto Rico, for however long she wants to stay. Maybe until the end. We can rent out both houses to pay for it, and I can work from there until the launch.

Andy said she couldn't let me do all of that for her, that it was too much, too soon, and I told her that it was about time I got off my ass and did something. And there was no *too much, too soon* about getting out of the house for a while. It was past time for me to take some chances, and there was no one I'd rather take them for than her.

Still. I don't want to leave Burke in the middle of this massive shitstorm. I texted the guys about my ideas for the game launch and then called Burke. I told him what I was thinking and offered to stick around until things settled.

"No, man. Don't you dare disrupt your life because of my parents. This is my shit to deal with. And you can be supportive from wherever you wind up. Just make sure you can get high speed internet, because *we're doing this thing.*"

I hadn't expected him to say any differently, but still. It'll take weeks to make the arrangements we need to make, and I'm hoping...

"Well," Nicole says, probably enjoying having us on the hook. It strikes me that she's not looking so great either, although I'd never say so. Particularly not with Damien sitting next to her. Sleep-deprived, like we are, though I doubt it's our problems that are keeping her up at night. She dips her head to her phone and pulls something up, pushes it across the table to us. A photograph of Leonard wearing an *I Heart Trees* T-shirt. It likes like he's with some sort of clean-up crew.

"That's probably why he left the first place he landed," she says. "That's from when he was Roland Duty. He wasn't too far away. Just down in Highland Hills. We think he stuck close for a while to give you a chance to find him, Drew. But they slapped his photo in the paper. I mean, who can blame them? Your boy's a looker. He left after that."

A hiss of air escapes Burke like he's a deflating balloon, but the look on his face is all relief. His parents didn't have Leonard killed, or at least not right away. Something eases off my shoulders, too, and Andy squeezes my leg under the table. It takes me a second to realize it's the last of the old guilt floating away. *I didn't kill him.* Moreover, he'd wanted to tell me about this. He didn't purposefully leave me thinking the worst.

He obviously started that fight with me on purpose. I was part of his cover story, but I was also his friend, and he didn't want me thinking I'd killed him. So he'd created a clue. A clue I never would have found if not for Andy—and Nicole, I guess, since she was the one who broke that frame.

I glance at Andy, who's grinning. "I guess this means you get to say I told you so forever."

"I'm glad you think so too," she says, then shifts her gaze to Nicole and Damien, "but I mostly want to say it to them. Suck it, fairy godmothers."

Damien looks amused but not annoyed. I guess he's leaving that for Nicole, who takes another sip of her beer.

"We never really doubted you," he says. "We wanted to see what you could put together for yourself. You did well."

"Luck played a big part in it," she admits, then lifts up her finger. There's still a Band-Aid wrapped around it. "Luck and broken glass."

"I feel like we had a high injury quotient on this one," Nicole says to Damien. "Is that our fault or theirs? Let's say it's theirs."

"Are you going to help me nail them?" Burke asks, his hand clenched around his beer glass.

Nicole cranes her head toward a couple of blond women sitting at the bar. "Who, those girls over there? You probably don't need my help, but I'll be your wing woman, sure. What's our cover story?"

"I'm talking about my parents," he says flatly, not even glancing in the direction of the women she'd indicated. Yep, he's going through some shit. He's not usually the sort of person to turn down that kind of opportunity.

"Yes," Damien says. "Finding Leonard's going to help. We've tracked him to a second identity, but he ditched that one too. We're getting closer."

"*If* he's still alive," Nicole says pointedly. "You need to keep in mind that your friend was the type to borrow trouble. It's more than possible that it found him."

"Well, let's hope we find him first." I finally take a sip of the beer, grimacing a little because alcohol was not my friend last night, and I'm not feeling all that partial to it today. Still, it would feel wrong not to lift a toast for Leonard. I hope I get to see him again.

I think Burke needs it.

There's a moment of silence, then Burke asks, "Why do you think he took the money from me? If he already had all that money from my parents, I mean."

"Maybe he's just a dick," Nicole says, with an eyebrow lift to say this isn't a question that's kept her up at night.

"He might be a dick," I say, "but not *that* kind of a dick."

"No," Burke agrees. "I think Leonard is his own personality type."

"Tell us some more about him," Andy says, her hand still on my leg.

"Well," I glance at my friend. "He got kicked out of the Biltmore for life because he snuck a beer into the house and brought it into a restricted area."

"He said he wanted to have a cold one on the roof," Burke says with a half smile. "Then there's the time he pretended to be an investor to get some rich asshole who'd nearly run Danny over to buy us all drinks. He had him begging to get in on the ground floor."

"So he's a con artist," Nicole says. "I figured."

"Maybe," I say, but that word doesn't seem to encompass him. There's no denying he makes poor life decisions. "He grew up in foster care. I guess he learned some things."

"If he's alive, we'll find him," Nicole says. "He might be slipperier than I thought, but no one's slippery enough to get away from me. I take this as a personal challenge."

"Poor Leonard," Andy says with a smirk.

"Poor Leonard with two million and sixty-five grand," Burke adds, messing with his beer glass.

Nicole snorts. "Don't expect to see a dime of it. He'll have spent that and more, I'm guessing. It's not easy or cheap to restart your life every couple of years."

Burke looks up. "I'm going to hold him accountable. More people should be held accountable for the shit they do. If they were, then no one would take things so far."

I know he's thinking about his parents, about what will come next, after he goes DEFCON 1 on them.

"What are you going to do?" I ask. "Have him arrested?"

"No," he says, a stubborn look on his face, "I'm going to hold him accountable. He said he wanted to flip a house with me, and he's goddamn well going to flip a house with me. He's coming home."

"If he's alive," Damien says.

"He'll only be able to come back as Leonard if he helps the authorities put together a case against your parents," Nicole cautions. "Because otherwise he could get convicted of multiple charges of fraud. Not to mention wasting police resources."

"I don't care," Burke says. "I'll call him Roland or whatever the hell name he's been going by. But he has to come home. It's time."

The thought gives me chills, because I don't dare believe in it. I'm glad when Andy lifts her glass. "To Roland, if he's alive."

We all drink to that.

———

> We found the slippery fucker. Hurrah! We're off to meet Leonard Smith. He must have gotten tired of coming up with names, because he's usually MUCH more creative. Who's up for a road trip?

It's a message from Nicole, addressed to me, Andy, and Burke. Damien's not on it, presumably because he's with her.

"Andy," I say. "Andy!"

It's Friday night, almost a week after we had drinks with Nicole and Damien at Griffin's bar. We're on the couch in the little purple house, watching a telenovela with her grandmother. It's terrible. They love it, though, and I love watching them love it together.

"What?" she asks, her eyes laughing. "Rinaldo just came back to life for the fifth time."

I flash her the screen. "Oh shit," she says, getting up and reaching a hand down for me. "You've got to go!"

"Language," Mrs. Ruiz snaps, although she doesn't seem too bent out of shape about it. In fact, she hasn't been all that bent out of shape about anything over the last couple of days. Andy and I have only moved our clothes, personal items, and computers out of my house, because I'm renting it out as a furnished rental. We've also been making the arrangements for our trip, which is taking longer because we need to get a nurse sorted for Mrs. Ruiz, plus I had to take care of a couple of other minor details, including quitting my job, which was *quite* enjoyable.

Danny suggested that I put a virus on my boss's computer so it would show a zombie walking across his screen every day at noon, and while I appreciated the ingenuity, and also the fact that it was something Leonard would have both done and enjoyed, I didn't want to waste the effort on him. So I just straight up quit. He blamed me for *Heads Will Roll* being behind schedule—in an email blasted to the whole staff. But I wasn't going to go out on his terms, not after being there so long, so I responded with screenshots of every single time I'd warned him he was talking up a game months from completion.

Andy and I also invited everyone for a last dinner at the house last night. And when I say everybody, I mean everybody—my sisters and their fiancés, Reggie and Aunt Helen, Mrs. Ruiz, Burke, Danny, and Shane. Nicole and Damien. Even Jack, Andy's brother. He didn't come—apparently he did get fired, and he's butthurt about it, but I think a reconciliation is possible. Eventually. Theo's an incurable asshole, I think, but I don't talk about it around Mrs. Ruiz, because I think she takes it personally that he's such a dick.

It felt like the right kind of temporary send-off to the house, and Marnie and I got teary-eyed as the night rolled to a drunken close. Because we'd lived in that house together for most of our lives, and that meant something. It also meant something that we'd both grown enough to move on, for now. Sinclair asked us if this meant she needed to take down the *90210* posters in her childhood bedroom, but I told her no.

"Give them an authentic experience."

Rafe smirked at her. "There's nothing she likes better than an authentic *90210* experience."

From the way she shoved his arm, all while smiling at him, I was fairly sure I don't want to know what that's all about. I didn't ask any follow-up questions, but Nicole whistled and said, "So you guys are into role-play shit too. I was wondering."

Fantastic. It's much too easy to walk into a *my sisters have sex* minefield these days.

Reggie also made sure to corner Andy so he could ask her questions about what finally made me win her over. When I asked him why he cared so much, he said that Aunt Helen's been encouraging him to start a life coaching service. God help us all.

Damien's been working on Burke's parents. He's found some shit, but Leonard is the lynchpin. "Without him, we can still get them for bad business practices," he told Burke. "But if you want to bring down the house, you've got to go for one of the bottom cards."

I'm wrested from my thoughts by Andy tugging on my arm. "Go," she urges me. "Wait, I'll pack you an overnight bag in case they're planning on driving to, like, California. I wouldn't put it past Nicole to leave a detail like that out."

"Wait, you're not coming?" I ask, dumbfounded.

She grins at me, her eyes full of her usual mischief. "You seriously want to sit in the middle seat for an unspecified amount of time?"

"Next to you? Sure. It gives me an excuse to cop a feel."

Mrs. Ruiz clears her throat, but she doesn't seem all that pissed off. Like I said, she's mellowed.

"You've got to come, Andy," I continue. "You started all of this." My throat feels thick as I say it, because it's true. If not for her, I would have gone through the rest of my life thinking I was responsible for my friend's death. Not to mention I would have lived out my whole life in the house I was born in without giving much thought to the fact that I'd landed myself in a rut and decided to take out a pillow and a blanket and live there.

"But...*Abuela*."

Mrs. Ruiz waves a hand. "I'll do you the service of not dying until you get home. I'm not going to miss our trip. Besides, my nurse says I'm doing much better, and Jack told me he would like to visit. Maybe I'll let him in the house this time."

"Really?" Andy says, looking from her to me. "Because I'm *dying* to go. I just felt like I should say no, but I want to see this through."

My phone buzzes with another text.

It's Nicole, telling us where and when to meet her.

Then Burke, expressing his disbelief-slash-excitement.

I look up at Andy. "This is really happening, isn't it?"

She pinches my ass. "Did that hurt?"

"Not really. Maybe you should do it again."

Mrs. Ruiz's lips flatten in one of her expressions designed to close down disputes. "Go pack your bags. You're ruining my show."

thirty-three

DREW

EIGHT HOURS. We've been in the car eight hours, Damien driving through the pitch dark, my knees twisted toward Andy, which makes my situation more acceptable if not more comfortable. We've made some pit stops to pick up junk food and gas up, but for the most part we've been on the road. We passed the state line into Florida half an hour ago, prompting Andy to snort and say, "I think this means that Leonard is officially Florida Man."

There's always some article starting "Florida Man," ending in some crazy shit like "rides an alligator" or "holds up a Wendy's because he was given sweet and sour sauce instead of barbecue." "Maybe he's every Florida man," Nicole had said with a laugh. "He's had enough names for it."

Our conversation has mostly petered out, but there's an audiobook playing that makes Andy's man-chest-cover books seem like Christian romance. My pulse feels like a hummingbird's. I know Burke's just as wound up. He hasn't said more than a couple of words since Nicole turned on the audiobook, although at one point, we look at each other at exactly the same time—because that's what you do when someone starts screwing a monster.

Finally, Damien takes the turn for a town called Featherton. "It's three in the morning," he says, glancing at the dash. "Should we stay somewhere for the night and look for him in the morning?"

"Nope," Nicole responds. "I'm not giving him a chance to bounce."

Five minutes later, he pulls into a trailer park. There's a manmade pond in the middle and a few of the yards have plastic flamingos stuck in the ground, as if they're handed out on the state line. Then he parks in front of a banged-up white trailer that looks like a can that got knocked around in the grocery store. There's a light on inside, so someone's home and awake, despite the late hour.

Andy opens her door and pulls me out. Burke comes out after us on our side of the car, as if he can't bring himself to exit through his own door, or maybe he's just on autopilot.

Nicole and Damien get out too, but Nicole nods to the door. "Go ahead."

Andy glances at Burke and me and then releases my hand. "You two should go up together."

We do. We walk up side by side. When we get to the door, Burke bumps my shoulder and nods to it. I can see what he's thinking—I was the last one to see him alive. I get to be the first one to see him.

I suck in a breath, and I knock.

There's a moment that stretches like taffy, then keeps stretching. I hear something from the back of the house, and I see someone go running.

There's only a flash of dark hair and a tall body, but I know it's him—and he's not getting away from us now, not after everything. I'm fit. It only takes me a couple of minutes to chase him down in the streets of Featherton and tackle him. It mustn't be an unusual occurrence in the trailer park, because no one comes out to yell at me. No one says a word, actually. It's almost unnaturally quiet, like a moment out of time.

"I didn't do it," Leonard says without looking up. "They're lying." Then he turns and looks at me, his eyes going wide with shock. A beat passes and then a huge grin creases his face. He looks the same but different—just like I must. Time has marched along, almost a decade of it. "Well, I'll be goddamned. I never thought I'd see the day."

I'm torn between wanting to punch him in the nose and hug him. "What kind of shit did you get yourself into now?" I ask, pulling him to his feet. And then I *do* hug him, because I need to prove to myself that his body isn't moldering at the bottom of that river somewhere, the way I'd thought for so many years—an image that had woken me up gasping more nights than I'd like to admit. And when he pulls away, I punch him in the shoulder. Not terribly hard. But he's a fucker, and he should know it.

"I deserved that," he says wryly, rubbing the spot.

"For letting me think you died?"

He scrunches his mouth to the side and nods. "Yeah, for that. You finally found the note, huh? But how'd you find me *here*?"

"We had help." I swallow. "We think we know what happened. Some of it. You left because of the Burkes didn't you? You knew something about the Newton building. Burke—"

Leonard flinches. "You told him?"

"Yeah, buddy, but he didn't know anything about it. He's on your side. He—"

Then Burke catches up to us on the sidewalk, looking at Leonard like he's some kind of oddity. For a second, I think Leonard is going to push me away and try running again, but as Burke comes closer, a streetlight reveals the tears in his eyes. I feel the hot answering press of them in my eyes, and to my shock, I see that Leonard's tearing up too.

"Dammit," he says, rubbing at his face. "I'm glad you're here. I've missed you guys."

And then we're all hugging each other. I hear Nicole in the background, saying something about circle jerks, but I couldn't give a damn.

"I didn't mean to duck out on you. When I told you about the flip house, I was planning on staying," Leonard says, glancing warily across the table from Burke. We're at a twenty-four-hour diner just outside of Featherton, the five of us blocking Leonard in in case he gets any smart ideas. He's in the middle, with Nicole on one side and Damien on the other. I'm directly across from him with Burke on one side and Andy on the other. We're all eating pancakes, which seems ridiculous, but you try driving for eight hours with nothing but M&Ms as sustenance and tell me you're not in the mood for a tall stack and a gallon of coffee.

"Oh?" Burke says, keeping the *Do expand on that, dipshit* to himself.

"I got jumpy," he says, rubbing the side of his nose. It looks like someone must have cracked him in it once or twice, and he's acquired a scar on his arm, plus a couple of new tattoos. "Someone was watching me. I saw a car tailing me. Caught sight of this guy with a mustache a couple of times. Real distinctive. It had curled ends and everything." Then he gives Nicole and Damien a sidelong glance—taking in her day-glo pink hair and his distinctive features—and shrugs. "I'd never seen this guy before, but they wouldn't have hired someone I'd recognize to take me out or keep an eye on me. I got to thinking they were trying to exercise some risk management."

Burke flinches, because it's not looking so good for Mama and Papa Burke. "But why ask me to cover the flip? You had two million. You could have paid for your half."

Leonard gives him a shit-eating grin. "Sure, but wouldn't you have been curious about why I suddenly had that kind of change in my pocket, especially after they'd just fired me?"

Andy and Nicole snort at practically the same time, and I struggle to hold back a grin.

"Do you have evidence they were involved in what happened with the Newton Building?" Burke asks.

He gives a humorless laugh. "If I'd had evidence, I would have used it anonymously after they broke their end of the bargain. No offense, man, but your parents are assholes. They knew they were building too close to the sinkhole, but they decided to take the risk rather than lose the value of the land. Then they arranged for that guy to take the fall."

"And they told you all of this?" Damien asks, obviously aware that they would have done no such thing. It's a test of Leonard's truthfulness.

"No," he says with a snort. His gaze moves from Burke to me and back. "I guess you can say I have a knack for picking up on information that might be useful."

"Will you testify against them?" Burke asks.

Leonard whistles. "You really want to hamstring your own company?"

"Despite what you must have thought of me," Burke says tightly, "I wouldn't have let them get away with that shit. I'm not going to let them get away with it now."

Leonard's mouth twists to the side. "The thing is...I'm what you might call an unreliable witness. Your parents told me as much when I confronted them. I wasn't sure whose side you would take, especially since they were right." He pauses, then contemplates Nicole and Damien. "But if you're good at finding things, I can tell you where to look. I'm not saying you'll be able to put them away, but they'd feel the burn."

"We're good at it," Andy says, glancing at me with a smirk. I put my hand on her thigh. "We found you, after all."

"Your girlfriend's hot," Leonard comments.

"Yup," I say happily, putting an arm around her. "Stay away from her."

"There's still the matter of the sixty-five thousand you owe me," Burke tells Leonard.

Leonard shrugs and takes a big bite of his pancakes.

"It's going to take you roughly fifteen seconds to finish that," Andy says. "You'll still have to answer him."

Sighing, he sets down his fork. "What do you want me to say, man? I'm broke. It's all gone. It's *been* gone. I've made some...I guess you could call them poor life decisions."

"Called it," Nicole says, reaching for a high five from Damien. He leans in and kisses her instead.

"You're coming home to Asheville," Burke says in his stubborn tone, which means he's not going to accept no or maybe for an answer. "And you're going to work for that money."

"Don't you have a trust fund?"

"Sure," Burke says, smirking now. Despite what he's facing, he looks more himself than he has in days. "But you don't."

"Your parents aren't going to like us very much, and even if you pull this off, they still have power. There's no way they're going to be the ones that get hung out to dry. I've seen shit like this play out too many times."

"They're going to be in the public eye," Damien says. "Scrutinized. Something tells me they're too careful to come after either of you." He nods to me. "We'll get some rest at a motel, then you and Andy take our car. We'll ride up with the con artist. Seems we have a lot to talk about."

"I wouldn't call myself a con artist," Leonard says, cutting into the pancakes again as if his appetite hasn't been much affected by all of this after all. "I'm a survivor."

"So being a con artist is your side gig is what you're saying?" Andy says with a smile.

He grins back at her. "That about covers it."

epilogue

ANDY

THREE WEEKS LATER

SUMMER NIGHTS IS CLOSED for our going away party. Grace is finally back from New York, thank God, and she and Enoch are coming. So are Danny and Shane, but they went on an epic hike earlier and came back filthy. Marnie and Griffin, Sinclair, Rafe, Reggie, and Drew's Aunt Helen are all already here—talking in clusters around the bar. So is my grandmother and Leonard "Smith," whom she's been eying with open disdain while he and Drew chat. He looks at home here, like he was born in a dive bar and it's his natural habitat.

He's been staying on Burke and Danny's couch, but we've agreed to let him stay in the purple house while we're gone, in exchange for him finishing some repairs. Leonard is impossible to trust, obviously, but I have a feeling Burke will be keeping an eye on him. He seems to have a vested interest in Leonard's future.

Nicole and Damien haven't arrived yet, but they promised they'd make an appearance. They've been busy lately—what with rounding up evidence that the executives at Burke Enterprises, headed up by Mama and Papa Burke, knew about the sinkhole and chose to build an unsafe distance from it, and also that they willfully placed the blame for their poor decision-making on someone else. Hell, we even managed to track down the detective they'd hired to keep an eye on Leonard—not an assassin, thankfully, but a private investigator who was being paid to follow him around the clock.

They turned their information over to the feds earlier this week, and they've used Burke as their inside man, asking him to find and scan certain files, including Leonard's severance agreement. Despite initially saying he didn't want his name involved, Leonard has spoken with them too. They've agreed not to press fraud charges, or look too deeply into his activities, in exchange for his cooperation. The Burkes and their empire are a much bigger fish.

It's been a thrill to be a part of it, and I'm going to miss that thrill while we're in Puerto Rico, but if I only have a few months left with my grandmother, I'm going to spend them *with my grandmother*. Nicole and Damien have already told me that I always have a job with them—perks of being one of their clients.

Burke comes in, grinning, but there's something sharp behind it, like a rose covering a thorn.

"What's wrong?" I ask as he comes up to us.

The grin falters.

Drew glances around and, seeing that Griffin's in the middle of a story, slips behind the bar to pour Burke a whiskey.

"Can I get one?" Leonard asks.

"Make it a round of shots," I say.

So he does, sliding them across the counter before taking his place next to me.

"So, let us have it," Drew says.

"That obvious, huh?" Burke asks, chagrined.

"It's in your face," Leonard says. "Your eyes."

Spoken like a person used to manipulating other people, but I don't say so. Leonard's untrustworthy as hell, but Drew and Burke also weren't wrong about him. He has his own code, if you can call it that, and it's become obvious to me that he does care about Drew and Burke and their buddies. Danny and Shane just about shit their pants when Leonard walked into their Dungeons & Dragons game night a few weeks back. It was a mean prank, but Burke was feeling low, and Drew and I came up with it to amuse him. Despite Nicole's threat that she can find him wherever he goes—proven by the fact that she *did* track down his many identities—I don't think that's why he's stuck around. I think he came back to Asheville because he wanted to. Because of the many places he's lived, this is the one that's felt most like home.

I understand that, because Marnie and Drew have always been home for me. Because there's something special about the group of friends that Drew has formed for himself. They're all the kind of men who will be there for each other through anything.

Even crime.

Call me biased, but I think it's because of Drew—because he's the kind of man who's loyal beyond anything. And people like that are capable of inspiring the same kind of loyalty.

Burke downs his shot. We follow suit.

"I quit today," he says, slamming the empty shot glass down on the bar.

"No shit," Drew says and pats him on the back. "How'd it go?"

Burke gives us a half smile. "About as well as you'd think. I couldn't tell them why. Not yet. Let them find out."

"Won't be long," Drew says, putting an arm around me. He gives me a squeeze, and I know what he's thinking because he's said it often enough. *Because of you, Andy. You freed him.*

I felt bad about it at first because, shit, Burke's losing his parents *and* his job, but both Drew and Burke himself pointed out that his parents had always made him feel like shit about himself and his job wasn't fulfilling—he'd always preferred doing house flips to working in his executive suite.

"So what'd you say?" Leonard asks, curiosity lighting his eyes.

"I said I wanted to experience more of life. They shuttled me into that office so fast, I didn't get to do anything. I never had a choice."

Leonard starts playing a tiny violin with his fingers, and we all laugh, including Burke.

"Fine, asshole. But I mean it. I want to try out different experiences. Have fun. Figure out why I'm here on this planet besides being a Burke." He swallows. "I want everyone to start calling me Lucas. I'm sick of being known for my family, and I have a feeling it's not going to be such a good thing pretty soon."

"Feels pretty good to change your name now and then, brother. I'll call you Lucas."

Drew nods. "We all will if that's what you want, but it might take a while to remember. About the hobby thing, talk to Sinclair. I think my sister's tried every hobby on the planet, and she and Rafe are opening this business where people get to try out different hobbies and arts and crafts. The Waiting Place."

"What's this now?" Sinclair calls out.

He waves her over, and she comes, bringing along Rafe. Reggie and Helen have cornered my grandmother and are telling her a long and very animated story that is almost certainly inappropriate. Marnie silently salutes me and stays over there with Griffin to keep an eye on things, but my grandmother is *laughing*. I've realized that a big part of her sadness in knowing the end is coming soon came from worry about me. She knew I depended on her every bit as much as she depended on me, and that there would be a gaping hole in my life when I lost her. That's still going to happen. But she knows I'm happy. She knows I'm in love with the best man in existence, and that he and I are going to take care of each other.

I'm hoping it also means we'll have longer with her. Her nurse told me that a good attitude makes a huge difference in outcome.

"Sinclair," Drew says, "Burke's newly fun-employed."

They all know about what's been going on—there are no real

secrets in this group, besides whichever ones Leonard is inevitably holding close to his chest—so there's not much surprise over this.

"He's looking to try new things. I was telling him about The Waiting Place."

Her mouth purses. "Well, we're not opening for a few months yet." Then her eyes light up. "Hey, I've got something for you."

"Don't feel overenthusiastic, bud," Rafe says, giving her a fond glance. "I know that look. She's up to no good."

Sinclair hip-checks him. "He has every reason for enthusiasm, because I have an awesome part-time job for him on the set of my new movie."

"Oh, yeah?" Burke says with a smirk. "What am I going to do, bring people coffee?"

"We need extras." She looks excited about the idea, and I'm hit with how much more expressive she's gotten since coming home. Back in the day, when she'd visit from Hollywood, it seemed like she'd go out of her way to avoid emoting unless she was in front of a camera. "I'll get you a recurring extra role. You'd be perfect. You've got one of those faces."

Meaning he's super-hot. But it's obvious she doesn't want to say so around Rafe. He grumbles something to express dissatisfaction, but truthfully, he seems amused.

I glance up at Drew. "Do you want to be an extra too?"

"Testing me, Ruiz?" he asks, tipping his head down to me. "We're going to have a house next to the ocean. Being an extra on a hot-as-balls movie set where my sister's treated like a queen and I'm a peon without any reasonable bathroom breaks has nothing on that."

I lift up and kiss him, because yes, I suppose it was a test. I still can't believe he's doing all of this for us—upending his comfortable life. Challenging himself. But then, I guess I've done the same for him. That's what happens when you meet the person you want forever with.

"You're not really encouraging me to take this gig," Burke says, his eyes dancing.

"Might be good for you to be treated like a peon," Leonard says. "See how the other half lives."

Burke rolls his eyes, but he still has an amused look, which is better than the look he had when he walked in, so it seems like a win. "I'll do it," he says, then glances at Leonard. "So long as you can get something for *him* too."

Sinclair's eyebrows lift, but she checks Leonard out and nods. "Sure. It's a deal."

"Do we get to ask what the movie's about?" Leonard asks, but he seems amused by the whole thing.

"Are you guys talking about the movie?" Marnie calls out, and she and Griffin walk over, followed by the others.

"Sinclair got me a job as the set photographer," Reggie says proudly —a little too proudly if you consider that he once did the set photography for *Star Wars*, and they're filming a made-for-TV romance.

Griffin grimaces, probably because he took a few photographs for him and Marnie a while back, and either he was drunk when he did it or he's lost his eye for it.

"Yeah," I say, "Burke and Leonard want to be extras."

Marnie laughs behind her hand. "She's been pushing all of us to do it."

"I'm starting to question what I've agreed to," Burke says, but I can tell he's game for it. He'd probably be game for anything that would keep his mind off what he's going through.

Marnie's gaze skips to me and Drew. "You know, I'm going to miss the hell out of you. I know we're going to FaceTime like we did with Gracie when she and Enoch were in New York for forever, but it's not the same. I can't wait until you come back home."

My grandmother clears her throat. "You're saying you can't wait for me to die?"

Marnie gives me an *oh shit* look that makes me laugh.

"Stop teasing her, *Abuela*." I give Drew a nudge. "I swear, she's picking up bad habits from you."

He gives me a squeeze in response. "I'm picking up bad habits from you too," he says into my ear. "That matchmaking show came on last night while I was making dinner, and it took me a solid five minutes to remember that I could change the channel."

"Very funny. And would you please, for the love of God, stop trying to make the Fabgadget work?"

He laughs into my hair, lighting up the nerve endings, because I love it when he pulls my hair while he drives into me. It's become a bit of an addiction, you might say. "It wasn't that bad," he lies. "I mean, I wasn't aware that rice could have that texture, but life can be surprising."

The door slams open, and Nicole and Damien walk in. "You started our party without us?" she says.

"*Our* party," I correct with a scowl, even though I'm damn glad to see her.

"I figured we could share it," she says, walking toward us. Griffin crosses behind the bar without being told and starts mixing drinks, a slight smile on his face. Maybe he knows what she's talking about already. Although he's not the sort to keep things from Marnie, he does have loyalty to Nicole and Damien.

Then it strikes me.

"Oh shit, is this where you remind me that I'm supposed to come up with some other sad case for you to help." I gesture to our gathered friends as Grace and Enoch slip in, Grace giving me a little wave. "Because all of my friends are doing pretty damn well. I mean, except for Burke, and obviously Leonard, but I was under the impression you only help women."

"What do you mean *obviously Leonard*?" Leonard asks with an amused look.

"It's obvious to all of us, Leonard," Nicole says. Then, turning to me, she says, "You're off the hook."

"It's a trick," Marnie says as Grace slips up to us.

"Nicole doesn't let people off the hook," agrees Enoch.

He should know. She did a number on him before Grace decided she loves him more than she hates him.

"This is going to be our going away party, too, kids," Nicole says with a grin. "As you said, you're all doing fantastic. Our fairy godmothering work is done. For now."

"You're leaving?" Marnie says, her gaze darting to Griffin, who's now pouring the drinks—enough for all of us.

He gives her a half-smile. "They told me this morning. Nicole wanted to make her big announcement to all of you, and I wasn't going to take that away from her."

"Thank you, Griffin. You get a gold star," Nicole says.

"I was told to fear for my life," he adds. "I did."

"Where are you going?" I ask. "And what happened to *'Andy, you'll always have a job with us'*? Shouldn't you have mentioned this to your employee?"

She grins at me. "You're the one who's abandoning us. We'd take you with us under different circumstances." She gestures to Drew. "But you just had to fall in love with the person we all already knew you were in love with. Super inconvenient for my plans."

"We'll be back," Damien says. "We just don't know when. But if you get home before us, I talked to Rufus—"

"The mustache P.I.?" I ask with genuine disbelief.

He smiles. "I think he'd like being called that. Yeah. And he says you've got a job with him if you want one. We had a little talk with him about you. He was impressed."

I glance at Drew, who's grinning down at me, then them. "You all do realize I didn't actually *know* something weird had happened with Leonard. I just wanted to do something for Drew. To show him—"

"That you were madly in love with me," he says, the hand around my back playing with my hair.

"That I appreciated him...and begrudgingly wanted to sleep with him."

His laughter lifts me up, the way it always has. The way it always will.

"You have instincts," Damien says. "That's the one thing you can't train."

"But if you're just dying to get back in the classroom," Nicole adds, "I hear there's a director position opening at that shitty daycare you used to work at."

"He lost his job?" I ask, intrigued.

She starts laughing, hard, but gets out, "His wife made him go to rehab for sex addiction. Some of the parents found out."

"Let me guess how they found out," I say, gratitude burning inside of me. These two. Goddammit, they'd done so much for all of us. I wouldn't say they're good people exactly. Like Leonard, they're somewhere in the middle. Somewhere gray. I guess that's where I live too. But they've given so much of themselves to make us happy, and if there are karmic points, I'm guessing theirs are more positive than negative.

Nicole gives herself a pat on the back, and we all laugh.

"They wouldn't hire me back after the OnlyFans thing."

"There's no actual proof those are your feet," Damien says. "And all signs of your former account have been mysteriously wiped."

"You guys are too much."

"But you should have told us you were leaving," Sinclair scolds. "I would have made a cake for you."

"Maybe that's why they didn't tell us," Rafe says, pulling her to him.

She gives him the stink-eye over her shoulder, and he kisses her nose.

"Will you tell us why?" Marnie asks.

"When we get back," Nicole says, her face breaking into a shifty grin. "Something tells me it'll make for a hell of a story."

"Can I write about it?" Grace asks, her face lighting up.

"Only if you make me sound like a badass."

"You know, leave it to you to hijack our going away party," I complain without heat. Because, honestly, it just makes me more fond of them. This is their way. Dramatic reveals. Underhanded favors. Saving people who didn't really know they needed saving. Being fairy godparents.

"I figured you'd appreciate one last dick move from me," Nicole says, her nose ring winking at me as if she's covered in fairy dust. "Consider it a parting gift."

"You're coming back," I confirm.

"Sometime."

It's bittersweet, the party. Because they're leaving. Because *we're* leaving. Danny and Shane show up, less smelly than before their showers, I'm sure. We have some more drinks. Reggie makes a long and meandering speech about what it took to make Drew datable that has me laughing so hard I almost pee my pants. Marnie reminisces about something I'd forgotten—that night over a year ago when we went bowling. Drew and Lilah broke up the next day. Marnie says she sees it in a new light, and Drew lifts his shoulder in a shrug and grins at me. "What can I say? You're the Queen of Bright Ideas."

Then, a couple of hours in, when my grandmother is starting to look tired, Drew takes my hand, glancing around to make sure our friends are busy, and leads me to the back stairs. We head up them and exit onto the roof. It's not a tall building, but then again, none of the buildings here are particularly tall, and because of where we're situated, we get a good view of downtown.

"Griffin told me it's nice up here," he says with a slow smile.

"Because he and Marnie have had *relations* up here?" I suggest playfully.

His expression slips into a grimace. "Do you *want* me to retaliate?"

"Yes, please."

"Reggie says he and Aunt Helen tried to convince your grandmother to have a threesome with them."

I gape at him. "No."

He shrugs, grinning at my horror-stricken expression. "That's what he said. She wasn't interested, obviously, but I wouldn't put it past them to try again tonight."

"When you said you were going to retaliate, I figured you'd lay me across your knee and spank me."

"I can still do that," he says, his voice low, pulling me to him. His lips are soft but demanding as they meet mine—their taste and feel both comfortable and always, always a turn-on that sends need curling through my body. I'm still so grateful that we can do this now. That we can pull each other close and kiss and make love and be together. That our lives are as intermingled as the weave of a rug.

I pull away, keeping myself within his arms, and soak in the sight of him. Those big brown eyes, his strong jaw. He shaved the beard after a week, saying that he already had me in his grasp and didn't want to make Reggie too full of himself.

"So you didn't bring me up here to have your wicked way with me?" I ask, looking up into his eyes.

"Not expressly." His mouth lifts at the corner. "What do you think about Burke and Leonard working on the movie?"

"I think it's going to be a mess," I say, laughing. "And I halfway wish we'd be here to see it. Now, why'd you really bring me up here?" I grab the front of his shirt as if to threaten him, and his grin spreads wider.

"Getting frisky, huh? They're down there bringing out a cake shaped like a Fabgadget. It's supposed to be a surprise."

"You didn't."

"Oh, I did. I had it special-ordered."

"I love you."

He wraps his finger around one of my curls, his arms still around my back, his eyes holding my gaze. "And I love you, Andrea Ruiz. You're my one and only." His mouth lifts again. "I'd say I've always loved you, but when I mentioned something like that around your grandmother, she reminded me that we met when you were only six. So I'll just say that you grew on me *a while ago*."

I laugh and kiss his nose.

"I'm giving you fair warning," he says, his gaze intense now. "I'm going to ask you to marry me. Not today. Not next week. But soon. I figured I'd give you a heads-up so you can freak out slowly, over time, instead of all at once."

My heart erupts and fills my body with light. With heat. "Then I'll give you fair warning too," I say, lifting up so our faces are less than an inch apart. "I'm going to say yes. Possibly even *hell, yes*."

He lowers that final inch, capturing my lips, and I pour myself into the kiss, happy in a way that's not brittle or liable to break. Happy in a way I've never been in my whole life.

"Get a room!" someone shouts from beneath us, and I laugh into his mouth because I recognize Marnie's voice. I look over the edge, and she, Sinclair, and Grace are grinning up at us.

"My shame is complete," Drew mutters, but he doesn't seem to mind.

I *definitely* don't mind, because it hits me that Marnie is going to officially be my sister.

"Come down," Sinclair adds, then Grace says, "Jack just got here."

I swivel to look at Drew.

"I may have invited him," he admits. "He came around the other day while you were out. He seemed remorseful, and your grandmother handed his ass to him. Theo, I did not invite. Mostly because that bruise lasted for weeks, but also because he's an unforgivable dick. Though if you choose to forgive him someday, I'll pretend to get along with him."

"*Drew.*"

His sisters and Grace wave and then head back inside.

He looks a little chagrined, the way he always does when someone catches him doing something kind. "I know it's been bothering you to leave things this way. Especially since we don't know how much longer Elena has."

Yes, Drew is one of the few people my grandmother has allowed to call her by her first name.

"You're a prince among men, Andrew Jones."

He traces a hand down my cheek. "I thought I was the court jester."

"*Never*. You're the one who said so, and you were *obviously* mistaken."

"Shall we?" he asks.

I steal another kiss and then take his hand. "We shall."

It feels perilously close to *I do*. But the thought of forever doesn't scare me anymore. We walk downstairs hand in hand, our sides pressed together, and I have the sensation that we're walking into a lifetime of adventure—or possibly misadventure. There's no one I'd prefer to have as my partner in crime and late-night infomercial purchases.

ANGELA CASELLA is a romcom fanatic. Writing them, reading them, watching them—she's greedy, and she does it all. In addition to her solo releases, she's lucky enough to collaborate with Denise Grover Swank. They have three complete series and more co-written projects to come.

She lives in Asheville, NC. Her hobbies include herding her daughter toward less dangerous activities, the aforementioned romcom addiction, and dreaming of having someone else clean her house.

Visit her website at www.angelacasella.com or Angela and Denise's shared website at www.arcdgs.com.